WILD
THING

BLUEBLOOD VAMPIRES BOOK TWO

MICHELLE
HERCULES

USA TODAY BESTSELLING AUTHOR

Wild Thing © 2020 by Michelle Hercules

Cover Design: Michelle Hercules
Photographer: Michelle Lancaster (@lanefotograf)
Cover Model: Lochie Carey

Editor: Theresa Schultz, Marginalia Editing

Proofreading: Cara Quinlan

ISBN: 978-1-950991-14-3

WILD
THING

BLUEBLOOD VAMPIRES BOOK TWO

1

AURORA

My mother told me to stay away from the catacombs, and what she says must be obeyed without question. Once upon a time, she used to be kinder, but that was before my father passed away. Then, I think the demands of her job stripped away any lingering softness from her. And since I'm her oldest child and destined to take her place as the High Witch, I get her worst.

But I've never been one to follow orders, and tonight, I'm sticking to my rebellious side. I want to know what the hell she and Solomon are hiding under the institute. I overheard the conversation between them after she came back from a meeting with King Raphael. They're going to attempt to trap the deadly ghost again, and I'm not going to miss it.

That wraith was a vampire once, and my guess is she was a Blueblood, maybe even first generation. She felt powerful but also malicious, evil. More so than Boone, and that's saying a lot.

But I can't simply follow my mother at a distance and hope she won't notice me. I'm taking precautions—and by precautions, I mean I'm using a concealment spell strong enough to fool even the High Witch. She would never approve of it. I acquired the potion from a member of the rogue mage guild, after all.

It would have been impossible for me to find them if the idiot who created the poisonous fog on the day of Boone's attack hadn't left behind a piece of his clothing. It was easy to cast a tracking spell with it. A bit harder to convince the guild to assist the daughter of the High Witch. Rogue mages can be hired, and some of them are powerful, but they're all cowards. I had to resort to blackmail to get what I needed. They'd had no idea their fog job would assist in Lucca's murder attempt by Boone. I promised them I wouldn't rat them out to King Raphael if they cooperated.

Maybe it was stupid of me to waste such a trump card just to get a concealment spell, but I'm desperate to know my mother's secret. I'm prone to making impulsive decisions. I hope this one doesn't come back to bite me in the ass like my previous one. I have the guild by the balls, but I can't keep blackmailing them. It's amoral and also dangerous.

I drink the bitter potion and then head for the catacombs. Everything is eerily quiet, and the small hairs on the back of my neck stand on end. *Shit.* Could the ghost have overpowered my mother and Solomon? I stick my hand inside my bag and pull out an enchanted crystal. It's used to ward off vengeful ghosts, but it will only keep a vampire ghost at bay for a limited amount of time.

My heart is thumping hard and slow against my rib cage. It's impossible not to feel the weight of fear when I know what's on the loose down here. The silence is broken suddenly by a terrifying shriek that sends my heart spiraling up to my throat. *Fuck.* That's the ghost. I freeze for a second, but then I hear my mother's voice. She's reciting a spell.

I walk faster, still mindful of being stealthy. Just before I reach the spot where my mother is, I flatten my back against the wall and stick my head around the corner. My mother and Solomon have the vampire wraith trapped in an orb of green light. She's as freaky as I remember. I never knew vampires could turn into ghosts.

"You can't keep us trapped forever," the ghost wails. "The Nightingales have returned. We will get our revenge."

Shit. The ghost is talking about Vivienne.

"You will return to your prison, Madeleine."

"Madeleine?" The ghost laughs. "Madeleine has ceased to exist. Lost in her madness, she made a deal with me. I control her body and her soul."

Solomon trades a glance with my mother. She nods, and together, they send the ghost back to the secret chamber. Her prison.

That's it?

I'm pissed. Not only didn't I get any intel, but I also wasted my leverage with the rogue mage guild in the process.

I quickly retrace my steps before my mother finds me. That would be the cherry on top.

When I get back to my apartment, I make sure all the lights are on. I hate that I can't open the shutters and let sunlight in. Designed for vampires, they close automatically and won't roll up again until nightfall. I sit on a high stool, leaning my elbows on the counter.

I'm not sure what I was hoping to achieve by spying on my mother. To gain a sense of control maybe, something that's clearly absent in my life. If I had a choice, I wouldn't be at Bloodstone,

I wouldn't be studying to take my mother's place, and most importantly, I wouldn't be promised to a douche canoe from an important magical family.

Running my hands through my hair, I yank back the strands. "Fuck."

The sudden knock on my door makes me jerk on my seat. *What now?*

"Who is it?"

"Aurora, it's me, Saxon."

A string of curses runs through my head. I don't want to deal with him, but at the same time, I could use a punching bag.

I cross the room with long strides and then open the door with a brusque movement. "What do you want?"

His hand is braced against the wall, and he looks positively ill. With a grimace, he replies, "The potion you gave me didn't work."

"Impossible. That should have worked."

"Well, it didn't." He stands straighter, imposing, feral. "You're still my damn mate, and if you don't fix this, you're going to be a widow before you exchange vows with your betrothed."

2

AURORA

—✦—

A month later

Incredulity. Disgust. Rage. All those feelings compete for space in my head as I park my car in front of Havoc. Growing up, I've always known I wouldn't have much control over my life. As the oldest daughter of the High Witch, much is expected of me. There was never time for play; studying witchcraft was my only priority. Responsibility and sacrifice were the bywords repeated constantly by my mother.

And damn, the woman can't complain. I've always done what she said, even if I broke her rules in secret. I enrolled at Bloodstone Institute, a school for vampires—and the last place I wanted to be— without offering resistance. But what she's asked me to do now is brutal.

Mother dearest wants me to marry a douche canoe from a

prestigious magical family. Apparently, not only do I have to pledge my life to serve the ruler of vampires, King Raphael, but I also have to make sure my offspring will be sufficiently gifted to carry on our legacy.

I left her house fuming, but I couldn't return to Bloodstone. I wanted to scream and break things. What would those bloodsuckers do if they saw the future High Witch losing her shit? I drove for hours until I saw the sign welcoming me to Boston. I could have simply spent the night in the big metropolis, but that wouldn't change my reality.

It wasn't until I was back in Salem that I made the last-minute decision to stop at the popular vampire club. I've never stepped foot inside before. I have my fill of vamps at the institute, after all. But I've heard stories about the place. Things can get wild in there and tonight that's exactly what I need.

I pull the visor down and check my reflection in the vanity mirror to make sure my makeup is not smeared. I cried tears of rage earlier, which I'm not ashamed to admit, but I don't need to flaunt the raccoon look. Surprisingly, my makeup survived the ugly crying. *Hooray for waterproof mascara!* I ditch my severe jacket and button-down shirt, glad that I forgot a bag from my latest shopping trip in my car. What I have isn't by any means club attire, but I'll take the tank top with the sassy quote any time over a lame combo meant for working in an office. Who knows, maybe the pissed-off unicorn saying "Back the fuck up, sparkle tits, or you get shanked" will deter vampires from annoying me.

There's already a line of humans waiting to get in. It's so long, it goes around the block. I veer straight toward the bouncer at the front—a tall, mean-looking regular vampire who is attired in a black suit and an earpiece. He glances in my direction, already sporting a frown, but before he can open his mouth to send me to the back of the line, I flash him the ring on my finger that bears the royal insignia of King Raphael. In an instant, his expression changes to one of respect. He nods, and then lifts the red velvet rope to let me through.

He must have alerted his coworkers inside because I'm ushered through the VIP entrance without having to pay the entrance fee. Finally, I get to reap the benefits of my association with the king.

The music is obnoxiously loud. I can feel the bass vibrations deep in my chest. It's definitely not the kind of soundtrack one can enjoy sober, so I head straight for the bar near the main dance floor. It's hard not to wrinkle my nose as I'm blasted with the scent of blood and sex in the air. That's what vampires do. They feed and fuck whenever the urge strikes. No false modesty with them.

I elbow my way through the throng of writhing bodies, getting nasty looks as I go. One stupid vamp skank hisses at me when I shove her to the side. Not a Blueblood, but even if she were, I wouldn't give a damn. Despite her lack of status, I sense she wants to start a fight. *Not tonight, bitch.* I let the magic run freely through my veins, which makes my eyes glow with a white light. Immediately, the vampire backs down. No surprise there. They're taught not to mess with powerful witches.

Thanks to my little demonstration, I have no problem getting a spot in front of the bar. A tall and extremely attractive vampire is busy mixing a cocktail. Judging by the ingredients he's pouring into the shaker, he's making something for a human. None of these regulars would be able to handle a Bloody Mary.

He looks familiar, but it's not until he speaks to another patron that recognition hits me. Derek Blackwater, the last vampire made before the Nightingales went away, and owner of Havoc. No wonder I didn't recognize him right away. He's not wearing one of his expensive custom-made suits and he has scruff on his face.

Without lifting his gaze to mine, he says, "I'm surprised to see you here, Aurora. I thought you didn't like to party with our kind."

I flatten my lips to prevent an angry retort from coming out of my mouth. I have to be careful about what I say to Derek. He's only a regular on paper. In reality, he's just as powerful as any Blueblood I've met, and equally lethal.

"I'm pissed at my kind. So, I figured I needed a change of scenery."

He raises his piercing eyes to mine. "Received bad news?"

Watching him through slits, I ask, "What do you know about it?"

He chuckles, switching his attention to another drink he's mixing. "I've only heard rumors that there would be an important engagement announcement soon in the magical community. You're the High Witch's heir, twenty-one, and single. It wasn't hard to guess."

I keep the glower in place, but it's not aimed at Derek per se. I'm still riding on the anger triggered by my mother's news. If it were up to me, I'd never get married. I don't see any good reason to shackle myself to any man. But tonight, I'm determined to forget the shit storm that's waiting for me in my near future.

"Hit me with your most powerful stuff," I say.

He seeks my gaze again, raising an eyebrow. "You can't handle my most powerful stuff."

The corners of his lips twitch upward, and his deep green

eyes become lighter. My spine turns rigid in an instant. *Did Derek just flirt with me?* He's definitely a sexy vamp, but hell, I'm smart enough to not go there.

"Oh, gag me. Save the innuendos for the blow-up dolls crawling in your club."

Grinning, he replies, "I don't need to waste any inferences on them."

"I bet you don't. Just give me a bottle of Patron and I'll get out of your hair."

He shakes his head. "No can do, baby girl. I don't need an intoxicated and pissed-off witch on my premises."

"Don't worry. I don't plan to drink it alone."

Derek's posture doesn't change as he opens his mouth to no doubt tell me no again. But someone interjects before he can.

"Just give the little witch the bottle, Derek. I promise she won't misbehave."

I turn, coming face-to-face with Saxon Hellström, a cocky Blueblood that I've had the misfortune to interact with on a few occasions. I never understood the allure of vampires until I met him. He had me tongue-tied and blushing like a schoolgirl until he opened his big mouth and ruined everything. The almost five-hundred-year-old vampire has the maturity level of an eight-year-old boy. Now he's watching me with eyes that are filled with glee and a shit-eating grin on his lips. And yet, my traitorous body does a number on me. My pulse quickens just being in close proximity to him.

"Why are you staring at me like that?" I ask.

"No reason at all."

Derek sets a sealed Patron bottle in front of me along with two shot glasses. "She's your responsibility now, Saxon. She hexes my place, I'm coming for you."

He reaches over, grabbing the bottle and glasses before I can. "She's in good hands."

What an arrogant ass. There are so many things I want to tell him, but I save it for when Derek can't hear us. Saxon turns away from the bar with my drink in hand, leaving me no choice but to follow him.

He chooses to cut right through the dance floor. The crowd parts to let him through, gawking at the blond vampire like he's some kind of deity. Women and men alike ogle him with clear desire in their eyes, but Saxon doesn't seem to notice or care.

We reach a set of wide stairs, which are currently roped off and manned by another bouncer in a dark suit. Silently, he lets us through. Saxon goes up the stairs two steps at a time, reaching the second floor in the blink of an eye. I race to catch up with him, and the little bit of cardio only adds fuel to my growing irritation with the male.

He's sitting casually in one of the couches by the time I reach the landing and has already poured the shots. *Damn vampires and their supernatural speed.* Still watching me with amusement, he offers me one of the glasses when I stop in front of his table.

I take his offering with a jerky movement, maintaining eye contact with him. Saxon seems to be fighting down a smirk. *Asshat.* My irritation expands, and it feels like an itch on my back that I can't reach. It's a prickling sensation under my skin. Getting alcohol into my system becomes the number one priority. I throw my head back to swallow the shot in one single gulp. Immediately, warmth spreads through my body, but it's not nearly enough to make me relax. I need more.

"Feeling better now?" he asks.

My answer is to sit down on the chair opposite him and pour myself another shot. It's only after I drink the fifth one and have a nice buzz going that I reply, "Yes."

He chuckles, and then raises his glass in salute before tossing his head back. My eyes drop to his exposed throat as he gulps down, and I get a funny feeling in the pit of my stomach. It must be the tequila at work. I'm still staring when Saxon drops his chin and our gazes collide. He rewards me with a knowing smile.

"Are you going to tell me what's eating you?" he asks.

Normally, I'd tell him to mind his own business, but alcohol has loosened my tongue.

"My mother wants me to marry."

Saxon's eyebrows arch, almost meeting his hairline. "An arranged marriage? Isn't that a little old-fashioned?"

"The magical community can be unpredictable, but one thing that never changes about them is their attachment to archaic traditions." I take another shot of tequila. So far, I've consumed almost half the bottle by myself. Maybe Saxon wants to see me drunk.

"That sucks. Who is the lucky guy?" His tone is casual, but his eyes have a different gleam in them, almost feral.

"Calvin Belmont. An asshole with a capital A. I hate him." I forgo the glass this time, drinking straight from the bottle.

I barely manage a couple swallows before Saxon takes the bottle away from me.

"Hey! I wasn't done."

He's standing in front of my chair, imposing and so damn close. I tilt my head back so I can scowl at him properly. I don't think it's working.

He sets the bottle back on the table and then braces his hands on each side of my head, leaning down. "Yes, you are."

He's all over my personal space and I don't know if the tequila has muddled my brain already, but I'm suddenly hit by a crazy urge to find out what a vampire kiss tastes like. It doesn't matter if Saxon can be a nuisance most of the time. He's a sexy pest and I want him. He stands straight again, stepping back, and I miss my opportunity. *Damn it!*

"Why do you care if I drink myself into a stupor?" I ask angrily.

"Maybe I like you." He sticks his hands in his pockets, pushing his low-rise jeans even lower. A peek of taut, golden skin appears, and my fingers are now itching to touch him.

"You're such a liar," I reply a little harshly to hide my reaction.

He offers me his hand. "Come on. You need to dance off all that poison you drank."

I should bat his hand away, but instead, I curl my fingers around his and let him help me up. The room begins to spin, making me sway on the spot. Still holding me, Saxon places his free hand on my waist, which brings me flush against his body.

With my palm flat against his chest, I can feel the accelerated beat of his heart. It matches the tempo of mine. A wisp of desire curls around the base of my spine, making me forget all the reasons I shouldn't entertain the idea of hooking up with Saxon. My breathing has become shallow, and I don't dare to move. This situation is changing fast and I'm not sure how I want to proceed.

You wanted a wild night, Aurora. There's nothing wilder than Saxon Hellström.

"Are you all right?" he asks in a voice that's much huskier than before. *Damn.*

I look up, seeking Saxon's gaze. His blue eyes are shining crimson now. *Danger. Danger, Will Robinson.* I've suddenly become a tasty snack to him. I need to pull away from his embrace, but it's almost like my body has a will of its own.

"What's the matter, Aurora? Did the cat get your tongue?" His fingers dig deeper in my skin as he leans in. There's definitely a bulge in his pants, pressing against my belly.

All common sense flies right out the window.

"Is that a gun in your pocket or are you just happy to see me?" I ask like a moron, regretting my outburst immediately.

His lips widen into a wolfish smile, revealing the tips of his sharp fangs. "You know I don't need a gun."

The song in the background changes to one of my favorite songs by Dua Lipa, snapping me out of his seductive trance. I finally find the will to step back.

"I thought you wanted to dance," I say.

Without waiting for his reply, I whirl around and practically run down the stairs to the dance floor. Heat has creeped up my face, just like my body is on fire. Tequila didn't do this. My overheated skin is all thanks to Saxon.

I'm almost in the middle of the club when a rough hand grabs my arm and twists me around.

"You're not escaping so easily, little witch," Saxon says. His blue eyes still have a tinge of red in them.

Hunger and arousal will do that to a vampire. I vowed to never allow a bloodsucker to drink from me, but my will is crumbling fast. It's common knowledge that a vampire's bite is quite erotic and when combined with sex is an unforgettable experience.

I lift my chin in defiance. "Who says I was trying to?"

Saxon lets go of me only to circle his arms around my waist and pull me closer. *Yep.* His erection is still there. He leans down, stopping an inch from my mouth and making my breathing hitch. *Crap. Is he going to kiss me now?*

He brings his lips to my ear instead. "I can smell your arousal, you know."

"Tequila makes me horny. Don't let that go to your head." I sway my hips to the beat of the song, knowing very well what the friction between our bodies will do to him.

He hisses. "Don't tease me, Aurora. You're playing with fire."

"Maybe I like playing with fire." Rising on my tiptoes, I lick the hollow of his throat.

There's a tiny voice in the back of my head saying this is a huge mistake, but I stomp on it until it dies. Saxon freezes, becoming as still as a statue. I don't think he's breathing. The moment only lasts a few seconds, and then his fingers are tangled with my hair and his tongue is in my mouth.

Sweet baby unicorns. This is heaven.

3

SAXON

———⟡———

Truth be told, I've had a thing for Aurora since the first time I met her at an official royal function at King Raphael's mansion years ago. Beautiful and with a sharp tongue, she's exactly the type of woman I'm drawn to. I don't like meek and boring. I need someone to keep me on my toes. Too bad she's a witch.

I was taught to never mess with them by my asshole father. If the brutal general was afraid of them, he must have had a reason. My whole life, I was careful to give any of the magical folks a wide berth until I came across Aurora Leal, the High Witch's daughter. It was impossible to stay away from her. And the fact that I crashed and burned on my first attempt to get her into my bed only motivated me more. Didn't have much luck on the second and third tries either.

When I spotted her in Havoc, I made a deal with myself. If I got another no, I'd give up. Little did I know the little witch was looking for some cock fun, and I was more than ready to volunteer.

Which explains why we are all over each other like animals in heat. All it took was one tequila-flavored kiss from her to set my body ablaze. I thread my fingers through her hair to bring her closer while my arm snakes around her waist to keep her in place. Her perky breasts crush against my chest as my erection presses against her belly. A shot of libido shoots straight down, making me wish we weren't in the middle of a crowded dance floor. I've never been more turned on by a female than I am now. One wrong move, just a little bit more friction, and I'm going to jizz in my pants. If she were a regular human, I'd fuck her right here while I fed from her. But Aurora is not a blood whore. She's different, special.

Fuck. What am I thinking?

She lets out a throaty moan as she angles her head, deepening our kiss. A strange, tingling warmth uncoils in my chest, spreading through the rest of my body like wildfire. It feels like my very bones are turning into molten lava. Then the loud music fades into the background, and all I can hear is Aurora's accelerated pulse. My mouth waters, and my fangs descend fully as her blood calls to me. The craving is not bloodlust, but it's powerful enough to make my head spin.

I let go of her lips, leaving a trail of hot kisses along her jawline, before dipping down to her neck. Aurora arches her back, whimpering as I lick her feverish skin. Her vein throbs under my tongue. One nick, one hard pull, and her warm blood will flood into my mouth. I'm on the verge of succumbing, but I hesitate—a first for me.

I suspect getting bitten by a vampire in the middle of a club is not something Aurora ever desired. She's not thinking clearly tonight, and hell, I don't want to give her any reason to regret hooking up with me.

Why do I fucking care?

She grabs a fistful of my hair, and brings my mouth back to where she wants, covering hers. My tongue pierces through her lips, and the tingling feeling all over my body returns, much stronger this time. I get hot and cold in the span of a second, and the desire to fuck Aurora senseless is almost overwhelming.

Maybe caught in the same heat wave as me, she curls her arms behind my neck, jumping into my arms. *Motherfucker.* Her legs hook around my lower back, bringing her pussy flush against the bulge in my pants. Self-control is quickly slipping through my fingers, but there's nothing that can stop me from savoring this moment. My hands glide to her sweet ass, not because I need them to support her weight, but because I want them there.

"What are you trying to do to me, little witch?" The words hiss out of my mouth in a hoarse voice right before I return to hers.

She bites my lower lip, and then peppers my jaw with open kisses, sending shivers down my spine. A chuckle from her sends hot air over my burning skin. It feels like she just poured gasoline over roaring flames.

Not missing a beat, she moves on to my neck and then my ear. "I want you to fuck me." She rotates her hips, sending me straight to my doom.

That's it. I can't take it anymore.

Still latched to her delicious mouth, I head back to the VIP area, shoving whoever is standing in my way. The restroom is empty, and I plan to keep it that way by locking the door. Aurora jumps off me, and then with deft fingers, begins to unbutton my shirt. I help her out because I'm dying to discover what treasure she's hiding under the unicorn tank top she wears.

My mouth and hands find her breasts at once. I don't bother with taking it slow; I stretch the neckline down, revealing her pink lacy bra. I love sexy lingerie, but right now it's a nuisance. I snap it down the middle, freeing the most luscious pair of tits I've ever seen. Aurora arches her back while reaching for my pants. *Damn it.* Sometimes, I hate clothing. I suck one of her nipples into my mouth, groaning when she finally manages to unzip my pants and free my cock.

She stills suddenly, then takes a small step back while holding on to my shaft.

"What?" I ask.

Her chin is dipped now, and her long dark hair is falling over her face, blocking my view. "Fuck," she says, then she lifts her eyes to mine. "You're huge."

I don't know if it's the look of astonishment on her flushed face or the compliment, but shit if she didn't gain a thousand more points on the scale of awesomeness. My lips curl into a wolfish grin.

"Don't worry, little witch. It will fit."

Her brows furrow together. "I'm not so sure. Look at me; I'm tiny." She points at her hips.

Aurora is indeed on the petite side, except for her breasts. They're nice and full and *hell*, I'm ready for another taste, but first things first. I pick her up, which consequently forces her to let go of my cock—*sad face*—and then I set her on the long marble sink, spreading her legs wide. *Happy face.*

I drop to my knees next, making sure our gazes are locked as I tug her underwear down her legs. Aurora's chest is rising and falling out of sync as if she has been running.

"Don't worry, little witch. You'll be fine."

Her pussy is all pink and smooth, and already glistening with her arousal. *Fuck.* One single lick and I'm a goner. She runs her fingers through my hair, yanking at the strands as a tortured moan escapes her lips. The growl in the back of my throat is savage and possessive. She tastes like the most divine nectar, velvety and sweet. I grab her by the hips, pulling her closer while I fuck her with my tongue.

"Saxon … damn it. Why did I wait so long to give in?"

I'd answer her, even if the question was rhetorical, but I can't move away from my feast. A tremor runs through her body when I suck her clit into my mouth. She bucks her hips, but I keep her firmly in place.

"Motherfucker!" she cries out, pulling my hair so hard it actually hurts. I don't care, though. She's falling apart under my touch and it's the hottest thing I've ever seen.

I don't stop licking and sucking until she makes me. Still holding a fistful of my hair, she tilts my head up and kisses me long and hard. Without breaking the connection, I unfurl from my kneeling position, lifting her off the sink counter to pin her against the wall. My cock presses against her core, making us both groan in a desperate way.

I'm torn between my rampant arousal and the painful need to drink from her. My world seems to be spiraling out of control, and Aurora is the vortex responsible for my imminent destruction.

She grabs my face between her palms, pushing me back. "If you don't fuck me now, I'm going to hex you."

My eyes grow rounder. "Don't even joke about it, little witch."

She narrows her lust-infused eyes. "Don't tell me you're afraid of magic."

"I'll show you magic when I plunge my enormous cock into your pussy."

A bubble of laughter erupts from her lips, making me tense up on the spot. That was not the reaction I was hoping for. *Shit. Am I losing my mojo?*

"Why are you laughing?" I frown.

She shakes her head. "I'm sorry. I didn't mean to. I'm not laughing at you. I'm laughing at this surreal moment. I'm about to fuck a vampire in a club's restroom. I never thought this would happen *to me*."

"Hey, we don't need to do this if you're not sure."

But pretty please don't say you've changed your mind.

Her eyebrows shoot to the heavens. "Are you crazy? I've never wanted anything more in my life than having your enormous cock inside of me."

A breath of relief whooshes out of me, but then she laughs again.

"Damn it, Aurora. It's really hard to believe you when you can't keep a straight face."

"I'm sorry. I have the giggles."

Narrowing my eyes to slits, I position my dick at her entrance, sliding in a little. In an instant, the amusement vanishes from her expression. Her whiskey-colored eyes become glazed and riveted on my lips.

"You were saying?" I ask.

She hooks her legs at the ankles behind my ass, nudging me toward her and crushing my lips with hers. In a single thrust, I slide in completely, hissing as every nerve in my body short-circuits. *Holy fuck*. I was never one to climax prematurely, but I'm in absolute danger here of pulling a quick-draw move.

Hell no. I can't let that happen. Aurora deserves to get the best of Saxon Hellström, and I intend to deliver. Fighting the urge to piston in and out of her, I pull out slowly, only to slam back in. My balls are tight as hell, and I'm seriously on the verge of exploding, but this feels amazing and it would be a shame to allow it to end too soon.

"Why are you torturing me?" she asks between kisses.

"Woman, do you know how good you feel right now? I'm about to die here."

"That's the intention. *La petit mort.*" She licks my jawline before switching her attention to my neck.

"Fuck," I say, moving my hips faster. This is a battle I can't win.

She bites my earlobe, and then whispers in my ear. "You want to drink from me, don't you?"

"Yes," I hiss.

Tilting her head to the side, she replies, "Go ahead. Do it."

The hunger I felt on the dance floor returns with a vengeance. I'm salivating already, and my vision becomes tinged with red.

"Don't tempt me, little witch."

"I'm not. I want the whole package, and a vampire bite is a must." She turns her face to mine, piercing me with a determined and lucid stare. "I want this, Saxon. And I want it from you."

Ah, hell. When she puts it that way, who am I to deny it?

She offers me her neck again, and this time, I don't hesitate. My fangs sink into her soft flesh, and when the first drop of her blood hits my tongue, I know I just made a terrible mistake. Too late now. My fate is sealed. And so is hers.

4

AURORA

After the romping session in Havoc's VIP restroom, Saxon and I went back to his place, a mansion deep in the woods that very few people know the location of due to security reasons. It's also the residence of Lucca Della Morte, King Raphael's nephew. But the Blueblood vampire has been in hibernation for almost a hundred years—not that I was too concerned about bumping into him, or another vampire in residence. I was still too caught up in Saxon to notice anyone else.

This midafternoon, it's a different story. My body might be relaxed and utterly satisfied—there *were* a lot of orgasms involved—but my mind is whirling. I spent almost the entire day in bed with Saxon, and now I'm trapped under his muscled arm across my stomach. He's spooning me, which I can't deny feels pretty good. But I can't allow myself to lower my barrier around him or feel anything besides indifference. He's a Blueblood and I'm a witch. Even if I wasn't "promised" to someone else, Saxon and I could never be together. Vampires and witches are a dangerous combination. Neither the coven nor the king would allow it.

Why am I even thinking about this shit? I've always considered Saxon an annoying and immature male. Just because he's a god in bed doesn't make him boyfriend material. My brain must still be clouded by post-coital bliss. It's the only explanation.

Enough with the pointless inner monologue, Aurora. You need to get out of his bed.

If I could reach my purse on the floor and grab an energized stone, I could attempt a levitation spell.

Saxon mumbles something in his sleep, and finally rolls on his back, releasing me. Holding my breath, I throw my legs to the side of the bed and stand up. My limbs are a little unsteady. I did things yesterday I didn't think I was capable of. I'm definitely more flexible than I thought.

Hastily, I collect all the pieces of my clothing scattered on the floor and get dressed. The only thing I'm missing is my underwear, which I find after a minute under a chair. Well, I find what's left of it, nothing more than scraps of torn fabric. I guess I'm going commando then.

Saxon makes another noise, and my heart leapfrogs to my throat. I turn around, but he's still sound asleep, although I notice a frown on his face. I should leave, but my feet bring me closer to his satin-sheet-covered bed. His eyelids are twitching; he must be having a dream.

"Kari…no," he mutters.

Kari. Who the hell is Kari? That sounds like a girl's name.

Jealousy spears my chest, confusing the hell out of me. Why

would I care if Saxon was dreaming about another girl? It's not like I have feelings for the guy. Until a day ago, I didn't want anything to do with him. And just because he gave me the best orgasms of my life, I'm not stupid enough to let that morph into affection.

I turn away, grab my purse from the floor, and sneak out of his bedroom without glancing back. The door closes with a soft click, which sounds much louder in the silent hallway. I don't see a soul as I head to the ground floor, not even a familiar, which is pretty lucky. No one to witness my walk of shame.

The front door is not locked from the inside, and once I'm out in the courtyard, I pull my cellphone out. There are several missed calls from my mother, and even a couple from Miranda. My mother must be truly desperate to talk if she's using my little sister to reach me.

Miranda left me a voice message, so I press the button to listen to it while I walk out of the dark mansion Saxon calls home. I can't call an Uber from here. I'd like to keep last night a secret if I can.

Fat chance of that happening, Aurora. Everyone at Havoc saw you sucking face with Saxon on the dance floor.

Oh God. I hope there aren't pictures. That would send my mother into a rage, and seriously destroy my image at Bloodstone. So far, I've been able to keep most of the douchebags away from me, but if word gets out that I hooked up with Saxon, I can bet I'll be swarmed by a wave of horny Bluebloods trying to score a piece of the High Witch's daughter. It's like I'm a prize to them or something. *Dumbasses.*

"Hey, big sis." Miranda's voice sounds in my ear. "Where have you been? Mom is going crazy trying to locate you. Call me as soon as you hear this message. She's not telling me anything, so I need to hear all the deets from you. Bye!"

I'm not surprised Mom is not talking. It's her MO to be secretive. I'll call Miranda later. She can't help me get out of an arranged marriage, but she'll listen to my whining without bitching about it. She's the middle child and the most chill in our family of deranged witches. Niko is another story. A total brat.

When I finally reach a road with more traffic, I pull up the Uber app and get a ride. Miranda would pick me up in a heartbeat, but I'm not ready to disclose where I spent the night. As a matter of fact, I don't think I'll ever tell a soul. I'm not ashamed that I hooked up with Saxon, I'm ashamed I broke my own promise to never get involved with any vampire.

I find a medium-sized rock near the side of the road and sit down. It's less conspicuous than standing like a hippie looking to hitchhike. I left in such a hurry that I didn't even have the chance to check my appearance. Using the video app, I glance at my reflection, immediately cringing at my state. Messy hair, smeared makeup, redness around my mouth and chin. I look like a dejected groupie or a whore. I'm not sure which is worse.

Aiming the phone at my neck, I inspect the damage Saxon left there. Surprisingly, it's not as bad as I thought it would be. There are only two small incisions that are already healing. A slight throbbing begins between my legs as I remember the feeling of Saxon drinking my blood as he fucked me. I close my eyes for a second, shivering. That moment resulted in the best orgasm of my life. Now I understand why humans fill Havoc night after night in the hopes of hooking up with a bloodsucker. There's nothing in this world that compares to a vampire bite. *Nothing.*

And I will never get to experience that again. I bet Calvin is awful in the sack.

Oh God. If we get married, I'll have to sleep with that asshole.

My stomach coils violently as sudden nausea hits me. I lean to the side, throwing up everything I consumed last night while the same thought keeps running through my head in a loop.

I can't do it. I can't marry Calvin Belmont.

By the time the Uber driver arrives, I have recovered from the nausea. But I'm more depressed than I was yesterday when I arrive at Bloodstone. The sun hasn't set yet, so it's a familiar manning the gates. I asked the driver to drop me off at the front to avoid going through the security check.

The familiar on duty, Mr. Goodwin, gives me an overall glance, but mercifully, keeps his expression devoid of disapproval. I know he must be thinking the worst about me, but as long as he doesn't display his thoughts, I'm fine with it.

I have absolutely no desire to get out of my small dorm apartment for at least two days. Fuck my duties and fuck my mother. The first order of business is taking a shower and erasing for good any traces of Saxon from my skin. Then eat something, because I need food to get rid of this damn hangover.

But all I manage to do in peace is to shower. There's a knock on my door as I head to the kitchen in my bathrobe. I panic for a second, thinking Saxon tracked me down already. But then I remember the sun is still out. *Oh shit, then it must be my mother.* Even worse. The last thing I want is to listen to a tongue-lashing from her, but it's not like I can avoid her forever. Might as well get this over with.

So certain that I will find Isadora Leal outside, I don't bother looking through the peephole. Big mistake. It's not my mother standing in the hallway. It's Calvin Belmont, looking smug as shit.

Damn it.

"Hello, Aurora." He smiles slyly, displaying his flawless white teeth, which go hand in hand with his perfect coiffed hairstyle and preppy clothes. *Barf.*

"What are you doing here? How did you get past security?" I pull the lapels of my robe closer together.

"Oh, wow. Is this how you treat all your guests?"

"Only the uninvited ones."

His cocky smile wilts as his fake warmth is all spent. "I'm sorry. You're right. It was rude of me to simply show up."

What a pitiful attempt to show remorse. He can't hide the arrogance in his eyes for even one second.

"You still didn't answer how you got in."

"I came with your mother. She's in a meeting with the principal now."

Of course, Mom dearest had to be involved.

"May I come in?" Calvin asks.

I'm tempted to shut the door in his face, but that won't do me any good. Besides, rebelling won't change my fate. As much as I'd love to say to hell with traditions, if I don't accept my engagement to Calvin, most likely, my training to become the next High Witch will cease immediately, and I'll be kicked out of the coven. I'll be forced to align myself with those rogue mages, selling potions and taking any assignment I can find. That's a pretty bleak future.

With a resigned sigh, I open the door wider and move out of the way. "Sure, since you're here."

He takes an overall glance of my living room and kitchen, before turning around. "It's my understanding you're not happy about our engagement."

Straight to the point. All right then. At least he doesn't waste time with inane chitchat.

"No, I can't say that I am."

His eyebrows arch. "Why? I come from one of the most powerful magical families in the country. Our children will be unstoppable. I'm also not bad to look at." He smiles in an arrogant way, and I can't help comparing him to Saxon.

Sure, at first sight, Calvin can be considered attractive with his all-American preppy looks, but it's impossible to admire his appearance once one catches a glimpse of his ugly heart.

Claiming attractiveness is something Saxon would say, but the difference is that his cockiness is sexy. Calvin's comment only rubs me in the wrong way. He lacks the charisma Saxon has. A strange flittering feeling spreads through my chest, followed by a pang. *What the hell is this? Do I miss Saxon?*

"I've made you speechless. Does that mean you agree with me?" He invades my personal space, touching my arm. I must have zoned out for a second because I didn't see him approach.

"Nope. I don't agree with you." I step back, but Calvin has me trapped between him and the kitchen counter.

Anger flashes in his eyes as he narrows them. "That's too bad. Like me or not, you *will* be my wife." He grabs my jaw in a rough grip, tilting my head up.

My heart goes to a hundred in a split second as adrenaline kicks in. Raw magic flares in my core, spreading at the speed of light through my veins.

"Let go of me," I say through clenched teeth.

"I think you need a demonstration of how things are going to work from now on." He crushes his dry lips against mine, nauseating me on the spot.

But he only has a second to enjoy the stolen kiss before I blast him with a thousand volts of electricity. He flies back, hitting the opposite wall with a loud bang. *Holy shit.* I can't believe I was able to summon that much juice at once without the assist of a crystal.

Calvin is on his ass, looking at me with a dazed expression. I don't even think he knows where he is right now. But he only remains stunned for a few more seconds. When he recovers from the blast, his eyes flash murderous intentions. I don't care. I'm not afraid of him.

I march to the front door, opening it wide. "Get out of here before I call security."

He staggers back to his feet, not once breaking eye contact with me. His nostrils are flared like he's some kind of rabid beast.

"You'll regret this, Aurora. But don't worry, we'll have a lifetime together. I'll teach you to be a good and obedient wife."

"Get the fuck out!"

He walks slowly, enjoying my loss of control if the chilling smile on his lips is any indication. I bang the door shut when he leaves, but I can't erase the feeling of doom his parting comment gave me. I hug myself, trying to stop the tremors that are rocking through my body. *Damn it.* I can't believe he got me rattled like this.

He'll punish me for denying him. Well, he can try. He clearly has no idea who he's dealing with.

5

SAXON

✦

I stretch my arm, thinking in my half-asleep state that I'm going to find Aurora next to me. But all I get is the feel of my cold satin sheets. I open my eyes, confirming that I'm alone in bed. She's not in the bathroom either—I'd sense it if she were. She's gone. Disappointment unfurls in the center of my chest, and not because I won't get my evening-after sex. This is different, but hell if I know why. Most of the time, I'm relieved when a hookup leaves on her own.

With a groan I sit up. My entire body aches thanks to the out-of-this-world sex marathon from the night before. My morning wood becomes a rock-hard erection in the blink of an eye just by remembering the feel of Aurora's pussy wrapped around my cock and the taste of her blood on my tongue. I still can't believe she offered me her vein.

My gums ache as my fangs descend. I'm suddenly starving.

thirsty for more from her. The powerful sensation leaves me lightheaded. My room begins to spin, and if I wasn't sitting down, I might have fallen on my ass. *What the fuck is going on?*

Closing my eyes, I press the heel of my hand against my forehead, trying to stop the room from revolving. The feeling passes after a moment, but I'm still worried this shit happened in the first place. Maybe Aurora's witch blood messed with me. I've never drunk from a magical being before. Or maybe she hexed me. But why would she do that? She can't possibly be suffering from buyer's remorse. I'm not being conceited when I say I rocked her world. Her many orgasms attest to that.

I get out of bed, feeling restless now. What I need is a good workout to forget about Aurora. As much as I would love a repeat, hunting season is over. I got what I wanted and that has to be enough. She's the High Witch's daughter, engaged to marry another guy. I have no business getting in the middle of it.

As soon as I reach the main area of the mansion that I've called home for a long time, one of the staff asks if I'm ready for my dinner. Unlike in most Blueblood households, there isn't a single familiar working here. Gerard Norton is a human in his late fifties who we hired two decades ago. He's a jack-of-all-trades and mega discreet.

"I've procured five young ladies who have not been sampled by any other vampire," he continues.

Yesterday, I'd be more than ready to drink from all of them. Gerard knows my taste; I bet every single one of those girls is gorgeous. Tonight, the prospect of drinking from any of them doesn't appeal to me, despite my hunger. *Damn it. Aurora better not have ruined me for others.*

"Can you just send a few warm blood bags to the gym?"

His eyebrows shoot through the roof. "Are you certain?"

"Yeah. Save them for Ronan. I'm sure he'll appreciate having first pick for once."

Gerard always comes to me first when he has fresh blood in the house. It's not because he favors me. I pay him extra for the perk, a fact Ronan either doesn't know or couldn't care less about.

"He has eaten already."

"From whom?"

"Not from any of the new girls," Gerard is quick to assure me. "He too opted for warm blood bags."

I hear the annoyance in his tone. Gerard thrives on being the best at what he does. The fact Ronan and I aren't willing to taste the nourishment he procured is probably rubbing him the wrong way.

"Well, don't take it personally. Ronan is a weirdo."

"And you must still be full," he replies.

I narrow my gaze, not appreciating the remark. "What's that supposed to mean?"

Quickly, an expression of contrition appears on his face. "Nothing. I'm sorry. I misspoke."

He must have seen Aurora sneak out earlier. I'm aggravated, but Gerard is not to blame. *Why am I annoyed that Aurora left without saying a word?* I'm seriously beginning to think her blood screwed up something in me.

To avoid saying something I'll regret to him, I head to the back of the mansion where the gym is. It's a sizeable detached building equipped with the most modern workout equipment there is on the market. We also have one of the largest arsenals of hand combat weapons at our disposal.

Since it's nighttime, I don't bother taking the underground tunnel. I head out of the house through the back door, enjoying the pine-scented fresh air. It takes me back to the past, when pollution and noise didn't overpower nature. I love modern times, but I also miss a simpler life where I could truly connect with the raw energy of the world. I also miss the era when there weren't so many rules in place, where honor mattered, and despicable beings didn't hide behind red tape and bullshit treaties.

Lucca is going to have a cow when he wakes up and discovers what his uncle did.

I'm not surprised to find Ronan already breaking a sweat, punching and kicking one of the punching bags. The male practically lives in the gym.

"Yo. How long have you been here?" I ask.

"An hour," he replies without taking his eyes off his target.

"You've been here before sundown?"

"I couldn't sleep." He swings a powerful punch, followed by a roundhouse kick. The chains attached to the ceiling rattle perilously. They're the strongest kind, but from time to time, either Ronan or I will break them off.

"Why not?" I pull my T-shirt off, preferring to work out bare-chested.

Ronan doesn't answer right away, which draws my attention to his face. He's usually a closed-off male, but I've known him long enough to recognize when something is worrying him.

"Did something happen?" I press.

"King Raphael contacted me last night. He's sending the High Witch here again tonight."

My spine becomes taut as if an invisible string were pulling it.

"She was here last month. Do you think she can wake Lucca from hibernation this time?"

"I don't know, Sax. He's been sleeping for far too long." The next punch sends the bag swinging high.

That's how Ronan copes with his feelings, by pounding and breaking things. We're all worried about Lucca. He's been gone for ninety-five years. Manu, his younger sister, is acting more deranged than usual due to that. There's a dark cloud looming over our heads. The possibility that Lucca might not wake up this time is something none of us want to discuss, but it's in our minds constantly.

Lucca is not only King Raphael's heir, he's my friend, my brother. We've been through so much throughout the centuries. He's the reason I'm not some soulless monster. I owe him everything. We've survived bloody wars, battlefields, and assassination attempts. It's not fair that we're losing him to a fucking curse.

I veer toward the sword display on the other side of the room. The shining katana mounted on the very top is my favorite blade in the collection. The curved single-edged sword is considered the most perfect and effective handheld weapon that humans have developed throughout history. I love how it's light, agile, and lethal.

The pounding against leather stops, and then I sense Ronan approach. He reaches for the other katana on display, removing it from its sheath with a metallic *whoosh* of steel cutting air.

"Are you sure you're up for it? You've been punishing that bag for how long?" My tone is light, almost joking. Someone has to keep the atmosphere positive around here or gloom will sink its claws into all of us and drag us down to a pit of despair.

In true Ronan style, he gives me a droll look. "Bitch, please. That was only the warm-up. I could take you after running a marathon."

I head to the tatami area. "Aren't you overconfident? I remember I kicked your ass the last couple of times."

He rolls his eyes. "I had to let you win, or you would be an insufferable whining brat."

The corners of my lips twitch upward. "Oh, the lies you tell yourself."

We spar in silence for the next hour. I usually like to irritate Ronan with endless trash talk, but I know when not to mess around with him. He's angry and out for blood. All my focus must be on keeping my head attached to my body. There's no room for error when your opponent is a beast and you're fighting at warp speed.

Neither of us show any signs of winding down. Gerard already came and went with the warm blood bags. I'm hungry, but the physical activity has numbed it a bit. Maybe after I get rid of all my irritation, I'll be able to drink from one of the humans he brought in.

A bang coming from the door makes Ronan slow down. He lowers his katana when it's safe and glances at the gym's entrance. Manu is standing there, wearing a long deep red dress that, against her pale complexion and white hair, makes her look like blood spilled in snow. She's a stunning female, even if she doesn't believe so. She was also cursed by the Nightingale queen for interfering when the ruthless immortal was doling out Lucca's punishment. Manu lost her natural coloring. She used to be a brunette like Lucca, a stunning beauty who broke hearts wherever she went. Now her formerly warm, golden skin is almost translucent, her hair is stark white, and her eyes are golden instead of rich brown.

She doesn't acknowledge me. Her stormy eyes are glued to Ronan's face. "Why didn't you tell me the High Witch was coming?"

"I didn't see you yesterday."

"You couldn't text or call?"

He lets out a heavy sigh. "I was sparing myself the pain of dealing with your tantrum."

"You're an ass." She crosses her arms. "Well, they're here."

"They?" I ask.

Manu cuts her stare to mine. "Yeah, the High Witch brought her stuck-up daughter along. Ugh, I really don't like that girl."

I ignore Manu. She doesn't like anyone. But by the way my heart has gone galloping at full speed, apparently, I do like Aurora. A lot. *Fuck.*

6

AURORA

I should have known my mother wouldn't leave me alone for much longer, especially after I kicked Calvin out. She doesn't try calling, she simply shows up at my door, not bothering with manners or my privacy.

I'm in the kitchen, staring at my fridge without any idea what I want to eat, when she invades my apartment as if she owns it. Forgetting the food, I bang the refrigerator door shut, turning to glower at her.

"What are you doing here?"

She fusses with the sleeve of her jacket. "Since you left our meeting in a hurry, and have been ignoring my calls, I had no choice but to show up unannounced." Calmly, she lifts her gaze to mine.

"No, what you should have done was take the hint." I walk around her, heading toward the couch.

Plopping on it like I don't have a care in the world, I reach for the open magazine on the coffee table. I need to keep my hands occupied or I may "accidentally" hex her.

She follows me, losing her peaceful composure. *That was quick.* "Aurora Yuki Leal, I won't tolerate defiance from you."

"How did you expect I'd react when you told me I have to marry an asshole in ten months? Grateful? Over the moon?"

"You knew it was coming. Don't act like it was out of the blue. You're the future High Witch. You must marry someone equally matched in magic and influence, like I married your father."

I snort. "That's rich. You and Dad were high school sweethearts. Don't stand there and pretend it was a huge sacrifice for you."

A flash of rare emotion shines in her eyes. For all her faults, I know she loved my father deeply, and when he died, it broke her heart. But this isn't about her pain, it's about my future and the bleakness of my existence if I marry Calvin.

"That's true. I was lucky," she replies. "But even if I hadn't fallen in love with your father, I'd still have married him."

"What if Dad wasn't the man you had to marry? Would you have given him up then?"

Mom flinches as if my question caused her physical pain. But in the next second, her shrewd eyes narrow. "What are you trying to tell me, Aurora? Were you foolish enough to fall in love with someone?"

Saxon's image pops in my head. Why is beyond me. I don't love him; I barely like the male. Just because his dick is enormous and he made me climax more times than I can count on my fingers doesn't mean I'm suddenly in love with him. Although, if I had to pick between Calvin and Saxon, *hell*, I'd pledge myself to the Blueblood.

"There's no one else. I'm just pointing out that you can't possibly know how I feel about this. I didn't ask to be the next High Witch. I'm not even sure I want the job."

"You're talking gibberish. You've always desired to be the most important witch in the world. Don't pretend the power this position brings doesn't excite you."

She has me there. I want the power and the influence, but not to satisfy my ego. I want to make a difference. There's too much unfairness in the supernatural community, too much suffering, and the witches and mages aren't doing anything about it. If you don't fall in line with their archaic agenda, you're shunned, forced to become a rogue.

When I don't offer a retort, she continues. "Come on. Get dressed. You're coming with me."

I'm on high alert in an instant. "Where?"

If she says she's dragging me to see Calvin, I'm going to lose my shit. I can't face that perv again so soon.

"Per the king's request, I'm going to attempt to wake Lucca. I'd like you to be present. It will be a good learning opportunity for you."

Suddenly restless, I jump from the couch. Saxon lives in that same mansion. *Shit. Am I ready to see him so soon after our hookup?* Crazy radioactive butterflies flutter in my belly, and the warmth that spreads through my chest feels like giddy anticipation.

Pull yourself together, woman.

"Fine," I snap, to keep up the pretense that her request pains me.

The truth is, I'm far from annoyed. I'm excited beyond reason.

Thirty minutes later, we're pulling up in front of Lucca's house. At nighttime, the gothic mansion with its pointy windows, dark brick tiles, and black rooftop is even spookier. Count Dracula would have been so proud. Bloodstone Institute has the same somber vibe. *What's up with vampires wanting to live as if they're in a black-and-white horror movie?*

An imposing human in his fifties lets us in. He's not a familiar, and I never understood why the king's nephew and his inner circle don't have familiars like most Blueblood vampires do. There are rumors that Manu, Lucca's sister, has one, but he hasn't been seen by her side in ages.

On the ride here, I tried to get into a business frame of mind. I can't let my mother suspect for a second that Saxon and I were fucking like rabbits last night. Technically, there isn't a rule that says witches and vampires can't hook up, but a relationship between species is frowned upon. For me, it's entirely forbidden. I'm the future High Witch; I can't be involved with anyone or anything that might jeopardize my position serving the king. If you ask me, that's a load of crap. But until it's my time to serve King Raphael, I have to keep my opinions to myself.

The marble-floored entry foyer opens to a grand staircase that leads to the living quarters on the second floor. But that's not where the stuffy human leads us. We veer to the right, and then down a set of stairs toward the basement. Lucca's hibernation room is underground for safety reasons. Vampires are mortally allergic to sunlight. Once underground, we meet a set of steel doors that require a password to unlock.

The staff member angles his body over the security pad so we can't see when he types in the code. I watch him with dispassionate curiosity. Does he think we're a threat to Lucca? A low beep comes from the machine, and then the distinct sound of a deadbolt unlocking. Our guide holds the door open for us, waiting until we're through to step ahead once again.

The surprisingly cozy hallway tricks one into believing they're still above ground. Light wallpaper covers the walls, which are peppered with oil paintings in dark frames. It seems no one cared to update the décor down here.

It's eerily quiet, that's for sure, and I dare to hope we won't cross paths with any of the current residents. But as soon as Mr. Stuffy opens the wooden double doors to Lucca's chamber, I discover it was stupid of me to think I'd be able to avoid seeing Saxon. He's sitting on a lavish red velvet chair, looking sexy as hell in his black sweater and faded jeans. There's nothing special about his outfit, but he makes everything look good. He'd probably be hot wearing a potato sack. His blond hair is wet and sticks out at odd angles. He must have showered recently and immediately my dirty mind conjures up an image of him in all his naked glory. *Crap*. My stomach does a backflip, and my mouth becomes as dry as coal. I don't know why I'm having such a visceral reaction to seeing him.

He turns, burning me with an intense and heated stare. Warmth creeps up my cheeks as a swirling ball of desire concentrates in my core. One look. That's all it took to get me all hot and bothered. This is insane. Maybe by giving him my vein, I got under his thrall.

I force my eyes from his, taking in the rest of the room. Ronan and Manu are also present, standing at opposite sides. Manu is sitting on the edge of a desk that, by the ornate carvings on the wood and its sturdiness, must be an antique. She has her phone in her hand, forgotten now that we're present. Her yellow eyes burn into me, smothering, almost as if she feels a deep loathing toward me. A quick search down memory lane shows me nothing out of the ordinary, no interaction between us that would warrant that scathing stare. *Whatever, I'm not here to win a popularity contest.*

Ronan is leaning against a wall with his arms crossed. But his casual stance doesn't fool me. He's wound tight, ready to spring into action if necessary. I'm beginning to suspect my mother's previous visits left a bad taste in his mouth. The high tension in the air is undeniable.

"Good evening," she greets everyone without making eye contact to any.

That's how she is. Cold and aloof when dealing with bloodsuckers—and in her personal life. She wants me to be like her, and I've been trying to project the back-the-fuck-off vibe at Bloodstone Institute, even if acting like that is not me. I've just perfected the art of pretending. But I don't want to live like I'm made out of a block of ice twenty-four seven.

"Has there been any change since the last time I was here?" She stops next to Lucca's bed, keeping her stare focused on his ashen face.

It's the first time I see the infamous Dark Prince in person, but it looks like I'm staring at a corpse. He's lying on his back, dressed in fancy silk pajamas with his hands clasped across his abdomen. His hair is long, reaching his shoulders, but his face is free of scruff.

When vampires weaken, they fall asleep and don't wake up.

Witches must cast a spell on them to prevent their bodies from deteriorating. Bloodsuckers can't die if they don't drink blood, but they'll shrivel to the point there's no coming back to their normal appearance. They mummify. *Yuck.*

My great-grandmother cast the spell on Lucca, and since then, our family has been monitoring the heir to the throne, trying to bring him back every few years. But King Raphael must be getting desperate for the return of his nephew. He wouldn't have asked my mother to come here again only after a month otherwise.

"No. Not even a stir," Manu replies.

"Hmm." Mom retrieves four river stones from her bag and sets them around Lucca's body. Each has a Wiccan symbol drawn on it, representing the four elements: Earth, Water, Fire, and Air. She then pulls a white crystal the size of an ostrich egg and sets it on his chest.

Movement in my peripheral catches my attention. Saxon walks over to the bed, keeping his eyes glued to Lucca's face. I can't help but watch him while he's distracted. His jaw is set in a hard line and his lips are nothing but a slash on his handsome face. It never occurred to me how difficult it must be for him and the others to wait decades for their friend to rise. Lucca's curse must weigh heavily on his mind.

"Do you think he will ever wake up?" Saxon asks in a tight voice.

"I don't know. I can't predict the future," my mother replies in her blunt way.

Is she dense? Can't she see how hard this situation is for Lucca's inner circle? She has the empathy capacity of a teaspoon.

He crosses his arms, still frowning at his friend. "What does that big-ass crystal do? You didn't use it the last time."

"Sax, quit asking questions and let the High Witch do her thing," Ronan, the towering vampire, says.

Saxon crosses his arms, rewarding his friend with a displeased look. I'm still watching him, which I'm sure he can sense, but he doesn't make eye contact with me. I swear he wasn't indifferent to me when I came in the room, but now, it's like I'm not even here. I should be glad that he's not trying to get into my pants again, but a part of me feels dejected.

"Aurora, please stand by Lucca's head."

My mother's stern voice snaps me out of my inner musings. I take a step forward, but Saxon is standing in my way. He glances at me for a fleeting moment, which is long enough for me to catch a myriad of different emotions swirling in his eyes. He seems conflicted, but about what?

Without a word and still sporting his somber expression, he takes a step back to let me through. As much as I'd like to know what's going on with him, I force my attention to the task at hand. This is a big deal for me. I've never participated in an awakening attempt before.

"Place your right hand above his head and focus all your en—"

"Wait," Manu cuts in. "Does she know what she's doing?"

"My daughter is training to take my place one day. I'm showing her what has to be done."

"That's unbelievable. You're training her on Lucca?" Manu's voice rises to a shrill.

Ronan moves in front of the female when she takes a menacing step toward my mother. Pity. I'd like to see her go head-to-head with my mother. That'd be entertaining.

"If you can't act like a civilized person, you have no business being here," Mom retorts.

"Come on, Manu. I'm sure Aurora knows what she's doing."

I'm surprised by his remark. I didn't expect the brooding Blueblood to come to my defense. We've never spoken before. The idiotic schoolgirl living in my head immediately assumes Saxon talked about me to his friend. The idea is absolutely ludicrous, so I shove the dumb girl in the trunk of a car, gagged and bound. I don't have time for high school nonsense. I'm a grown woman on the verge of getting hitched.

God, I had to go and think about that jackass.

"What are we doing? Creating a shield of energy around Lucca?" I ask to get myself back on track.

"Precisely. I want his body covered from head to toe while I recite the spell."

Determined to prove to the bitchy vampire that I'm not an amateur, I eliminate all distractions from my mind and concentrate solely on the blessed power of Mother Earth that resides deep in my center. My skin becomes warmer, and my ears buzz with crackling electricity. A burst of scintillant power unfurls in my chest, like I just opened a jar filled with colorful butterflies and they're now fluttering their wings inside the confines of my rib cage.

It would be too easy to lose control and allow the energy to flow freely through my body. But I must divert everything toward the palm of my hand, hovering over Lucca's head. When I'm sure I have plenty of juice to create an energy field to cover his entire body, I unleash the strands of glowing light. Quickly, they form a mesh, and then, as the light becomes blinding, the mesh closes, turning into a shield.

The world ceases to exist. My body has become a vessel, a conduit for the planet's energy. My gift comes from everything surrounding me. Witches are born with the ability to harness the primal power from Earth.

There's a low humming in the background, but it's not until it ceases, and I hear my mother's voice in my head, that I know she finished casting the spell.

I pull my powers into my body once more, dissolving the shield. When I open my eyes, I'm a little lightheaded, but I manage to stand straight without swaying on the spot. I can't show weakness in front of anyone, especially Blueblood vampires.

"Did it work?" Saxon asks, moving closer to me.

Immediately, I feel a strange pull toward the male, almost as if he's a magnet and I'm steel. My skin begins to tingle again, and it seems like little wisps of electricity are snaking from my hand toward him.

"No. It didn't work," Mom replies. "I sense no change in his vitals."

Saxon makes a strangled sound in the back of his throat, reminding me of a wounded animal. Then he storms out of the room, almost pulling the door off its hinges in the process.

Mom doesn't even register the occurrence as she begins to collect the stones and the crystal. Ronan crosses the room, walking over to the vampire princess. Her face is twisted in an expression of agony when she locks gazes with her friend. I still sense tension between them, but whatever it is, it vanishes when she throws herself into his arms. He engulfs her in a bear hug while fixing his gaze on the sleeping prince.

I should wait for my mother, but my body has other ideas. I

head out, letting the pull guide me to Saxon. The corridor is empty and quiet, and yet, I know exactly where to go. The steel doors we came through are not locked from the inside, but they're effing heavy. Security in this place is tight.

I'm not sure where I'll end up. If Saxon returned to his bedroom, do I dare follow? But the invisible cord leads me to the great room that I can't call a living room because it's too grandiose. It more resembles a place where monarchs would receive special guests. A number of sofas and chairs are spread around the room, all in deep jewel tones that match the dark furniture. Classic paintings hang from the walls, including a life-size portrait of Lucca looking like he just sprang from a Jane Austen novel—if she wrote about brooding vampires.

Saxon is standing in front of the dormant fireplace. His hand is braced against the mantel and his head hangs low.

"Are you okay?" I ask.

He looks up, but in the gloom, the only thing I can see is the crimson glow of his eyes. *Shit.* Maybe I shouldn't have followed him.

"No. I'm not okay." His voice comes out stifled.

I walk over even if common sense is telling me to keep my distance.

"I'm sorry. We'll keep trying to get him back, every week if necessary."

Why am I making this promise to him? It's not up to me to decide, or even my mother. The king could very well tell us to wait another decade or longer.

Saxon doesn't reply for a moment, and then comes the sneak attack. His arm curls around my waist to pull me closer, and his lips crash against mine. I should resist, but when his tongue darts into my mouth, possessive and hungry, I'm a goner. My wanton body surrenders completely, melting into his, until I remember my mother could walk in on us at any second. With enormous regret, I push him off me.

"Stop it! I didn't come after you for this."

"Your mouth said otherwise," he replies roughly.

I take a step back even though I want to soak up his body heat. "You caught me by surprise. What's up with all the jackasses in the world trying to steal kisses from me today?"

"Excuse me?" Saxon's demeanor changes in an instant, going from I-want-to-sex-you-up to I'm-going-to-murder-a-motherfucker.

Shit. I shouldn't have said anything.

"Did someone harass you?" he presses.

"Forget I said anything." I begin to turn, but he grabs my arm.

"Answer me, Aurora. Did a vampire at Bloodstone try anything? Or was it your betrothed?"

His tone drips with disgust around the word "betrothed" and he hasn't even met the guy yet. When I don't answer, he continues. "It *was* him."

"What's going on here?" my mother asks from the entrance of the room.

Saxon drops my arm as if he has been electrocuted, stepping away.

"Nothing," I say, sounding incredibly guilty.

Mom spares a couple of beats scrutinizing us. The light from the foyer casts wicked shadows on her face, and also allows me to see the calculating gleam in her dark eyes.

"We're leaving now." She whirls around, striding away without a glance back.

No scene, and no questions. That means I'm screwed. She'll be watching me like a hawk now.

I follow her, but not before I glance at Saxon. There's a promise in his eyes that this isn't over.

7

SAXON

I tried to forget Aurora. In fact, I did my very best by returning to Havoc on the same evening she and her mother failed to wake Lucca. It was bad enough that every time there's a failed attempt to rise him, my guilt quadruples. It was my fault Lucca went to hibernation early. If I had not abandoned my post to chase some random skirt, I would have prevented Boone from striking Lucca with a blade that had been forged with vampire's bane.

The upscale club was brimming with humans, ready to have a good time either on the dance floor or in the arms of a vampire. My idea had been to fuck someone else to erase Aurora's taste from my memory, but for the first time since I could remember, my dick wasn't even remotely interested in any of the humans present.

I should have driven back home, but unconsciously, I end up at Bloodstone Institute. My pulse accelerates as I cross the gates of the building. I don't understand my reaction. It's definitely not the school that's making me feel this way. I haven't been here since I woke from hibernation forty years ago, and I was more than happy to keep my distance from the place until now. The world has certainly changed, but standing here, in front of the building erected as an ode to days past, it seems like the time hasn't passed.

I'm not surprised to find Solomon Corvicus waiting for me in the entry foyer, wearing his trademark perpetual scowl. After all, he was just as glad to see me depart Bloodstone as I was to go. He's the headmaster and the first familiar to ever be created, which means he's immortal like us.

"Good evening, Saxon. I'd like to say it's good to see you, but that'd be a lie."

I place a hand over my heart. "Ouch. You wound me."

All my mockery does is irritate the headmaster more. I can't blame the guy for not being happy to see me. I *did* burn down the north side of the building the last time I was here. I learned my lesson, though. Do not try to build the tallest bonfire in town during a windstorm.

"Cut the crap. What are you doing here?"

"I came to visit a friend."

"You don't have any friends currently attending school."

I raise an eyebrow. "How do you know? I'm a social guy."

The headmaster snorts. "Yeah, I know what kind of socializing you like to do." He looks at me intently, narrowing his beady eyes.

Solomon's insinuation amuses me. I have to bite the inside of my cheek to avoid laughing. He could kick me out of here if he wanted to, so I'm not taking any chances.

"Uh, I don't know what you mean." I try to keep a straight face, but the corners of my lips twitch up.

"Oh, for heaven's sake. Go ahead." He steps out of my way and waves his hand. "I know a mated vampire when I see one."

My entire body becomes a block of ice, frozen. All but my jaw, which currently hangs almost to the floor. "Come again?"

His bushy eyebrows furrow. "You don't know?"

"I'm not mated to anyone," I reply through clenched teeth. "That's ridiculous."

The male throws his head back and laughs, clutching his stomach. *Fuck.* He's taking too much pleasure from this. It's pointless to argue with him, so I keep walking, listing in my head a thousand reasons why his statement is bullshit. I'm not mated to Aurora. What a ludicrous notion. We're not even the same species. Was there ever a case throughout history where a vampire found a mate in the human population? I don't think so. And I'm pretty sure when the Nightingales left this world, the magic that created the mating bond went with them.

Yeah, Solomon has definitely gone mad.

It's not until my feet lead me to the library and I see Aurora sitting at a table that I realize I didn't make a conscious decision to come here. I had every intention of finding out where her apartment was. I still don't believe in Solomon's crap, but I have to concede this is weird as fuck.

To prove that his theory has no merit, I don't walk to her immediately. If I was bonded to her, I'd be unable to keep my distance. But as the seconds tick by, it seems my entire body, down to its tiniest cell, is being pulled toward her. My skin tingles, my stomach is a hot mess of twisted knots, and my mouth is watering already, remembering the taste of her blood. The feeling is similar to bloodlust. The difference is, I don't want to drink from her until she's dry. I just want to be near her.

Come on, Saxon. Don't let Solomon get in your head.

My foot moves an inch forward and it's a herculean effort to stop in my tracks. I switch my attention to the clock mounted on the wall to my right. Five minutes. If I can stay still for five minutes, I'll call it a win.

I don't last one.

AURORA

I knew Saxon wouldn't leave me alone, but I didn't expect him to come after me on the same evening of that stolen kiss. I wish he had waited longer because I sure as hell have not recovered from it yet. As a matter of fact, I've been doing nothing but replaying the moment in my head since I got back.

When I raise my eyes from the book I've been trying to read for the past hour, I find him looking all smug and fine, staring at me with a wolfish grin on his lips.

"Evening, Aurora."

"What are you doing here?" I shout-whisper.

He pulls up the chair next to mine and takes a seat awfully close to me. "I'm considering enrolling here. I think I need a refresher."

I shut the book with a loud thud, trying to mask how much my heart supports that idea. My body begins to hum at his proximity, which doesn't bode well for me. The last thing I need is Saxon living in the same building as me, tempting me with his delicious body and smoldering eyes. There's a high chance that I might develop some kind of attachment to him as a way to reject my impending doom. But it wouldn't be real.

"Why?"

"Why not? It's been a while." He leans back on the chair, folding his arms behind his head, which makes his shirt rise up and reveal a patch of golden skin.

I've licked that area and farther south. Now I want to taste it again. *Crap.*

"That's ridiculous. You can't simply enroll whenever you feel like it."

"Oh? I can't? Says who?" He raises an eyebrow.

I don't really have an answer for that. "When was the last time you were here?"

"Forty years ago. Why do you ask?"

It's so easy to forget Saxon has hundreds of years over me when he looks like that. "No reason."

I begin to collect my things. It's getting harder and harder to keep pretending I don't want to jump his bones again.

Saxon picks one of the books from the pile and opens it to a random page. "What were you reading with such intensity?"

Intensity? I want to laugh. *I was thinking about how good your dick felt inside of me, you idiot.* My face is on fire. I'm glad I don't blush easily, but surrounded by vampires, it makes no difference. They can sense any change in a human's body, which means Saxon knows exactly how fast my heart is beating.

"This is a druid book about vampire hibernation. You were looking for a way to help Lucca." He meets my gaze. Gone is the cockiness. All I see now is a male who is vulnerable and in pain.

"I know how important it is that Lucca returns. My mother is set in her ways. She won't look for an alternative that's a little unorthodox."

"And you think druid magic has the answer? How different is their magic from witches', anyway?"

"Extremely different. We draw our powers from Mother Earth. Druids were gifted their magic."

"By whom?"

"I don't know."

Saxon's gaze darkens. "You don't think the Nightingales, do you?"

I let out a heavy sigh. The source of druid magic, like many other secrets, is something the witch and mage elders don't like to share. They keep the information for themselves, like dirty little hoarders. Information is power. No wonder a witch's grimoire can fetch a high price on the black market. The older the grimoire, the more valuable.

"It's a possibility, but the Nightingales aren't my specialty. Can I have my book back, please?" I turn my hand palm-up.

The solemn glint fades from his eyes, giving way to a heatwave. He returns the book, making sure his fingers brush mine. There's an actual shock at the contact, and we both pull our hands back at the same time.

"What the hell was that?" I ask.

"You tell me. You're the witch."

"I didn't do that."

His eyes widen a fraction, almost as if he's suddenly realizing something. He abruptly stands, pushing the chair back so hard it screeches against the wooden floor.

"I have to go."

Without giving me a chance to reply, he whirls around and zooms out of the library, becoming a blur. He ran away and I want to know why.

I sense two female regulars staring at me, and I don't like it. I've been here for two months and I've worked really hard to avoid gossip. I'm required to spend a year in this godforsaken place, attending classes with the bloodsuckers and studying with the headmaster. I can't allow my personal life to become fodder for fork-tongued bitches.

"What are you staring at?" I snap.

They look away, shrinking in on themselves. *Shit.* They're the meek kind. I feel sort of bad for biting their heads off, but what's done is done. I shove my belongings in my bag and head back to my apartment. I'm supposed to attend a boring Keepers training class, but I'm not in the mood to hear Hanson, the instructor, yap about honor and gratitude. I'm not a regular, I don't need the brainwashing.

I'm determined to forget the last few hours, but it seems destiny has other ideas. A fancy envelope was shoved under my door, and it bears the insignia of the coven of witches. *Hell. What now?*

I rip the envelope open, and then pull out the invitation written in gold letters. My jaw locks tight. The elders are throwing a ball, and in my experience, they never organize those parties without an ulterior motive. I can guess what they're celebrating this time. My engagement. *Damn everything to hell.*

8

SAXON

⟞⟝

It's been five days since I last saw Aurora and I can say with absolute certainty it's been fucking hell. I feel achy, irritable, needy. It's pointless to remain in denial. I have to accept that Solomon's assessment about my condition is accurate. Aurora is my mate and now I'm fucked.

I've avoided everyone in my household, which was easy to accomplish. My mood has been so foul, I've been dolling out insults left and right. Ronan and Manu were smart to give me a wide berth. Of course, my reprieve from their well-meaning meddling must come to an end.

After hours in the gym, and then a run through the woods behind our house, I return to the mansion to find Ronan waiting for me on the steps of the back patio. The outdoor lights are out, and the new moon provides zero illumination. All I can see is the ember butt of his cigarette.

He takes a big drag, holding the smoke inside for a few seconds before releasing it in symmetric circles. I ignore him as I veer toward the door, but he stops me in my tracks with a question.

"All right. I've let you sulk in silence long enough. What's eating you?"

"Nothing."

"Come on, Sax. Let's not do this. You've been in an awful mood since the High Witch and Aurora came to visit."

"You know why I'm upset. They failed." I glance away, staring at the pitch-black forest.

"We're all upset, but you've been … off."

I whip my face toward him. "What do you mean by that?"

He flicks the cigarette stub away. "I don't know. I was hoping if you told me what else is bothering you, I could help."

"No one can help me."

"Dramatic much? I don't like this mopey version of you. I want the old Saxon back."

"You mean you want the sexy back?" I half smile, but it does little to make me feel better. This mate thing is serious shit.

"That was a pitiful but valid attempt at a joke."

"Where's Manu anyway?" I ask to change the subject.

"Dealing with missing Lucca the only way she can." Ronan snorts.

He doesn't need to elaborate. Whenever Manu is upset, she tries to break her own record of how many humans she can fuck in one night. Is it a healthy habit? Probably not, but Ronan always gets uber upset when it happens. Sometimes I think he's in love with her, but he's such a hard male to read, I can't be sure. And there's also the deal with the other female in his life, the one he never talks about.

"Well, I'm going to hit the sack. Sunup will be here soon."

"Oh, I almost forgot." Ronan pulls an envelope from his jacket. "We're invited to a ball organized by the coven of witches. King Raphael will be in attendance, and we're expected to be there too."

Fuck. A ball run by witches? Aurora will be there too. And her fiancé. My fangs elongate and my vision becomes tinged in red. I yank the envelope from Ronan's hand, almost ripping the paper in the process.

"Why are they throwing a damn ball? What's the occasion?"

"Do the witches need a reason to throw a party in this town?"

I quickly read the invite, but there's nothing mentioning Aurora's engagement. It doesn't matter. My heart is beating at full speed and shakes are running through my body.

"Sax? Are you okay?" Ronan asks.

"I'm fine," I grit out.

"Then why are you crushing the invitation like that?"

I toss the crumpled paper to the ground. "I have to feed."

Not looking back, I stride into the house, and veer toward the kitchen where a huge fridge stores bags of blood. I haven't been able to drink from a human since Aurora, and right now, it's not the moment to try. Ronan follows me, but he doesn't say a word as I clear through at least five bags. I didn't even bother to heat them up.

"It's the young witch, isn't it? You two hooked up," he says.

"Yeah. So what? It was just a one-time thing."

"Hmm. If you say so. Whatever it is that you're going through, you'd better be on your best behavior tomorrow night."

"Wait. The ball is tomorrow night?" I didn't read all the details on the invite. My eyes were scanning for the word engagement or wedding.

"Yep."

"And why did we only receive the invitation today?"

"It arrived five days ago. Gerard gave me all the mail. I simply didn't remember it until tonight."

Frustrated and angry, I run a shaky hand through my hair. I've been denying seeing Aurora for this long, which only made my craving worse. What's going to happen when I see her face-to-face again? Am I going to claim her caveman-style by tossing her over my shoulder and taking her away?

"Why are your eyes glowing like that?" Ronan stands straighter, his body now coiled tight in high alert. "Are you going into bloodlust?"

"No. It's not bloodlust." I glance away, embarrassed. "Solomon told me I'm mated to Aurora."

"What?" His voice rises.

"Somehow, when I drank from her, I ended up mated to her." I laugh without humor. "I thought Solomon was pulling my leg, trying to get back at me for all the headaches I've given him throughout the years."

"He'd never make a statement like that as punishment."

I snort. "He laughed his ass off, so I'm not sure I agree with you. Anyway, I didn't believe him at first. But I've been getting physically ill by staying away from Aurora. I don't know what to do."

"Sax, she's promised to another. You have to find a way to break the bond."

"I know that! Do you think I want to be mated to her? She's a witch, Ronan. A fucking witch. Only a crazy vampire would want to shack up with one."

"And she's mortal too. Even if there were no fiancé in the mix and you got together, you'd have to watch her die."

A sharp pain in my chest robs me of breath. The idea of her dying on me is akin to a steely knife puncturing my lungs.

"What am I supposed to do? Have you ever heard of anyone breaking a mating bond?"

"No. But if there's a way, the witches would know."

"I can't tell Aurora I'm mated to her."

His eyebrows arch, almost meeting his hairline. "Why the hell not? She has as much skin in the game as you do. She needs to know."

I shake my head. "No. As far as I'm aware, this situation is one-sided. I'm going to deal with it on my own."

"Suit yourself. But maybe you'd better skip the ball."

He's right. I shouldn't go. But we both know I won't be able to stay away.

9

SAXON

———◈———

"These balls are such a bore. There's rarely any human in sight." Manu scans the crowd from the entry foyer of the Conservatorium Hotel, no doubt looking for her hookup for the night.

"I see plenty of humans," Ronan grumbles.

"I meant non-magical humans," she amends. "I'm not crazy enough to drink from a mage."

I wince, even though her remark is not aimed at me. She doesn't know I've hooked up with Aurora. If she did, Manu would have mentioned it. She wouldn't pass up the opportunity to tease me.

Ronan fixes the lapels of his tuxedo, then glances at me briefly, probably to check if I'm about to take off in search of Aurora.

"Let's get this over with," I say.

I appreciate his concern, and I'm glad I told him the truth. He might have to drag me out of here tonight. I can already feel the yearning increasing by leaps and bounds. Aurora is inside the building, and the magic of the mating bond is pulling me toward her. But I hold my ground and follow Ronan in the opposite direction instead.

Manu, with her pale skin and long white hair, draws the attention of every single person she passes. Her allure has not vanished despite the curse from the Nightingale queen. We owe the Nightingales our existence, but no one can make me like that bitch.

The Conservatorium Hotel is a grandiose building, a landmark in Salem. It belongs to the Montenegros, a powerful family of witches and mages, and one of the first settlers here. The decoration is lavish, all whites, creams, and golds. It reminds me of the Palace of Versailles and I believe it was inspired by it, down to the corridor with mirrors encased by golden frames to the large chandelier hanging from the frescoed ceiling.

King Raphael is already holding court, which is no surprise. He'd command the attention of anyone in any room. Tall and imposing, he's a force to be reckoned with, and the most powerful vampire I've ever met. I don't know how anyone can look at the male and not think he's the rightful king. The thought brings me bitter memories that I'd sooner shove back to a dark corner in my mind.

Manu reaches the king first. He ceases the conversation at once to greet his niece with a kiss on her cheek. Ronan and I are not that chummy with him, despite have known him our entire lives. We simply bow our heads.

From the corner of my eye, I spot several of the king's Red Guard soldiers. They're not dressed in uniform, but their symbol—a red rose pin—is attached to the lapels of their jackets. Ronan, Lucca, and I have trained with them. They're all badasses, even the regulars in their ranks.

Ronan and Manu are talking to the king now, but my attention is diverted elsewhere. I sense Aurora getting nearer. My neck strains as I try to see over the crowd of people mingling in the grand saloon. When I finally spot her, my heart somersaults to my throat, getting stuck there. She's a vision in a formfitting sparkling gold dress that accentuates her tanned skin. Her long hair is pulled back in a complicated style, which leaves her neck exposed.

I move in the blink of an eye, using supersonic vampire speed in a room full of people. I'm breaking etiquette, but the bond is too strong to resist. I only stop moving when I'm standing right in front of her. She gasps, widening her eyes in fright. *Oops, I guess I did appear out of nowhere.*

"Saxon, what the hell!" she snaps, but then looks sheepishly at the two guests standing nearby.

"Sorry."

"What are you doing here?" she asks in a much lower tone.

"I was invited." I step closer, taking a deep breath of her sweet scent.

She glances around in a cagey manner. "You shouldn't have come."

A dark feeling unfurls in my chest. It's dangerous and aggressive, not quite jealousy, but a hundred times worse. "Because of your fiancé?"

She looks straight into my eyes. "Yes."

"Are you afraid he's going to find out you have the hots for me?" I joke, a terrible attempt to distract me from the need to kill the bastard.

She doesn't answer for a couple of beats, but she also doesn't break eye contact. "I don't think he would care about that. This is a political alliance."

"You seem resigned to your fate."

With a shake of her head, she glances away. "I'm not sure I am."

Like an idiot, I touch her naked arm, and once again, our contact causes an electroshock. But I don't move my hand away. I can't.

"Just say the word and I will rip his throat out. I mean it."

Her plump lips part, sending a zing of libido down my cock. I'm about to make a scene and crush my mouth to hers when someone with a mic interrupts.

"Good evening, ladies and gentlemen, and welcome to our little soiree," a woman with bright red hair and more cosmetic surgeries than Cher says.

Aurora turns toward the stage, her body now super tense. Her heartbeat changed too; it's pounding a little slower, almost as if it's suddenly heavier. The crazy need to pull her to my side and soothe whatever is distressing her is almost too much to bear. But she will push me away if I try anything, and mating bond or not, my ego won't take the rejection well.

"Who is she?" I ask.

"One of the members of the witch council," she replies.

The lady is still talking, but I'm busy observing Aurora. It's only when she mentions Aurora's name that my attention diverts to her.

"It's showtime," she murmurs.

With squared shoulders, she walks toward the stage. I'm about to follow her, but a strong hand clasps around my arm.

"Don't," Ronan warns.

There's an angry retort on the tip of my tongue. I'm fucking pissed that Ronan is keeping me from going after Aurora. I know he's right. But my savage instinct is clouding everything.

"Let me go," I grit out.

"Your eyes are glowing red. If you don't control yourself, you'll be hexed faster than you can blink."

He's not wrong, but damn, it hurts so much. I look at the stage, and that's when everything and everyone fade into the background. My pulse is now pounding in my ears and my body is infused with pure red-hot rage. There's a man standing next to Aurora, looking smug and shit. Their hands are linked together. That must be her fiancé.

Not even Ronan with all his muscles will be able to keep me in place. A roar is in my throat, ready for the battle cry as I launch myself at the enemy. But suddenly, a pair of dark eyes appear in front of me, and with a few whispered words, I black out.

AURORA

It's official. I'm engaged. My mother warned me they would announce it tonight. But no matter how hard I worked to accept my fate, to not let the news crush me, I can't pretend I'm not screaming inside. How can I marry this jerk? A unworthy man who I loathe.

If the union was only on paper, a true political alliance, it'd be easier to stomach. But I have to have sex with him, bear his children. I'm beginning to doubt if being the High Witch is worth the sacrifice.

To make matters worse, Saxon is here. I couldn't believe my eyes or how my entire being was craving him like he's the air I breathe. It isn't only because he looks like sex on a stick wearing a tuxedo. The need goes deeper. It's raw, primal.

Calvin is gripping my hand in a tight hold, but all I feel is disgust at the contact. Unlike the actual sparks that seem to fly every time Saxon touches me. I seek his face in the crowd, noticing immediately something is terribly wrong with him. His eyes are bright red, trained on Calvin, and his fangs are exposed. Oh my God. He's going to murder Calvin in front of all these people.

Suddenly, King Raphael appears in front of him. I'm not sure what he does, but a moment later, he and Ronan drag a stunned Saxon out.

"Earth to Aurora," Calvin says next to my ear, making my skin crawl. Yeah, that will bode well for our honeymoon.

On instinct, I pull away. "Back off, perv. We're not married yet."

Calvin's expression turns dark. "You'd better start treating me with more respect, darling. I won't tolerate this kind of behavior once we're married."

"That's a long time away and many things can happen before then." I storm off the stage, not caring that I'm blowing the charade this is a happy union.

I know that as soon as I leave, the gossip will start. My mother will be mortified that I behaved in such a disrespectful manner, but she can't have her cake and eat it too. I agreed to this alliance, but

I'm not going to pretend I don't hate Calvin.

Back in the La Morte mansion, I could sense Saxon—as crazy as it sounds—but as I search for the connection now, I find nothing. Unsure where Ronan and the king took him, I have to cast a quick location spell. He just touched me, so it's easy to do it without the help of a magical stone or crystal. They're outside, probably about to leave. *Shit.* I need to know if Saxon is okay. As soon as I walk out of the ballroom, I lift my skirt and break into a run.

A black SUV has just pulled over when I burst through the hotel's entrance. Ronan is helping Saxon into the car, but the king is nowhere to be seen.

"Wait," I say, breaking the final distance.

Ronan turns around. "What are you doing out here? Go back inside."

"What happened to Saxon? He was about to go berserk."

I try to peer over Ronan, who is blocking my way. I can only see Saxon's feet sticking out of the car.

"Don't worry about Saxon. He'll be fine tomorrow." Ronan closes the back door, then circles around the vehicle to get behind the steering wheel.

Damn it. He's really not going to tell me anything. The car peels off with a loud screech of tires burning rubber, making me suspect that whatever happened to Saxon is not over yet.

A chilly wind comes out of nowhere, reminding me I'm not wearing a jacket. I knew this party was going to be a bust, but I didn't imagine it would suck in such a monumental fashion. When I turn toward the building to go back inside, I find Elena Montenegro, the matriarch of the family, staring at me from the top of the stairs.

She must be nearing ninety years old, but she still has the energy to participate in council meetings and attend parties like this. She's a freaky lady, intimidating as fuck, but if I'm to be the High Witch someday, I can't show weakness in front of anyone, especially her.

"You should be more careful, child," she warns when I reach the top of the stairs.

"I'm sorry?"

"You'll catch a cold. Come inside and keep me company, will you?" She turns around, using her cane for support.

She doesn't return to the party; instead, she veers in the opposite direction, toward the lobby. When she stops in front of the elevators, I ask her where she's going.

"I can't handle grand balls anymore. I get weary easily these days. But I'd like to get to know the future High Witch better. So we're going back to my penthouse for tea."

That's a development I didn't expect. I've never exchanged more than a few words with the woman, but on every occasion, she made me super uncomfortable. Her gaze is so penetrating that it feels like she can see into my soul. But I can't refuse her invitation.

She doesn't engage in small talk during the ride all the way to the top floor. Once we're in her cozy apartment, she begins to prattle on about a myriad of things. Where some of her furniture and artwork came from, what kind of tea she likes best, who I think will win the next *Bachelor*. Maybe she's lonely and really only wants company. I begin to relax.

It's not until I'm comfortable sitting on her couch with a steaming cup of tea in my hand that the lady pounces.

"You need to end whatever it is you have going on with that blond Blueblood."

I choke on my tea. "Excuse me?"

"Don't waste your breath denying it. If anyone in that room had a brain, they'd have noticed too."

"There's nothing there. You don't need to worry."

"Oh, I'm not worried. But you should be. You can't jeopardize this union, Aurora. Surely your mother explained to you how crucial this alliance is."

"You don't need to give me the spiel about honor and sacrifice. My mother covered that ad nauseum."

Elena squints. "I'm sensing here she has not told you everything."

"What do you mean?"

"What do you know about the Belmont family?"

"They're one of the oldest magical families in Salem. Uber powerful and rich."

"There are other equally prestigious families with sons of age that would make a good match for you, maybe even one you could grow to love."

"I haven't thought about that. I suppose this is leading to your revelation why the council picked Calvin for me."

"Oh, the council didn't vote for Calvin. He wasn't even a contender. I was the one who had the final say in it."

Fuck. Now I'm getting pissed.

"You're the reason I have to marry that asshole?" My voice rises to a shrill.

"That's right. It was me. Do you want to know why?" She smiles in a wicked way.

My warmth toward her has vanished. So has my patience. "No. I don't want to know why you decided to shackle me to that hateful man. What do you think?"

She chuckles. "I like your spunk. I was right about you."

"Gee, thanks."

"The Belmont family is in possession of the oldest grimoire in history. It belonged to the first witch and it contains spells that you can't even begin to imagine."

Okay, now she has my attention.

"How do you know they have it?"

"Calvin's great-grandfather showed it to me once when we were betrothed. The grimoire is protected by a spell; only a member of the family can open it. I only know of its existence because I was about to become part of the family. But poor Ludwick died a week before our wedding." The lady sighs. "I never got the chance to look inside the grimoire. Such a pity."

Wow. She seems more upset about that than the loss of her fiancé. Maybe she cared about him as much as I care about Calvin.

"That's why you want me to marry Calvin—so I can have access to the grimoire."

"Oh no, my dear. That's too shortsighted. You're going to steal it."

"I may not like Calvin, but that's wrong. The Belmonts have done nothing wrong."

"Are you sure?" She raises an eyebrow. "Who do you think taught Tatiana's son to forge a sword using vampire's bane?"

Fuck. I thought that was just a story. It was rumored that a wound inflicted by Boone had sent Lucca into early hibernation.

"If that's true, then the Belmonts are traitors!"

"Yes, but there's no proof of that."

"How do you know then?" I narrow my eyes.

"Ludwick was only too eager to share all his family's dirty secrets with me in return for a little bit of affection." She smiles

71

slyly.

Elena Montenegro is as shady as it gets. We're members of the same coven, but damn, I'm not going to trust her with anything from now on.

"I'm not going to let you use me and destroy my future so you can steal from them. And what's the point? You wouldn't be able to read the grimoire anyway."

She waves her hand in a dismissive way. "I don't need to read it, child. I just want our coven to own it, keep it safe."

Yeah, like I'm buying all her bullshit. I wasn't born yesterday, lady.

I place my teacup back on the table and stand up. "I'm not doing it. As a matter of fact, I'm going back to the party and announcing the engagement is over."

"You're not going anywhere." She makes a circular motion with her index finger, conjuring a magical gale that sends my butt back on the couch.

"What the hell!"

"Be quiet, child. And don't even try to counter-spell me. Whatever nifty tricks you think you have, they're child's play compared to my arsenal."

I'm seething now, breathing through my nose and mouth as I glare at the woman. And to think, for a second, I considered her a harmless old lady who only wanted company.

"You're evil."

Her glassy eyes become rounder as a genuine expression of shock sweeps over her face. "I'm not evil. I'm one of the good guys here. Can't you see? The Belmonts are the ones who have done despicable things throughout the years. Only no one talks about them because they're so powerful."

"The Montenegros are powerful too. If the Belmonts are so terrible, how come you've never done anything to smoke them out?"

"They have the grimoire. As long as that relic is in their possession, no one stands a chance against them."

I shake my head, knowing she's manipulating me. But it won't work. As soon as I get out of here, I'm going straight to my mother. I don't know what I should believe anymore. Based on my experience with Calvin, I don't doubt Elena when she says the Belmonts aren't innocent darlings. But I don't think she's so blameless either.

"I can see you're not convinced." She stands up, leaning on her cane heavily. "Come with me. I want to show you something."

Reluctantly, I follow the old lady, painfully aware of my surroundings as I expect a trap to spring up on me from behind a flowery vase or a corner. My sixth sense is urging me to get out of here, but for starters, I doubt she'll let me, and also, my curiosity has been piqued.

She leads me to a study room that looks like it belongs to a librarian. Stacks of books cover every single surface, even an old chair, and bookshelves are filled to the brim. In a corner stands an old mirror, framed by a dark gold baroque border. Swirls of leaves and flowers compound all around the spotted mirror.

Elena stops in front of it and stares at her stooped and wrinkled reflection. "Do you know what this is, child?"

"It's an old mirror, but you're going to tell me it's more than just an antique, so get on with it."

She makes a disapproving clicking noise with her tongue. "Your lack of respect is appalling. I knew Isadora was slacking in your education."

I swallow the angry retort, not wanting to waste time discussing my mother.

"How old is this?" I ask instead.

"Very old. This is a relic from the golden era when the Nightingales walked among us."

My eyes become rounder. "Wait. Are you telling me this mirror is a Nightingale design?"

She smiles smugly. "Yes, my dear. It has been in my family for generations. But I didn't bring you here to boast about my priceless possession. I want you to look into the mirror and tell me what you see."

She steps away, allowing me to take her spot. I'm leery. If this object belonged to the Nightingales, who knows what it will do to me? But like a cat that can't resist a laser pen, I move closer. At first, all I see is my reflection. I don't sense any glimmer of magic coming from the mirror. My head begins to feel like cotton candy as my image dissolves in wisps of translucent fog. A vertiginous sensation takes a hold of me and then I'm falling forward into the mirror. I can't feel my body anymore, only my mind is sharp. A reel of images begins to flash in front of me, like a movie. I can't make sense of them until a familiar face appears. It's Saxon, kneeling in front of a burned-down building, crying desperately as he clutches a broken sword in his hand. I can't tell if that's something that took place in the past or if it's a glimpse of the future until King Raphael appears in the picture, covered in soot and blood, and holding in his hand the severed head of Manu, his own niece. His clothes look modern. So this is the future then.

Saxon turns to him and asks why but there's no sign of recognition in the king's crimson eyes. He looks demented, terrifying. He tosses

Manu's head to the side, then raises his broadsword, ready to swing at Saxon. When the blade descends, cutting an arch in the air, I cry out and the gruesome vision fades to black.

I'm freefalling, and then, I'm back in my body. I stagger back, still reeling from the vision I saw.

"So, what did you see?" Elena asks too eagerly.

"What the fuck is this mirror?"

"It shows what was and what can be."

I'm shaking, and my heart is thrumming like a moth trapped inside a mason jar. "What can be? Like a possible future?"

"Yes."

"So that means what I saw might not come to pass?"

She narrows her shrewd eyes. "You saw your vampire lover's demise, didn't you?"

My eyes burn and my throat tightens to the point I almost can't breathe. "Yes." I force the word out.

"Was it the king who dealt the killing blow?"

I nod, unable to form words.

"I also saw the king's downfall."

"How? He looked changed, almost possessed."

"I don't know, child. The only thing I know with certainty is that if his nephew doesn't return to the world of the living, that will be the future."

"How can you be so sure that if Lucca returns, the king won't turn into a monster?"

"I didn't say he won't turn into a monster. I've looked into the mirror countless times, and the outcome is always the same. The king goes mad. But if Lucca is back, there won't be so much bloodshed."

"Are you certain what this mirror shows is true?"

She shrugs. "All the visions it showed me throughout the years have come to pass. I have no reason to believe it isn't the case this time. But you can stop it."

"Me? How?"

"I have the spell that will bring Lucca back from hibernation."

"If you're in possession of the spell, and you know the awful reality that awaits if he doesn't return, why haven't you given it to my mother yet?"

She laughs, shaking her white head. "Oh, child. Why would I give away such a great bargaining chip like that? I couldn't care less if King Raphael killed his entire family and all his friends."

"You're awful."

"No. I'm practical. There's no good reason why we witches should bend over backwards to please the bloodsuckers. Don't stand there and tell me that you didn't think the same before you fell in love with a vampire."

I press my lips together, knowing that I can't refute her assessment. Similar thoughts have crossed my mind many times.

"I have a proposal," she continues. "I'll give you the spell in exchange for the promise you *will* marry Calvin."

A violent clench of my stomach sends bile to my mouth. "So you can get your hands on the grimoire."

"Yes, it's the end goal."

"How can I be sure the spell you have will work? My mother has been trying for years to bring him back without success."

Elena chuckles. "Well, I have a few more years of experience than your mother. This deal will obviously require a magical binding. Promises without it are only empty words."

A trickle of dread licks the back of my neck. The last thing I want is to be magically bound to her.

"I'm not going to bind myself to you."

She shrugs. "No blood vow, no spell. Remember, child, your lover's life is on the line. If Lucca doesn't wake, the blond Blueblood dies."

A stabbing pain pierces my chest as vises of fear curl around my neck, cutting off my air supply. That scene I saw in the mirror is imprinted in my mind and the emotions it evoked in me have carved a hole in my chest. I haven't figured out yet what I feel for Saxon, but I can't be responsible for his demise. The idea of him dying such a cruel death crushes me. How could Elena Montenegro have known what those visions would do to me unless she saw my connection to Saxon herself? What else has she seen using the Nightingale relic?

"I could tell my mother and the rest of the council what I saw, and what you're withholding."

She snorts in derision. "Good luck with that. Who do you think they'll believe? A living legend or a young, rebellious witch?"

Fuck. Knowing how those fools operate, they'll side with Elena for sure. Sadly, even my mother will have a hard time believing me. I also don't know when the vision I saw will take place. I could try to find another solution, but am I willing to gamble with Saxon's life like that?

I swallow the tightness in my throat and spit the words out bitterly. "Fine. You have a deal."

MICHELLE HERCULES

10

SAXON

———◆———

I'm groggy as fuck when I finally wake up in my room. It takes me a moment to notice I'm not alone. There's a dark figure sitting in the corner, and immediately, my survival instinct kicks in. I jump out of bed—or try. My coordination is shot, and I end up getting tangled in the sheets and falling on the floor.

"Please try not to hurt yourself on my account, son," King Raphael says.

Ah, shit.

I get up in a most ungraceful manner, only to stand awkwardly in front of the male. I've known him for a long time, but still, there's a trace of deep discomfort and shame whenever I'm in his presence.

"My king, what can I do for you?" I ask.

"You can start by telling me what the hell happened back at the gala."

I swallow the embarrassment and clear my throat. "Aurora is

my mate." It's pointless to lie to him, and I shouldn't anyway.

My answer hangs in the air like a net of barbed wire while the king just stares at me without uttering a word.

"And how did that happen exactly?" he finally asks.

"We hooked up last week, and I drank from her. I didn't mean for it to happen, nor do I want to be mated to her," I'm quick to add.

"It doesn't matter whether you want this or not. It's done."

Fuck.

"So there's no way to reverse the situation? Aurora doesn't know. I believe the bond is one-sided."

"No. It's not. She might not be aware of it yet because she's not a vampire. I'd usually consult with the High Witch about these matters, but considering it involves her daughter, it's better to leave her out of it for now."

"With all due respect, my king, how does that help me? Aurora is engaged, and I almost killed the guy tonight."

"I know. I was there," he grumbles. "I brought you this." He taps the table next to his chair, drawing my attention to a vial with a green liquid inside.

"What's that?"

"A potion that will numb your mating bond instincts and keep you from committing murder. Mind you, it wasn't designed for that purpose, so I'm not sure it will work well."

"What is it for then?"

"Curing vampires who have fallen under the spell of sirens."

Fucking great.

"It was the best I could find on short notice," the king continues. "Aurora's engagement must not be compromised by one of my own. I can't afford to lose the support of the magical community."

He stands, fixing the front of his tux. *Shit*. He left the party early on my account. *Way to royally fuck up, Saxon.*

"One vial should be good enough for a week," he continues. "It's a temporary fix, not a real solution."

"What if we can't find a real solution?"

He narrows his gaze while I sense a darkness crowding around him. "That would be unpleasant."

I don't know what to make of his statement. Does that mean he would have to kill me? I'd like to believe I've proven myself to the king. I'm not my father's son. But maybe the bad blood runs too deep, and I'm cursed to pay for his sins.

"I'll find a way," I reply.

"I've spoken to Solomon. I want you to re-enroll in the institute immediately."

My eyebrows shoot to the heavens. I didn't expect that. "Why?"

"Because being away from Aurora will only make matters worse, even with the potion. Also, he can help you find a solution."

The king walks to the large window in the room. Those would be a big no-no in a vampire's lair, but the house is equipped with impenetrable shutters that close automatically ten minutes before sunrise. Even so, my bed is nowhere near the range of streaming light.

The window opens on its own. That's one of the super cool tricks the king has up his sleeve. In the next second, he turns into black smoke, vanishing in the dark. The male and his abilities never cease to amaze me, but tonight, there's no room in my mind for admiration. The next time I see him might very well be when he comes to off me.

With that depressing thought hanging over my head, I head

over to the table and grab the vial. Now that the king is gone, the overwhelming compulsion to go after Aurora, the crazed need to kill her fiancé, is returning. My skin prickles all over as if I'm covered from head to toe in needles.

I pull the cap off the vial and stare at the greenish liquid. "Here goes nothing."

Throwing my head back, I drink everything in one gulp. Bitterness fills my mouth, and a crazy burn goes down my throat. I cough, covering my lips with the back of my forearm.

"Fuck!" I say when I'm sure I'll be able to keep the liquid down. *Why do witch potions have to taste so foul?*

I drop on the chair the king was occupying earlier, feeling lethargic all of a sudden. If this is what he meant by numbness, it sucks balls. I don't think I can even walk back to my bed. How am I supposed to function at all?

There's a knock on my door. Since Manu rarely visits me in my quarters, I guess it must be Ronan.

"Come in," I say in a scratchy voice. He walks in, doing a quick search of the room first.

"He's gone."

"I thought as much. I sensed a huge drop in power coming from inside."

"Fuck off," I grumble.

Ronan changed clothes already, and now he's back in his regular outfit of dark jeans and a generic T-shirt. He shoves his hands in his pockets and stares at me with a question in his eyes.

"Don't worry. I'm not about to rip Aurora's fiancé's throat out. The king gave me a potion."

"Is it going to remove the bond?"

"No. I think only powerful magic can do that. He ordered me to enroll at Bloodstone Institute again."

"Whatever for?" His eyes widen.

"I have to be near Aurora, even with the potion." I pull my hair back, yanking at the strands. "This situation blows."

"We'll come with you. You can't face it alone."

"No. You have to stay here with Lucca. Protecting him is the main priority."

Ronan clenches his jaw so hard that I can hear his molars grinding together. "And who is going to protect you from yourself?"

I look out the window, not in the mood to withstand Ronan's knowing gaze. Being wild and reckless is in my nature, but with supernatural forces trying to control my body and mind, I'm now a ticking bomb, ready to explode.

Will I finally live up to my father's legacy and destroy everything the king has worked for?

"When are you leaving?"

"Tomorrow."

"So soon? Shouldn't you rest for a few days? Get things in order?"

I turn to him. "No. I don't want to stay too long away from her. That might jeopardize the potion's effect."

If it works. The pessimistic thought pops in my head. It's best if I don't tell him what the main purpose of the potion is. He'd never let me go alone if he thinks it's not safe.

Ronan crosses his arms, emphasizing his huge pectorals and biceps. "What can Manu and I do?"

A humorless laugh bursts from my mouth. "Do you know a rogue mage powerful enough to break a mating bond?"

"Aurora could probably do it."

His logic is sound, but I don't want her to know. The idea that she might not want to break the bond terrifies me. That would for sure cause a blood war between vampires and her kind. I can't risk King Raphael's crown like that.

There isn't a shred of doubt in my mind that if Aurora says yes to me, I'm going to let them all burn.

11

AURORA

———✦———

Committed to my deal with Elena Montenegro, I decide the best course of action is to bury the hatchet and try to get along with Calvin. My decision goes against everything I believe in, especially after Elena's insinuation that the Belmonts have assisted Boone in the past.

I've been waiting in the lobby of the law firm his father owns for almost an hour, and the douche canoe hasn't showed his face yet. This isn't a surprise visit. I called in advance, but it seems he's determined to make me grovel. *Fucker.*

I'm about to leave when he walks into the lobby, laughing with a tall blonde latched to his arm. She's wearing a business suit, but the skirt is so tight it could be mistaken for a tube top. And her white blouse is unbuttoned to the point I can see her lacy bra peeking out. So, that's how he's going to play the game, by parading in front of me with a random bimbo. I groan in my head, fighting the urge to roll my eyes.

He kisses Blondie on the cheek before turning to me. "Hello, darling. Have you been waiting long?"

"No, I just got here." I put on a fake smile. If he was hoping for a fit of jealousy, he has no idea who he's messing with.

Blondie walks away, but I don't break eye contact with him. I'm enjoying his disappointed face too much.

"I have to say that I was surprised you called after you stormed out of the gala last night."

"I didn't storm out. I had to use the ladies' room, and then Elena Montenegro asked me to accompany her to her apartment. You know I can't say no to her."

"Oh, did she say anything to you?" Calvin's eyes gleam with sudden interest.

Wouldn't you like to know, buddy?

"She just wanted to get to know the future High Witch better. It *is* the highest-ranking position in the magical community." I smirk, knowing the remark will piss off Calvin.

He can't conceal his scowl, which doubles my pleasure. But then I remember the reason I'm here, so I try not to display too much glee.

"I was wondering if you have time for lunch. I'm afraid we got off on the wrong foot."

The squint of his eyes tells me he's not buying my change of attitude. "That's true, but only because you were being a bitch."

Anger swirls in the pit of my stomach. No one calls me a bitch without retaliation. But thanks to the blood vow I made with Elena, I have to swallow my pride. I curl my hands into fists, digging my nails into my palms.

"I'm really trying here, Calvin," I grit out. "But if you, if *we*, don't change our attitudes toward one another, I don't see the point of going ahead with this union."

"You can't back out of our engagement, sunshine. The council voted. It's happening."

"Do you think you're the only eligible bachelor from a powerful magical family? I can always claim we aren't compatible, and they'd have no choice but to marry me to someone else. All they care about is that the future High Witch marries a candidate from a good family. It doesn't need to be you."

This is a total bluff. The council members would rather cut their own wrists than go back on a decision they all voted in favor of. They're that stubborn.

But Calvin is a moron, and clearly doesn't know about the inner workings of the elders. Sparks of fury are coming out of his eyes now. "Bullshit."

"Would you bet on it?" I raise an eyebrow. "It'd be a hassle to get rid of you, for sure. But I'll do it if you keep acting like a jerk. Let's face it, *darling*, you need me more than I need you."

Watching the pompous ass turn beet red is more than I could hope for. But I can't gloat. I'm balancing on a tightrope here, and if I push him too far, I'm going to lose the game.

"Fine. I'll try to be nicer. How about I take the rest of the day off and we spend it together?"

It's impossible to miss the implication of his suggestion. *Hell to the no, jerkface. You're not sampling the goods until I have no choice.*

"Let's not be hasty. We'll start with lunch."

After a gruesome two-hour lunch where I tried not to stab Calvin in the eye with a fork, I stopped to see my sisters. I miss the brats, and I also knew Mom wouldn't be home. It was good catching up with them, and they made me forget my fucked-up life for a little bit. But I also had another reason for my surprise visit. I had to plant the spell Elena Montenegro gave me in one of my mother's books.

When I return to Bloodstone, my heart is heavy, and I have no desire to attend any of the classes on the schedule tonight. But I can't keep blowing them off. Solomon will definitely keep me here longer if he thinks I need more training. In hindsight, it would postpone my wedding to Calvin, but that would be like spending another thirty days on death row in prison.

I run to my apartment to change clothes, then hurry to Hanson's class—Keepers training. He's another asshole I'd rather not deal with, but at least I don't have to endure him one-on-one. Besides, he barely pays attention to me. I'm not there to become one of his brainless soldiers. In my opinion, Solomon should have never allowed this ridiculous program. Back in the old days, regulars trained to join the king's Red Guard. They were warriors. The students in this class are the equivalent of mall cops. Pathetic.

A cluster of five regulars are chatting when I enter the gym. They stop talking at once to gawk at me. I should be used to the stares by now. There's a lot of lore about witches that vampires fear, especially regulars.

I wave at them, grinning from ear to ear like a maniac. They look away without waving back. *Sheep.*

Hanson is not here yet, so I start with the warm-up exercises. The other students resume their chitchat, but it's easy to tune them out. My deal with Elena is at the forefront of my mind. I hate that she cornered me into a blood vow. Magical bindings are not something anyone should enter without careful consideration, and even so it's risky as hell. In my case, it feels like I sold my soul to the devil.

She ripped a page from her own grimoire and gave it to me. All I had to do was magically include the page in one of the grimoires my mother has access to. She can't know where the spell came from or what I had to agree to in order to get it. That was one of Elena's conditions, and she made sure it was included in the vow's agreement.

I'm in the middle of a calf stretch when the murmurs in the background stop. My head is down, so I can't see who disrupted the class, but tingles down my back warn me the regulars didn't shut up because Hanson arrived. Saxon is here. I don't know how I know it's him.

I lift my head, and sure as hell, I find Saxon standing on the opposite side of the gym wearing workout clothes. My heart begins to thump faster, not as heavy as before. I stand straighter, caught in the desire to run into his arms or flee. Heat creeps up my cheeks and electricity seems to crackle in the air.

What the hell is going on?

I expect Saxon to walk over, but he veers toward the regulars instead. The two girls in the group perk up, and almost at once, they begin to play with their hair and smile like idiots. Jealousy hits my chest like a bulldozer. The words of a wicked spell gather in my tongue. One sentence and those two regulars will be shitting in their pants.

Oh my God. What am I doing? Am I seriously considering hexing those poor regulars only because Saxon said hello to them? He's not my boyfriend. He's just a vampire I fucked.

Hanson comes in, stopping in his tracks when he sees Saxon there.

"What are you doing in my class?" he asks.

"Solomon asked me to train with the regulars."

"What do you mean? Does he have a problem with my curriculum?"

"Not that I know of." Saxon shrugs.

"I don't understand. You woke from hibernation years ago. Didn't you already complete your rehabilitation or … wait. Is Lucca awake?"

No. He can't be. I just added Elena's spell to my mother's stuff. She couldn't possibly have found it and had the chance to perform it.

"No. Lucca is not awake yet. Come on, dude. Stop asking me questions. I'm back. That's all you need to know."

Hanson grumbles. My stomach spirals.

My worst fear has come to pass. Saxon is here, and I'm woman enough to admit the temptation will be hard to resist.

He finally comes over, and before he has even crossed the distance, my body begins to shake violently. I feel physically ill, like I have a fever. I press my palm against my forehead. *Shit.* I'm burning up.

"Are you okay?" He's now in front of me. Too close.

I shake my head. "I can't be here. I don't feel well."

To my dismay, he touches my cheek with the back of his hand.

Swiftly, the shock comes—much more potent this time. I cry out, and that's the last thing I remember doing before I pass out.

12

SAXON

———◆———

I've been pacing in Aurora's living room for the past half hour. She passed out during Hanson's class after I touched her, so naturally I whisked her into my arms and bolted to Solomon's office. She regained consciousness there, but I refrained from touching her again.

The potion King Raphael gave me worked. I could sense the mating bond, but it was weaker, it didn't take over my senses completely. It's obvious that the magic binding us is beginning to affect Aurora too.

Finally, Solomon walks out of her room, looking extremely displeased. I lied to him and said the king had forbidden me or anyone to tell Aurora we're mates. It was a stupid move and I'm sure the headmaster didn't believe me.

"I gave her something for the fever." He answers the question that's shining in my eyes. "Now you're going to explain to me why she can't know, and don't try to sell me that crap about the king again."

My shoulders sag forward as a resigned exhale leaves my body. "Look, Aurora doesn't want to get married to the asshat the council chose for her. What if she sees the bond as the perfect excuse to break off the engagement?"

Squinting, Solomon rubs his chin as he seems to ponder my reply. "I hadn't thought about that. If she calls off the engagement because of you, King Raphael will surely lose the support of the witches and mages. We can't allow that to happen."

Wow, Solomon is agreeing with me. I never thought I'd see the day. Too bad everything that I said is a load of crap. Sure, I don't want to screw things up for the king, but I'm having a terrible time letting go of Aurora even under the influence of the potion. I want to touch her and protect her. The idea I can't keep her from marrying someone she hates is crushing me.

"I know," I say.

"And with your blemished past, some people might even think you did it on purpose. Like father, like son."

Fuck. He had to go there. I've always suspected Solomon didn't like me, and it seems I've been right all along. Why else would he pour salt into the wound that never healed?

"I'm not my father," I grit out. "I'd never betray my king."

"That remains to be seen," he says in an offhanded manner.

"What's that supposed to mean? What are you insinuating?"

"Perhaps not on purpose," he counters, not one bit affected by my aggressive stance. "What kind of potion did you say you took to help with your primal mating urges?"

"Something against a siren's spell."

"Hmm. Not good. Not good. I'll have to think of a better alternative. In the meantime, stay away from Aurora. And definitely no touching of any kind."

"What am I supposed to do if she comes after me?"

He gives me a droll stare. "You're a second-generation Blueblood, you've survived several bloody wars, don't tell me you can't evade a twenty-one-year-old witch."

Irritated, I cross my arms while glowering at the small male. "I can evade her."

He shakes his head. "I'm sure your head could. Your dick? That's another matter."

AURORA

I don't know what kind of malady hit me, but I must have spent days in bed recovering from the sudden cold. My body is achy when the fever finally breaks, and I can feel the hollowness in my stomach.

There's someone making a ruckus in my kitchen, opening and shutting cupboards. A minute later, my sister Miranda walks into the room, carrying a tray of food in her hands.

"Oh good. You're awake. Feel like some chicken soup?"

Wincing, I sit up. "If you didn't know I was awake, why did you bring me food?"

"I was hoping the smell would raise you from the dead." She

smirks.

My stomach rumbles as loud as thunder, making her laugh.

"How long was I out?"

"Two days. You got a nasty bug. I've been taking care of you since Solomon called Mom."

"I'm sorry."

Miranda frowns. "Why are you apologizing? It's not your fault you got sick."

"No, I'm sorry our mother sucks and you had to pick up the slack."

In true Miranda fashion, she rolls her eyes. "God, you're starting to sound like Niko. So dramatic."

I reach for the tray, dying to dig in, even though there's steam coming out of the bowl and I'm likely to burn my tongue.

"Did Mom come visit me once at least?"

"Yep. She said she will come later today."

"I'd better recover my strength, then." I take a full spoon of soup. It's hot, but I welcome the warmth down my throat.

Miranda allows me to eat in peace for a few minutes as she begins to straighten up my room. But then she has to bring up the male I've been trying so hard to forget.

"A blond Blueblood came by to check on you. He's a hottie. Did you tap that?"

"Miranda! That's none of your business."

"Okay, that answers my question." She laughs. "I knew you wouldn't be able to resist trying a bloodsucker at least once. Did you let him bite you?"

I cover my face with both hands. "Oh my God. I don't want to talk about that with you."

"Why not? We've never kept secrets from one another, and you promised me you wouldn't change before you came here."

She's right. I did promise that.

"If you must know, we did hook up the evening Mom dropped the engagement guillotine."

Miranda's gaze darkens. "Good for you. I'm so fucking mad that she's forcing you to marry that toad. Do you want to be the High Witch that badly?"

I clench my jaw as I debate telling her what's at stake. In the end, I decide to leave Miranda out of it. Elena Montenegro is a cunning, dangerous witch. I can't risk involving my sister in her shady schemes.

"Yes, I do."

It kills me to see disappointment shine in her eyes. She thinks that I'm a sellout, that all I care about is power, which couldn't be further from the truth. I'm not sure I can make her understand without telling her the whole truth, but the sound of a key turning interrupts our conversation.

"Mom is here." Miranda takes the tray from me without making eye contact. "I'll tell her you're awake."

A minute later, Isadora Leal comes in, dressed in one of her finest ensembles. Her black hair is pulled back in a severe bun, highlighting her sharp cheekbones and almond-shaped eyes. We look alike, but I don't have the resting bitch face she does.

"Hey, Mom. You're looking sharp. Do you have a hot date?" I smirk.

She rewards me with a haughty glance. "No. I was meeting with the king. I came to check on you before I drive to Lucca's mansion."

"Are you going to attempt bringing him back again?"

"Yes. I've found a new spell I'd like to try."

I push the covers off me and throw my legs to the side of the bed. "I'm coming with you."

"Absolutely not. You're in no condition to assist me on anything."

"I'm fine," I insist, but my body doesn't want to get with the program. I sway on the spot and end up with my butt back on the mattress.

"Clearly. Well, you do seem recovered enough to be arguing with me, and that's what matters. I heard that you had lunch with Calvin before you fell ill."

Ugh. Did she really have to bring that up?

"Yes. Since he's my future husband, I wanted to get to know him better."

Mom raises an eyebrow. "Oh? I thought your rebellion would last longer. I'm glad that you're past childish tantrums."

"Yes, Mother. I've finally grown up."

She ignores my sarcastic comment and glances at her watch. "I'd better get going. Take care, Aurora. I don't want you falling behind on your training."

And just like that, I'm dismissed. She's already on her way to the door and misses my death stare.

Don't worry, Mom. There's a blood vow hanging over my head ensuring I can't disappoint you now, even if I wanted to.

13

SAXON

I promised Solomon I'd leave Aurora alone, but I've come to check on her every day that she was sick. And I also have been skulking near her apartment like a total stalker. I hid when the High Witch came to visit, obviously. If she finds out I'm mated to her daughter, she might turn me into a slug or something equally disgusting. But not much longer after the scary witch leaves, her younger daughter follows suit.

This time, I don't stay hidden. Instead, I jump in her path, making her gasp while she clutches at her chest.

"Son of a bitch. Where did you come from?"

"Going home already?" I ask.

"Good grief, dude. Do you make it a habit to scare the crap out of people?"

"Sorry. Didn't mean to." I reward her with my most charming smile, but it doesn't have the desired effect.

Still sporting a frown, she walks around me. "Aurora is better."

Unable to play it cool, I follow the girl. "Really? Is her fever gone?"

"Yeah. She's fine. You don't need to lose your beauty sleep anymore, okay?"

I open and shut my mouth, not knowing how to reply to that. It seems sassiness runs in the family.

"Aurora and I are just friends. That's all."

Why am I explaining myself to this kid? I sound like a moron.

"Yeah, yeah. I know what kind of friends," she mumbles under her breath.

"Wait." I touch her arm, making her stop. "Did Aurora talk about me?"

She narrows her eyes, watching me with suspicion. "What do you want with her? You know she's engaged, right?"

The reminder is akin to a spear piercing my chest.

"I know." My voice comes out strangled.

Suddenly, her eyebrows shoot up, almost meeting her hairline. "Oh my God. You *like* Aurora."

Shit. Am I that transparent? I let go of her arm, stepping back. "Don't start getting crazy notions in your head, girlie."

A manic glint appears in her eyes, right before her mouth splits into a wide grin. "This is perfect."

"Why are you looking at me like that?"

"Because Aurora is making a huge mistake and I'll do anything to stop her, even if it means helping you win her over."

Ah, fuck. That's exactly what I need right now. A naïve teen who has seen way too many romcom movies.

"Just stop right there." I raise my hand. "Let me make things clear. I don't like your sister. We just banged, that's all. So take that notion out of your head."

"Right. I believe you." She pulls a small notebook from her purse and scribbles something on it. Then she rips a page and hands it over. "Here. This is my number. Call me when you're out of denial land and ready to strategize. We have ten months to avert a wedding."

She saunters away while I just stare at the piece of paper, perplexed. A teenager has just floored me, an over five-hundred-year-old Blueblood. *Damn it.* My only saving grace is that Manu wasn't here to witness the exchange. But even knowing I can't entertain Aurora's sister's proposal, I shove the note in my pocket.

The sun has just set, and classes won't start for at least an hour. I haven't eaten anything substantial in days, so I veer toward the feeding room. But I don't take two steps forward before my body turns around of its own accord.

What the hell.

There's an invisible cord pulling me back to the dorm section of the building—more precisely, pulling me back to Aurora's apartment. *Shit.* I think the potion the king gave me is wearing off because all the fucked symptoms associated with this damn bond are returning: the tingling sensation, the fevered skin, the ache in my bones.

I break into a run—at vampire speed—and in a few seconds, I'm knocking on her apartment door so hard that I might end up knocking it down. I can sense her moving inside, and a moment later, she opens the door with a yank.

Her hair is wet, and she's wrapped in a bathrobe. She smells like vanilla-flavored shampoo, and even though that particular spice does nothing for me, when mixed with her natural scent, it drives me insane.

"Saxon…"

I walk in, invading her personal space, forcing her to walk back to maintain a gap between us. I kick the door shut, not wanting any interruptions. I have no fucking clue what I'm doing, or how I'll keep my promise to not screw things up. My fingers itch to touch her, but for now, I can manage to keep my hands glued to my sides.

"How are you?" I ask in a strangled voice. *God, I sound like an animal.*

"Okay. You shouldn't be here."

"I know."

She's standing in the middle of her small living room now, staring at me with eyes that are round and alert. Her heart is beating so fast, I'd be able to hear it even without my enhanced vampire senses.

"My sister told me you came by to check on me."

"I did. You scared me."

"I scared you?" Her voice rises an octave. "How?"

"The way you collapsed in Hanson's class scared the crap out of me."

I step forward, losing the battle against the mysterious forces of the mating bond. Aurora has nowhere else to go. Her hands settle on the back of the couch, clutching it tightly, like she needs an anchor.

"I hear you're getting married in ten months."

I don't know why I said that. Thinking about her fiancé just makes everything worse.

"Who told you that?"

"I bumped into your little sister."

"Miranda has a big mouth. But yeah, the wedding is happening as soon as I finish my training here."

"So that means I have time." I step into her space, leaving barely any room between our bodies.

"Have time for what?" She tilts her head up, staring straight into my eyes.

I cup her cheek with my hand, caressing her soft skin with my thumb. "To make you change your mind."

No. No. No. Saxon, what the hell are you doing?

"I'm not changing my mind." Her reply is so weak, it's like vapor.

I smile ruefully. "We'll see about that."

She doesn't try to stop me when I lean down, sealing my lips to hers. On the contrary, she grabs my arms, melting into my body. In an instant, I'm on fire and my sense of duty and responsibility flies out the window.

I grip a fistful of her hair, tilting her head to the side to kiss her deeper. Aurora lets out a moan when I nudge her legs apart with mine, feeling her heat through my jeans. With my free hand I part her robe, then cup one of her breasts, loving how it fits perfectly in my hand.

Her fingers curl into my shirt, and when I understand that she wants to get rid of it, I pull back to help her out. My gaze connects with hers, unleashing a myriad of emotions through me. Her beautiful, wild eyes are swirling with untamed desire. She has surrendered to the bond, even though she doesn't know anything about it. If I were a better person, I'd tell her. But I'm not. I'm a rascal only too happy to take everything she's offering.

I kiss her again, hard and demanding, before I switch my

attention to her neck. Her vein is calling my name, but I ignore it, just happy to place open kisses there before I continue the path down her breasts. I latch on to one of her nipples, alternating between licking and sucking until she arches her back and yanks at my hair, her silent plea for me to continue.

There's nothing in the world that can stop me from doing as she wishes. She's my queen, and I'm at her command. When she whispers my name in a throaty voice that could very well be confused for a siren's call, my cock is injected with pure libido—as if it weren't already rock hard.

My name on her tongue, her fingers in my hair, the feel of her soft skin against my callused hands, these are memories that will be forever imprinted on my mind. Dying to taste more of her, I release her nipple with a soft pop and drop down to my knees. Leveling me with a smothering stare, Aurora unties the sash of her robe, pushing the fabric apart. The corners of my lips curl, and without breaking eye contact, I dive into her folds. She cries out when I lick her clit, already trembling as if she's on the verge of an orgasm.

Fuck. I'm close too.

I try to keep the pace slow and prolong her pleasure, but either I'm a fucking magician with my tongue, or the mating bond is enhancing everything.

Suddenly, there's a loud scream—not one of pure ecstasy. It's a scream of excruciating pain, and it's coming from me.

AURORA

There's a terrible sound buzzing in my ears, like banshees screeching, out for blood. I cover them while shutting my eyes, not knowing what to do to make it stop. All I know is that I was on the verge of an earth-shattering orgasm when a foreign power surged within me.

"Ugh!" someone says nearby.

Oh my God. Saxon!

I uncover my ears and open my eyes. The noise in my head begins to fade finally. Saxon is on the floor, bracing forward with one hand while the other clutches his middle.

"Are you okay?"

He lifts his face, which is twisted in a grimace and red. "Fucking hell. What did you do to me?"

"I have no idea."

Slowly, he gets back onto his feet, still watching me with annoyance. *Did I strike him by accident?* That's never happened before in my entire life.

"You hexed me," he says through clenched teeth, his tenor voice split between annoyance and disbelief.

"I didn't mean to."

He glances away, rubbing his chin. "It serves me right. I shouldn't have come here anyway."

I drop my eyes to the floor. *And I shouldn't have let you get that far.* Maybe the blood vow triggered the spell. I promised Elena that I'd marry Calvin, and succumbing to my feelings for Saxon was definitely not me upholding my end of the deal. The crazy thing is it wasn't only carnal desire that spurred me on. My heart was one hundred percent invested in the male in front of me—still is—and that's a major problem.

"I'm sorry that I hexed you. Maybe we should stay away from each other from now on."

He glances at me, rage simmering in his eyes. "Yes, I think that would be best."

"Please don't hate me," I blurt out.

My statement seems to stun him for a second. I don't understand either where it came from, only that it would kill me if he did. *For heaven's sake, why am I having these strange feelings for Saxon out of the blue?* Not a week ago, he was just a cocky Blueblood who annoyed me. Now it feels like he's my soulmate. *Ugh.*

"Trust me, Aurora, as much as I would love to hate you, that would be impossible."

He heads for the door, stepping out of my apartment before I can think of anything to say to him.

I can't believe it. This is how it's going to end for us. With a bad case of blue balls and a hex. And now he's in residence at Bloodstone, which means I'll be forced to see his sexy face everywhere and pretend I don't give a fig about him.

It should be easy. We didn't spend enough time together to develop any real feelings. But *should* is the imperative word here. Somehow, I'm tethered to Saxon, and deep down I know there's no hex or blood vow that will change that.

14

AURORA

I stare at Saxon like a moron as my brain processes his words. "I'm what?"

"You heard me."

He pushes me to the side so he can walk into my apartment without an invitation. His body is coiled as tightly as a spring, and if I learned anything in the past weeks it's that anything can trigger his savage beast mode while he's wound taut like that. The last time he behaved this way was when he found me after my altercation with Boone's lackeys. He went berserk, ready to tear up Salem in search of the vampires involved in the ambush.

Not wanting anyone eavesdropping on this conversation, I close the door before I reply.

"You told me the female you were obsessed with was a siren," I say calmly.

It's hard to keep my voice even; the past month has been hell.

On top of dealing with Lucca's reawakening and all the political crap and murder attempts that followed, I had to suppress my growing feelings for his best friend, also known as the idiot in front of me. And now he just dropped the bomb that there is an explanation for my crazy attraction to him. He's my mate.

He rakes his fingers through his hair with a jerky movement. "Well, I lied. I didn't want anyone to know, especially you."

I wince despite myself. Saxon was supposed to be a hookup, a drunken mistake. Now I'm finding out this is much bigger, but apparently not big enough for him to be honest with me.

"How long have you known about this?"

"Since the beginning."

I shake my head, feeling the sharp sting of betrayal deep in my soul. "You're such a jerk!" I snap, forgetting that I'm supposed to be the levelheaded person in this conversation. "I can't believe you kept this secret from me."

"I had no choice, okay? I couldn't risk you deciding to use the bond as an excuse to break off your engagement."

Ouch. Way to sucker punch me in the chest, Saxon.

I can't breathe for a second, but when I recover from the blow, all I can say is, "I see."

His angry countenance morphs into something else. I don't know what he sees etched on my face, but whatever it is, it changes his attitude. He seems regretful now, but it's impossible to tell the reason for that look. *Is he regretting his statement or regretting acting like an ass?*

"I'm sorry. That sounded way harsher than I intended." He puts his hands on his hips, dipping his chin. "I can't be responsible for you breaking off your engagement to that nimrod. That would turn the magical community against the king."

Oh, Saxon. I know that. It stings that you don't seem to care about me. But hell if I'll let you see how much you're hurting me right now.

"You're so conceited," I hiss. "What makes you think I'd consider you a better alternative than Calvin?"

Now it's his turn to grimace. Even without some crazy-ass vampire bond controlling my hormones, I'd pick Saxon over Calvin any time, given the chance. Too bad I tossed away that option when I made a deal with Elena Montenegro.

"Well, we can spend the entire evening trading insults, sunshine. But it doesn't change the fact that we're mated, and we can't be."

"What do you want me to do about it? I know nothing about vampire mating bonds."

"You're a witch, aren't you? Solomon believes there's a spell that can annul the bond."

"Oh, Solomon knows about us too?" I throw my hands up in the air. "That's fucking great."

"He was helping me in the beginning, but with all the drama involving Lucca, Vivienne, and Boone, my problem wasn't his top priority anymore. That's why I had to come to you for the potion. I've been using it to numb the effects of the bond."

I pull my hair back, yanking at the strands in frustration. "Oh my God. Whose brilliant idea was it to use a potion against a siren's thrall to fight a vampire mating bond?"

"King Raphael's."

I freeze, and then, like a deranged woman, I laugh so hard that my belly hurts. I must be losing my mind. "Of course. Vampires and common sense. Clearly not two things that go together."

"Are you done making fun of this situation?" Saxon asks, irritated.

"Shut up, jerkface. You're not going to boss me around in my own home, bond or not."

In the blink of an eye, Saxon is on me, hand around my throat, face inches from mine. His hold is not tight; the fury in his eyes is threat enough.

"Let go of me before I hex you again."

"No. Don't you understand? This is no joke. Do you have any idea what it feels like to be near you and not be able to touch you? Protect you? I almost lost my mind when I found out you faced Boone's followers alone. I'm in constant pain. I can't taste the blood that I drink from others, I can't fuck anyone else."

My stomach does a backflip at his admission that he can't screw other women. My crazy heart is doing cartwheels in celebration.

"I've been in pain too, okay? Perhaps not as much as you, but I didn't have a potion to numb whatever I was feeling, because I didn't know what the problem was."

"I don't understand how someone so stubborn, so infuriating, can beguile me this much. Half the time I don't know if I want to punish you or love you."

I inhale deeply. *Is that a declaration of love? No, it can't be.* "I think it's clear which way you're leaning."

Clarity returns to his eyes, then his expression changes into one of regret. He steps back, releasing me, and like an idiot, I miss his closeness. The yearning hits me hard then. Every molecule in my body is drawn to Saxon. He's the sun, and I'm a lonely planet getting pulled into his orbit.

"I'd never hurt you," he replies softly.

"Because I'm your mate."

"Not because of that. I'm not a monster who beats females for fun. It would be different if you were a seasoned warrior like Manu and we were at war."

"I thought she was a spoiled princess," I say callously, only because I need a distraction from the overwhelming impulse to attack Saxon's mouth.

Crossing his arms, he squints. "I know what you're doing. It's not going to work. I'm aware of how aroused you are right now."

Balls.

"I can't help it. It's all because of this stupid bond. How did you become my mate, anyway? Was it because I let you drink from me?"

"I don't know, Rora."

Rora? Sweet baby unicorns. Does he want me to melt where I stand? I think my ovaries just exploded.

"No cutesy nicknames, please. Let's not make this situation worse."

He smiles, revealing the tips of his fangs. "Sorry. Slip of the tongue."

Ah, fuck. Now I want his tongue to slip inside me.

I cover my ears. "Quit putting images in my head."

"I have no such power." His smile is brighter.

A moment ago, he seemed to be in excruciating pain, and now, he acts like this is a stroll through the park.

"I thought you were in dire need of help."

The amusement wilts from his face at once. "I am. I guess being close to you is making things a little bit more bearable."

Only for you.

"We need a plan. I can look through my family's grimoires and see if I can find anything on vampire mating bonds."

"That sounds good. But I also think we should spend as much time together as possible."

At first, I think he's joking, but his expression is dead serious. "Why?"

"Didn't you just hear me, woman? Just by being near you, I feel better. And also, the urge to kill your fiancé is not as acute. But if you want to risk his precious life…"

"Oh, shut up. You know I don't care about him that much. I'm more concerned that you'll get in trouble."

Saxon's eyes swim with glee, and even though he's trying hard to not smile, I catch the tremble in the corners of his lips.

"You're worried about me?"

"Don't sound so smug. Of course I am. Like you said, there's a lot at stake here. Jacques pretty much declared war against King Raphael, and we can't allow our problem to make matters worse for him."

"What if instead of fighting the bond, we surrender to it?"

My jaw drops. "Are you out of your mind? Was I speaking to the fucking walls just now? We can't allow this bullshit bond to mess things up for *your* king."

"Hey, this bond is not bullshit. Inconvenient, but not bullshit. It's actually a big deal that it happened to us. This hasn't occurred to any vampire since the Nightingales left."

I raise my hand. "Wait a second. Are you saying this bond thing is Nightingale magic?"

Was it how Elena knew how deep my feelings for Saxon went? Because that fucking mirror of hers showed Saxon and I were bonded?

He shrugs. "Well, everything related to our existence links to them. It's an educated guess. Too bad the only Nightingales we know have lost their powers."

"True, but Vivi has recovered her memories. Maybe she can help."

It's the best idea I can come up with, but Saxon's expression is as solemn as ever.

"What's the matter? Why are you looking at me like the world is about to end?"

With a shake of his head, he glances away. "I don't know. I don't fucking know."

15

AURORA

I tell Saxon to go back to his apartment while I go talk to Vivienne. Naturally, he insisted on tagging along, but I put my foot down. I have to tell her the whole truth and it will be easier if my *mate* is not around. This is going to be a humiliating conversation. I can't even think about the word mate in relation to Saxon without my face bursting into flames in a mix of humiliation and excitement.

When I stop in front of the apartment Vivienne shares with Manu, I find the door semi open. I wouldn't think much of it if there wasn't a prize in exchange for Vivienne's head. Boone is dead, but Tatiana still has sympathizers at Bloodstone.

Now on high alert, I pull a small crystal from my purse and enter without knocking. If there's someone inside up to no good, I don't want them to know help is coming.

I only need to take two steps in to realize I made a huge mistake. Vivienne is sitting facing the side of the couch with her hands braced against its arm. Her face is tilted toward the ceiling, but her eyes are closed and she's moaning. I can only guess who is lying between her legs. I try to backtrack without making any noise, but I end up bumping into a high chair.

She gasps, whipping her face to mine. Then she covers her breasts and pretty much falls off the couch with a soft thud. Lucca sits up at once, briefly glancing at me before helping his girlfriend from the floor.

"I'm so sorry. I didn't mean to invade your privacy like that," I say while looking at everything but them.

"How did you get in?" Lucca asks.

"The door was open. I was afraid that someone had broken in."

"Lucca, you told me you shut the door," Vivienne complains, but it sounds half-hearted.

They're in the honeymoon phase of their relationship. *I bet all they do all day is fuck and cuddle.* Yikes, that thought makes me sound like a bitter old woman. I'm happy things have worked out between them. Vivienne has become a close friend and I don't begrudge her happiness.

"Sorry. I thought I did," Lucca replies sheepishly. "I can't concentrate properly when you decide to parade naked in the living room."

I chance glancing in their direction again. Vivienne is now wearing a T-shirt, and Lucca has put some pants on. I can still see the tent in the front, though. *Shit. Focus on his face, Aurora. On. His. Face.*

"Oh, have you embraced the vampires' lack of modesty, Vivi?" I tease, remembering how appalled she was the first time she saw a vampire fuck a human in the middle of a party while he fed.

"No." Her face turns beet red.

"So, you're not worried that Manu could catch you?" I return the crystal to my bag since the only danger facing Vivienne was being impaled by Lucca's cock.

"Manu doesn't live here anymore," she replies.

"Seriously, then ... oh. You guys have moved in together? When did this happen?"

"Last night." Lucca pulls Vivienne to his side and kisses her soundly on her cheek.

Okay, I'm getting mega jealousy surges now, even though I don't want to. Saxon's image pops in my head and I have to fight hard to banish him to a dark corner in my mind. That reminds me of the reason I'm here.

"I was hoping I could talk to you in private, Vivi," I say. Immediately, Lucca makes a face, so I add, "Chill, Prince of the Night. This is a personal matter concerning me."

"Ugh. Is it a female thing? Then I'm out of here." He jumps over the couch instead of walking around it like Vivienne does. He kisses her again, long and hard, making me uncomfortable enough that I have to look away.

I'd tell them to get a room, but then I'd have to come back later. Breaking the mating bond with Saxon is too important. I know he won't leave me alone, and eventually, my feeble barriers are going to crumble completely.

Lucca bangs the door shut this time as he leaves, but I wait a few seconds to make sure he's not within eavesdropping distance. Vampires and their enhanced senses can be a drag.

"Do you want to drink something? I can finally store food and drinks in the apartment without fear of being found out."

"I'm okay. I'm really sorry that I barged in like that. I feel horrible."

She waves her hand dismissively. "Don't worry about it. I think I'm getting used to not giving a crap about modesty."

"Were the Nightingales as promiscuous as vampires?" I ask, regretting my question immediately. There's a visible grimace on Vivienne's face now. "Gah. I'm so sorry. I shouldn't have asked that."

"Oh, don't apologize for being curious. To answer your question, no, the Nightingales weren't like vampires. They loved rules and decorum. Maybe that's why some looked down on vampires and called them savages."

I didn't know how I was going to broach the subject of a vampire bond, but if that's not the perfect opening, I don't know what is.

"That's interesting. Was that the reason why your kind created the mating bond?"

"What do you mean?"

"You know, the magical bond that makes two vampires perfect for each other."

"Oh. I'm not sure if that was something the Nightingale elders did on purpose, unlike the familiars who were created by design."

"So, are you saying it was a side effect?"

"It's possible it was residual magic. Fated mates is something that happens quite often among my people—I mean, former people. I don't consider myself a Nightingale anymore."

I catch the sadness in her tone, and I should ask her about it, but I don't want to deviate from the mating bond yet.

"What if people weren't happy with their fated mates, was there a way to break the bond?"

"Fated mates were a big deal back in Ellnesari."

I notice she totally evaded my question. *Why?*

"But there has to be a way. What if suddenly the Nightingales returned, and a dashing Nightingale prince claimed you were his fated mate?"

The look of pure horror that appears on Vivienne's face makes me suspect she was mated to someone.

"Then I don't think I'd have a choice. Bonded mates don't have eyes for anyone else besides their mates."

Okay, maybe she didn't have a mate. *Duh, Aurora, of course she didn't.* She wouldn't have left Ellnesari behind if she was mated to someone. I know I wouldn't have been able to walk away from Saxon and cross into a different realm.

"So the fact that you're madly in love with Lucca wouldn't matter?"

"I'd probably cease to be in love with him." Vivienne narrows her eyes. "Why are you asking me all these questions about fated mates?"

Shit. I thought I could get all the information I needed from her without having to tell the truth. I guess not.

Letting my shoulders sag forward and heaving a loaded sigh, I say, "I'm mated to Saxon."

She stares at me without blinking for a few seconds. "Are you sure?"

"I'm positive. We hook—"

"You hooked up with Saxon? Oh my God. When did that happen?"

"Gee, take it easy, will you? It was about a month ago."

She smacks her open palm on the counter. "I knew there was

something going on between you two."

"There's nothing going on between us. I'm his mate, but I can't be."

"Why not? Because he's a vampire and you're a witch? Besides the whole immortality bit, is there a rule that says you can't be together?"

"No, not a rule, only my upcoming wedding to someone else."

"You're engaged?" Her voice rises to a pitch, making me wince.

"Yeah. To a douche canoe. Arranged marriages are still a thing among witches and mages."

"Oh my God, Aurora. I'm so sorry. Is that why you want to break your bond with Saxon? What does he have to say about it?"

"He wants the mating bond gone as much as I do." I try to keep my voice steady, but it pains me to say that.

"Really?" Her delicate eyebrows furrow together. "Mated males are super possessive. I can't believe he hasn't killed your fiancé yet."

"He almost did. If King Raphael hadn't intervened, Saxon would be facing a trial right now. Murder is murder, no matter the cause or the victim."

"How are you coping? I mean, I assume you're not sleeping together."

"No, although it's pretty hard to resist the pull." I look at the floor. "And Saxon is a hot piece of ass."

Vivienne laughs. "Yeah, he's not bad to look at." There's a poignant pause, and Vivienne's expression becomes grim again. "But in all seriousness, I get why you need to end the bond, but those things don't simply happen at random, Aurora. The mating bond happens to bring the right people together. Are you sure you want to find a way to destroy it?"

"I have no choice, okay? I shouldn't be telling you this, but I made a deal with a very powerful witch. She wants me to marry Calvin so I can have access to the first grimoire in history, which his family possesses. In exchange, she gave me the spell that brought Lucca back from hibernation."

That's as much as I dare reveal to Vivienne on the matter. I can't say what I saw in the Nightingale mirror. That future is too gruesome, and I hope that Elena is wrong and it doesn't come to pass.

"You found the spell? Everyone thinks your mother was responsible for it."

"And it should stay that way. No one can know about my deal with Elena, not even Lucca."

Vivienne shakes her head. "This is really messed up. I'm so torn right now. Grateful that you brought Lucca back, but distraught that you have to marry someone you don't love as a result."

"Don't feel bad about me. I come from a long line of High Witches. Sacrifice for the greater good is in my DNA."

Her frown tells me she's so not buying my lame excuse. "I wish it didn't have to be this way for you. But don't worry, your secret is safe with me."

"I appreciate your discretion, but I also need your help. We have to find a way to break the bond."

She drops her gaze, biting her lower lip. She's definitely hiding something.

"You know of one, don't you?"

"Kind of. Rikkon was bonded to someone before he crossed over to the human realm with me. It nearly killed him to be apart from his mate. I think…" Her voice becomes chocked up. "I think it's why he deteriorated faster than I did. Why he became a junkie in the end."

"Vivi, it wasn't your fault. He made that choice."

When she glances at me again, her eyes brim with unshed tears. "I don't think so. The bond settled only moments before we crossed the veil. And my mother had already used her magic to banish us. There was no time for him to make the decision, and honestly, I don't think he'd have crossed with me if it hadn't been already too late."

"What do you think finally broke the bond in the end?"

"I think the memory spell did. But I don't know if the bond is severed or simply buried. It's possible that it will come back with all its horrible symptoms if he remembers who he is."

"Shit. That's not good at all. So maybe it's best if he doesn't recover his memories."

"No. I can't allow him to keep living as he is now, a shell of the male he used to be. He was the most courageous, beautiful, and kind person I've ever met. His mind was the sharpest in the entire kingdom. And look at him now. He's a junkie, a liar, and a thief."

I understand Vivienne's determination to restore Rikkon's memory. I would do the same if I were her.

"All right. Then you have to help me find another away to break the bond, for my sake and your brother's."

16

SAXON

———❖———

When I return to my apartment in a sour mood thanks to unfulfilled mating pains, another unpleasant surprise is waiting for me. All the living room stuff is packed up and there are several strangers moving around and dismantling furniture.

"What the hell is going on?" I ask to no one in particular.

Ronan walks out of his room, carrying a huge box in his hands. "You didn't get my message? We're moving to a bigger apartment."

"Why? I like this one."

"Because we're getting new roommates."

I arch my eyebrows. "Who?"

"Vaughn and Rikkon."

"What? Are you serious? I didn't realize there was an apartment with five bedrooms at the institute."

"Not five, four. Lucca moved in with Vivienne."

"Whoa. That's huge. And where is Manu going to live now?"

"She got an apartment for herself," Ronan replies with a note of criticism.

"How did she manage that?"

He shrugs. "You know how. By acting like she always does, with tantrums and threats."

"She probably wants privacy now that her familiar is back in the picture," I say jokingly, forgetting for a moment how weird Ronan gets every time Karl is mentioned.

His response is a grumble, and he walks away before I can say anything else. I think the next nine months are going to be very interesting—that is, if we all survive the drama. Yeah, I'm more concerned about the inner circle's integrity than the conflict outside the institute's walls. I'm not an idiot. I know Tatiana will retaliate after Lucca killed her son, but if our small group is not tight, if we're unstable, we'll crumble at the slightest pressure.

I head for my room, pissed that I didn't find out about the move sooner. I didn't bring a lot of my stuff here, but I don't want strangers going through my personal belongings. I'm glad to see no one touched anything in my room. Ronan must have warned the human helpers to stay clear of my stuff. He knows me too well.

With supernatural speed, it takes me five minutes to pack up my shit, and another five to bring everything to our new digs, and only because I had no fucking clue where I was going.

It turns out, our new apartment is much closer to Lucca and Vivienne's love nest, and only two doors down from Aurora's apartment. But the closer proximity doesn't make things easier for me. On the contrary, I can sense the exact moment she walks by our front door, and the awareness doesn't decrease with the distance. My yearning seems to double, and it gets so bad that I begin to shake like a fucking palm tree getting slammed by an incoming hurricane.

Ronan is busy getting the TV system set up and doesn't witness me grab the kitchen counter and rip a piece of the marble. *Damn it.* I totally forgot to get a new potion from Aurora. I got too distracted by her.

"Um, hello?" a male says as he pushes the front door open.

I turn around, ready to bite the newcomer's head off, when I see Rikkon, Vivienne's brother, standing there like a fucking lost kid in a park. He looks better than the last time I saw him. He's gained weight and lost the gaunt appearance. Looking at him closely, his Nightingale roots are impossible to miss. It's not the longish, light blond hair or his wiry and tall stature. It's his face. The male is too perfect to be confused for a mere human. He'd probably make loads of money in the fashion industry. Too bad he lost his mind and probably never had the idea.

"Hey. Welcome to Bloodstone Institute." I open my arms in a grand gesture.

He only has one duffle bag with him, and it looks kind of empty.

"Thanks." He sets the bag down and looks around. "This is pretty nice. I confess, I was expecting a darker vibe."

"Well, the gothic and scary exterior is only for show, you know, to keep the good old folks of Salem terrified of us."

"It's definitely an improvement over my lodgings at Ember Emporium."

"Dude, you have to tell me what that was like."

He raises an eyebrow. "You want to know what my prison cell was like?"

"Err…" I rub the back of my neck.

"Ignore Saxon. He can be an idiot sometimes." Ronan

approaches, apparently to save Rikkon from me. "Is that all your stuff?" He eyeballs the bag.

Rikkon glances at it and then shrugs. "Yeah. I don't need much. To be honest, I'm not sure what I'm supposed to be doing here."

"You're pretending to be a vampire, so just try to relax and follow the flow. There's really not much to it."

"I don't quite get it. Why do you have to attend school? Aren't you, like, hundreds of years old?"

"You do know that we have to hibernate from time to time, right? Thanks to *your* elders leaving us here to hang dry." I give him a meaningful stare.

"Yeah, Vivi explained that to me. I still can't believe what she told me or that I was stupid enough to procure a memory spell."

His reply gives me pause. Whoever sold him the spell must have been someone powerful enough to be able to come up with it. Maybe they know a way to break a mating bond too.

"Where did you get it?" I ask.

Rikkon stares at me as if I'm stupid. "I don't know. The spell erased all my memories, remember?"

"Oh, right."

I should be disappointed, but deep down I'm not invested in breaking the bond. What if Aurora and I are meant to be together and we're going to unleash a much bigger problem if we succeed in our plan? But the damn pain, though. Fuck, I could do without that.

"How did you get here?" Ronan asks Rikkon.

"Cheryl dropped me off."

There's a visible tension around the corners of Ronan's mouth now, which is no surprise with the way he's clenching his jaw. Ronan and his females. For a brooding vampire, he sure knows how to pick them. The quiet ones are always the worst.

"Did she just leave you to fend for yourself?" I ask. "The females in admin can be quite dreadful."

"Oh, I didn't register yet. Vivi said she'll take me. And Cheryl went to visit Karl." Rikkon runs a hand through his hair. "I still can't believe Karl and Cheryl are wolf shifters."

"There are two rooms left," Ronan interrupts. "Pick one and get ready to hit the gym."

"Shit. I haven't worked out in ages."

"Noticeable," I say. "Don't worry, Ronan will whip you into shape in no time."

Rikkon twists his face into a grimace. I wonder if he ever received combat training when he lived in the Nightingale realm. It doesn't matter now. Ronan will make sure he can kick some ass when the time comes.

"Knock, knock. Is this where the cool kids hang out?" Vaughn, the newly turned vampire, says from the door, sporting a stupid-ass grin on his face.

"Hey, Vaughn. Are you staying here too?" Rikkon asks.

"It looks like it." He walks in, staring at everything with his mouth hanging open. "This is neat."

"You seem to be handling your new existence well," Rikkon adds.

"Dude, it's amazing. The stuff that I can do now. Mind-blowing." He tilts his head to the side, squinting. "You feel different. What happened to you?"

"He's pretending to be one of us. I went over this with you already," Ronan grumbles. "Enough with the chitchat. Let's get going. King Raphael tasked me to get you in shape within an impossibly short time and I don't plan on disappointing him."

"I'm in shape." Vaughn flexes his arms, showing off nothing.

"What am I supposed to be looking at? Hold up, let me get a magnifying glass," I pipe up.

Rikkon chuckles, which earns him a scowl from Vaughn.

"What are you laughing at? You look scrawnier than a scarecrow."

"For fuck's sake." Ronan stares at the ceiling, resting his hands on his hips. "I must have pissed off some angry deity in my previous life to deserve you two."

I'm about to give Ronan one of my trademark smartass comments when my spine goes rigid, and the hairs on the back of my neck stand on end. Aurora is in distress. I can pick up the sudden acceleration of her heartbeat through the bond. She needs my help. With red tinging my gaze, and my fangs fully exposed, I zoom out of my apartment in a flash, ready for battle.

17

AURORA

I feel drained after my conversation with Vivienne. She agreed to help me with my problem, but until then, I have to deal with all the changes in my body. It seems like I'm suffering from an ice-cold fever. I've got the aches and the shakes. But the worst part is the throbbing between my legs, the urge to fuck Saxon nonstop, that's making everything ten billion times worse. I can't walk around the institute all hot and bothered all the time. Thanks to vampires' enhanced senses, everybody will know about my *condition. How mortifying is that?*

As soon as I enter my apartment, I know something is different. I'm not sure what's going on, but Saxon feels closer to me somehow. Either he's coming here or the bond is getting stronger. If so, how long until both of us break down and make a huge mistake?

Come on, Aurora. It wouldn't be the end of the world if you slept with Saxon again.

Ugh. Shut up, demon! Where's the fucking angel on my right shoulder telling me to remain strong?

I don't move for a minute, waiting for the knock on the door. When it doesn't come, I can only come to one conclusion. The mating bond magic is increasing by leaps and bounds. *Is it because I'm now aware of its presence?* Vivienne told me how much Rikkon suffered in the first years of their banishment. He would have high fevers and sometimes not be able to move at all. I definitely don't want to wait until things get that bad. I have to do something to alleviate my craving.

I pull my personal grimoire from my bag. It's not as thick as some of the older ones, and definitely not as valuable to others. But to me, it's precious, almost like an extension of myself. Every witch receives a blank grimoire when they turn six and start to learn how to harness their powers. The leather is plain when gifted; it's up to the owner to customize the cover as they please. Mine depicts a phoenix rising from the ashes. I did the carving and painting of the leather by hand without the use of magic, and I'm extremely proud of it.

I've been recording every new spell and potion I learned throughout the years. And one of them is the antidote against a siren's thrall. That's not something I would ever search for out of the blue. Saxon came to me and begged for it.

I get mad all over again. The stupid male should have told me about our bond sooner.

The potion I made for Saxon was specific to vampires, but I can modify it to work for me. It's not ideal, but it's better than this feeling of wrongness within me.

The page is already marked. I just hope I have all the ingredients

I need. Since I'm the only witch living at the institute, it's not like I can get more ingredients easily. If Solomon doesn't have it, then I have to order online or head into town. I begin to open cupboards at random, wishing I were more organized and kept my potion-making ingredients separate from my food.

I'm in the middle of the task when there's a knock on my door. It's not Saxon, I know that much. Maybe Vivienne has news. With a simple spell, I open the door from where I stand, and my mood immediately plummets when Calvin walks in.

"Hello, darling." He smiles in a phony way.

My skin crawls just by staring at him, and I feel sick. It's like my entire body is rejecting his presence.

"What are you doing here? It's the middle of the night."

"It's not like I have a choice. You're living here now, and thus, on the bloodsuckers' schedule."

I can't argue with that. "Okay, but you didn't tell me what you're doing here. I don't like surprise visits."

His gaze darkens and I get ready for an angry retort from him. But he seems to be able to rein in his irritation a bit. "I'll remember that next time. I heard you were sick, so I came to check on you."

"I fell ill two days ago." I cross my arms. "And you could have called."

"Nobody bothered to tell me until today. And what kind of fiancé would I be if I didn't come in person to make sure you're okay?"

He walks over, and on reflex, I step back. He notices it.

"You said you wanted to make things work between us, and yet, you act like you're scared of me."

I snort. "Oh please. Like I'd ever be scared of you."

What's making my heart beat out of control has nothing to do with fear. It's the damn bond rejecting the knowledge that I'm supposed to marry someone who is not Saxon. *Shit.* What's going to happen during the honeymoon? If I'm getting the creeps now, will I go into shock if Calvin touches me?

My stomach decides to revolt just then. I run to the sink, almost not making it in time. My eyes and nose sting as I puke my guts out.

"Fuck. You're still sick," Calvin says. "Are you contagious?"

I wish I could tell him yes so he'll bail, but I'm not done spewing out the contents of my stomach yet.

Suddenly, a growl echoes in my apartment. It takes me a second to register that Saxon is here, ready to shred Calvin to pieces. The sickness passes at once.

"Who the hell are you?" Calvin asks.

Wiping my face with the back of my arm, I whirl around. Saxon's eyes are glowing bright red and his lips are pulled back. *Damn it.* He's gone berserk.

I jump in front of Calvin with my hands up. "Saxon. Calm down. Everything is fine."

His breathing is coming out in bursts and he still won't meet my gaze. His murderous eyes are focused on Calvin behind me.

"What's that deranged vampire doing here, Aurora?"

I sense a burst of magic behind me, which only makes Saxon take a menacing step forward, body poised to strike.

"Shut up, Calvin, and stand down."

"Hell no. That bloodsucker is going crazy and he's going to kill us both."

"Saxon, look at me." I walk over slowly, afraid any sudden movement will set him off. He's like a wild animal in protective mode, ready to strike.

But my proximity doesn't seem to register. Saxon doesn't lower his gaze to mine, so I reach over and touch his cheek as tenderly as possible. A zap of electricity shoots up my hand, but instead of causing pain, it soothes everything. My muscles relax and a peaceful warmth spreads through my body. Finally, his attention switches to me. The red in his eyes fades when he looks into mine and his fangs retract.

"I'm okay," I say.

"I thought you were in danger," he replies gruffly.

Goose bumps spread all over my skin when sparks of electricity seem to crackle around us. The desire that has been ever-present unleashes at full strength, making the world around us disappear. Saxon leans down, bringing his mouth an inch from mine.

"What the hell!" Calvin's annoying voice pierces through the bubble of the mating bond, jarring me back to the here and now.

Shit. I was about to make out with Saxon in front of my fiancé.

I jump back, covering my face, which now feels as hot as lava. My pulse has skyrocketed and my heart is beating in an erratic manner.

Slowly, I turn around, not knowing how I'm going to explain what he just witnessed without telling the truth.

"Did you fuck this bloodsucker, Aurora?" Calvin asks with an air of incredulity.

"You bet your ass she did," Saxon replies, stepping to my side.

Damn it, Saxon. Way to make things worse.

"What happened between Saxon and me is none of your business, Calvin. I had a life before our arrangement."

He doesn't need to know I fucked Saxon's brains out only after

I knew I'd be shackled to his Douchey Excellency.

"Right. You want me to believe your illicit affair is over?" Calvin narrows his beady eyes, while a vein in his temple throbs.

Illicit affair? I'm so fucking angry right now that any common sense I have leaves my brain.

"You know what? We're not getting married for another nine months, which means I can do whatever I please until then."

"No, you can't!" His eyes bulge from his skull, and I fear he's about to have an aneurism. *Boy, wouldn't that be convenient?* "You're my fiancée."

Saxon wraps his arm around my shoulder, and my traitorous body melts into his. "You heard Rora. She can do whatever she pleases."

Calvin's face twists into a horrifying mask of hatred. "You're a filthy whore."

Saxon is gone from my side in a split second. In the next, he has Calvin by his neck, holding him off the floor.

"You're not going to disrespect Aurora in front of me, weasel. Apologize," he growls.

Calvin doesn't say a word for a few seconds, but his face is definitely turning red. Saxon is squeezing his windpipe.

"He can't breathe, Saxon."

Only when he eases off his hold does Calvin say with a whimper, "I'm sorry."

To my surprise, Saxon doesn't rip Calvin's head off. He drops the asshole with an air of disgust and walks back to my side. I can sense the aggression coming off him in waves, though. He must be using all his willpower to not kill Calvin on the spot. Somehow, his restraint makes me want to jump in his arms even more, and the giddiness that's now making my heart skip a beat feels different somehow. More real.

Calvin doesn't say another word as he hurries out the door, but I catch the promise of retribution in his eyes. I just made a huge mistake, but it's not his retaliation that I fear. It's Elena Montenegro's.

If Calvin breaks off the engagement, what's going to happen to me?

18

SAXON

The motherfucker is gone, but my rage still churns inside. The only thing that kept me from turning him into human pâté was Aurora's presence. I close the distance between us, ready to pull her in my arms, but the hardness in her eyes makes me stop in my tracks.

"Why did you tell him about us?"

She doesn't sound mad, but she looks worried.

"I couldn't help it. You're my mate, and my instinct is to claim you as mine. I know, it sounds barbaric. I'm sorry."

With a shake of her head, she veers toward the kitchen sink, reminding me that she was throwing up when I barged into her apartment. She rinses her mouth with water, then plucks a leaf from a mint plant on the counter, shoving it in her mouth.

"It doesn't matter now. The damage is done. Besides, Bloodstone is a gossip factory. Someone was bound to find out about us eventually."

I'd believe her if her body language didn't tell me a different story. Unable to control myself, I stop behind her, leaving barely any space between our bodies. Her spine becomes taut while she grabs the edge of the counter.

"Saxon, please. You're making it worse."

I lean down, bringing my nose closer to her neck. Her scent shoots straight to my head, making me dizzy for a moment. Needing her as an anchor, I hold her arms, creating the familiar crackling energy that surges every time we touch. The action has the opposite effect of keeping me grounded. I feel like I'm flying, soaring through the skies. Her back is suddenly flush against my chest, and I don't know if it was me who pulled her closer or if she melted into me by herself.

One of my hands slides down her belly, and then disappears underneath the waistband of her leggings. Her pussy is hot and wet when I part her folds with my fingers. Letting out a kitten moan, she arches her back, and then reaches for the back of my head.

"Saxon, this is a terrible mistake. We can't let the bond win."

"Just this once, Rora. We're hurting so badly." I insert a finger inside of her while pressing my thumb against her clit.

She gasps loudly, shuddering in my arms. I push her long hair off her shoulder, and place soft, open kisses on her neck while I finger-fuck her. My cock is so damn hard, ready for action, but there's another urge that's winning. I need her blood. My mouth is watering already. I'm about to sink my fangs into her skin when I feel a change in her body. She tenses and not because she's about to climax.

"Rora?"

"Step away, Saxon," she grits out. "Now!"

I jump back, seconds before Aurora's body becomes enveloped by an energy field. The occurrence only lasts a moment, and when it vanishes, she turns around, staring at me with eyes that are round with fear and regret.

"Did I hurt you?" she asks.

"No. What the hell was that?"

She drops her chin, staring at the floor. "I think I've made a terrible mistake." Her voice is small, defeated.

I walk over, but she raises her hand. "No, don't come closer. It's not safe."

"What's going on? What other terrible mistake did you make besides agreeing to marry that insipid clown?"

She lets out a shaky breath that I feel deep in my soul. I never thought I'd be a protector to anyone, but for her, I'll step into that role happily if she lets me. I don't even know if my feelings are a result of the mating bond anymore, or if they'd be here, swirling in my chest, even without it.

"On the evening of my engagement to Calvin, I made a deal with Elena Montenegro, one of the most powerful witches in Salem. I agreed to not call off the wedding in exchange for the spell that brought Lucca back from hibernation."

An invisible giant fist punches me in the chest, crushing my thorax. "Why would you do that?"

She presses her lips together and her eyes reveal such turmoil and darkness that a sense of despair seeps into my brain. *Am I feeling what she's feeling?*

"Because King Raphael needed his nephew back, and also…" She trails off, looking away.

"And also what?"

"I saw how hard you took it when we couldn't awaken your friend the first time."

There's more she's not telling me. I'm aware of it. But even her half-truth is making me shake, torn between crushing her into a bear hug and yelling at her for being so stupid.

"What kind of deal did you make, Rora?"

"A blood vow. It's unbreakable."

I cover my mouth with a closed fist, fighting the urge to break something. When I thought this nightmare couldn't get any worse. *Fuck me.*

"I think the magic that created the vow is preventing me from being with you."

Rage surges within me, turning my vision red. "We're going to find a way to break that stupid vow."

"Saxon, I can't. We need to spend our time finding a manner to end our bond."

"No." I stalk her, pushing her into a corner. "I'm not going to let some old hag have that kind of leverage over you."

Aurora lifts her chin in defiance. "You can't make that decision, Saxon. This is my life."

"I'm your mate, damn it! Whether you like it or not. And until that changes, I'll protect you from anyone who wants to harm you."

She doesn't wince or cower from my outburst. On the contrary, she matches my intense stare. "If she hexes you, don't come to me crying."

"There's nothing she can do to me that's worse than being mated to someone who's determined to see me gone."

Her forehead crinkles. "That's not true. I don't want to see you gone."

"Tell me then, Rora. What *is* the truth?"

She watches me for a couple of beats, and with each second that passes, my heart squeezes harder in anticipation.

"The truth is I wish you had come into my life sooner."

Ah, fuck.

Risking another electrocution, I pull Aurora to me, crushing my lips to hers, invading her mouth with my tongue, branding her as mine. Her passion matches mine stroke for stroke. I know what's coming, I can sense the magic gathering in her core, but I need more than just a savage kiss. My fangs nick her lower lip, and the little bit of blood that drops into my mouth is better than the nectar of the gods. My balls become tight as hell, and my cock is about to explode.

Then *zap!* I'm thrown back by the strength of the magical hit and crash against the door. My body convulses, and I try not to cry out while I'm getting fried by the repel spell. It takes at least a minute for the tremors to stop and the awareness of my body to return.

Aurora drops into a crouch next to me. "Shit. Are you okay?"

"I will be in a minute."

She gives me a once-over, fixating on my crotch. "Uh, Sax. What's that stain on your pants?"

I glance down, seeing the dark circle in the front. "Well, what do you know? There's a first for everything."

"Did you piss your pants?"

I snap my eyes to hers. "Are you crazy, woman? That's not pee."

"But it's a lot."

"I jizzed in my pants."

Her gorgeous lips part, a devilish temptation that, sadly, I must resist right now. I can't get fried again.

"You want me to believe that's never happened to you before?"

"I never went long enough without pussy for this to happen."

She rolls her eyes. "Sorry for the inconvenience."

I crack a smile. "Don't apologize, sweetheart. You're totally worth it."

She gets up, stepping away from me. "I was about to make a batch of the potion against a siren's thrall when Calvin interrupted. If you promise to keep your hands to yourself, you can wait here for it."

It hurts to get back on my feet. All my muscles protest, but it doesn't compare to the pain of not being able to touch my mate.

"I promise to behave." I move to the counter, pulling a barstool to sit down.

Aurora gets into the zone, alternating her attention between her grimoire and the ingredients she has spread in front of her. I could stare at her all night. I've always been drawn to her, since the first time we met. Being turned down by her only made me want her more. I couldn't have predicted that my little obsession would turn into this enormous complication.

"Fuck," she says suddenly, staring at her notes.

"What?"

"I don't have all the ingredients for the potion."

"What are you missing?"

"The rarest of them all. Siren's tears."

"Real tears?"

"Yes, of course real tears," she replies, exasperated.

I scratch the back of my neck, probably looking as dumb as I feel. "Where can we get that?"

"I can ask Solomon. If he doesn't have it, I'll have to pay a visit to the Nightshade Market."

"What's that? Never heard of it."

"You wouldn't have. It predominantly caters to witches and mages. Sometimes you'll find a lost druid there, but no one likes them."

"Why doesn't anyone like druids?"

Aurora freezes, and her eyes shine with a new glint. "Holy shit. I can't believe I didn't even consider them."

"Consider them for what?"

"The bracelet Rikkon procured with the memory spell had druid runes carved in it. Witches and mages don't like them because we don't know where druid magic comes from."

"But if they're powerful enough to wipe out the memory of a Nightingale…"

"They might be powerful enough to break our bond."

This revelation should be good news, but I'm not motivated at all. I try to keep my feelings on the matter concealed, though. Aurora is dead set on breaking our bond thanks to the crazy vow she made. I'm more interested in breaking that vow than our bond.

"What are we waiting for? Let's go find some druids."

She gives me a droll stare. "I wish it were that simple. Druids tend to disguise themselves, especially when they're around witches and mages."

"But you said sometimes they'll venture into the Nightshade Market."

"Right. Well, let's see if Solomon has our ingredient first. If not, we'll head to the market tonight. Maybe we'll get lucky and kill two birds with one stone."

I'm totally on board with her plan, but if we find a druid, I'm not asking them to help destroy my bond to Aurora. They're freeing her from the blood vow and this ridiculous engagement, even if I have to resort to the vilest tricks I know. I'm not giving her up. Not now, not ever.

19

SAXON

×━━▶═══════━

It's just our luck that when we're on our way to see Solomon we catch the break between classes. The hallways are filled with students, Bluebloods, regulars, and even familiars, either in groups gossiping or heading somewhere.

As Aurora and I walk side by side, we attract curious glances, and even some frowns. I wonder if they're picking up the mating bond too. To me, my bond to Aurora is obvious, but is it the same for others, or can only Solomon sense it because he's a familiar on steroids?

I spot three Blueblood females who look familiar ahead. I've come across many people throughout my long life, and very few— if any—made a big enough impression on me for their faces to be imprinted in my memory, especially the ones I fucked. It sounds bad, but it's not a one-sided situation. I bet the majority of the Blueblood females I slept with don't remember me either. It's just the way vampires are, with a few exceptions. But when we fall, we fall hard.

However, the females in question are watching me with wide smiles and hungry eyes, and when I get near them, the tallest of the group steps in my way.

"Hi, Saxon. Remember me?"

"Uh, should I?"

She giggles and starts playing with her jet-black hair. "Well, it's been what? Fifty-one years?"

It's been exactly fifty-one years since I went into hibernation, so when could I have possibly met this creature? I pick up on Aurora's irritation immediately. I want to reassure her there's nothing to worry about, but now I'm curious. I walk down memory lane, searching the darkest places in my mind for an event where I could have possibly crossed paths with this vampire.

"Oh my God. You don't remember, do you?" She laughs. "It was at Woodstock in 1969. We decided to try every single drug they had at the festival, which in hindsight was such a bad move. We all went into hibernation after that."

Fuzzy memories slowly begin to trickle out. No wonder I don't remember her or her friends.

"Ah, that's right."

She switches her attention to Aurora without losing her friendly face. She must be shockingly dense if she can't pick up my mate's animosity toward her. I'm going to pay for this conversation, but I can't help basking in Aurora's jealousy. It's a nice change in our dynamic.

"Oh, you're human. You must be the future High Witch. I'm Teodora Barros, and these are my best friends, Jane Welsh and Lee

Schroeder."

Aurora doesn't say a word, just glowers at the females as if she's considering which hex to use against them. I'd better get rid of the trio quickly before we end up with another problem on our hands, like Aurora turning them into toads. I open my mouth to cut the conversation short, but Teodora talks over me.

"Did you just wake from hibernation too?" she asks me.

Her question makes me frown. "Uh. No. I've been up for forty years already."

Her dark eyes widen. "Wow, really? I just came out of mine like a month ago. Jane and Lee, the same."

"You were hibernating for fifty years?" Aurora breaks her silence. "Is that normal?"

A shared grimace appears on the females' faces. They exchange a glance, and then Lee, the stocky brunette with a too-wide face, answers, "It was my longest hibernation period."

Aurora's eyebrows crinkle, and her lips become nothing but a thin flat line. Her train of thought must have gone to the same place mine did. Usually, vampires only need to hibernate for ten to twenty years, thirty tops. Lucca was the only exception, and only because of his curse. A change in the number of years required for a vampire to regain their strength is troubling.

Jane glances at her wristwatch, an accessory reminiscent of a different era. No one uses those anymore. "We need to head to our next class, something about computers." She wrinkles her nose.

Teodora makes a similar face, before she switches back to flirtatious mode. She steps closer, and then touches my arm. "Don't be a stranger, Sax. We need to catch up."

A surge of red-hot rage hits me full force. It takes me a second to realize those aren't my feelings, but Aurora's. I step away from Teodora and link my arm with my little witch before she blasts the vampire back into hibernation.

"I'm a bit busy these days, but welcome back to the land of the living." I walk away, dragging Aurora with me.

She doesn't fight me until we round a corner, and then it's showtime. She pulls away, stopping in front of me with her hands balled into fists by her sides. Wisps of magic gather around her wrists, which tells me I have to be very careful here.

"Who was that vamp?" she grits out.

"You heard her. Someone from my past."

"She was all over you and you didn't do anything."

I lift my palms up. "Whoa. She wasn't all over me. Calm down."

"Don't tell me to calm down!" Aurora makes a jerky movement with her arm, and a bolt of lightning shoots from her hand.

It misses my head by an inch, hitting the wall next to me instead, leaving a charred hole in its wake.

"Fuck!" I say.

"Oh my God." She covers her mouth with her hands. "What did I do?"

"You almost blew my head off."

The rage swimming in her eyes recedes, guilt taking its place. "I'm so sorry. I didn't mean to lash out at you. I don't know what happened to me. I was never one to suffer from such intense jealousy before, but I wanted to hurt those vampires for even looking at you."

Amused as shit, I press my lips together to avoid laughing out loud. "I know."

She glowers at me. "Quit being so pleased about it."

"I can't help it. I'm a vain male who likes to have his ego

stroked."

I didn't mean to sound dirty like that, but immediately, my cock hardens, and once again, I want to push Aurora against the wall and fuck her senseless.

Her pulse quickens, becoming a beacon to me. *Damn everything to hell.*

She shakes her head, looking away. "Let's get to Solomon's office before someone ends up losing their head."

Clenching my jaw tight, I follow after her, trying my hardest to keep a healthy distance. When we finally arrive at the headmaster's office, he doesn't look too pleased to see us. He doesn't even allow us to walk in, stepping into the hallway instead.

"What do you want?" he asks, annoyed.

"I need siren's tears to finish making the potion for Saxon."

"I can't look for it now. Come back tomorrow."

"We can't wait until tomorrow. Saxon is in agony."

I take a deep breath, noticing immediately a different scent in the air. I'll be damned. "He doesn't want to look for it now because he's not alone. We've interrupted his date."

Solomon's bushy eyebrows shoot to the heavens, giving him a comical look. Keeping my laughter bottled up is almost impossible, but I try. He's already embarrassed. I don't need to make him angrier on top of that.

"Please, Solomon. Can you just check to see if you have the ingredient?" Aurora pleads.

"Fine. Wait here." He shuts the door in our faces, and then, I hear whispering. I don't recognize the female voice.

"Who do you think is in there with him?" Aurora asks.

"I don't have the faintest idea."

Two minutes later, the headmaster opens the door again, only sticking his head out this time. "Sorry, lovebirds. I'm out of siren's tears. I guess you'll have to make a trip to the Nightshade Market."

"Balls." Aurora turns on her heels, striding away.

"So we go to the Nightshade Market. What's the big deal?"

"The big deal is that we're both on the verge of doing something stupid. I almost blew your head off by accident." She points at the damaged wall as we walk by it.

"There's nothing for it. We need the ingredient. I say let's make a trip out of it."

"This is not a date, Saxon. As a matter of fact, I think you should stay behind."

"Hell to the no. With the way the bond's magic is increasing exponentially, I can't stay away from you without going insane. I'm coming."

"Coming where?" Lucca asks, appearing in the hallway out of thin air. It's probably not true, but I was so distracted by Aurora that I didn't notice his approach.

He's not alone, Vivienne and Rikkon are with him.

"Shit, man. Where did you come from?" I say.

"I didn't spring up on you. What's going on here?" He alternates between looking at Aurora and me, suspicious.

"Nothing is going on," Aurora grits out.

"Bullshit. There's something strange happening between you. I can sense … Holy fucking shit! You're bonded."

"Shh! No one is supposed to know that," Aurora retorts, glancing around to make sure no one is nearby.

"How did you guess?" I ask, surprised. Ronan would never share my secret with anyone, not even Lucca.

"I just felt it. When did this happen?"

He just felt it? *Fuck*. Then there's no keeping a lid on this anymore. By tomorrow, the entire institute will know about Aurora and me.

"We don't have time for this," she interrupts. "We're going to the Nightshade Market."

"What's the Nightshade Market? The name sounds familiar," Rikkon chimes in.

"I've never heard of it before, but again, I'm recently awakened," Lucca adds.

"It's a market that caters to the magical community," Aurora replies.

"Can I come too?" Rikkon asks eagerly. "I have this feeling that I've been there before. Maybe I got my memory spell there."

"Really?" Vivienne arches her eyebrows. "Then we should all go."

I can tell Aurora is not happy with this new development without even looking at her. Man, with the bond getting stronger, it's like our minds are connected. But honestly, I don't see the harm. "Sure, the more the merrier."

Her irritation level rises up to the point it feels like she smacked me upside the head. She doesn't offer a verbal retort, though. She growls like a feral cat before stomping away. I'm about to follow her when Lucca steps next to me. "Seriously, when did this happen?"

"About a month ago. We hooked up, I fed from her, and the next thing I knew, we were bonded."

"But I saw you with another girl at Havoc on the night of my awakening party. Bonded males can't—"

"I know!" I snap, then regret my outburst. "Sorry. This situation has me on edge. Nothing happened that night. I couldn't do more than kiss the human before guilt and self-loathing kicked in. But I had to pretend because…" I pull my bangs back. "Well, I was trying to find a way to break the bond then and I didn't want anyone to know about it."

"Wait, so you and Aurora aren't together?"

"She's engaged to a mage." The words drip out of my mouth, drenched in disgust.

Aurora stops ahead in the hallway, right in front of the main exit. She looks over her shoulder, glowering. "Are you coming or not?"

"Coming, babe!" I joke.

Her eyes narrow to slits, and when I get near, she whispers to me. "Bond or no bond, you call me babe again, I'll rip your nut sack off."

20

AURORA

—————✦—————

"How long are you going to pout like that?" Saxon asks from the driver's seat.

"This was supposed to be a quick visit to the Nightshade Market. Not a damn trip to Disneyland," I retort angrily.

"Are you insinuating that we are children?" Lucca grumbles from the backseat.

I turn around, trying to level him with my most scathing glare. "You're friends with Saxon. Enough said."

"Hey!" Saxon protests. "I take offense to that."

"I think this is all my fault. I shouldn't have asked to tag along," Rikkon says apologetically.

It makes sense for Rikkon to come with us. If he got the memory spell there like he suspects, maybe visiting the market will jolt his memory. That's why when he asked to join us, I didn't put up too much of a fight. I should have known Vivienne and Lucca would want to come too. She's worried about him, I get that. They both have a target on their backs. Jacques, Tatiana's right hand, accused Vivienne of attacking Boone, and then Lucca killed him. Jacques will do anything to get his hands on the Nightingale siblings in order to get to Lucca and the king. But I could have protected Rikkon on my own. And there's Saxon too. I witnessed firsthand how feral he can get.

There's no chance to roam the market without being noticed now. The news will reach my mother as soon as I step foot there. We'll also draw the attention of people we shouldn't. The place is brimming with unsavory characters trying to find a shady way to make money. If anyone suspects for a second Vivienne and Rikkon are Nightingales, they'll have more to worry about than Jacques.

Their concealing spell is solid, though. My mother brewed the potion herself, making it stronger so not only vampires will see the glamor, but all other supernatural creatures too. When Vivienne first came to Bloodstone, I could see past the concealment. Now, I can't. They look like bloodsuckers. They were also instructed to carry extra potions with them at all times, just in case the magic begins to wear off sooner than normal.

"Okay, we're downtown. Where to now?" Saxon asks.

"Park anywhere near Salem Common. We'll walk from there."

It's past three in the morning, and the park is completely deserted. A shiver runs down my spine when a chilly wind comes from the north, bringing the cold bite of winter. Saxon walks around the car, stopping next to me. There's a good gap between our bodies, but the air between us crackles with energy.

"Whoa," Lucca exclaims. "You can't stay close like that."

"Why not?" Saxon scowls at his friend.

"It's like you have a neon sign saying you're mates. Plus, it's kind of affecting me too." Lucca's eyes flash crimson for a second, and when he glances at Vivienne, it's impossible to miss the intensity of that stare.

"Are you kidding me? Our bond is making *you* horny?" I ask.

"It seems so," Vivienne answers in a husky voice.

"Oh my God. I can't be witness to this," Rikkon protests. "If Saxon and Aurora's proximity is the problem, I'll be a buffer."

He nudges Saxon to the side, sliding in between us. Saxon lets out a growl, peeling back his lips to reveal his fangs.

"Relax, dude. I'm not after your mate," Rikkon says.

"It doesn't matter," he grits out. "You're too close to her. It's triggering my instincts."

Pinching the bridge of my nose, I say, "I should have come alone."

Without looking back, I stride toward the Salem Common Bandstand, a Colonial Revival style, its domed and temple-like construction built in commemoration of the city's tercentennial. That's the hidden entrance to the Nightshade Market. The inhabitants of Salem might be aware of the supernatural world, but that doesn't mean we allow humans access to all our secrets and magic.

My companions follow me in silence. Determined to help, Rikkon is right behind me, serving as a barrier to the mating bond magic that's now seriously affecting my mood and my ability to concentrate. *How foolish was I to have agreed to let Saxon come with me?* Irritated as I was with our large party, I'm fucking glad now I'm not alone with him.

Once everyone is inside the bandstand, I recite the short spell that will reveal the Nightshade Market. The familiar tingle of magic gives me goose bumps, and then there's a sudden sensation of dropping out of the sky. I'm prepared for it, so it doesn't take me by surprise.

Vivienne gasps, clutching Lucca. Saxon stretches his arms and bends his legs, trying to keep his balance. But Rikkon falls into me. He barely has time to stand straight before Saxon yanks him back by the collar of his jacket.

"Get off her!" he snarls, throwing him to the floor.

Rikkon hits his head hard on one of the columns, getting stunned for a moment. *Shit.*

"Saxon! What the hell!" Vivienne runs to her brother, dropping into a crouch next to him.

Lucca sends him a glower before following her.

The red haze fades from Saxon's eyes as guilt washes over his face. "Fuck. I'm sorry. I don't know what came over me."

"You know what? Maybe I should go into the market alone. I can't risk you going crazy every time a guy gets near me." I try to sound firm, but my heart feels like there are thorns around it. *Shit on toast, I can't even think about being away from him without triggering this God-awful pain in my chest.*

Saxon furrows his brows together, creating a deep V in his forehead. "I don't disagree with you. But it's too late. I won't be able to not follow you in there."

I don't think I could leave you behind either.

I blow out a resigned sigh. "Fine." I glance over his shoulder to check on Rikkon. "How are you?"

He's already back on his feet, but there's a grimace on his face as he rubs the back of his head. "I'll be okay. I might need a painkiller soon, though."

"You don't think you have a concussion, do you?" Vivienne asks.

"I don't think so. But good thing I'm on a nocturnal schedule now. I won't be falling asleep anytime soon."

I whirl around and exit the bandstand, heading toward the market, which now is in plain sight. Nightshade Market is open every day of the week, from midnight until six in the morning. At a first glance, it's similar to any regular street market. It's got booths and tents from different vendors, all selling a variety of items. The difference, of course, is the nature of the items for sale. There are charms, amulets, obscure ingredients, grimoires, potions, and if someone has enough cash and knows who to ask, they can even get wolf's bane or vampire's bane here.

"How can a market this size remain hidden to the human population?" Vivienne asks.

"Thanks to a very special and intricate piece of magic. It required two circles of witches to conjure up the spell. Nightshade Market exists in a parallel dimension. The magic created a pocket in that dimension, and the spell I cast opened a portal to it."

"Wow. That's amazing," Rikkon says in awe.

"You said two circles of witches were needed. Do you think that if we got more witch juice, we could open a portal to Ellnesari?" Lucca asks.

"Why would you want to open a portal there?" Vivienne asks with an edge to her voice. All her memories were restored, and I bet many of them weren't pleasant.

He shakes his head. "I thought that maybe if I managed to talk to the Nightingale elders, I could convince them to return."

"My mother would kill you on the spot," she says.

"Would she kill me too?" Rikkon asks.

"Most likely. You chose me over her."

"Shit, I wish I remembered any of that." He runs a hand through his long hair, glancing away. "What was I thinking when I decided to erase my memories—and yours, to boot."

"I'm sure at the time you felt it was the right thing to do," I say, remembering my conversation with Vivienne about his fated mate.

Saxon grumbles under his breath, a sound that sends tingles down my spine, even if it was triggered by pure male jealousy. Under normal circumstances, it would make me mad as hell. I was never attracted to possessive guys. But I know Saxon is not like that. He's just under the control of the bond, just like I was when those females back at the institute were all over his personal space. Even thinking about them gives me dark thoughts. Images of me gouging their eyes out with my bare hands is one of the possible scenarios in my mind.

"I don't think there are enough witches in the world to open a portal to the Nightingale realm," I reply. "And I'm pretty sure the king already tried."

Lucca grunts in response. I could have been less blunt in my response, but the fact I can even have a normal conversation when all my senses are fried is a miracle. I resume walking, stopping only when I reach the edge of the market. I quickly scan the booths that I can see. It's been a while since I was here. Most of the vendors usually stay in the same spot, but sometimes, things change. The problem is, I don't know who sells siren's tears. The stock I had in my apartment I snatched from my mother.

"Do you know where to go?" Saxon asks in a tight voice. I think he's also hanging on to his sanity by a thread.

"No." I turn around to glance at the others. "We need to split up. I don't know how much longer Saxon and I will be able to stay away from each other."

Rikkon frowns. "If it's getting that bad, why don't you just … well, you know." Redness creeps up to his cheeks. He reminds me of Vivienne, getting flustered by vampires' lack of modesty when she started at Bloodstone.

I glance at Saxon, finding him scowling. Yeah, he's still angry about my deal with Elena Montenegro. Nothing either of us can do about that now.

"It would probably make everything worse," I answer. "The best we can do is find the missing ingredient for the potion until we can break the bond."

"Okay. How about Lucca, Rikkon, and I take the east side, and you and Saxon the west?" Vivienne suggests.

"Actually, I think Rikkon should come with us," Saxon says, surprising the hell out of me.

"Really? You want me to come?" He stares at him with round eyes.

"Yeah, I might need you to serve as a buffer again."

"You almost killed him before when he tried," Vivienne interjects.

"I'm sorry. I promise I'll try my best not to kill your brother."

I pull a small vial from my purse and offer it to Rikkon. "Here. This is vampire's bane, just in case."

Both Lucca and Saxon shoot daggers at me with their eyes. "Why do you carry vampire's bane in your purse?" Saxon asks.

I return the frown. "Do you think I'd agree to live among a bunch of bloodsuckers without protection?"

"Don't worry, bro. I'll only use it as a last resort," Rikkon pipes up.

Shaking his head, Saxon turns toward the market. "Let's find some fucking siren's tears already."

21

SAXON

———◆———

I didn't insist on coming on this trip only because the bond is making it impossible for me to be apart from Aurora. I had ulterior motives. I wanted to find information about this blood vow deal Aurora made, but hell, finding the siren's tears is my main focus right now. It's hard to describe what's going on in my body. I alternate between feeling hot and cold in the span of seconds, my skin feels raw and prickly, my throat is parched. I'm walking with a semi, and the friction of my erection against my jeans, instead of offering comfort, is hurting more. *Fuck, if I don't find some kind of relief, I'll go insane.*

Rikkon offered to come with us, but he's not walking between us. He learned his lesson the hard way; you can't come between bonded mates. He's walking next to me instead. When Aurora stops by a vendor to ask about siren's tears, I take the opportunity to ask the male a few questions.

"Anything coming back to you yet?"

He shakes his head. "Nothing. Maybe I didn't come here after all. If the market was hidden to the human population, how would I find it?"

"Come on, dude. It wouldn't be hard to hire a rogue mage to bring you here."

"I suppose." He sticks his hands in his pockets. "Why do you want me to recover my memories so much anyway? What's in it for you?"

Aurora returns, not pleased, and I don't have the chance to answer him.

"They didn't have it. But the lady said the guy at the end of this row might."

"What if we can't find siren's tears? What's going to happen to you two?" Rikkon asks.

Aurora twists her face into a scowl. "Let's not think about that."

We walk for another minute when Rikkon stops suddenly, his attention riveted on something. I follow his line of vision, finding a gray tent booth that has dreamcatchers hanging in the front.

"What is it?" I ask.

"Those dreamcatchers look familiar."

"We don't have time to stop now," Aurora snaps. "We'll come back later. We really need to get the final ingredient."

She resumes her brisk pace, but Rikkon remains frozen. As for me, I'm torn. I want to investigate that booth, but as Aurora puts distance between us, the ache increases. I can't believe she hasn't slowed down. Can't she feel the agony? Maybe it's stronger for me.

I pull on the male's jacket. "Come on, dude. We have to go."

"Okay," he says, but he still doesn't move. I have to drag his ass from the spot.

I can't see Aurora anymore, and I'm seized by a moment of panic. But then I feel the invisible band that links us together. I think it's stretched out to the max. I push people out of my way without care. I'm sprinting, and the only reason I don't take off with vampiric speed is because of Rikkon. It sucks that his mother stripped his powers away. Nightingales could travel with the wind, popping in and out of places in the blink of an eye.

Aurora is waiting for us, but the moment that I see her face, I know I'm going to receive a tongue-lashing. Her expression is contorted in a mix of pain and rage. She's hugging her middle too. *Shit.*

"Why didn't you follow me right away?" she grits out.

"I had to make sure Rikkon didn't get lost. We can't lose him in the crowd. Lucca will have my head."

"I'm not a child who can get lost," he objects.

Ignoring Rikkon, she continues. "Fine. The guy who presumably has the stuff is in the booth around the corner."

We walk side by side this time, only because even falling behind a step could cause me to have a seizure. I don't think I can drive back to the institute in this condition. Good thing Aurora already prepped everything, and she only needs to add the final ingredient. When we finally stop at the booth, a frail old man is finishing up a sale, but Aurora interrupts him.

"Do you have siren's tears?"

"Oh dear. I just sold the last vial to her." He points at the tall woman with a gaunt face and thinning black hair that's standing next to Aurora. *Yikes.* She looks like the bride of death.

"I'll pay you double for it." Aurora turns to the woman, not hiding her desperation.

She snorts, glancing down at her. "Absolutely not. I need this for my beauty potion and there's been a shortage of siren's tears for months."

"You're going to need more than a potion, lady," I say.

With a hateful expression etched on her face, she says, "The siren's tears are mine." She turns to leave, but I'm not having it.

In a split second, I'm in front of her, blocking her way. "You *will* sell us the siren's tears."

The aggression vanishes from her gaze as her eyes glaze over. The tension around her mouth eases. "Of course."

I give her all the money I have on me as I don't have a fucking clue how much the vendor charged her. The exchange is quick, and after it's done, I tell her to go home.

Aurora and Rikkon are watching me with their mouths hanging open. I don't make it a habit to use compulsion like that, and definitely not in front of so many witnesses. But hell, I got what we needed. My lips begin to crack into a smile, but the vendor jumps from behind his counter, waving his scrawny arms in a menacing way at me.

"Filthy bloodsucker. How dare you use your devilish powers on my customers?"

His ruckus is drawing a lot of attention to us. Aurora quickly comes to my side, and tugs on my sleeve. "Come on, let's go before he hexes us."

We break into a run, but the problem is, I grabbed Aurora's hand by instinct. We only manage to turn around a corner before we latch on each other like wild animals in heat. I don't know where we are, or who is near us. All I care about is doing what the bond demands.

"Fuck! Guys, cut it out," someone says, but it sounds far away.

While my mouth devours Aurora's, my hands are busy stripping her of her clothes. There are too many fucking layers. She's just as eager to do the same to me. I know there was a reason why we couldn't be together like this, but I can't remember anymore. It wasn't important. There's a sudden current of energy zapping into my body. It feels like I've been hit by lightning, but the power of the bond is stronger. It gives me the endurance to withstand the blast. Eventually, the zing fades into the background too.

I'm about to tear Aurora's pants so I can plunge my cock inside her hot pussy when rough hands yank me away from her. At once, the savage beast mode takes over. I roar at the motherfucker who dared to interrupt, fangs bared and ready to shred him to pieces. He looks familiar, but I don't care. I pounce, hitting an invisible barrier that sends me flying in the opposite direction.

I hit my head against something when I fall, which stuns me for a moment. The lights hanging above me are blurry. Or are they stars? They look like pesky fireflies. The buzz in my ears is annoying as hell too. Suddenly, Aurora's face appears in my line of vision. I smile, reaching for her face.

"Not now, Sax. Quickly, drink this," she urges me.

Then she shoves something into my mouth. A bitter liquid hits my tongue, almost making me gag. She keeps the vial against my lips until I've drunk it all. At once, a familiar numbness takes over my body, and at the same time, my mind becomes sharper. She moves away, giving me room to sit up. There's a small crowd around us, staring, pointing, gossiping. But the only people I recognize are Aurora, Rikkon, and Aurora's younger sister. *Wait. Why is she here?*

"What happened?" I ask.

"You and Aurora went crazy," Rikkon answers.

Slowly, the memories of what we were about to do return. *Damn it.* I almost fucked Aurora in the middle of the market. She must hate me now.

"Can someone explain to me what the hell is going on?" her sister asks.

Aurora steps in front of me with her arms crossed. I think she's trying to cover the top I'm sure I tore open.

"Not until you tell me what you're doing here," she replies.

The teen makes a face that spells guilty. We don't get to hear her answer, though. Lucca and Vivienne arrive just then, and it's clear they have something important to say.

I jump back to my feet with my body already tense. "What now?"

"You need to get Vivienne and Rikkon to the institute at once. Jacques is here and he's not alone," Lucca says.

Of course. When it rains, it pours.

22

AURORA

❦

"What do you mean *I* have to take them back? What about you?" Saxon asks, clearly not happy with Lucca's orders.

"I'm not running away from Jacques. If he wants a fight, he'll get one."

"Oh, that's fucking stupid. You can't turn the Nightshade Market into a war zone. Do you know how many mages and witches are here? They would hex you so hard it might send you back into hibernation."

Vivienne steps closer to Lucca. "No. He can't go into hibernation again."

"I'm not a coward. I'm not running away," Lucca replies through clenched teeth.

"What if we hex the crap out of Jacques?" Miranda suggests.

"We can't attack him unprovoked, especially you and me. We would be breaking the Accords," I retort.

164

"He doesn't need to know the hex came from you," Rikkon suggests. "Can't you cast a spell from afar?"

Miranda glances at him with a mischievous smile on her lips. "That's a great idea."

"What's the fun in that?" Saxon whines. "That's sneaky and cowardly."

His remark should annoy me. We're trying to avoid a major conflict here and save lives. But even under the effects of the potion, he beguiles me like no other. He's my mate all right, but there's more to the feeling than just ancient magic. The warmth that spreads through my chest when I look at him feels natural, real. *Oh God.* I can't be falling for him. When we break the bond, I'm marrying Calvin.

At least the aches are gone. I'm glad that I had the foresight to bring the potions with me. I don't know what would have happened otherwise. I pull the lapels of my jacket closer together. Saxon ripped it open in his lust-infused frenzy, and now the zipper is busted.

"This is not a show, Sax," Vivienne retorts. "It's life-and-death. I'm not risking Lucca's or Rikkon's lives so you guys can dick around in a testosterone contest."

A chilly, unnatural gust of wind licks the back of my neck, making me shiver. I glance over my shoulder, certain that I will find someone lurking in the shadows. But the only things I see are the stacked-up boxes of the booth nearby.

We're still surrounded by a crowd of curious people. There's no chance in hell our little performance won't reach my mother's ears and the rest of the cronies in the council. I have no clue how I'm going to explain almost fucking Saxon's brains out in the middle of the Nightshade Market to everyone, but that problem will have to wait.

"Where was Jacques the last time you saw him?" I ask.

"Right at the front of the market. By now, who knows?" Lucca replies.

Someone pushes through the crowd, creating a commotion. It's the scrawny vendor who went ballistic when Saxon compelled the witch to sell us siren's tears. He's not alone. Two members of the Warlocks of Ivern Guild are standing next to him. I recognize them instantly by the dark power emanating from their tall frames. They're the most ruthless magic users in the community, feared by pretty much everyone. I didn't know they were in Salem, much less that they were working as security in the Nightshade Market.

"Those are the bloodsuckers who broke the sacred rules of Nightshade Market." The old man points a shaky finger in our direction.

"Sacred rules? It was just a little bit of compulsion," Saxon retorts. "No one got hurt."

Oh, for fuck's sake. He had to open his big mouth. Am I the only one who senses the danger emanating from those warlocks? I reach for Saxon's hand to draw his attention. The crackling when we touch happens again, but with much less intensity. "Sax, don't say another word," I whisper.

He turns to me with a frown, no doubt ready to argue.

"You're all coming with us," one of the warlocks says in a baritone voice that leaves no room for argument. This is not a request. It's an order, and we'd better obey or the consequences will be dire.

Lucca takes a step forward, hissing. "Who the fuck are you to tell us what to do?"

Am I surprised Lucca and Saxon don't know who we are dealing with? Not really. The warlocks very rarely mingle with vampires. They have other, more pressing issues to occupy their time, like keeping demons from taking over the world. Which begs the question. Why are they in Salem?

I step in front of Lucca while giving Vivienne a meaningful glance, hoping she will understand my message that she needs to control her guy. Those warlocks can wreak some serious damage, and they don't care if Lucca is royalty or not.

"We didn't mean to break any rules," I say. "I'm sorry my friend used compulsion on your customer, sir." I look at the vendor. "It was an emergency."

"Some High Witch you will be one day. You're supposed to be an example to the community."

I wince, feeling his criticism deep in my soul. He's not wrong.

"Hey, don't talk to Aurora like that," Saxon replies angrily. "You know nothing about her."

I wish he would stop speaking, but damn, it feels good to hear him defending me. But I can't allow my mushy feelings to interfere now. I have to save our asses.

"We'll come with you," I tell the warlocks.

"What?" Saxon exclaims. "Are you crazy?"

Leaning closer, I whisper, "I know what I'm doing. Trust me."

"At least now we don't have to worry about Jacques anymore," Rikkon adds with a shrug.

I can tell his comment is not well received by Lucca and Saxon given the glowers they're sporting now. And things become even tenser when the second warlock points two glowing fingers in our direction and whispers words in a foreign language. I reach for

Saxon again, hooking my arm with his to keep him in place. A bright green light surrounds our group and it feels like my entire body is disintegrating. I'm caught by a nauseating sensation of vertigo that mercifully only lasts a few seconds. When I recover the full awareness of my body, we're no longer in the market, but in a place I know all too well. *Fuck.* The warlocks brought us to the Council of Witches headquarters, and standing before us is my mother, looking positively pissed off.

Her furious stare switches from me to Saxon, and it's only then I realize I'm still clutching him. I step away from his side, glad that thanks to the potion, I'm no longer lusting for him like a dog in heat.

"Son of a bitch. What the hell was that?" Saxon presses the heel of his hand against his forehead. "I feel sick."

"Aurora Yuki, you have a lot of explaining to do," my mother says with a deadly calm that preludes the unleashing of her wrath. I'm not looking forward to it.

"About what exactly?" I ask to buy time. I have to come up with a pretty good excuse to avoid telling her the truth. She can't know under any circumstances that Saxon is my mate.

"About what?" Her voice rises to a shrill. "You were spotted behaving in the most disgraceful manner with that blond vampire in the middle of the Nightshade Market. You're engaged to be married in nine months. Do you know how badly your rebellion reflects on me?"

My blood's temperature is rising to a boiling point. She doesn't care one bit about us. All that matters are what our actions will do to her reputation. I'm about to blow the lid off this can and tell her my engagement to Calvin can go to hell, but the words get stuck in my mouth. It takes me a moment to understand the blood vow is what's making me tongue-tied.

"Rora did nothing. This whole fiasco was all my fault." Miranda steps forward with her chin raised high.

What is she doing?

Mom raises an eyebrow. "Oh? Is that so?"

"It's kind of embarrassing, really. I needed an ingredient for a love potion and went to the Nightshade Market to buy it. I met Aurora and her friends there by chance, and thanks to my clumsiness, Aurora and Saxon ended up covered in Venus Dust."

I don't miss the traded glance between the two warlocks who brought us here. I can't begin to imagine what they must be thinking about this situation. From killing demons to witnessing a scene straight from a daytime soap opera. What a change.

"And you expect me to believe that's what happened?" Mom asks.

"She's not lying, ma'am," one of the warlocks chimes in.

At once, we all turn to stare at the man. I try to school my expression into a neutral one, but I'm completely astonished by his bald-faced lie. *Why would he do that?*

"Are you saying you were there? You witnessed with your own eyes those events?"

"Yes, ma'am."

I think Mom still suspects Miranda's story isn't true, but like me, she probably can't fathom why the warlocks would lie to save my ass.

"Very well. You're all dismissed, except you, Miranda."

She lowers her gaze to the floor, but I catch the grimace on her face just the same. *Shit.* I hate that she's going to be punished for something she didn't do. But if I tell the truth now, it won't save her from punishment, it will only make matters worse for everyone.

"We'll take you back to the institute," the tallest of the warlocks says.

"Oh hell no. I'm not traveling like the first time again," Saxon protests.

"Fine. You can walk from here. We don't care."

"Sax, just shut up and let's go home," Lucca says. "We have much to discuss."

The warlocks use their magic again to send us back to Bloodstone, but this time, I land inside my apartment alone. Well, not alone. One of them came with me. The second trip was just as jarring as the first one, so before I do anything, I pull up a chair and sit down.

"The dizziness should fade in a moment," he says.

I bite the inside of my cheek to speed up the process. Glaring at him, I ask, "Why did you lie to my mother?"

"For the same reason we came to Salem."

"What reason is that?"

"We know about the deal you made with Elena Montenegro and what she covets. We can't allow her to have it."

23

SAXON

———⚔———

"**W**hat in the fucking hell!" I stagger to the nearest chair as the world around me spins out of control.

Not far from me, Lucca and Rikkon grunt as well. It takes me a few seconds to notice Aurora is not in the room. I pivot around too fast and end up losing my balance, crashing against the second chair next to me and then falling straight to the floor.

"Careful, you shouldn't move too fast after traveling through a wormhole," says the asshole who brought us back.

I jump back onto my feet, ready to tear him to pieces if he doesn't tell me where Aurora is in the next second. But Ronan, who must have been in his room, sneaks up behind the warlock and presses a blade against his neck.

"Don't fucking move, motherfucker, or I'll slit your throat before you can say *expelliarmus*."

The warlock doesn't seem one bit nervous about Ronan's threat and I don't think it's because he quoted Harry Potter. The corners of his lips twitch upward and amusement dances in his pale gray eyes.

"Ronan McLaren. It's been a while."

Say what? He knows Ronan?

My friend presses the blade closer to the warlock's neck. "Don't even attempt pleasantries, Declan. I want to know what you're doing in my apartment. How did you pass through the wards protecting Bloodstone?"

Whoa. Ronan knows the freaky warlock too? How is that possible? I wasn't even aware they existed until an hour ago.

"I was carrying precious cargo. The future High Witch's magic was enough to break through the wards."

"Where's Aurora?" I growl.

Declan raises an eyebrow. "You can't feel her anymore?"

Fuck. Does he know we're mates? He must, but I don't know how. The High Witch didn't seem to suspect about my link to her daughter.

I concentrate, remembering the invisible line that connects me to Aurora. I finally sense her. She's back in her apartment. The potion has really dampened the effects of the bond. I wonder how long it will last this time. It seems the more I consume it, the less effective it becomes.

"What do you know about my relationship with Aurora?" I take a step toward him.

"I'll answer you if you tell Ronnie boy here to bring his aggression down a notch."

"Don't release him just yet, Ronan. I have some questions I'd like answered," Lucca chimes in.

"You do realize I'm just indulging your friend for old times' sake," Declan replies with a smirk.

With a grumble, Ronan removes the blade from the jackass's throat and steps away. "Don't waste your time trying to get answers from him. Most of the words out of his mouth will be lies anyway."

"That's true." The warlock shrugs.

"Where do you know this guy from?" Rikkon asks, watching the stranger intensely.

"It's a long story. What I'd like to know is what he's doing here in our apartment."

"There was a situation in the Nightshade Market," I answer. "Declan and his friend showed up and took us to see the High Witch."

"Friend?" Ronan's eyebrows shoot to the heavens. "Who else is in Salem, Declan?"

"It's just Ryker and me for now."

"Wait. Where is the other douche?" I ask.

"And where's Vivienne?" Lucca adds.

"The blonde girl is back in her apartment." Declan attempts to smooth the wrinkles on his jacket as if he doesn't have a care in the world. He's surrounded by three Blueblood vampires, but he doesn't seem to give a rat's ass about it.

"And Ryker is having a private conversation with Aurora," he continues.

The instinct to protect sweeps over me. "Hell to the fucking no." I turn toward the door, but I only manage to take two steps forward before I hit an invisible barrier that I can't break through. "What the fuck is this?"

"You're not going to interrupt that meeting, Saxon. Don't worry. Aurora is safe with Ryker."

"And you think I trust your word?"

"Shut the fuck up, everyone!" Lucca yells. "Ronan, just tell us who we're dealing with since you and those warlocks seem to go way back."

Glaring at our unwelcome guest, he replies, "Declan and Ryker belong to the Warlocks of Ivern Guild. I met them when King Raphael sent me on a solo mission about three hundred years ago. You and Saxon were in hibernation at the time."

"Are you saying those assholes are immortals?" I ask, unable to contain the surprise in my tone.

"Yep." Declan takes a seat on the couch, crossing his legs at the knees. "Perk of being a warlock."

"What's the difference between warlocks and mages?" Rikkon asks.

"Warlocks deal with dark magic." Ronan watches our unwanted guest through slits.

"Isn't that bad?"

"It can be, if the mage is weak-minded," Declan replies. "But it's a necessary evil. You can't fight demons using the garden-variety magic witches and mages do."

Lucca shakes his head. "This doesn't make any sense. How come I never knew your kind existed?"

"We don't like the spotlight. We can do our job much easier in the shadows."

I turn to Ronan. "I can't believe you never told us about them."

"Don't give me that accusatory glance. By the time you and Lucca woke up, my encounter with those assholes was way in the past and almost forgotten. Besides, the subject never came up."

"Why are you here, though?" Lucca asks Declan. "Did my

uncle send for you?"

He snorts. "We aren't servants of the king like the witches and mages in this town."

"You lied to the High Witch to protect Aurora and now your buddy is talking to her. What do you want with my mate?" I almost shout.

"We're not after your mate. But she's in the way of our goal. It's up to her if she wants to be an ally or a hindrance."

Without thinking, I leap, ready to tackle the warlock down. But he simply moves faster than I can reach him, appearing on the other side of the room, unfazed.

"Don't waste your time trying to pick a fight with me, buddy. You'll lose. Besides, if Aurora agrees to help us, it will benefit you too."

"What do you mean?" I ask.

"We can free her of the blood vow she made with Elena Montenegro. But she must agree to our terms."

I wasn't born yesterday. I know their terms might not be something Aurora would get on board with. But until she's free of the deal with the old witch, we can't be together.

"What terms are those?"

"I can't tell you. You'll have to ask her."

"Then let me through," I demand.

Declan tilts his head to the side, narrowing his gaze. "Not yet. Ryker needs another minute."

AURORA

"How did you know?" I ask through the lump lodged in my throat.

"It was careless of you to agree to a blood vow. No sane witch would do it, especially not with the likes of Elena Montenegro," he says in a reproachful tone instead of answering my question.

The criticism makes my heart feel even tighter in my chest. "What do you know about her?"

"More than you do, clearly."

"Don't presume I'm a naïve person. I know Elena is bad news, but..." I trail off, leery of sharing what I saw in the Nightingale mirror with him.

"But what, girl? If you know something, you'd better tell me. You're way over your head already."

"Why should I tell you anything? I just met you. I don't even know your name."

"The name is Ryker Marx. I've been fighting demons and other nightmarish creatures for centuries. If there's one person you should trust, it's me."

"What are you implying? Is Elena Montenegro a demon?"

My heart is thumping so loud in my chest, I'm sure the douche canoe can hear it.

"No, but she's been after the relic your fiancé's family possesses for generations. Did you know she bewitched Calvin's great-grandfather into proposing to her?"

"That's against the council's law," I say, but I'm not surprised she's done it.

"No kidding. She didn't care. Her obsession with the first witch's grimoire trumped everything else."

I shake my head, having a hard time believing what this guy is telling me is true. "Her fiancé died."

"Yes, he did."

Suspicion takes hold of me. "You didn't kill him, did you?"

He gives me a droll stare. "If we were allowed to kill people, don't you think we would have eliminated Elena instead?"

Maybe they should have.

"Did you know she has a magical mirror of Nightingale origin?"

My question drops onto the warlock's head like a bomb. He doesn't speak for a moment, but his eyes turn rounder and his face blanches. "Are you sure?"

"Yes. She made me look in it."

"What did you see?"

I close my eyes for a second, not wanting to relive that awful scene, but it's too late. "A terrible future. King Raphael went mad."

When I look at the warlock again, he's so still he could be confused with a statue. Only his eyes seem alive, blazing an electric blue.

"Just like the Boucher family," he mumbles.

"Yes, just like them."

He passes his hand over his face, looking rather rattled, which doesn't help with my anxiety. "The situation is worse than I thought."

"Why is that?"

"Elena already has the mirror, which was believed to have been destroyed. And now she wants the first grimoire."

"What's so terrible about her wanting the grimoire? Any witch would kill to have it."

"And several have killed for it. The first grimoire contains terrible spells, girlie. Secrets that should never see the light of day. The Belmonts have been entrusted to keep the grimoire safe for centuries. Unfortunately, anyone marrying into the family automatically gains access to it."

"Elena wants me to steal it when I marry Calvin, which doesn't make any sense. She wouldn't be able to read it."

Well, she seems to believe she can, but I keep that thought to myself. Ryker already thinks I'm a stupid woman, there's no need to give him more reason to keep believing that.

The warlock's gaze darkens, matching the frown on his tanned face. "She tricked you into a blood vow. That means your blood is her blood. Once you marry Calvin Belmont, she can do whatever she pleases with the grimoire."

That's why she didn't blink an eye when I pointed the problem out. She had already thought of a solution. Suddenly, my legs can no longer support my weight. I reach for the nearest chair, needing to sit down. I knew I was making a deal with the devil, but the implications of what I allowed her to do to me go beyond my fears. She set me up, played on my emotions, and I let her. I was so fucking stupid.

With my head in my hands, I fight the urge to cry. *What the hell am I going to do now?*

"What's your plan?" I ask. "I assume you have one."

"You're going to keep acting as if nothing has changed. We can't do anything against Elena Montenegro until she shows her hand."

"Are you saying I have to continue with the sham engagement and marry Calvin?"

"I'm afraid so."

I let out a shaky breath as my world collapses on top of me. *What about Saxon?* The potion has dulled the power of the bond temporarily, but it's still there, vibrating in my chest. God, I wish he were here. I miss him, even though we've only been apart for a few minutes.

"You're thinking about your mate," the warlock says.

"Yes," I reply without making eye contact.

"I have the power to break your bond, if you desire."

A sharp pain pierces through my chest as my entire body rejects the idea. I should say yes; it would make things much easier. That was the goal—finding a way to end the mating bond. And now that's been offered to me on a silver platter, I can't take it.

"I don't want to break the bond." I lift my eyes to his. "Saxon is my mate. I'm not going to give him up."

"But you have to marry Calvin. What you're doing is madness. It's torture."

He's not wrong. But knowing how badly that old bitch played me has given me a moment of much needed clarity. She knew what was in my heart before I did. I love Saxon. It's why I couldn't bear to lose him.

"Can't you end the blood vow instead?"

The man squints while his jaw is clenched hard. "I can, but Elena would know the moment it happened that she'd lost the connection to you. We can't have that."

Undiluted anger rushes through my body, making me see red. I'm tired of awful things snowballing out of control and being unable to stop them.

"Are you saying that I'm your pawn now?" I grit out.

"Don't you realize, Aurora? You've always been a pawn. But now, you're playing in my boardgame."

On unsteady legs, I get up. "I'm nobody's pawn. You just told me you can't act against Elena until you have proof, which means you need my help. If you're as powerful as you claim, you *will* find a way to free me of this vow without Elena knowing before I have to marry Calvin."

His nostrils flare as he stares at me in a cold and calculating manner. "I don't take orders from anyone, girlie, especially from a barely-of-age witch."

"Then don't consider this as me ordering you around. Think of this arrangement as a collaboration. Neither of us can get what we want without the other, so why not partner up?"

He doesn't answer for a couple of seconds, and in that time, I keep my gaze steady, locked on his. Warlock or not, I'm not going to be intimidated by him.

"Fine. I'll need a few days to come up with a solution. In the meantime, I'd suggest you keep your trysts with your mate private. Your little sister won't be around to cover for you next time."

24

AURORA

The annoying warlock is gone. He'll get in touch when he can figure out a way to break the stupid blood vow I made with Elena. His promise should have relieved some of the weight crushing my chest, but blood vow or not, I'm still expected to marry Calvin.

If that wasn't already a death sentence before, now that Saxon has come into the picture, the situation feels more impossible than ever.

I text Miranda to see how she's doing. She shouldn't have lied like that to cover my ass, but I'll be forever grateful that she did. There's no answer, which could indicate part of her punishment means no access to her phone. I send a text to Niko as well. If Miranda is on social lockdown, Niko will have all the details. She's usually the one dealing with our mother's wrath, but only because she's a brat.

She doesn't text me back either and I begin to worry, but then

I remember it's the middle of the night and she's probably asleep. *God. Where is my brain?*

I drop the phone on the kitchen counter, feeling frustrated and angry as hell. My life is spiraling out of control and it seems there's no stopping it. A second later, these feelings begin to give way to a sense of giddiness spreading through my chest. I whirl around, facing the door, suddenly out of breath. A single knock sounds, injecting my heart with euphoria. Saxon is on the other side.

I could open the door for him using a simple spell, but I need the short walk to get a grip on my emotions. My stomach is twisting, all thanks to the horde of little trolls having a rave party in my belly. This is definitely not the mating bond at work. Its magic is still dulled. What I'm feeling is one hundred percent me.

Saxon's hands are in his pockets and his chin is tucked low when I open the door. His long bangs are covering part of his face and I can't get over how fucking sexy he is. Slowly, he glances up, looking at me from under his eyelashes. I lean against the doorframe because my legs are dangerously close to turning into jelly.

"Hey," he says in a husky voice that sends tingles down my spine.

"Hi."

"Are you okay?"

"Yeah. And you?"

Shit. This is the most painful conversation I've ever had with Saxon. It's like we're strangers on a blind date.

"Do you want to come in?"

His eyes widen a fraction, the only hint of his surprise. "You know I do. But is it wise?"

My heart is going ninety, a fact Saxon must be aware of. "No, but I don't care."

His lips curl into a mischievous grin. "Aren't you the rebel?"

I open the door wider, stepping to the side to let him through. When the door clicks shut again, I lean against the hard surface, not daring to move closer to him. He stops after a few steps and turns around.

"What's the matter? Did that son of a bitch warlock do something to you?" There's an edge to his tone now.

"Yes."

His body becomes tense as hell while his eyes turn crimson. "What did he do?" he grits out with barely contained rage.

Crap. I should have stopped to think before I opened my big mouth. "Nothing bad. Just calm down for a second."

"You're shaking. How can that not be bad?"

A loud exhale leaves my mouth. "I'm not shaking because of him. It's you."

The anger leaves his face, giving way to misplaced guilt. "Are you afraid of me? Is it because of what happened in the market?"

For fuck's sake, Aurora. You're making a mess out of this conversation.

I take a step toward him. "God, no. What I meant before was my conversation with the warlock made me realize something."

"What?"

The words are on the tip of my tongue, but I'm too scared to confess. *Damn it. I don't know what I'm doing anymore.* Looking away, I run my fingers through my hair. "I don't think I want to end our bond."

Not the whole truth, but it's all I dare say for now.

I expect Saxon to have a comment to my statement, but when

he doesn't speak for several beats, I glance in his direction. *Holy cannoli.* Talk about being blasted by the most intense heated stare ever. Shining in his eyes I see a combination of lust and admiration.

"What does that mean for your upcoming nuptials?"

My throat begins to close up. "I don't know."

"If we're still mated by then, you know what will happen, don't you?" Crimson shines in his eyes again.

"You'll slay Calvin." I move closer, dying to come into his orbit, his heat.

"Do you want me to kill your fiancé, Rora?" His eyes narrow. "Is that what this is about?"

I despise Calvin, but do I want him dead? No, I'm not that ruthless. But even if I were, I'd never use Saxon to do my dirty work.

"I wish it were that simple. No, I don't want you to kill the jerkface. If I wanted him dead, I'd do it myself."

"Then what do you want from me?" He sounds frustrated now.

I knit my fingers together, unsure of what to say. *Damn it. Why am I all of a sudden so insecure?*

"I didn't expect any of this to happen, Sax. I'm confused as hell. The warlock said he had the power to break our bond, and I said no."

The muscles around Saxon's mouth tense as he clenches his jaw hard. "What about the blood vow?"

"I asked him to find a way to free me of it."

"So no more zapping." The corners of his lips twitch upward.

"No more zapping." I smile.

He walks over, grinning from ear to ear now. "You don't want to end our mating bond, and you're trying to remove the pesky invisible chastity belt some old hag put on you. Does that mean you want to ride the Saxon sex machine again?"

"Oh my God. You had to go and ruin it."

His arms circle around my waist, pulling me against his body. His enormous cock is up and alert, ready for action, which only stokes my own fire.

"I'm not trying to ruin anything, Rora." He caresses my cheek. "But I do say stupid shit when I'm nervous. And that is how it is with you. I feel like I'm way out of my depth."

"Why? You have, like, hundreds of years of experience over me."

His brows furrow. "Way to make a guy feel old."

"You're not a guy. You're a vampire."

He slides his hand to the back of my head, twisting a lock of hair around his fingers. "And you are a sassy little witch. What am I going to do with you?"

"How about you quit talking and kiss me already?"

He raises one eyebrow. "Is this a trick? Are you trying to get me fried again?"

"For fuck's sake." I curl my fingers around his T-shirt, pulling him to me.

Our lips and tongues fuse together, and it's like the Fourth of July exploded in my apartment. There are fireworks everywhere, lighting up the sky. I want to meld myself to him so we'll never be apart. Our kiss quickly becomes a ferocious dance that has me panting for more. My body is in flames, and my pussy is clenching in anticipation.

Without breaking the kiss, I walk backward until I reach the couch. Then I fall on it, dragging Saxon with me. Thanks to his vampiric reflexes, he twists his body so that he doesn't crush me, bracing his hand against the back of the sofa.

With impatient hands, I try to get rid of his T-shirt without letting go of his lips, which is pretty much impossible. He leans back to yank his shirt off, revealing the carved perfection that is his chest and abs. A wicked smile blossoms on his face when he catches me ogling him.

"Is it still safe?" He leans down, bracing his forearms on each side of my head.

"Yeah," I say, out of breath. "For now."

"Good enough."

He lowers his pelvis down as his tongue darts into my mouth. I bring my knees up, allowing Saxon better access to my throbbing core. His cock presses against me, already so hard and big that the friction alone will make me climax in the next minute. But as I get near the edge, I sense the blood vow magic building within. *Shit.*

I push Saxon off me, sending him to the floor. He ends up hitting his shoulder against the coffee table with a loud *clunk.*

"Ouch." He massages the sore spot, pouting.

"Sorry. It was happening again. I didn't want to hurt you."

"Didn't want to hurt me *more*, you mean."

"Come on. You didn't hit the table that hard."

"I wasn't only talking about the fall." He rubs his face in a fitful manner. "This fucking sucks. Do you know how badly I want you right now?"

"Yeah, I do. Trust me. The feeling is not one-sided."

He narrows his eyes, watching me with a newly predatory gaze. "Take off your clothes."

"What?" I sit up.

He jumps to his feet and then proceeds to strip down completely. My eyes immediately zero in on his cock, which is bigger than I remember. I want to taste him so badly, I'm almost weeping. He fists his shaft, rubbing his thumb over the head to spread pre-cum over the sensitive skin.

"If I can't touch you, then I want you to pleasure yourself as I watch."

Heat creeps up to my cheeks. I'm not a prude, but I've never masturbated in front of a guy before. It sounds so intimate, even more than sex.

Saxon moves his hand up and down his erection, not taking his eyes off me. "See how hard I am for you, Rora? Don't make me beg."

Come on, Aurora. You've fucked Saxon six ways to Sunday in the bathroom of a club. You can get off with him watching.

I take off my top, and then my leggings and underwear. When Saxon's hungry eyes sweep over my naked body, it's almost like he's touching me for real. I lie down, propping my head on a pillow so I can watch him better.

"Damn it. You're so beautiful," he says in a husky voice.

I lick my middle finger, then slide my hand down my belly until I reach my clit. I'm so horny that just the simple touch makes me arch my body. A moan escapes my lips as I continue to make circles with my fingers across the sensitive bud. Saxon grunts, moving his hand faster now.

"God, Sax," I purr like a kitten. "I wish you were the one in between my legs."

"Me too, Rora. Me too. But watching you is the next best thing."

The pressure keeps building below, and if I were alone, I'd have my eyes closed now, probably picturing a delicious fantasy starring him. But I don't need to do that today when I have the real deal in front of me.

"I'm so close, sweetheart. I'm just waiting for you."

I don't know if it's the tenderness in his voice, or the way he's looking at me, but a wave of pleasure sweeps over me in the next second, making my entire body shake. I cry out his name. He cries out mine. I only stop moving my fingers when he collapses on the other side of the couch, spent. We don't speak for a moment and all I can hear is the combined sound of our erratic breathing.

When my heartbeat returns to normal, I curl my legs, sitting up. Saxon turns to me with a pleased grin on his lips and sleepy eyes. "That was hot."

I glance at his crotch. "And messy."

He's still sporting a semi, which doesn't surprise me. His endurance was off the charts when we hooked up for the first time.

His face turns a lovely pink shade. *Oh my God, I made Saxon blush.*

"Yeah. Sorry about that. I should have thought things through."

I scooch closer, unable to keep my distance from him when he looks adorable like that. I kiss him on the cheek. "Don't worry about it."

He closes his eyes, making a humming sound in the back of his throat.

"What is it?" I ask.

"Nothing. I'm just … happy." He looks at me again, burying me with so much tenderness that I feel undeserving. "You make me happy, Rora. And I think that's why fate chose you as my mate."

My heart overflows with emotion, leaving me speechless.

Falling in love wasn't something I ever expected to happen to me, and definitely not falling in love with a vampire.

"I didn't see you coming, Saxon. But you make me happy too. I don't care what my mother, Elena, or the fucking warlocks say, I'm not marrying Calvin."

"Damn straight you aren't. So what's the plan?"

"I don't have one yet, but we have nine months to think of one."

25

AURORA

───━══╫══━───

I had to kick Saxon out of my apartment with the sunrise. We both needed to rest. Besides, being near him without the option of touching is beyond torture, it's cruelty. But I could barely sleep. I felt the sense of wrongness returning, and all the aches with it. As I feared, the potion's effect is already beginning to wane. I don't know if it's because Saxon and I kissed last night, or the bond is getting stronger.

It's no surprise that I'm a hot mess in the morning, sporting dark circles under my eyes that would make any raccoon proud. I head straight for the coffee pot, knowing I need to drink several cups before I can function properly. As I wait for it to brew, I check my phone, which I left on the kitchen counter before going to bed.

I have two text messages. One from Niko and one from Miranda. Niko was clueless about Miranda's punishment. All Miranda's message says is to call her ASAP. *Damn it.* I shouldn't have checked my phone before coffee. Now I have to call her while caffeine deprived.

The phone rings three times before she answers. "Finally. What took you so long to call me back?"

"I just got out of bed."

"Sunset was over an hour ago. Shouldn't you be heading to class?"

Fuck. Is it that late already?

"I overslept. What happened? What did Mom do to you?"

"Don't worry about me. My punishment was actually milder than I expected. I wanted to tell you that despite my excuse and that warlock covering for us, the council members are furious, especially the Belmont rep."

I pinch the bridge of my nose, already feeling the telltale signs of a massive headache coming. "Fuck. What did they say?"

"They don't want to wait for you to finish your studies at Bloodstone before the wedding takes place. They're demanding you two get hitched within a month. I think they're afraid you're a flight risk and they want to secure the match at all costs."

My blood runs cold. "No. That's too soon."

"Oh, and there's more. They demanded that Calvin receive the same training as you do."

"What's that supposed to mean?"

"I don't know. I couldn't get all the information with all the simultaneous shouting that was going on. Eavesdropping is a lot harder when everyone is talking at once. But I did hear them mention Bloodstone. My guess is that Calvin will be joining you there."

"That's absurd and completely unheard of. Only those destined to become High Witches can attend Bloodstone. This is not fucking

Hogwarts. This is a school for vampires, for fuck's sake."

"I know. You don't need to shout in my ear. But thanks to the fiasco that was your visit to the Nightshade Market, the Belmonts have leverage now."

"Solomon will never agree to it," I say, but I don't believe my own words.

"Maybe not, but I thought you should know. At least now you won't die of shock when you bump into Calvin."

This is going to end up terribly. Calvin and Saxon can't be living under the same roof. Saxon will kill Calvin and start a conflict that King Raphael can't afford. *Oh my God. That's it.* If there's one person who can stop this madness, it's the king. Bloodstone is part of his domain.

"What were you doing in the market last night anyway?" I ask, just remembering that she wasn't supposed to be there.

"I was looking for an ingredient, but not for a love potion."

"What was it for then?"

"Please don't get mad at me. I'm trying to brew a potion that will make Calvin repulsed by you."

"What?" I yell, giving myself a headache.

"I figured that if he couldn't stomach you, he'd call off the engagement."

I pinch the bridge of my nose, counting to ten in my head. Poor Miranda doesn't know that being repulsed by me won't deter the idiot. "I appreciate the effort, but I don't think it will matter much to him. He already loathes me."

"You seem resigned to marrying the guy. What about Saxon?"

"We are … I don't know. It's complicated. Thank you for letting me know about Calvin. I have to get ready."

"Wait. Don't hang up yet. I wanted to ask you something."

I don't really have the time to chitchat with my sister, but considering she got in trouble to save my ass, I owe her that much.

"Fine. What is it?"

"What's the deal with Vivienne's brother? He's cute."

"Oh no. Don't even think about it, Miranda. Rikkon is not someone you should be even remotely interested in."

"But he's your friend's brother."

"Yeah, and he's also a recovering junkie with a bad case of memory loss."

"Okay, okay. I won't ask about him again. Jeez."

"I'm sorry. I didn't mean to snap at you. I'm under a lot of pressure here."

"I know. If I hear more, I'll let you know. Talk later."

I'm not sure what I've done to deserve a sister like Miranda. Risking my mother's wrath to help me goes beyond sisterly duties. I do hope her ill-conceived attempt to save me from Calvin ends there. It's a dead end. But I can't worry about that now when I have to find a way to speak with the king. I suppose I could ask Lucca to arrange the meeting.

I get ready as fast as I can, not only because I'm late for a lecture with Solomon, but because I must get this new problem taken care of immediately. After that, the next item on the agenda is to call my mother and ask if they're moving the date of my wedding forward. If it's true, then I have to find a way to break off my engagement and help the warlocks catch Elena in a month's time.

It turns out, all my hurrying to get ready is for nothing. When I reach Solomon's office, none other than Calvin is walking out of it. He smiles in a chilling manner when he sees me.

"Good evening, darling."

I stop in my tracks while vises of dread take hold of me. "Did you come here to see me? I said I didn't like surprises."

"Oh no. I didn't come for a visit, but I do have a surprise for you. I'll be joining you here at Bloodstone. Isn't that grand?"

I stare at him without blinking, not even daring to breathe. How could they have made this decision so fast? And why did Solomon agree to it when he knows Saxon and I are mated?

"Oh my God. I think I've shocked you into silence. I should do that more often." He chuckles.

"When are you starting?" I ask.

"Tonight. I'm moving in tomorrow. It's a pity that we can't share the same apartment, though. But rules are rules. Solomon made it clear couples can't live together while here. It's okay, we'll have plenty of time when we're married."

Well, for starters, Solomon lied. Lucca and Vivienne are living together. I suppose I have to thank him for that. Still, bile fills my mouth. If Calvin doesn't stop talking, I'm going to barf all over his clothes.

"I'd love to stay here and chat, but I'm late for a meeting with Solomon," I say.

"Sure, sure. I don't want to get you into trouble with the headmaster. God knows how much mayhem seems to follow you, right, darling?" His eyes take on a threatening glint. He must be talking about last night's incident.

"What are you insinuating? If you have something to say to me, get on with it."

He opens his mouth to reply, but he's interrupted by Solomon, who steps into the hallway. "Ah, Aurora. I see that you already heard the news."

"Yeah, sure have. Are we still having a meeting or what?"

"Naturally." He turns to the Lord of Doucheville. "Well, Calvin. Good luck."

I completely ignore him as I enter Solomon's office fuming, and immediately begin to pace. I'm so angry that sparks of magic leak from my fingers. Solomon closes the door softly and, at a leisurely pace, heads for his chair behind his desk.

"How could you let that snake enroll here?" I start.

"I had no choice in the matter. The order came directly from the king."

"What? King Raphael sanctioned this? Is he crazy?"

"Child, you'd better learn to control your temper if you hope to last as the High Witch."

"I don't want to control my temper," I yell. "And right now, being the High Witch is not a priority anymore."

"You'd better not say that near your mother." He arches his bushy brows.

"Fuck her. This is her fault too."

"No, Aurora. Your irresponsible actions last night triggered all this. Your reckless behavior put us all in an extremely delicate situation. King Raphael can't lose the support of the Council of Witches."

"You don't need to repeat what I already know. And my behavior yesterday wasn't reckless. You know why I went to the Nightshade Market. Or have you forgotten already that Saxon and I are mated, and fighting the bond is driving us both insane?"

"You didn't have to bring an entourage to procure that ingredient. Not only have you exposed the nature of your relationship with

Saxon, but you also risked Vivienne and Rikkon's secret. If the wrong people find out they're Nightingale royals, keeping them safe will be impossible."

He's not wrong about that. I swallow the angry retort that's on the tip of my tongue. It sucks balls being chastised by the headmaster as if I were a small child, but my ego will have to deal with it.

"I admit I made a bad judgment call last night. But you know that Calvin's presence here could have worse consequences for King Raphael."

"Declan and Ryker came to see me after their meeting with you and Saxon. They offered to break your bond and you refused."

I know exactly where he's going with that, but I'm not going to be coerced into doing things I don't want to anymore. I'm nobody's pawn. Lifting my chin higher, I say, "Yes, I did. And I'm not changing my mind."

He leans back, linking his hands over his round belly. "Then you, my dear, have to find a way to keep your mate from killing your fiancé."

"Some headmaster you are," I grit out, not hiding the contempt in my voice.

"Save the attitude for someone else, Aurora. I've already kept Calvin from moving in with you. That's the best I can do. Now, enough on this topic. Let's get on with your lessons."

I'm so furious with Solomon that I could just storm out of here. But I can't let my anger prevent me from soaking up as much information from the familiar as possible. Knowledge is power, after all.

"What's on the agenda today?" I cross my arms.

He slides a small book across his desk. "I'd like you to get familiar with this."

The leather cover is scratched and dry, and the golden symbol etched on it is almost entirely faded. I can distinguish only the letter *B*.

"What is this?"

"Just an overview of one of the most notorious and savage families of Bluebloods in the entire history of vampires. The Bouchers."

I open to the first page, cringing at the art depicting a vampire female bathing in blood. The drawing is in black and white, but the severed heads hanging above the bathtub, dripping blood, clues me in that the liquid in the tub is not water.

"Ew. Who the hell is this?"

"A first-generation Blueblood. Her name is Madeleine Boucher. I believe you've met her already, haven't you?"

I lift my gaze from the page, meeting Solomon's intense stare. "I have?"

He raises an eyebrow. "You were clever to use a concealing spell to spy on your mother and me, child. Unfortunately, nothing those rogue mages produce will affect me. You were in the catacombs when we imprisoned Madeleine again."

"You knew and you didn't rat me out?"

He smiles. "You see? I'm not such a terrible headmaster after all."

I switch my attention to the book again. The following pages contain text, but there is more disturbing artwork sprinkled throughout the book. "What happened to these vampires?"

"The Nightingales' departure affected vampires in different ways. While second-generation and regulars must hibernate to recover their strength, first-generation vampires are slowly losing their minds. The Boucher family was the first one to succumb to the madness."

My blood turns ice cold in an instant. King Raphael had gone mad in the vision I saw. *So that's why.* I seek Solomon's gaze again.

"The creatures trapped in the catacombs are ghosts, not vampires."

"They're not ghosts. They're specters, which is far worse than your generic poltergeist."

"But how did they get like that?"

"We're still trying to figure it out."

"That lady looked possessed by a demon. Do the warlocks know about them?"

Solomon nods. "Only the head of the guild, Zachary Morel. He helped us with the wards."

"What about the king? Does he know about this?"

He furrows his eyebrows. "What kind of question is that? Of course the king knows."

I shut the book, taking a steadying breath. "Is he already showing signs of change?"

"Not yet, but Tatiana is."

Ah, hell.

26

SAXON

I wake up with a big smile on my face, and a much bigger evening wood. The memory of Aurora naked on that couch pleasuring herself is not something I'll likely forget for a long time. It begs a repeat, but only when I can fuck her senseless after. Not being able to be near her is agony.

Speaking of agony, it seems the effect of the potion is already wearing thin. I can definitely feel the bond's tug and the uncomfortable sensation that comes with it. I get out of bed and head for the shower. It has to be a cold one, and paired with a hand job.

Five minutes later, I'm ready to face another cumbersome day in the institute. If it weren't for Aurora, I'd beg Lucca to simply be done with it. Pretending everything is normal just for appearance's sake is not how I roll. I miss the ages of blood and chaos when we could deal with our frustrations in the best way possible—on a battlefield. Now conflicts are solved behind closed doors via treaties and diplomacy. Well, there's Jacques, itching for violence. He's bad news, but secretly, I do want him to go savage. I'd like nothing more than to kill the bastard.

But Aurora has to remain at Bloodstone for another nine months, so that's my sentence too. I hope those two warlocks can find a solution for the blood vow. Staying cooped up in the institute won't be as bad if I can be with her.

I'm smiling again. I've never felt this way before and I'm a little freaked out to be honest. When I step into the living room, my roommates are already up. Ronan is actually escorting his breakfast out of the apartment while Vaughn is playing a video game with Rikkon.

My stomach rumbles, reminding me that I haven't eaten in a while. I'll have to resort to blood bags because there's no way in hell I can drink from another human. I just want Aurora's blood. I pluck a blood sucker from the bowl in front of me and stick it in my mouth. Normally, blood has to be kept chilled, but there's enough chemicals in the lollipops to keep it from going bad.

"What are you smiling about?" Ronan asks as he returns to the kitchen.

"Nothing."

"Right. I take things with Aurora went well last night."

"Yeah. Better than I expected."

Rikkon pauses the game and turns to me. "Did you hear anything about her sister?"

Immediately, my mood sours as I go into protective mode. Aurora is my mate, and therefore, I also feel responsible for keeping her sisters safe.

"What do you want with her?"

His eyebrows arch a little while his jaw slackens. "I was just checking if she's okay. She *did* lie to cover for you."

Ah, hell. I totally forgot about that. Some protector I am.

"I don't know. I haven't checked with Rora yet."

"*Rora?*" Vaughn pipes up. "Is she your girlfriend or something?"

"She's my mate, so don't even entertain any ideas about her."

He lifts both hands. "Dude, relax. I'm not an asshole who goes after someone else's girl. But I *am* surprised. I thought you were some kind of Casanova."

Ronan snorts. "Casanova. The correct term is manwhore. Saxon's dick precedes his reputation."

"Sounds like someone is jealous of my legendary size," I say through a grin.

"Not likely. Just be glad vampires can't catch STDs."

"Really? We can't?" Vaughn perks up from the couch.

I give him a droll stare. "Dude, you're practically immortal. The only things that can kill you now are sunlight, heart extraction, or decapitation."

He twists his face into a grimace as he touches his neck. "I'll make sure to stay away from sharp blades then."

"No can do. We're hitting the tatami in ten minutes and we're training with swords tonight," Ronan chimes in.

The door to our apartment opens, and Manu enters as if she owns the place. Tonight, she's wearing a deep-red leather catsuit that leaves nothing to the imagination.

"Good evening, losers."

"Where's the hero convention, Manu?" I ask.

She fires her death glare in my direction, but my good mood has returned, so all I do is smile broader.

"I'm going to Havoc tonight. I don't need to attend any classes, unlike Lucca."

"You should be training with us," Ronan retorts.

She gives him an annoyed glance. "Why, when I can practice with the Red Guard?"

Ronan's stare becomes darker. Manu loves to insinuate he's not as lethal as he thinks, which is bullshit. He could be one of the famous elite warriors if he hadn't pledged to protect Lucca. I try to stay out of their bickering most of the time. Watching from afar is entertaining enough, but tonight, I can't help but be a brat to her too. There are no victims here. We're all a bunch of assholes.

"And where is your familiar tonight?" I ask, just to piss her off.

"Don't know. Probably visiting his annoying sister. She did come by during the day to see him."

"What was she doing here?" Ronan's tone changes, showing a hint of worry.

"How am I supposed to know? I was asleep. I pay the security guard to keep me informed of visitors. Besides, shouldn't you sense when Cheryl is near?"

"Why would Ronan be able to sense her?" Vaughn asks.

We all ignore the new vampire. Trying to explain the Ronan-Cheryl factor is too fucking hard, plus it always puts Ronan in a foul mood.

"Oh, by the way, Sax. Thanks for letting me know you were mated to the High Witch's daughter. I love being the last to know."

"I was trying to avoid the unnecessary drama."

She flips her long white hair back and puts her hands on her hips. "I'm not dramatic."

"Yeah, yeah, Lady Gaga."

Her eyes turn to slits, and I brace for something horrid to come out of her mouth. "Go ahead, keep making fun of me, asshole. But while you're here sucking on your lollipop, your mate's fiancé is busy enrolling at Bloodstone."

"What?" I jump out of my chair so fast it tips over.

"Oh, you didn't know?" She smirks. "See how it sucks to be kept in the dark."

"Manu, quit being a bitch," Ronan retorts, but I'm out of the apartment before I can hear her reply.

Letting the bond guide me, I run in Aurora's direction, which leads me to Solomon's office. A quick whiff tells me Calvin was here at the same time as she was. Uncontrollable jealousy takes over me and it awakens the bloodlust. I'm going to rip Calvin to shreds. I'd take off to hunt the mage down if I didn't sense Aurora inside Solomon's office.

The door opens and the headmaster steps outside. "Saxon, you'd better come inside now."

Instead of answering him, I hiss like a rabid animal.

"Sax?" Aurora's voice pierces through the red haze, and like a balm, it calms me down a little. But not enough to make it safe for me to be around her.

My body is shaking nonstop while I fight two very distinct impulses. The urge to kill Calvin, and the desire to engulf her into a bear hug.

"Solomon, don't just stand there. Do something."

"No. He's your mate. He's your problem, not mine." He steps away, and then Aurora comes out the door.

She stops in front of me and stares into my eyes. "It's okay, Sax.

I'm not in any danger."

"Your fucking fiancé was here."

She touches my cheek tenderly, and sparks fly between us. I'd pull her into my arms if my nails weren't like claws now. I must look like a veritable monster.

"That's just a pesky formality. He's nothing to me. *You* are my mate."

Her words finally penetrate my brain and I begin to relax. When my vision is clear and my fangs retract, I lean down and kiss her because I need this connection right now. I wish I could do more than just savor her lips, but when she steps away from me, I try not to show my disappointment.

"I suggest you keep your PDA to zero while you're in public areas. Nobody knows you're mated, and no man likes to be cheated on," Solomon pipes up.

"I don't give a damn about that weasel," I bark.

"But you do care about what your actions will do to your king, don't you?" Solomon raises an eyebrow. "You're still a traitor's son, after all."

Fucking hell. Solomon had to go for the jugular. He always knows exactly what to say to bring me down.

"Traitor's son? What are you talking about?" Aurora asks the little possum man.

"I believe you're due for another history lesson, child." He turns to his office, shutting the door in our faces.

Aurora glances at me with a thousand questions shining in her eyes. Shame makes me turn away. I never wanted her to know about my disgraceful past.

"Sax, are you okay?"

"No. He had no right to bring my past up like that."

She touches my shoulder, sending liquid fire down my back, which I have to ignore. Dipping my chin low, I cross my arms in front of my chest as I fight the urge to whirl around and crush Aurora into me.

"It's okay if you don't want to talk about it."

I laugh without humor. "I don't, but it was foolish of me to believe I could keep such a dark secret from you. You have the right to know who your mate is."

She circles around me, and placing her finger under my chin, she forces me to look into her eyes. "We don't need to do this now."

I'm relieved that she's not demanding I spill my guts out. There are so many things I want to tell her, but my thoughts get scrambled when my stomach decides to roar loudly.

"What was that?"

I step back, hugging my middle. "I haven't fed yet."

The acknowledgment pulls my senses into one single direction, Aurora's neck. Now that I'm no longer driven by murderous instincts or consumed by shame, all I can think about is drinking her blood.

She touches the side of her neck. "Let's go back to my apartment."

"Are you sure? What about the side effects of the blood vow?"

"You don't need to drink straight from my vein, do you?"

My eyebrows furrow. Drinking directly from a person is one thing but cutting them open and ingesting spilled blood is barbaric. Blood bags are a little different because you don't know who the donor is, plus it's all very clinical.

"Are you willing to bleed for me?" I ask.

"I'll gladly do much more than bleed for you, Sax."

27

AURORA

I'm not sure why Saxon was so shocked when I offered to give him my blood. I'd much rather him drink from my neck because it feels so damn amazing, but cutting my palm open is not a big deal for me. I'm a witch, I'm used to the sharp bite of a steely knife against my flesh. But quickly I realize a simple cut to my hand won't yield enough blood, so I have to slash my wrist.

His eyes become rounder. "What the hell are you doing? Are you trying to die on me?"

"Relax, I can stitch myself back together with magic." I keep my bleeding wrist above a clear teacup.

He runs with vampiric speed to the other side of the room and flattens his back against the wall.

"What are you doing?" I ask.

"I have to stay back; the smell of blood is going to my head already."

His eyes are red now, and there's a new tension around his mouth. "How long since you've fed?"

"I've been drinking from blood bags, but from a live source? It has been a while."

"Saxon, that's not smart."

Ignoring my remark, he points at the cup. "I think you've got enough blood there."

I lower my gaze. "It's only half full. You need more than that."

"Aurora…" he growls. "That. Is. Enough."

Oh shit. I think he's really losing it. I'd better listen to him. I cover the cut with a paper towel, and then proceed with the spell to seal it shut. Saxon returns to the kitchen, and in the blink of an eye, he inhales the little I gave him.

"I can give you more blood," I say.

"No. This will hold me over for a few hours."

"Why are you being so stubborn about this? You've drunk more from me before."

He sits down, resting his forearms against the counter. "It's not the same. Watching you bleed like that, even if voluntarily, was hard. Back in the dark ages, there were savage vampires who would cut humans and let them bleed out. Some would even bathe in their victims' blood."

My spine goes rigid in an instant. He must be referring to Madeleine Boucher. Saxon doesn't miss the change in my demeanor.

"What is it?" he asks.

"Solomon told me about them today. They were first-generation Bluebloods."

"Yes. Why was he telling you about those vampires, though?"

"Okay, what I'm about to say is a big deal. I'm not even sure if

Lucca knows."

"Does it involve King Raphael?"

"Yep."

He squares his shoulders, and frowns so hard that deep lines form on his forehead. "Go on."

"The Nightingales' departure is affecting first-generations in a different way. It's making them crazy. You were referring just now to the Boucher family, right?"

"Yeah."

"They were the first ones to be affected by the disease."

"Son of a bitch. Is the king going crazy too?"

I grimace, remembering my vision. The king went mad and killed everyone close to him. But that was an outcome that would happen if Lucca hadn't wakened.

"Rora. What do you know?" Saxon presses.

"Do you want to know why I agreed to the blood vow?"

"To get the spell to help Lucca."

"Yes, but there's more to it." I wriggle my fingers together. They're clammy already. "Elena Montenegro has a magical Nightingale mirror. It shows scenes from the past and the future. She made me look into it and I saw King Raphael completely changed. He seemed possessed by a demon."

Saxon's eyes are as round as saucers as he stares at me in horror. "What else did you see?" he asks through a choke.

"He had killed Manu, and..." I let out a shuddering breath. "And I saw him strike you down with his sword. He killed you, Sax."

"Where were Lucca and Ronan?"

"I didn't see them. But that was a future that would come true if

Lucca didn't wake up. At least that was what Elena told me. That's why I agreed to the blood vow. I couldn't risk your life."

He makes a motion forward but catches himself. "I want to crush you into my arms so terribly, Rora. But I don't think I can yet."

"Because of the repel spell?"

He shakes his head. "No. I don't trust myself. The hunger is still present, lingering nearby."

"You should drink more," I insist.

"Only when I can do it the right way."

"You're so stubborn."

"Pot, meet kettle." He smiles ruefully, making my irritation melt—and other parts of my body.

I clear my throat, a feeble attempt to rescue my mind from the gutter. "The king has not shown signs yet of deteriorating mental faculties, but Tatiana has. She's currently locked in her house, watched by the king's Red Guard. None of her followers know about her condition."

My news erases any mirth left in Saxon's expression. His eyes darken as he rubs his jaw, and then he begins to pace in an agitated manner. He pulls his hair back with both hands, yanking at the strands. "Now everything is beginning to make sense."

"What is?"

He pierces me with a glance that spells heartache. "I believe my father was also affected by the disease."

"What happened to him?"

"When the feud between King Raphael and Tatiana started, my father took Tatiana's side."

Holy shit. Saxon's dad was a traitor?

209

"That happened before I was born. I was taught to be believe Tatiana was the rightful heir to the throne. As I grew older, I blindly followed him. But soon after the Nightingales left our world, my father began to act in a brutal manner, killing without mercy, slashing humans and leaving them to bleed dry."

With hands on his hips, he glances down, letting out a shuddering exhale.

"I'm so sorry, Sax."

"I didn't know what was happening to him. No one did. Then I was captured by Lucca's party. I was twelve at the time. Lucca was older and already a highly trained warrior. He could have killed me on the spot. He had every reason to do so. I was the enemy."

"But he didn't."

Saxon shakes his head. "No. I was his prisoner for two weeks, but he didn't treat me as such. Spending that amount of time with him, Ronan, and Manu far from my father's dark influence made me question my blind loyalty to him and the merit of Tatiana's claim."

"That's when you became part of Lucca's inner circle?"

He laughs without humor, scratching the back of his neck. "No. Two weeks wasn't enough to completely enlighten me."

Shaking his head, he focuses on the wall opposite him almost as if he's looking for the strength to continue. His beautiful face is contorted in so much pain that all I want to do is reach over and erase that expression.

"There was a huge fight and I managed to escape. It wasn't until months later, when my father finally committed his most atrocious sin, that I finally woke up. He killed my sister, tore her to pieces when he found out she had fallen in love with one of King Raphael's soldiers. My sister's murder broke my mother. She met the sun the following day."

Fat tears roll down my cheeks when Saxon wipes his wet face.

"Saxon…" The words get lodged in my throat. Nothing I could say seems appropriate.

He turns to me, not hiding the pain in his tear-filled eyes. "I wanted to make my father pay for what he'd done, but I knew I wasn't strong enough to challenge him in a fight. I had to wait for the right moment. You have no idea how much it killed me to pretend I was still a loyal son after what he'd done to my sister."

"When did it happen?"

"A few weeks later. My father had caught up with Lucca's small group. He outnumbered them three soldiers to one. It seemed an easy victory was within his grasp, but my father underestimated Lucca's, Ronan's, and Manu's fury."

Saxon's gaze becomes unfocused. I can tell he's right back in that memory.

"Despite their skills, my father did manage to corner Lucca. He might have succeeded in killing him if I hadn't chosen that moment to exact my revenge." His voice grows cold and his nails become sharp talons. "Lucca was down, injured. I asked my father to deliver the killing blow. But instead of dropping my sword on Lucca's neck, I swung it in a different direction. The bastard died instantly. My only regret is that he didn't suffer. Didn't even have the chance to scream as my blade severed his head, unlike my sister. To this day, I can still hear her desperate cries for help." His voice becomes choked up. Shaking, he covers his lips with a fist.

I walk over because despite Saxon's warning about his hunger, I'm not afraid of him. He won't hurt me. I pull him into a hug, and when his arms circle around my waist, he hides his face in the crook of my neck. I melt into him, soaking up as much of his warmth as I can. The bond's magic flares up, enveloping us completely. It seems much more potent now, almost complete. But there's the pesky blood vow magic, trying to disrupt the moment.

No. I'm not going to let this damn pact ruin this for us. I use all the power I have in me to keep the magic from blasting Saxon away. It's hard, though, and I understand now the spell isn't coming from me. The source of magic that feeds it is foreign. It belongs to Elena Montenegro. *Son of a bitch.* I'm clenching my jaw so hard it hurts. There's a ball of energy swirling inside of me, ready to be unleashed. *Shit.* It's too strong to be contained without the use of a crystal or magical stone. I begin to tremble with the effort.

Saxon pulls away, looking worried. "Rora? What's going on? Is it the blood vow?" He tries to step away from me, but I don't let him.

"Yes, but I'm fighting it."

"Your nose is bleeding." He does pull away, watching me with guilt in his gaze.

I touch my nose, finding it damp. The blood vow's wicked magic recedes, but not my resolution to stomp on it until it dies. Saxon grabs a napkin from my kitchen counter and then gently cleans up the mess. His eyes are bloodshot, and his cheeks are still damp from tears. He just shared gut-wrenching memories, but here he is, taking care of me.

"I love you," I blurt out.

He freezes while his eyes search mine. I don't dare to breathe while I wait for him to say something, anything. *Oh, God.*

"I don't expect you to say it back," I add quickly. "I just want you to know."

He steps back and I catch the slight shake of his head. "Thanks. But that's the mating bond talking."

My heart plummets. He doesn't believe me. I think that's worse than him not saying it back.

"It's not."

"I believe you believe the feeling is real. That's quite normal. The mating bond magic is strong; it can muddle things up."

"Don't presume to know what I'm feeling," I grit out.

"I'm sorry. I didn't mean to offend you. But it's the same for me too."

"Are you saying you think you love me, but in reality, you don't?"

The way Saxon opens and shuts his mouth like a fish out of water would have been comical if I wasn't hurting so badly.

"I'm sensing there's a trap here."

I throw my hands up in the air. "Ugh! Never mind, Saxon. If you don't want to believe me, fine. I don't care."

"I'm sorry, okay? I don't know what to think, or what to trust. This is new to me, and honestly, I don't see how you could love me for real knowing what you do now."

"Knowing what I know?" My voice rises to a shrill. "That your father was a fucking psycho who betrayed his king and killed his own daughter? How could knowing that possibly change the way I feel about you?"

"Don't you get it? I wasn't an innocent bystander, Rora. During the time I spent by my father's side, I committed a number of atrocities too."

"Did you cut a bunch of humans and let them bleed to death?"

"No, but I did kill innocent people. I just made sure they died quickly."

Shit. I'm not going to deny it. The knowledge that Saxon did despicable things hurts. It was naive of me to not realize that part of the story until he pointed it out. But I also get why he doesn't believe that I love him.

"You're so fucking stupid," I say.

His eyes widen. "Excuse me?"

"You heard me. You should go now. I need to process all this."

"All right. I think I'm going to train with Ronan for a bit."

"You do that. Just stay away from Calvin."

If the mood was awkward before, now it just reached tense-as-fuck levels. Saxon squints. "I'll try my best."

He strides out of my apartment, banging the door with so much fury, the picture hanging next to it falls to the floor. The glass shatters, but I don't move to clean up the mess. I simply keep staring at it, wondering how this evening got so messed up in a matter of minutes.

It's the fucking L-word, Aurora. You should have never said it out loud.

28

SAXON

⚔

Bloodstone Institute has two gyms, one used by Hanson for his pitiful Keepers Training class, and an older one, which smells of sweat and blood and definitely needs a fresh coat of paint. The appeal of the old gym room is its location in the east wing, which is currently closed off. We can train as hard as we want for hours without interruption.

This part of the building was open when I was here the last time, but I can see why Solomon decided to shut it off. It's in serious need of renovation. Peeling wallpaper, dripping pipes, and the obnoxious smell of rotten wood and mildew are prevalent in this area. Ironically, I've never seen anyone working on anything here in the past month.

The lights in the hallways are old and dim, and in some spots, they've gone out completely. Not that it matters to vampires. We can see perfectly in the dark. As I approach the gym, brighter light pours through the cracks of the double doors. Grunts and then loud cursing reach my ears. Lucca's distinct laugh echoes in the empty corridor. It's been fucking centuries since I heard him amused like that. Vivienne did more than lift the curse, she breathed new life into him.

I wish my love life wasn't in such shambles. I totally fucked up with Aurora. She told me she loved me, and I said she was confused. *Who does that? Oh, yeah, dumbasses like me.*

Riding on my frustration with myself, I open the doors with enough force that their hinges creak loudly. Everyone stops what they're doing to stare. I had every intention to say something idiotic, but I'm too busy processing the scene in front of me.

Ronan and Lucca are holding Vaughn and Rikkon respectively by their ankles, using them for weightlifting.

"What the fuck," I say.

"Oh, great. Now Saxon is here to witness my humiliation," Vaughn whines.

My friends let go of their … weights, victims, whatever. Vaughn drops onto the tatami like a potato sack while Rikkon gets back onto his feet in a more graceful manner. He doesn't seem as mad as Vaughn does.

"Hey, Saxon," he says. "Everything well with you and Aurora?"

The guy seems genuinely interested to know. The little I've heard about Rikkon had painted a completely different image of him in my mind. He was a petty drug dealer and junkie who needed his little sister to bail him out. I'd expected him to be this shady guy, untrustworthy, not a friendly, innocent-looking candidate for the most beautiful man in the world award.

"I didn't kill her fiancé if that's what you want to know," I grumble.

"We figured you didn't. Bad news travels fast, but what's with the sourpuss face?" Lucca asks.

"I don't want to talk about it. Now, explain what the hell you were doing with Vaughn and Rikkon."

Ronan hitches a thumb at the newbie vampire. "Smart mouth here lost a bet. That was his punishment."

"And Rikkon?" I raise an eyebrow.

He shrugs, glancing at Lucca. "Future brother-in-law bonding?"

He smirks. "Yeah, let's go with that. If Vivi thinks I'm manhandling you, she'll have my balls."

"I thought she already had your balls," I reply.

Lucca's easygoing expression vanishes as he squints at me. "What's up, Sax? Are you looking to hurt?"

"Ha-ha. You're fucking hilarious." I crack my knuckles. "I bet domestic bliss has made you soft."

Lucca curls his lips into a dark smile, showing hints of his fangs. His eyes flash red for a second. "Weapon of choice?"

"Katana, obviously." I glance at Rikkon, who is standing closest to the table with weapons. "Can you toss me one?"

"I don't think I should be tossing you anything." He selects one in the middle of the assortment, holding the weapon almost reverently. "Wow, the pattern on this sheath is incredible."

I walk over since it doesn't seem like he's going to let go of the sword anytime soon. "That's not even one of the nic—"

"Ugh!" Rikkon bends over, dropping the weapon to the floor. He presses the heels of his hands into his eyes with a groan as his face twists into an expression of extreme agony.

"Dude, are you all right?"

"Fuck," he answers, and then twists to the side to throw up.

I glance at Lucca. "Maybe holding him upside down wasn't the greatest of ideas."

He comes over, stopping next to Rikkon, who is still stooped over, clutching his stomach. "What's the matter? Did you get vertigo or something?"

"No." He stands straighter, wiping his mouth with the back of his hand. "I…" He runs his fingers through his hair. "I think Manu is in trouble."

Huh? Of all the things we expected him to say, that wasn't it.

"What do you mean you think she's in trouble?" Ronan butts in, displaying more aggression than worry.

Rikkon's face is pale now. His blue eyes are round with fear. "I get … visions. Premonitions. My head feels like it's going to split in two when it happens. It used to get really bad and the only thing that kept them away was the drugs."

"Is that a Nightingale thing?" I ask.

"I don't know."

Lucca grabs his arm, turning him around. "You have powers? I thought your mother took everything from you and Vivi when she banished you."

"That's what everyone keeps saying, but I don't remember anything about my life before the memory spell wiped my brain clean."

"You think Manu is in trouble," Ronan interrupts. "What did you see?"

"It was just a flash. She was surrounded by several males wearing dark clothes; I couldn't tell what they were. There was blood on her face."

218

"Fuck. It must be Jacques and his followers," Lucca growls.

I wanted Jacques to finally show his hand, but not at Manu's expense. I was already filled with pent-up aggression. Now I'm on the verge of exploding. There's no need for words. Lucca, Ronan, and I grab as many weapons as we can carry and head for the door.

"Should I come too?" Vaughn asks.

"No. You're not ready," Ronan replies. "Take Rikkon back to our apartment and stay put."

Lucca has his cell phone glued to his ear. After a moment, he lets out a string of curses. "She's not picking up."

"I'll try Derek. She was going to Havoc," I say.

I call the club's owner, hoping he will answer the phone. I can't say we are buddies, but I'd like to believe I hold a special place in his cold heart considering I'm one of his best patrons. After an eternity, his baritone voice comes through.

"Saxon, what do you want?"

"Have you seen Manu tonight?"

"Yeah, she came in about an hour ago. Why?"

"Is she still there?"

"Fuck. How am I supposed to know? The house is packed. What is this all about? You've never called looking for her before."

We walk out of the institute building through a side exit, getting blasted immediately with the chilly autumn air. I'm only wearing a muscle shirt and the cold seeps into my bones. Running as fast as we can helps a little.

"I have reason to believe Jacques is going to try something tonight," I say in a low tone, not wanting to chance being overheard.

"I haven't seen any of Tatiana's sympathizers here tonight, but I'll try to find Manu."

"Okay. We're on our way."

Ronan is already behind the steering wheel of his black SUV and Lucca is riding shotgun. I slide into the backseat, ending the call.

"Is she at the club?" Lucca asks.

"Derek doesn't know. But she was there earlier."

That's a good enough answer for Ronan. He presses the pedal to the metal, burning rubber as he speeds off down the lane.

"Easy there, Speedy. There's a fucking gate ahead." I brace against the supple leather seat.

Ronan presses on the brakes, sending me flying forward. I hit my face against the back of his seat, which sends white-hot pain up my nose. "Motherfucker!"

"Buckle up, idiot," Lucca growls.

"Did he give me the chance?"

As soon as the gate opens, Ronan takes off, pushing the engine to the limit. Going at this insane speed should bring us to Havoc in less than five minutes. We ride in silence, but it's impossible to miss the tension in the car. I can only guess my friends' brains are whirling as fast as mine. My thoughts are scattered everywhere, but mainly, I'm worried about Manu. Despite her being a badass fighter, she can't survive an ambush. *Fuck.* We shouldn't have let her go alone anywhere.

Maybe she isn't alone. I text Karl, hoping the familiar is with her. Instead of texting me back, he calls.

"What do you know?" he asks without preamble.

Fuck. It's true, then. Manu is in danger. Karl would be able to sense it. "Not much. I was hoping you would have more intel."

"I don't even know where she is. I've been dealing with other issues all week."

"We're headed to Havoc. It's the last place she was seen."

"I'm on my way." He ends the call before I can get another word in.

Lucca turns on his seat. "Was that Karl?"

"Yeah. He sensed something was wrong with Manu."

Ronan curses under his breath. "Why wasn't he with her?"

"Have you met my sister?" Lucca grumbles. "Damn it, Manu. Why do you have to be so fucking difficult?"

"Uh, maybe because the apple doesn't fall far from the tree?" I snort.

"Are you still looking for an ass-whooping, Saxon?" Lucca snarls.

"For fuck's sake!" Ronan hits the steering wheel hard. "Shut your piehole. Both of you."

I swallow my angry retort. Ronan is justified in getting pissed off. It seems I can't help but say stupid shit. Lucca remains quiet too, looking out the window. In another minute, Ronan parks right in front of Havoc, and I say a silent prayer. I'm jonesing for action.

Derek is waiting for us in front of the club. One close look at the male and I know he has bad news.

Lucca reaches him first. "She's not in there, is she?"

"No. I looked at the security camera footage. She left about half an hour ago accompanied by a human."

"Do you know the human's name?" Ronan asks.

"He didn't buy anything with a credit card, so no."

"Maybe we should have brought Rikkon with us. Another vision would be helpful."

I'm blasted immediately by Lucca's and Ronan's glares, which alerts me to my error. Derek is watching me with interest now. *Fuck me and my big stupid mouth.*

Ronan's spine becomes taut as his gaze travels past my shoulder. I turn around, but I already know who caught his attention. Karl, and his sister Cheryl. Well, I was looking for a distraction from my problems, and it seems I got more than I wished for. Cheryl and Ronan together, looking for Manu. It's shaping up to be an explosive night.

29

AURORA

I've been staring at nothing for the past half an hour while my brain keeps replaying my conversation with Saxon. Regret is a jagged little pill. I should have followed my instincts and kept my mouth shut. But it's not only my stupidity occupying my mind. It's his story and the possibility there are more first-generation Bluebloods suffering from insanity that the king doesn't even know about. At least Saxon's father is dead. But what about the Boucher family? Solomon said she's a specter, not a ghost. I'd always used the term interchangeably.

I know I shouldn't return to the catacombs, but maybe I can trick Madeleine into telling me what the hell happened to her. She wants freedom, and I'm not above lying to a murderous specter to get what I want.

I open the small book about her family that Solomon gave me. The gruesome images still make me cringe, but I try to focus on the text only. The English is archaic, and it doesn't flow well. Sometimes I have to google a word I'm not familiar with. The story is nonetheless fascinating in a morbid way.

They were aristocrats, but they didn't frequent King Raphael's court. They preferred to mingle with Marie Antoinette and King Louis XVI, who I'm guessing weren't aware the Bouchers were vampires. The Bouchers only started acting strangely after the French Revolution. By then, they had already immigrated to England's countryside, where they committed most of their atrocities.

I'm about one-third into the book when my phone pings loudly, announcing a text message. My heart leapfrogs to my throat, dropping immediately back to its place like a rock sinking into a lake. "Fucking hell." I press my hand against my chest.

When I glance at my phone, the notification has already vanished from my screen, so I have to slide my finger across to unlock it. The text is from Vivienne, asking me to meet her in the old gym on the east wing. She wrote emergency in capital letters. *Shit. What now?*

I hastily shove the book I was reading in my bag, then collect a few river stones and crystals I energized earlier. She didn't specify what type of emergency, but my guess is it requires witchcraft to fix it. I curse that it's still night and there are people milling about campus. If I run, it will draw too much attention. These damn bloodsuckers live for gossip. Certainly, I'd be followed.

When I get to the old gym, I find Rikkon on his back, and Vivienne and Vaughn crouching on each side of him.

"What the hell happened?" I run the rest of the way.

"Rikkon got sick after getting a vision about Manu being in danger. Lucca, Ronan, and Saxon went after her and told me to take Rikkon back to the apartment. But then he started to spasm and puke again. I didn't know what to do," Vaughn replies.

"Why didn't you take him to Solomon?" I drop next to the guy, who has his eyes closed and is moaning deliriously. A sheen of sweat covers his forehead. Placing my hand against his skin confirms that he has a fever.

"I-I called Vivienne," Vaughn replies.

"Can you help him?" she asks.

"I'll try. Do you think he's going through withdrawals?" I begin pulling items from my bag until I find the vial I was looking for.

"I don't think so. Unless he relapsed without me knowing." She gasps. "Oh shit. Maybe that's what happened."

"I don't think so, Vivi. I'd know if Rikkon had been high," Vaughn chimes in.

I force Rikkon's mouth open and pour the concoction down his throat. He begins to cough immediately.

"What was that?" Vivienne asks.

"The equivalent of ten shots of espresso. Don't worry. It's harmless."

Her brother opens his eyes, and at first, he doesn't seem to know where he is.

Vivienne touches his face. "How are you feeling?"

"Vivi, what happened?"

"I don't know. Vaughn said you got sick after having a vision?"

He closes his eyes, frowning. "Shit. It's happening again."

"What is?" I ask.

He grunts as he sits up, resting his arms on his knees. "The visions. I've been having them as long as I can remember."

"How is that possible? You never had that ability before," Vivienne says.

"I don't know. I can't tell you if they started before the memory spell or only after." He turns to her, his eyes glistening with anguish. "They're brutal, Vivi. You think I turned into a junkie because I couldn't cope with being cut from Ellnesari. But the truth is, the drugs were the only thing that kept them at bay."

"Oh, Rikkon. Why didn't you tell me?"

"Because I didn't want you to think I was crazy. Come on. Visions? What kind of human has them?"

"But you're not human," Vaughn pipes up.

"No shit, Sherlock. I wasn't aware of that until Vivi recovered her memories," he retorts angrily.

"Can you stand? We need to get you back to your apartment, and then you can tell me more about your visions," I say.

"I think I can, but I need help."

Vaughn and Vivienne assist Rikkon, and then he throws his arm around his sister's shoulder for support. I have a bunch of questions, but we shouldn't be talking about any of it in public. Vampires have super hearing, and anyone could be eavesdropping from a distance.

Unfortunately, in order to get back to the dorm section we have to go through the main building. I step closer to Rikkon and whisper, "Try to look alive."

Because the evening couldn't turn any worse, Therese, Lucca's former lover and now Vivienne's nemesis, approaches with her posse.

"What's wrong with your brother?" Therese asks, twisting her nose. "He reeks."

"None of your business," Vivienne hisses, earning Therese's death glare in return.

The atmosphere becomes saturated with animosity, and

unfortunately, the only person able to keep Therese at bay is me, which doesn't bode well, not with the way my nerves are already fried.

"Nothing to see here. Run along." I motion them away with my hand.

"You're not the boss of me. This isn't your territory, witch."

Don't let them get to you, Aurora.

I take a deep breath before replying. "Seriously. I'm doing you a favor. You do not want to test my patience tonight."

Therese's friend, whose name I can't remember for the life of me, tugs the vamp queen bee's sleeve. "Maybe we should go."

Therese pulls her arm free with a jerky movement. "I'm not afraid of her. Besides, she can't harm us. She's a guest here."

Vaughn steps forward. "Ladies. There's no need for all this hostility. Why can't we all be civil?"

"Who the fuck do you think you are?"

"Uh, I'm Vaughn. I'm in a band." He stuffs his chest out like what he just said is a big deal.

Poor idiot. He has no idea that being in a band is not something those bitches care about. They're Bluebloods, and for appearances' sake, he's a regular without pedigree. If they knew he had just been made, I'm not sure how they'd react. As a matter of fact, why is Vaughn telling them he's in a band? *Fuck, doesn't anyone have common sense anymore?*

Now the stupid bitch is staring at him with renewed interest. *Way to go, Vaughn.*

"What band?" she asks.

"An underground band from the hellhole town he comes from," I say before he can dig his grave deeper. I'm not sure how anyone has not recognized him yet. Salem is not a big city.

"And where is that?" Therese insists.

"I need to lie down. I think I'm going to be sick again," Rikkon interrupts.

"You do look positively dreadful. You don't even feel like a vampire." Therese steps closer, flaring her nostrils as she takes a whiff.

Hell. Is Rikkon's concealment spell weakening already?

"He was pranked like I was. Forced to eat human food," Vivienne grits out. "Now get out of my way before I kick your ass."

I know her threats are not empty. She's acting like the Nightingale princess she is. But Vivienne has only recovered her memories, not her Nightingale powers. In a fight, Therese would win.

"You little piece of shit. Just—"

"Aurora, darling. I didn't expect to see you again tonight." Calvin approaches, smiling from ear to ear.

I never thought I'd be glad to see the guy, but I can't complain about his timely intrusion. Therese and her friends visibly tense at the addition of another magic user.

"You're a mage. What are you doing at Bloodstone?" Therese narrows her eyes.

Calvin glances at me, smiling in an intimate way that I don't like. "I've just joined the institute. I couldn't stay away from my fiancée."

I keep my mouth shut even if every fiber of my being is fighting against Calvin claiming me as his anything.

"That's completely absurd. It's bad enough that we have to put up with Aurora, and that's only because she's the future High Witch."

"If you aren't happy, go take it up with the headmaster," I retort, hoping that she does complain. Not that it would do any good. King Raphael caved to the pressure of the Council of Witches. The Thereses of the world aren't going to change his mind.

She lifts her chin in an arrogant way, but I notice she has lost her bravado. No matter how powerful vampires are, they all secretly fear witches and mages. I wonder what they'd do in the presence of a warlock. Probably shit their pants.

"You bet your ass I will." Therese turns around and strides away, her high heels rapping the wooden floor.

"What a nice girl," Calvin says.

"She's not a girl. She's a Blueblood. You'd better remember that," I snap.

My critical response does exactly what I was hoping it would: it aggravates him. His brown eyes become hard, matching the set of his jaw. I meet his sharp stare without flinching. In the end, he's the one who looks away first, switching his attention to Vivienne and Rikkon.

"What's going on here? Is that regular sick?"

Relief washes over me. Rikkon's glamour is still in place. "Yes, he's sick. Freshman prank."

"Can we go now?" he moans again, clutching his stomach.

"Yes, absolutely."

We continue our trek to his apartment, but unfortunately, Calvin decides to tag along.

"You don't need to accompany us," I say.

"It's no trouble. I'm done for the evening." A yawn sneaks up on him, which he tries to hide by covering his mouth. "I just came from a meeting with Hanson. He was telling me about his Keepers program. Fascinating stuff."

Furtively, I glance at Vivienne. Her expression is shut off. No surprise there. Hanson put her in the hands of Boone not too long ago. I don't know how Lucca had the self-control to not kill the guy.

"I don't know what's so fascinating about it. I've been forced to attend his classes. They're a snooze fest. I've learned more by taking self-defense lessons at the local YMCA."

"Why would you need to enroll in a self-defense class?" Calvin asks, sounding truly surprised.

"Really? Do you have to ask? I'm the future High Witch. You don't think that position comes with risks?"

"That's why you're marrying me. I'll make sure you're protected."

"With what skills? I'm far superior to you when it comes to magic, and you look like you need to hit the gym more often."

Calvin's pale face becomes red in the blink of an eye, and a vein throbs on his temple. He looks like he's having an aneurism. *Ha! Wouldn't that be nice?*

"First of all, you're not better than me at using magic. Don't fool yourself. And the gym? Seriously? Are you out of your mind? We're not vampires who deal with our issues using fists and fangs. We're magic users, darling. We're above savagery."

I glower at him. I can't believe he just spewed that prejudiced garbage out loud in a building full of vampires. His arrogant comment may have flown right over Vivienne's, Rikkon's, and Vaughn's heads because the first two aren't vamps, and Vaughn is too new to the whole thing to feel the jab. But he does earn a few glares from the regulars that are in the hallway.

"Just stop talking," I say.

We're almost at the end of the corridor when Rikkon stops suddenly. He glances over his shoulder, frowning. "Did you hear that?"

"Hear what?" Vivienne asks.

"This eerie voice calling my name."

"I heard nothing," Vaughn replies.

I follow his line of vision, and at once, my blood runs cold. He's staring at the stairs that lead to the catacombs. *Shit. Is the specter calling to him? But how can he hear it all the way up here?* Vivienne couldn't hear Madeleine unless she was near the secret chamber.

"What is he talking about?" Calvin looks over my head, probably trying to see what caught Rikkon's attention.

"He must be delirious thanks to the human food he consumed." I turn to Rikkon. "Come on, buddy. We need to get that poison out of your system."

We resume our slow progress, but it seems the clusterfuck of problems has only begun. Rikkon cries out again, falling to his knees when Vivienne can't support his dead weight. He clutches his head with both hands while grunting in pain.

"Rikkon!" She crouches next to him. "Talk to me."

"It's happening again."

Shit. Shit. Shit. I look around, grimacing at the attention we're gathering. The few regulars in the hallway move closer, eyes shining with interest. I can't let them get nearer and discover Rikkon has special powers. What I'm about to do is going to come back to bite me in the ass, but I don't see any other option. I reach inside my bag, curling my fingers around the first crystal I can find. Using the object as an amplifier, I summon the power within me. Words pour out of my lips in an unfamiliar voice.

"What the hell are you doing, Aurora?" Calvin asks.

I ignore him and finish reciting the spell. The demeanor in the crowd changes from curiosity to sheer panic. At once, they disperse, running in different directions, but far away from us.

Calvin's beefy hand clutches around my arm. "What did you do?"

"Let go of me!" I pull myself free.

"Dude. What the hell!" Vaughn takes a menacing step forward, but Calvin doesn't seem threatened by the young vampire.

"You used magic against those vampires without cause. What are you trying to hide?"

I'm about to hex him too when Rikkon mumbles Saxon's name. A splinter made of ice pierces my chest. I whirl around. "What did you say?"

His eyes are closed and he's delirious, but Vivienne's troubled gaze tells me plenty. I turn my attention inward, searching for the mating bond's magic. Thanks to the potion we took, I can't sense Saxon across a great distance. However, there's a tightness in my chest and my stomach is spiraling. He's in trouble.

"I'm sorry, Vivi. I have to go."

Her eyes are torn when she replies, "Please make sure they're okay."

I nod before running toward the exit.

"Where are you going?" Calvin calls after me.

"I'm going to see my mother," I lie, hoping that will deter Calvin. No such luck. He follows me outside the building.

"Something is going on that you're not telling me. We're getting married, we can't keep secrets from each other. I'm coming with you."

That's it. The straw that breaks my back. I stop in my tracks, pivoting on my heels in the next second.

"Sorry, darling. You're not."

I blast him with the strongest knock-out spell I know. The bright energy sphere hits him square in the chest, making him stagger backward, and then finally, he drops to the ground, out cold.

Mr. Goodwin, the familiar security guard, comes running with mouth agape and eyes round.

"Don't worry. He'll be fine in an hour or so," I tell him.

"What should I do with him until then?" he asks.

"He hasn't moved in yet. Stuff him in his car."

He blows a frustrated breath out as he stares at Calvin. "That's what I get for complaining about boredom."

Another sharp pang hits my chest, making me forget the guard and Calvin. I find my car in a hurry, praying to all the gods that I'm not too late.

Damn it, Saxon. You'd better not die on me.

30

SAXON

⸺⊹⊱━━━━◆━━━━⊰⊹⸺

Ronan moves toward Karl, aggression clear in his stance, but one glance at Cheryl makes him halt suddenly. She narrows her fiery eyes at him, and for a couple of beats, it seems no one dares to breathe.

"Where have you been? Why weren't you with Manu?" Ronan snarls.

"Because she doesn't want me by her side," Karl barks back.

"The king gave you an order."

"Back off, Ronan," Cheryl butts in. "You have no right to accuse my brother of anything. Your obsession with the vampire princess is pathetic."

Whoa. That escalated fast. Why am I even surprised? Cheryl matches Manu in intensity beat by beat. No wonder Ronan couldn't fucking say no to her all those centuries ago.

"Don't you two start now," Lucca interrupts. "Let's find my

sister first and then maybe, Ronan, you can finally resolve your issues with Cheryl."

She peels her ruby lips back, showing off her impressive fangs. "There's nothing to resolve here."

"I don't want to point out the obvious, but you're drawing quite a lot of attention," Derek chimes in, glancing pointedly at the line of humans and regulars waiting to get into his club.

"I'd like to see the security camera footage. Maybe one of us will recognize the human Manu left with," Lucca says.

"No offense, Lucca, but you're not likely to recognize anyone. You've been up for how long? Three months?" Cheryl pipes up.

Karl breaks from the group and walks toward the front of the club. He begins to sniff the air like a damn dog, not caring that he has an audience. After a moment of acting like Rin Tin Tin, his back becomes rigid as he jerks his head to the left.

"I think he got something," I say.

Lucca walks over to the guy and takes a deep breath. "I got nothing."

"Something was done to mask her scent. But I have it now. Follow me." Karl takes off, running faster than any human could.

Super speed is not a trait familiars usually possess, but Karl wasn't an ordinary animal when he became a familiar. He was a wolf shifter, the son of an alpha. That gives him extra perks. Despite that, he's not faster than any of us. Vampires can move in a blur, like The Flash. We keep pace with Karl, though, because he's clearly the one with the better sense of smell. The landscape rushes by, but I don't pay too much attention to it. It's not until Cheryl mutters a string of curses that I take in my surroundings. *Hell and damn.* We're in dragon shifter territory.

That doesn't bode well. Why would Jacques drag Manu here? He must be in cahoots with the scaly shifters.

Karl veers in the opposite direction of the busiest section, and soon, we're nearing the outskirts of a wooded area. He stops abruptly, raising a hand to signal us to stop. His body is as tense as a coiled spring while he scans our surroundings. The forest is not dense, but on this moonless night, we're staring at a pitch-black wall. I concentrate on all my senses, trying to control my breathing so it doesn't make too much noise.

Cheryl stops by her brother's side and they exchange a meaningful glance. There's a sudden shift in the air. A chilly breeze hits us, bringing with it the unmistakable smell of spilled blood. *Fuck.*

Without words, we follow the scent of death, careful not to make a sound. Charging straight ahead would be foolish. We don't know what kind of situation we're walking into. Soon, we reach a clearing where two forms are laid six feet apart. It's impossible to miss Manu's white skin and hair contrasting sharply with the darkness around her.

"Manu!" Lucca says in a strangled outburst, right before he runs across the field without care.

Karl and Ronan follow close behind him, but considering Karl hasn't dropped dead where he stands, it's safe to say Manu is alive. When vampires gain a familiar, their life forces are linked together. It's what allows familiars to live as long as they do, but it also means if the vampire bites the dust, so does their familiar.

I veer toward the second body sprawled on the ground, the one that reeks of death. Cheryl has the same idea as I do. At first, I thought the dead man was the human who left Havoc with Manu, but as I step closer and really pay attention to the scent of his blood, I realize my mistake.

"Son of a bitch," I murmur.

Cheryl turns to me, showing in her eyes the same what-the-actual-fuck glint that's probably glistening in mine. "This is bad."

"What is?" Ronan stretches his neck toward us, and at the same time, Manu groans back to life.

"What happened?" she asks as she sits up.

"You have to be fucking kidding me." Cheryl balls her hands into fists just before she walks over to her. Her body is shaking, and I'm not sure if she's about to shift.

Fucking hell. I run after her, but Karl blocks his sister's path before she has the chance to get closer to Manu. "Hold up, Cheryl. Don't go jumping to conclusions."

"Don't go jumping to conclusions?" She points at the dead dragon shifter. "Take a look."

Karl's expression blanches. He rubs his jaw, and then looks at Manu, who is already getting up with Lucca's help. There's blood on her face, just like Rikkon had seen in his vision. But where are Jacques's associates?

Manu, now back on her feet, walks around Karl. Her ashen face is glued to the young dragon who has been ripped to shreds by, no doubt, a vampire. The bite marks on his neck can't be mistaken for anything else.

"Oh my God. You think I did this?" she whispers.

"You have his blood all over you," Cheryl points out.

Manu touches her face, and then glances at her blood-smeared fingers. "How is that possible? I don't know who he is."

"You mean was. The dragon is dead," I say.

"I didn't kill him!" Manu yells.

"What is the last thing you remember?" Lucca asks.

"I left with a guy, a human. I was going to bring him back to Bloodstone. Then…" She pauses, frowning. "It's all a blank. I don't remember how I got here or what happened to him."

The gravity of the situation has dropped like a bomb over our group. "You don't remember being ambushed by Jacques or his followers?" I ask.

"No. But my mind feels like it has been messed with." She rubs her forehead.

Karl puts his hands on his hips, staring at the carnage. "This was clearly a setup. Someone wants to start a turf war between King Raphael and the dragons. Cheryl and I have been dealing with unrest in the Salem pack too."

Ronan narrows his gaze. "What kind of unrest? And how come this is the first time I'm hearing of it?"

"Don't let your ego go to your head," Cheryl sneers at Ronan. "This is wolf's business."

"Everything that pertains to supernaturals affects the entire community," Ronan growls.

"King Raphael is aware," Karl replies calmly.

"What is the problem with the wolves?" Lucca asks, stepping in between the wolf siblings and Ronan.

"A new pack has arrived in town. Wolves, as you know, are very territorial. There's been some confrontations already. Marcus Novak, the Salem Pack's alpha, demanded the newcomers leave immediately. He was challenged instead."

"And why are you involved? I mean, you and Cheryl left wolf pack life many years ago," I say.

"Because this new pack has pledged allegiance to Tatiana. If they gain ground here in Salem, it tips the scale in her favor."

This situation sounds all too familiar. That's how my father used to conquer villages that supported King Raphael. He weakened them from the inside, created doubt and animosity, turned friends against each other. I glance at the dead dragon again, finally understanding the reason behind his murder.

"Jacques is trying to weaken the king by making him lose all his allies."

"The dragons never picked a side," Ronan says.

"Not officially, but Larsson and my uncle have an understanding," Lucca replies.

"That will go up in flames if they believe Manu killed one of their own," I chime in.

No sooner do the words leave my mouth than the ground trembles and a roar as loud as thunder echoes in the forest.

"What the hell was that?" I ask, looking into the distance.

"A very pissed-off dragon," Cheryl replies, getting into a defensive stance.

A bright orange flame erupts not too far from us, illuminating the sky. A few seconds later, a huge gray beast breaks through the trees, feral and deadly. Its ember eyes are glowing, and smoke is pouring out of its nostrils and mouth.

"Holy shit. When was the last time we saw one of them in their dragon form?" I ask no one in particular, walking backward slowly.

My friends do the same because no matter how fast and strong we are, we can't beat a fucking dragon.

"I didn't know they could still shift," Cheryl mumbles.

The dragon opens its wings to their full span, and glances at the body. I don't dare to breathe or move as I watch the monster step forward. Lowering its huge head, it nudges the corpse with its snout. When its friend doesn't wake up, the dragon lets out another terrifying roar, louder than the previous one, and then turns its attention to Manu. It can smell the dragon's blood on her.

"It's going to attack!" I yell, a second before a jet of fire shoots from the dragon's mouth.

Lucca leaps just in time, shoving Manu out of range. They roll together on the ground, but Lucca's sleeve still gets singed by the fire. The dragon's chest expands again as it draws air in. It's going to fire another deadly assault. There's no way Lucca and Manu can escape a second time.

I draw my katana, then let out a battle cry and charge the beast. The dragon turns, directing its flames toward me. With a power jump, I leap above them with my katana poised high above my head. As I drop, I swing the blade against the dragon's shoulder. It pierces through the thick skin, eliciting another deafening rumble from deep in its throat.

I fall into a crouch, but I didn't plan my move with precision, and end up not taking into account the dragon's spiked tail. The hit comes too fast for me to move or protect my upper body. The impact sends me flying back, and when I land roughly a few feet from its talons, I know there's something terribly wrong with me. I can't breathe. It feels like I'm drowning in dry land.

"Saxon!" Ronan yells from somewhere.

With difficulty, I lean on my elbows and stare at the massive hole in my chest, which is spewing blood. *Fuck.* Blood also slowly fills my mouth. This can't be good.

My vision is turning blurry, but I can see when several large males burst into the clearing, shouting and brandishing assault weapons. No swords for the dragons. They have embraced the modern world completely. I recognize Larsson among them, but I don't think familiarity is going to help us right now. They seem pretty pissed off, but at least the beast dragon has stopped attacking.

Suddenly, Cheryl drops next to me. "Damn it, Saxon. Why did you charge that dragon?"

"It was going to fry Lucca and Manu. I had no choice."

Cheryl opens her mouth, but something catches her attention. She unfolds from her crouch, bending her knees and keeping her hands at the ready. I have to twist my body to be able to see who's approaching. A tall male with brown hair and an expression that's not one bit friendly is standing in front of her.

"Tell your friend to back off, Jagger," Cheryl warns.

Okay, then. Cheryl is on a first-name basis with the guy. It seems everyone in the supe community mingles besides we vampires. And when I do decide to dip my toes into a different pool, I end up mated to a witch.

"Jemma has every right to be furious. That vampire killed her son!"

"Oh my God. Manu didn't kill anyone. She was set up."

"Set up by whom?" The dragon raises his eyebrows.

"By Jacques Tellier," I say with difficulty. Clutching my chest, I get to my knees.

"Saxon, don't try to move. You're hurt pretty badly."

"You were a fool for getting in Jemma's way," the dragon says.

Cheryl whirls around so fast, she's in the guy's business in a split second, holding him by the lapels of his jacket. "If that beast hadn't burst into the clearing, spitting fire, we would have been able to explain what happened."

"You say the vampire didn't kill the kid, but where are the witnesses? Sorry, love, I don't think your word is going to matter much to Jemma or Larsson."

Despite his harsh words and Cheryl's threatening position, the dragon's angry expression relaxes a fraction. I'm sensing they're more than simple acquaintances. *Oh man.* Ronan is going to have a cow when he finds out.

The dragon covers her hands with his and gently pushes Cheryl away. Neither speak for a couple of beats, but they're still too close to one another.

Ignoring Cheryl's advice, I get up. I only remain vertical for a couple of seconds, enough to see that the gray dragon has shifted back into her human form. She's now cradling her son in her arms, crying so desperately that it puts a chink in my heart. My mother cried like that when she saw my sister's mangled body.

Right before my legs give out from under me, the familiar tingles of the mating bond ripple down my spine. I try to locate Aurora in the gloom, but my vision is slowly fading to black, and the last thing I see is the ground getting near as I fall forward, boneless.

31

AURORA

I let the bond guide me to Saxon, driving like a maniac without regard for speed limits or safety. The closer I get to him, the stronger it becomes, but also the sense that something is terribly wrong with him. He's hurt. That much I know.

The invisible link leads me to a forest on the outskirts of town. There's no road going through it, which means I have to ditch the car. Running the rest of the way it is. Pushing my muscles to the max, I run into the woods, not caring one bit that it's pitch black and my human sight can't adjust to the darkness fast enough. But nature doesn't care about urgency. I trip over an exposed tree root and fall on my knees and hands, scraping both. The pain of the impact is jarring. The cuts on my skin burn. But I shake it off. The agony swirling in my chest is stronger, and it eclipses everything else. Saxon needs me.

My breathing is coming out in bursts when, after running for about two minutes, I reach a clearing. My pulse drumming in my ears prevented me from registering the sounds of turmoil until I come upon the scene. I halt for a moment to take it all in. It's a fighting ground, but the players are a surprise. This isn't a war between vampire clans. This is a war between species. Vampires and dragons, to be exact.

The tug in my chest becomes stronger. I barely register all the individuals in the meadow as I look for Saxon. He's standing twenty feet away from me next to Cheryl and a dragon shifter who looks familiar. Sensing my presence, Saxon glances in my direction, but instead of stepping forward, he collapses face first.

"Saxon!"

I take off, crossing the distance between us as fast as I can. There's no slowing down when I reach his side. I drop to my knees so fast that it's another fall. My knees throb, but it's my heart that's bleeding. With shaking hands, I turn him over, wincing at the sight of his pale appearance.

"Is he breathing?" Cheryl asks.

"I don't know."

My vision is blurry, and I can't tell if his chest is rising or not. It has been punctured by something rather large. The hole is the size of a fist, which allowed blood to spill freely. If he weren't a vampire, the wound would have killed him instantly.

"His chest just moved," the dragon chimes in.

Then I see the slow rise and fall of Saxon's ribs. Holding him by the shoulders, I shake him. "Saxon, wake up."

I sense when our group becomes larger, but I don't dare take my eyes off him to see who joined us.

"He's on the verge of going into hibernation. He needs blood,"

Lucca says in a raspy voice. He must have been screaming at the top of his lungs.

"I haven't been able to feed him from my vein," I reply through a choke.

"You're the only human around. It has to come from you," Cheryl insists.

She's right. I reach inside my bag and pull out a small dagger. Without hesitation, I slash my palm and press it against his lips. But he remains unresponsive.

"Come on, Sax. Drink up," I murmur.

"That's not enough blood. You have to force it down his throat." Cheryl crouches next to me.

My hands are shaking so terribly that when I press the blade against my wrist, I'm afraid I'll end up cutting my hand off. Cheryl reaches over, prying the dagger from me.

"Here. I'll do it."

She slits my skin with a swift move, not giving me any chance to pull away. It burns like acid, and when she applies pressure above the cut, the blood that spills out is hot and thick. Droplets fall over Saxon's lips, dripping down his chin. I force his mouth open, holding the makeshift blood fountain above it.

The seconds seem to tick by slowly until Saxon's eyes fly open and he gasps loudly. His eyes turn a deep shade of red, and for a moment, I don't think he recognizes me. I'm wrong.

"Rora, my love." He lifts his hand to cup my cheek. "You came."

My face feels warm and wet. *Shit, I'm already bawling my eyes out.* "Of course I came. You're my mate. Now stop talking and feed." I shove my wrist against his mouth.

His fangs pierce my skin, and immediately, the pain from the cut fades away. With each pull, something blooms inside of me. It takes me a moment to understand that the strange feeling is nothing more than the euphoria of connecting with Saxon at a deeper level. My blood is his lifeline.

The sensation doesn't last long before the magic from the blood vow rears its ugly head and attempts to ruin everything. Once again, I fight for control with every fiber of my being. Saxon needs my blood; I won't let this stupid decision I made get in the way of helping him.

My head feels light, and suddenly, the world seems to tilt off its axis. The loss of blood combined with the fight I'm waging within me is sapping all my energy. The repel spell is growing inside as I lose the battle against the unwanted magic. In another second or two, the electroshock will zap from my hands, and knock Saxon out. In his current weakened state, I might send him straight into hibernation, which means I might not ever see him again.

With my free hand, I blindly search for a crystal inside my bag. My fingers brush over a few river stones, but a crystal can store more magic, so it will give me a bigger boost. Finally, I touch sharp edges. I curl my fingers around the object quickly, and at once, power rushes through me. The sense of vertigo vanishes, and I can focus on isolating the blood vow magic, keeping it contained until Saxon is done.

Then something peculiar happens. I can't feel my body anymore, nor hear any sound around me besides my own breathing. It's almost like I'm immersed in a sensory deprivation pool. A second later, I'm shoved forward, landing in a different place. I'm in Elena Montenegro's apartment. The old witch is kneeling in front of an altar, praying to a statue that wasn't there when I visited. My heart lurches forward. Above the statue there's a symbol painted on the wall in red. A symbol I just saw in the book about the Boucher family.

I only linger in the scene for a couple of seconds before I'm yanked back by an invisible elastic band. I snap back into my body with a jerk. My senses return in a rush, making my skin tingle. I'm lying on my back, and above me, hovering with a worried expression on his face, is Saxon.

"Rora, I'm so sorry. I didn't mean to hurt you."

"Hurt me? I don't understand."

"You let out a cry and then collapsed."

I press the heel of my hand against my forehead. "It was the blood vow magic. Did I hex you?"

"No."

I'm still feeling out of sorts after my bizarre experience. Did I travel all the way to Elena's apartment for real? Then does that mean she's somehow worshipping a demon? Solomon gave me the tome about the Bouchers for a reason. I have to ask him what that symbol in the book means.

I try to sit up on my own, but Saxon links his arm with mine and gently pulls me up. My eyes immediately drop to his chest. He bled so much that the stain has covered the entire front of his shirt.

"I'll heal, my love."

It's the second time he called me that, but only now the coin drops. "Why are you calling me 'my love'? I thought you didn't believe our feelings were real."

Guilt shines in his eyes. "I'm sorry I said that."

I hold my breath, dying to hear more from him, but the world decides to interrupt again when King Raphael himself plus four of his highly trained soldiers march into the clearing. The dragons present seem to grow larger as they square their shoulders. At least they're pointing their weapons down. The king's Red Guard flank their boss, keeping their hands casual and loose by their sides. But despite their stance, their hard expressions leave no room for doubt. They will kill anyone who tries to harm the king.

Lucca moves toward his uncle, but he stops halfway when Ronan and Manu join him. I was so focused on saving Saxon that I completely forgot the reason he was here in the first place. A quick overall glance tells me Manu is not harmed.

"Larsson," the king says in his rich tenor voice that carries in the open. "I trust you weren't going rogue again."

King Raphael's comment is met with obvious deep-rooted anger. The relationship between vampires and shifters, especially dragon shifters, has never been as strong as his relationship with witches and mages. Somehow, all the supernatural types have managed to co-exist in Salem without any real conflict. As long as everyone stays on their turfs, everything is fine. Things are not the same outside of Salem. Boston, for example, is famously known for the constant bloodshed caused by gangs of different species fighting. Since humans outside of Salem don't know jack about the supernatural communities, they think the violence is caused by regular criminals.

"It wasn't any of my people who stepped outside of their turf. A young dragon was killed, and your niece has his blood all over her."

"I didn't kill anyone!" Manu retorts angrily. "I was set up."

"Manu." The king levels her with an intense stare, dousing her fiery indignation in an instant.

Larsson steps closer to him, lips peeled back, aggression rippling over his body. "I warned you when I agreed to your terms that I didn't want to be dragged into your clan war. Now look at him!" He points at a dead guy in a woman's arms. "Gus was only seventeen!"

Ah, shit.

"I'm sorry for your loss."

"Spare me the sentiment. Consider this your final warning. If you don't deal with your enemies on your own, I will not restrain my people. They will come after all vampires, regardless of allegiance."

The woman who was holding the dead dragon in her arms rises to her feet. "Do you know who did this to my son?"

"Not with one hundred percent certainty," Ronan replies.

"I want a name."

"Ma'am, I can't give you a name. You—"

"Give me a fucking name!" she roars so loudly she might be in her dragon form.

"Jemma, you *will* have your revenge," Larsson says calmly, before turning to the king. "I want his head, Raphael. I don't care what that is going to cost you."

"You'll have it, Larsson. You have my word."

32

AURORA

It's almost daybreak by the time we arrive at Bloodstone. Saxon was all jittery in the car, moving in his seat almost as if he wanted to jump out the door and run. It's an ingrained instinct in vampires to seek cover when sunup is near. Saxon chose to drive back with me, but I kept my distance from him, even though I was itching to reach over and squeeze his hand.

When I think how close I was to losing him to this unfair condition vampires suffer from, my heart twists savagely in my chest. I'm not sure how long he's been awake since the last time he hibernated, but I still have plenty of years left of him until I ... *fuck*. If I manage to be free of the vow I made, and thwart my unwanted marriage, there is the immortality detail to deal with. I'll grow old and Saxon will remain the sexy god that he is. I'm not sure if I will be able to handle that. And would he want to stay by my side and watch me wither and die?

The sky is getting lighter, but it doesn't mean our evening is over. The mood within our group is depressing as we walk up the steps of the dark stone building. Silence is prevalent. Even Saxon, who has been always quick with a joke, doesn't say a word.

Once we're inside, Lucca glances at Manu, breaking the silence first. "I have to see Vivi. Are you going to be okay?"

"Yes, I'm fine. I just need to feed and rest."

"You should have gone home with the king," Ronan grumbles.

"And you should have gone after Cheryl," she snaps. "She's sleeping with that dragon, you know."

It's right then that I remember where I recognize that dragon from. He's the bartender Cheryl screwed when we went to rescue Rikkon from Larsson's clutches.

"How do you know that she is?" I ask.

She gives me an arrogant look. "I could tell."

"From the one-second glance you spared in their direction?" I raise an eyebrow.

There's no reply from her unless I count her death glare as one. Maybe she's so in tune with Cheryl because Ronan is definitely linked to the she-wolf, and only a blind person wouldn't notice Manu has a thing for the brooding vampire. And there's Karl in the mix too. I'd bet a limb he's more than just a familiar. No wolf shifter would pledge an eternity linked to a vampire if some serious feelings weren't involved. *Damn.* This is not even a triangle anymore. It's a square of unresolved issues and complications. It almost makes my relationship with Saxon seem easy in comparison.

He brushes his fingers against the back of my wrist, sending a blazing ripple up my arm.

"I'm going to see Solomon. Will you come with me?"

"Yeah, of course."

We say goodbye to our companions and head over to the headmaster's office. Saxon was able to drink from me, but that's far from enough to recover from the wound he suffered. His appearance is still too pale for my liking, and he has dark circles under his eyes.

"Stop looking at me like that," he grumbles. "I'm okay."

"You scared the hell out of me. Don't do it again." I force my eyes to remain focused ahead, even though every fiber in my body pulls to him.

"I scared you?" His voice rises a little. "You were the one who collapsed and stayed catatonic for a whole minute. I thought … fuck, I thought that I had drunk too much from you."

The choke in his reply makes my heart twist in a vicious manner. But it's the inability of reassuring him through touch that hurts the most. I know it has only been a day since I snagged the promise from the warlock to free me from the blood vow, but after we see Solomon, I'll have to find a way to contact him.

I get lost in my head for a minute, and don't notice right away Saxon's change of demeanor. He stops abruptly and snarls as he stares at Solomon's closed door.

"What is it?"

He doesn't reply, but Solomon's door opens, and I understand why Saxon is going berserk. Calvin steps out, spearing me with a look of so much hatred and loathing that I could choke on it.

"Well, well. So he's the fucking reason you hexed me, bitch."

In a blur, Saxon moves, pouncing on Calvin before I can stop him. The force of the impact sends both careening to the floor. Saxon is on top, clawed hand high above his head, ready to strike while he keeps Calvin pinned down by holding him by his neck.

Solomon comes running out of his office, eyes bigger than saucers and bulging out of his skull. At once, he uses his special familiar power to knock Saxon off Calvin in the nick of time.

"Fuck!" Saxon cries out, hugging his middle. Then he rolls onto his side, and I see that his wound is bleeding again.

My heart shoots up to my throat, getting stuck there. I close the short distance between us as fast as I can, dropping to my knees next to him. This feels like déjà vu. *Weren't we in a similar position not even an hour ago?*

"Saxon, are you okay?" I lift his head onto my lap.

"Everything hurts." He twists his face in pain, pressing his cheek against my belly.

Furious, I whip my head toward Solomon, who is now helping Calvin up. "Did you have to blast him off like that?"

"He was going to kill this idiot here. I had to act fast."

"I'm not an idiot. That vampire is a menace. He needs to be put down."

"Fuck you, Calvin," I snap.

"How dare you talk to me like that? I'm your fiancé. I deserve respect!" He takes a step in my direction, shaking in anger while a vein on his forehead seems about to pop.

"Respect?" I snort. "You have to earn that, asshole."

He laughs derisively. "You think you're so special. You look down on me because you're the future High Witch. Let me tell you a secret, darling. That position is political—it's not awarded to the most powerful or deserving person. It's given to the witch who can suck the king's cock hardest."

Saxon tenses, but I don't give him the chance to attempt a retaliation. I'm the one who fires the most powerful attack spell

I know without holding anything back. My entire body radiates with energy; my skin feels hot as the violent surge of power rushes through me. Sparks of electricity converge on my outstretched hand a second before a blast akin to lightning whooshes from my fingers. A blinding light illuminates the hallway. There's a cry and then a string of curses.

When the light fades the air still crackles with the vestiges of magic. My skin is tingling, and my ear is buzzing. It takes a moment for my eyesight to adjust, and when it does, I find Solomon looking like a mad scientist who has just been electrocuted. His hair is sticking out at odd angles, and there's black soot on his right hand and sleeve.

"Holy shit!" Saxon exclaims. "You fried the headmaster."

Oh my God. I think I did. Solomon must have stepped in front of Calvin and received the full blast of my spell. *Fuck.* I'm in a heap of trouble.

Calvin staggers back to his feet. I'm not sure how he fell, but it's clear by the animosity shining in his eyes that his retaliation will be severe.

"You tried to kill me," he grits out.

"No. I only wanted to hurt you. *A lot.*"

"The council will know about this. You can say goodbye to your chances of ever being High Witch."

A bubble of crazy laughter erupts from my throat. "Do you think your threats scare me? Go ahead. Bitch about me to the elders. Besides, if I'm no longer in line to become the next High Witch, then I don't have to marry you."

I won't marry him either way, but he doesn't need to know that. Not until I get rid of the deal I made with Elena.

"That's fine. I like your sister better anyway."

My blood runs cold. "What?"

"Oh yeah. Once the council deems you unfit for the High Witch role, your sister is the next contender." He smiles maliciously, making me wish I had more juice in me to explode his head.

Saxon sits up but keeps his hand on my leg. He has no idea how much I appreciate that connection, even if it's an innocent touch that, so far, has not triggered anything wicked in me.

"You're not getting Rora, or any of her sisters, motherfucker," he snarls.

Understanding finally dawns on Calvin's demented face. "You're fucking that bloodsucker, aren't you, little whore?"

Saxon tries to get up but I hold his hand, keeping him in place. "No. He's not worth it."

"Enough!" Solomon finally decides to butt in. "I don't care who you are or how you got a spot in my institution, but I won't tolerate that kind of foul language in my presence. Get out of my sight before I forget I'm not supposed to use magic to torture people."

Calvin's eyes narrow to slits while he locks his jaw tight. But he doesn't open his mouth again before he strides away. The rush of adrenaline slowly recedes, leaving me completely depleted.

Saxon turns to me, capturing my face between his hands. "That blast … Holy shit, Rora. It was awesome!" He crushes his lips to mine, taking my breath away in an instant. I want to melt into his arms, but we only have time for a quick peck before Solomon ends the fun with an annoyed throat-clearing.

Saxon and I break apart, and glance at the short man who is looking the opposite of amused.

"Get in my office." He points at the open door.

Like scolded children, we get back on our feet and march into the room with our heads hanging low. We both messed up royally. Neither of us should have attacked Calvin. But I have no regrets. His insinuation that if he doesn't marry me, he'll marry Miranda has left me reeling. I wish Solomon had let me fry the bastard.

Over my dead body he'll marry my sister.

Saxon and I remain standing in front of Solomon's desk, waiting for him to sit behind it and doll out his punishment. But the familiar walks to the right, and pushes the heavy burgundy curtain open, revealing a small alcove where he has set up a mix of lab and infirmary. There's an examination table, shelves with books, glass pots, and boxes, and a number of other objects I can't identify.

"What are you waiting for, fool? Get in there." He gestures at Saxon.

He minces into the alcove clutching at his midsection. I follow him, getting hit by a mix of strong scents. Herbs, rubbing alcohol, mildew, and … What the hell? Wine. *What kind of shenanigans has Solomon been doing here?*

Saxon sits at the edge of the table, wincing as he does, which makes me mad at the headmaster again.

"What was Calvin doing here?" I ask.

"What do you think?" he replies without making eye contact. "You hexed him with a powerful sleeping spell."

"I had to get rid of him in a hurry. But he should have slept for at least ten hours."

"I found him passed out in his car."

The familiar continues moving around the small room, grabbing vials and bottles from the overcrowded shelves, and setting them on the table next to Saxon.

"You brought him back?" My voice rises to a shrill.

He levels me with a glare. "Of course I did. Everything that happens on Bloodstone grounds is my responsibility. I don't care about your issues with the man. You can't go around attacking people."

"If you can call that vermin people," Saxon chimes in. "If he doesn't stay away from Rora, he's going to die."

"Oh shut up. You're not going to kill anyone." He stops in front of Saxon, eyeballing the big hole on his chest. "Jesus, how did you get hurt like that?"

"I faced a pissed-off dragon."

He shakes his head. "How come every time there's a problem in the community, you and your dumbass friends are involved? We haven't seen a dragon shift into their beastly form in decades."

"Hey! This time wasn't our fault. Manu was set up for murder. Jacques is trying to weaken King Raphael by making him lose his allies. My father used to do the same thing when he wanted to conquer an enemy village."

"I know. Your daddy was a piece of shit."

There's no visible reaction on Saxon's expression, but when our eyes meet, I see the deep-rooted pain in his. I wish there was something I could do to erase that.

"Let's see what we're dealing with here," Solomon continues.

He rips Saxon's blood-caked T-shirt in the middle, revealing a sight more gruesome than I expected. The hole seems to be closing, but there's still plenty of torn muscle to make me nauseated.

"How can you still be breathing?" I say.

"The right question to ask is: how hasn't he gone into hibernation yet?" Solomon mutters.

"He drank from me."

Solomon switches his attention to me, displaying wrinkles on his forehead. "Feeding wouldn't necessarily help, but perhaps since you are his mate, that made a difference. Still, Saxon is not out of the woods yet. He should feed again."

A barbed wire seems to wrap around my heart. How can I do that without hurting Saxon in the process.

"No. Rora almost died tonight trying to help me. I won't put her at risk again like that."

"What do you mean she almost died? Did you enter bloodlust?"

"No. There's something within me that's repelling Saxon," I say with a heavy sigh. "I fought it and it backlashed. I was foolish enough to make a blood vow with Elena Montenegro. In exchange for the spell that brought Lucca back from hibernation, I agreed to marry Calvin."

Solomon's jaw slackens and he seems to freeze in that stupefied expression for a moment. Then his bushy eyebrows furrow together. "Foolish? That wasn't foolish. That was downright stupid and irresponsible. Has your mother taught you nothing? Under no circumstances should a High Witch enter in a blood vow with anyone. It's the most binding and invasive contract there is."

"I know that now!" Angry tears form in my eyes. "At the time, I didn't think I had a choice. Elena has a mirror from the Nightingales that shows possible futures. I saw with my own eyes King Raphael going mad and killing Saxon."

Solomon's eyes go rounder. "She has the Taluah Mirror?"

"I didn't ask if it had a name. I was too distraught by the vision. She said the only way to stop that future from happening was if Lucca came back from hibernation."

"Lucca coming back won't stop the king from going crazy. Only the return of the Nightingales will fix that."

"What are we going to do, then?" Saxon pipes up. "They aren't likely to return."

A shadow crosses the headmaster's eyes. "Don't worry about that now. We have to find a way for you to break that vow. It's the number one priority."

"The warlocks of Ivern are looking into it."

He rewards me with an eyeroll. "Sure, let's involve the brethren that deals with dark magic."

I put my hands on my hips. "Do you have a better idea?"

"At the moment, no." He dabs a piece of white cloth with a clear liquid, then turns to Saxon. "This is going to hurt. Try not to cry like a baby."

33

SAXON

———⚔———

"Where do you think you're going?" She crosses her arms, stepping in front of me to block my way when, instead of walking into her apartment, I make a motion to continue down the corridor.

"Back to my place. I need to grab some blood bags."

"You're not drinking from those stupid bags. You heard Solomon. You need to drink from me."

"And I told you, I'm not risking your life like that."

Her whiskey eyes flash with fiery determination. She's not going to back down. I rub my face, trying my best to not let my frustration win.

"You can drink from a cup like you did before."

I knew she was going to suggest that. "I can't stand to see you get hurt because of me."

"Well, you'd better get over it. I'm a witch. Cutting myself is part of the job."

Hands on my hips, I stare at her through eyes narrowed to slits. "You're not going to relent, are you?"

"Nope."

"Fine. But when this is all over, I'm going to make love to you so hard, you're not going to remember what planet we live on."

Shit. I shouldn't have said that. Aurora's heart rate spikes as she stares at me like a deer caught in headlights. Her arousal is immediate, and it hits me like a cannonball. My cock is as hard as a rock, and my mouth waters, dying for a taste of her.

"Make love to me? Not fuck me?"

Her question takes me by surprise until I realize what I said. It was a slip of the tongue, but not untrue. I breach the distance between us, not caring that it's dangerous for us to touch. Her breathing hitches as she tilts her face up. Holding my own breath, I wrap my arms around her waist, pulling her closer.

"There will be many, many occasions when I'm going to fuck you senseless. But as soon as you're free of this shitty blood vow, I'm going to cherish every single inch of your body, take my time drawing every gasp, every moan of ecstasy from your lips. I'm going to make love to you."

"Why?" She looks deep into my eyes, searching for the answer.

I'm about to give it to her—the truth I've known for a while, but I was too afraid to say out loud—when suddenly, I feel a cold ripple on the back of my neck. I whirl around faster than the speed of light, positioning myself in front of Aurora, using my body as a shield.

The hallway is empty, though, and I don't smell anyone approaching.

"What is it, Saxon?"

"I don't know. I sensed something strange. Didn't you?"

No sooner do I utter those words than the lights begin to flicker, going out completely for a few seconds before turning back on. Now there's a tall man standing a few feet from us. He's wearing a hoodie over his head, which is concealing part of his face. I can only see his sharp jawline.

"Who the fuck are you?" I ask.

Pulling his hoodie back, he lifts his chin, and pierces us with his bright blue-eyed stare. *Son of a bitch.* It's one of the warlocks who lied to the High Witch to cover for us.

"Ryker." She walks around me. "I hope you're here because you have the spell."

"I have *a* spell, but not what you were expecting." He switches his attention to me, or better yet, to my bandaged chest. "So it's true. You did get impaled by a dragon."

"How do you know?"

He gives me an amused stare. "Everyone in the supe community knows by now. You and your friends are getting quite a reputation. That's not why I'm here, though. Should we continue our conversation in a place more private?"

Sudden dizziness hits me, making me sway on the spot. Aurora is quick to link her arm with mine, stabilizing me. I wouldn't mind her assistance if we didn't have an audience. I hate being weak.

"You need to feed, don't you?" the warlock pipes up.

I grumble, but it's Aurora who replies. "Yes, from me. Let's get going."

She drags my ass back to her apartment. In hindsight, I don't know why I was arguing with her about drinking from blood bags. It's obvious that it wouldn't have helped me at all. A yawn sneaks up on me, which I try to cover with my fist. Aurora's hard stare immediately zeroes in on my face, almost burning a hole through it.

"You're not going into hibernation, are you?"

I'm beginning to feel fatigued, but that could be attributed to the fact that it's already morning. But sometimes, the process of hibernation can sneak up, and before I know it, I'm waking up a few decades later. *Fuck.* There's no way Aurora would wait for me for that long—that is, if she's still alive when I come out of my forced slumber. The thought alone makes me sick to my stomach.

"I don't think so," I lie.

There's a chance it's happening, but I don't want to worry her. She already has too much on her plate. Besides, if the process has begun, there isn't much she can do to stop it.

Once inside her apartment, I steer us straight toward the couch. I need to lie down because my eyelids are getting heavier and heavier.

"Sax, are you sure you're okay?"

I yawn again. "Yes, Rora. I'm fine. Go see what Ryker has come up with." She remains standing next to the couch, watching me intently. "Go on. I'm fine."

"Don't lie down then. I don't want you falling asleep before you feed."

With effort, I return to a sitting position. *Damn it.* This lethargy is not normal. I pull my cell phone out and text Ronan. He needs to bring me blood ASAP. I don't know how long Aurora will be busy with the warlock.

"I thought you were going to look into breaking the blood vow." She turns to him.

"We couldn't find a way to do it without alerting the old hag. She can't know we're investigating her."

"So what's your solution?"

"We're going to remove the blockage that prevents you from … *mating* with the vampire. I understand that's causing you a lot of headache."

I sit up straighter. "That would be very helpful."

To my surprise, the warlock smirks. I didn't think he had any sense of humor within him. All I ever got from him on the few occasions we met was his deadly vibe.

Aurora furrows her eyebrows and folds her arms. "I have a question about the blood vow."

"Go on."

"You said Elena can have access to the grimoire through it. Does that mean our minds are connected somehow? Can she spy on me too?"

"I've never heard of a blood vow granting that kind of connection. Why do you ask?"

"Something strange happened earlier. I had to feed Saxon and fight the repel spell at the same time. Somehow, I got a glimpse of Elena. She was in her apartment, praying to a strange statue. There was a symbol painted on the wall too."

"What kind of symbol?" The man takes a step forward, narrowing his eyes.

She shakes her head. "I can't remember the details anymore. It wasn't a pentagram, that's for sure, but the color was red."

"Blood?" I ask.

"I'm not sure. Maybe."

Ryker passes a hand over his face. "If Elena is worshipping a demon, we need to know what kind."

"Wait. Are you saying the witch Aurora made a deal with is messing with demonic magic?" I get up from the couch, the fear for her safety giving me a burst of energy.

"Most likely."

Aurora pulls her hair back. "Fuck. If I could see her through this sickening link, then I have to expect she can see me too. You have to do something about her."

"She has been extremely clever covering her tracks. Using the grimoire as bait is our best chance. You need to gain access to it," the man retorts.

"The only way I can do that is if I marry Calvin!"

"What? That's your fucking plan?" I yell. "Aurora is not marrying anyone but me."

Ryker's eyebrows shoot to the heavens while his eyes widen in surprise. "Oh, I didn't realize you were secretly engaged."

Heat creeps up my face. To hide my embarrassment, I run a hand through my hair, dropping my chin.

A knock on the door saves me from explaining to Aurora my outburst. We're mated, but I haven't even told her how I feel, and now I'm talking about marriage. *What's wrong with me?*

"What now?" She strides to the door.

"I texted Ronan. Asked him to bring me some blood."

She whips her face in my direction, glowering, before she opens the door. *Yeah, she's pissed at me now.*

"I got the blood." Ronan lifts the bags, but then freezes when he spots Ryker standing in the middle of Aurora's living room. "What is he doing here?"

"Oh, just come in already. I'm not going to explain while you're standing in the hallway." She opens the door wider to allow him to pass.

Ronan glances at me with a question in his eyes.

"The warlock is here to help Aurora." I shrug.

"Okay." He walks over and offers me the bags. "Here. I got everything we had, but I'm not sure these will help. You need to feed from a live source."

I cut a glance in Aurora's direction just in time to catch her wince. "I will as soon as our illustrious visitor does what he came here for."

It's an effort to forget—for the time being—the other part of Aurora's deal with him. I don't have all the details, but what matters to me is Aurora is expected to marry that motherfucker. There's no chance in hell I'll allow that to happen. I already carry the last name of a traitor. If I kill that good-for-nothing mage and it costs the king his alliance with the magical folk, would it matter? Most of King Raphael's supporters expect me to screw up. I might as well prove that the apple doesn't fall far from the tree.

She takes a step closer to the warlock with her chin raised high. "Just do what you have to do."

Ryker glances at me, and then at Ronan. "I was going to tie up lover boy there, but since you're here, just keep him restrained."

"Why?" we all ask in unison.

The warlock turns to Aurora. "Because this is going to hurt, and I won't put it past your mate to attack me while I'm in the middle of the incantation."

He's right about that. "Tying me up wouldn't have worked. Ronan is a better solution."

The warlock nods and then focuses on Aurora. "Are you ready?"

"As ready as I will ever be."

He presses two fingers in the middle of her forehead, and almost immediately, I sense the wisps of magic take over the room.

The warlock's eyes glow bright green while the light pouring from Aurora's eyes is white. Ryker's lips are moving, but I can't hear the words he's muttering, even with my vampire senses. Besides them lighting up like a supernova star, nothing seems to happen for a moment. Then I hear Aurora's small whimper, a sound that pulls my spine tight. The muscles around her mouth tense, her expression becomes twisted. Her hands turn into balled fists by her sides. She's in pain and trying to hide it. All my instincts are telling me to end her suffering.

Ronan, sensing the change in my stance, positions himself in front of me. "Sax, do I have to physically restrain you?"

I want to say no, that I can control myself, but just then, Aurora lets out a bloodcurdling scream that reverberates through my bones. I'm moving forward before I know it, only to collide with Ronan's brick wall. His steely arms wrap around me in a vise, turning me around to contain me in a choke hold. My right arm is twisted behind my back, and Ronan's forearm presses against my neck.

"Let me go!" I attempt to wrestle my way free, which is futile. Ronan is a beast.

In the background, Aurora continues to scream, driving me more insane. I thrash, trying to push Ronan against a wall, but my friend's grip on me doesn't waver. I end up pinned on the floor by him.

"Sorry, buddy."

"She's hurting," I grit out.

"Not anymore."

I stop struggling and listen beyond the pulse beating in my ears. He's right, Aurora is quiet now.

"It's done," Ryker announces. "You can release him."

Ronan jumps off my back, then offers me his hand. I'm still riding high on the adrenaline when I glance at Aurora. She looks paler than before, but in one piece.

"Are you okay?" I ask.

"I think so." She turns to Ryker. "Is the repel spell gone?"

"Yes. I stayed longer inside your head than necessary to investigate the possible mind-to-mind link you mentioned. It hurt more because of that. I'm sorry."

She rubs her forehead. "Did you find anything?"

"I couldn't find any traces of her inside your head. She's not spying on you through the bond. But she has the Taluah Mirror, which is troublesome. Here, wear this amulet at all times. It should keep her from spying on you via the mirror." He offers Aurora a silver chain necklace with a small pendant, which she puts on right away.

I open my mouth to comment, but the little wind of energy I got when trying to protect Aurora vanishes in the blink of an eye. I lose the feeling of my body first, and then there's nothing.

34

AURORA

⸺✦⸺

My head hurts like I've been hit by a sledgehammer. As uncomfortable as the throbbing is, it doesn't compare to the excruciating pain I endured during Ryker's mind invasion. It felt like he reached inside my brain with clawed hands and scratched it raw.

I'm trying to keep my discomfort from showing on my face for Saxon's benefit, when he passes out on me again, falling face forward, lifeless.

"Saxon!" I yell at the same time that Ronan catches him in his arms.

The towering vampire lets out a curse under his breath as he lays Saxon on the couch. My heart gets stuck in my throat when I see his deathlike appearance. The golden hue from his skin has turned into a washed-out gray color, a look that's common with vampires in a comatose state.

"Tell me he didn't go into hibernation."

"Not yet. His breathing hasn't slowed down that much, but considering the injury he suffered, I'd say he's very close. He needs blood ASAP."

"If he started the process, good luck getting him to wake in order to drink," Ryker pipes up.

"You're not helping!" I snap.

"On the contrary, I am. I can strike him with the right amount of voltage. It will revive him long enough for you to entice him with your blood."

"You mean electrocute him?" Ronan asks.

"Think of it as something akin to using a defibrillator to resuscitate a flatlining patient."

"Fine. Do it," I say. "Anything to keep Saxon from going where I can't follow."

"Okay. Step away."

Ryker raises his hand and begins to speak in a strange language so softly, it's almost a whisper. Strands of electricity form on his palm, crackling as they converge into a green sphere of energy. When he hurls it in Saxon's direction, it looks like lightning is shooting from his hand. I don't know what warlocks must give up in order to yield that kind of power. My guess is their souls. I can't deny that Ryker's abilities are fascinating and terrifying at the same time.

Saxon's chest lifts upon impact, and then he jerks into a sitting position with a loud gasp. His eyes are round and red-rimmed, but also unseeing. His mind is not back to us yet.

"Go on. Do what you have to do before he collapses again."

I run to him, sitting at the edge of the couch. I don't have anything sharp on me, so I just pull my hair to the side and offer him my neck, hoping that it will be enough to kick in his hunger.

"Bite me, Sax. Do it now."

With a snarl, he pulls me closer to him, sinking his fangs into my soft skin. I try not to wince when the sharp pain follows. It didn't hurt the first time he fed from me, but then he was one hundred percent in the moment, not half-asleep. With each pull, the pain recedes, until another feeling takes its place. A swirl of desire starts from my chest, quickly spreading through my body to concentrate mostly between my legs. A wanton moan escapes my lips, bursting my face into flames. I don't suffer from false modesty, but I'm not a vampire who doesn't mind voyeurism.

"I think we're good now. You can show yourselves out," I tell Ronan and Ryker.

My eyes are closed, so I don't see when they walk out, I only hear the door shutting. Saxon takes a couple more hard pulls before he licks the incisions with his warm tongue, and leans away from me. Goose bumps have broken out on my skin, and my heart is hammering like mad inside the confines of my chest. I blink my eyes open, suddenly afraid that my blood didn't help Saxon after all, and he's in danger of leaving me again. Relief washes over me when I find him staring with hooded eyes and lips partly open. Color has returned to his cheeks too.

"Are you okay? Did you have enough?"

"I'm much better now. How are you feeling?"

"I'm fine." I reach for his hand, squeezing it in mine. "I've never felt more terrified in my entire life. I thought you had left me."

"I was close, Rora. But you brought me back." He cups my face, a tender gesture that makes my skin sizzle nonetheless. "Is the repel spell gone?"

"I think so. I didn't feel anything foreign building inside when you were drinking from me."

A grin spreads over his lips, and his eyes shine with mischief. "You know what that means, right?"

I nod, because if I try to speak now, it's probably coming out as a croak. He stands up and I try my best to keep my gaze fixed on his face instead of the huge bulge in his pants. Smiling more broadly now, he offers me his hand. "If we're doing this properly, we'd better get to your bedroom."

He helps me up and I'm grateful for it. My legs are seriously malfunctioning now. Actually, my entire body has gone haywire. My skin is ablaze, my heart is going ninety, and my very bones are on fire.

"Are you sure you want to do this now? I mean, aren't you tired?"

I must be the biggest idiot in the world for saying this, but among all the wonderful, giddy feelings that are making me float in the clouds, there's also fear. This is a big step for us; I can sense the mating bond magic getting stronger. We're about to seal the deal. There won't be any going back from this.

"You're nervous," he says.

"I don't mean to be."

"It's okay. I'm nervous too. I never thought I'd ever feel this way about anyone, Rora. I didn't think love was in the cards for me, and I was fine with that. But you came along and it was game over for me. I didn't know what was missing from my long life until you showed me."

"Is that the bond talking?"

"No," he answers in a soft breath. "The bond makes me crazy for you, but there's something apart, a small spark that's all me. I love you, bond or not."

Maybe it's all the stress that accumulated in the last twenty-four hours, but instead of throwing myself into his arms, I break down in a torrid current of ugly sobs. I step away, covering my face with my hands.

"Rora, why are you crying?" He turns me around, pulling me into a hug.

I melt against him without reservations, without fear of hurting him. An enormous sense of peace and security wraps over me. I've had to be strong for so long that I forgot what it's like to feel protected. I realize in that moment what Saxon means to me.

"I love you too, Sax. And you want to know how I know?" I lift my face to his, getting lost in his eyes.

"How?"

"It will sound crazy, and we haven't really spent that much time together, but when I'm with you I feel free. You're the only one who has ever seen the real me, my vulnerable side, and that's okay. You're home to me."

He captures my face between his. "You have no idea how much your words mean to me, my love. No idea."

His lips meet mine for a kiss that's tender at first, but like always when we're together, we're unable to take things slow. When his tongue darts in my mouth, possessive and demanding, I have no choice but to match the intensity. Saxon grabs a fistful of my hair, tilting my head to the side to deepen the kiss. My arms go around his back, and as my fingers brush against his bandage, I'm reminded that he still has a hole in his chest that needs healing. Reluctantly, I pull back.

"Where do you think you're going?" He keeps me trapped in his arms.

"You're recovering. Let me take care of you."

I manage to break free from him, but only because he lets me. With our hands linked together, I steer him to my bedroom, bringing him to my bed. He sits on the edge of the mattress after I nudge him with a light shove.

"What are you doing, little witch?"

"You're hurt, so today, I'm doing all the loving." I smile.

The red in his eyes shines brighter. "Oh, I like that."

It's almost impossible not to combust while blasted by his intense stare. I think that even with my tan complexion, he can see the blush. But I'm determined to not mess this up. Recreating one of my favorite movie scenes, I unhook my bra, then work the straps while I'm still wearing my oversized top. Once free of the undergarment, I lob it toward Saxon, who grabs it with a deft hand.

"Is slow torture part of your loving?" he asks in a husky voice.

"What?" I fake innocence. "I'm just getting more comfortable for bed."

I take off my pants next, and then my underwear. All my most enticing bits are still covered by the oversized top, but at this point, Saxon's face is already beet red, and his hands are holding the bedcovers in a merciless twist. "Fuck me."

I sashay toward him slowly, which is much harder than I expected. The bond is pulling me to him, stronger than ever, demanding that I throw myself into his arms. With my fingers, I trace his forehead, then the angles of his cheeks, following along the line of his sharp jaw. "You're the most beautiful male I've ever seen."

He grabs my shirt and pulls me closer, while his other hand disappears underneath the fabric. "And you're the sexiest, most tempting witch I've ever met."

Sneakily, he reaches over my pussy, and using his thumb, he swipes over my throbbing clit.

"Sax, I'm the one who's supposed to be in control here," I breathe out.

"You *are* in control. I'm at your mercy," he replies with a devilish smile before he swipes my clit again, quickly turning me into putty in his hands.

I jump back from his wicked ministrations, dancing away when he tries to capture me again.

"Hey!" he complains.

Wiggling my finger, I say, "No. You're not going to do that to me. I told you that I'm the one taking charge today. And the first order of business is to get you out of those jeans."

He arches his eyebrows, fighting a grin. "You want these gone? All right then." He stands up, and moving too fast for my human eyes to register, he yanks his pants off, throwing them to the side torn in two pieces. All that's left are his boxer briefs.

"Now it's your turn. I want to see those gorgeous tits of yours."

With a shake of my head, I say, "Not so fast, love. There's something I want to do first."

I walk over, and then push him back on the mattress. Keeping our gazes locked, I drop onto my knees, and pull down the last barrier between me and his erection.

Saxon hisses when I curl my fingers around his shaft. Without breaking eye contact, I lick his head, and the moan that leaves his parted lips is the most amazing sound ever. He threads his fingers through my hair, giving me tingles not only where he's touching me, but everywhere. Not wanting to wait a second longer, I suck his cock into my mouth until the tip hits the back of my throat.

"Oh my God, Rora."

I take my time licking and sucking, loving every hiss, every grunt and moan that escapes his lips. He's getting bigger and harder, and I'm more than ready to make him explode in my mouth, but he grabs me by the shoulders, halting me. "Wait, sweetheart. Stop for a second."

I let go of him with a loud *pop* and look up. "What?"

He scooches back, then, hooking his index finger, he says, "Come here. I want to feast on you too."

My pussy throbs in anticipation. I couldn't get more turned on if I tried. I decide then that I've tortured Saxon enough. I pull my shirt off, not moving for a moment to soak up Saxon's heated gaze on my body. He isn't touching me, he's nowhere near me, but it feels like his hands are everywhere.

"If you don't get in this bed now, I'm going to pounce," he growls.

"Hmm, I love your wild side," I purr, but because I can't stay away from him for much longer, I join him on the mattress, slowly crawling in his direction.

"I'll show you my wild side." He reaches over, pulling me to his level for a searing, take-no-prisoners kiss.

I'm too far gone to offer any resistance. My plan was to do most of the work, but it seems my mate has other ideas. I lean back, breaking the kiss, only so I can straddle him, and finally fulfill what has been denied to us for too long. I'm so wet that his cock slides inside of me with ease. He grabs my hips, digging his fingers in my skin while I try to ride him nice and slow. "Try" being the operative word. It's impossible. My body is taken over by a fever that reaches stratospheric levels. It leaves tingles of pleasure in its wake; it goes straight to my head, making me dizzy in the most delicious way. I don't know anymore where I end and he begins. We're finally one and it's the most wonderful thing in the universe. My heart overflows with emotion.

Still pistoning in and out, Saxon sits up and claims my mouth again. I wish he would bite me, but maybe he can't take more from me before I recover. Even without his love bite, I know exactly when the bond clicks into place, when it solidifies. It's the moment when Saxon and I climax at the same time. I'm detached from my body, soaring through the sky tangled with him. We shatter into a million pieces, becoming stardust. We're suspended in time and space, and maybe the experience only lasted a few seconds, but it will be branded into my memory forever.

35

AURORA

I've got an hour until I have to start my day at the institute, so after more lovemaking and a shower, Saxon and I head back to his apartment where the whole gang is assembled—and not only the vampires, Vivienne, and Rikkon. Karl and Cheryl are here too. Just because Saxon and I won a personal battle, that doesn't mean the war is over.

"Evening," Saxon says as we walk into the living room, holding hands.

He sounds chipper; either he hasn't picked up on the tension in the room, or he's ignoring it. The ongoing conversation ceases abruptly, and everyone turns to gawk at us. I don't get embarrassed easily, but being blasted by all those knowing stares and smirks makes my face burst into flames.

"What are you all staring at?" I snap.

"There's something different about you," Vivienne says

"Yeah, post-coital bliss," Manu laughs.

She earns a glare from me. "Why are you so entertained? Have you forgotten already the mess you caused last night that almost cost Saxon's life?"

The amusement vanishes at once from her face. "I didn't cause anything. I was set up."

Saxon lifts his hands in a gesture of peace. "Okay, okay. Let's not start arguing. I'm in too good of a mood. Don't ruin it."

"Does that mean you guys are together now? For real?" Vivienne perks up on her seat, sporting a wide grin.

Saxon turns to me, smiling from ear to ear. "Yeah, we're together now."

"Well, sorry to put a damper on your good spirits, but we have a major problem on our hands. Jacques won't stop until he has turned Salem into a blood-drenched battlefield." Ronan's stare is hard and troubled, which only serves to increase my anxiety.

"Salem is not that big of a city, why can't the witches use a location spell to find him?" Cheryl suggests.

Even though Cheryl's idea wasn't aimed as criticism, I feel ashamed just the same. I've been so embroiled in my own issues that I fell out of the loop of the coven's business.

"I'm not sure if my mother has tried yet," I say.

"The High Witch has, unsuccessfully," Ronan replies.

"That means he's using a powerful concealment spell," I mutter to myself.

"What did he do? Hire a rogue mage?" Karl asks.

Suspicions creeps into my head. "Maybe, but there's also a chance he's receiving help from someone within the Council of Witches."

A low growl comes from Saxon, which earns him everyone's attention.

Manu cocks her head. "Why is Saxon looking like he's about to turn into the Tasmanian Devil?"

"Because we have a suspect. Elena Montenegro," I say.

"That name sounds familiar." Ronan frowns, rubbing his chiseled chin.

"She's a respected elder in the council, but we know she's up to no good." I refrain from telling them about the blood vow. I can't deal with everyone knowing about my stupidity. Plus, it doesn't change anything for them.

"The asshole warlocks believe she's made a deal with a demon," Saxon chimes in. "She also knows that first-generation Bluebloods are going crazy."

I watch the blood drain from Lucca's face. "What?"

"Uh? Come again?" Vaughn pinches his eyebrows together.

Saxon sucks his bottom lip in, looking incredibly guilty now. "You didn't know?" he asks Lucca.

"I did. But how could you or Elena possibly know that?" Lucca grumbles. "My uncle only told me recently. He's keeping a tight lid on the issue."

"He didn't tell me!" Manu crosses her arms, pouting, then turns to Karl. "Did you know?"

"Yep. I've known for a while."

With a mischievous grin on her lips, Cheryl chimes in, "Me too."

Fury sparks in Manu's eyes, and I bet if there weren't so many of us here, she might have tried to wipe the grin off Cheryl's face by force. Karl shoots his sister a reproachful look, which she ignores.

Rikkon is standing as still as a statue, but his eyes are vacant. My eyes immediately seek Vivienne's. She doesn't seem surprised by the revelation. Lucca must have told her. Now that she has recovered her memories, she might shed some light on the mysterious Nightingale relic Elena possesses.

"She has the Taluah Mirror," I say.

Vivienne widens her eyes as her spine goes taut. "She has one of them?"

"There are more?"

"Yes. Each court in Ellnesari had one. It allowed them to spy on the human realm without them having to leave their kingdoms."

"Kind of like a big brother thing?" Karl says.

"Precisely. A Nightingale must have brought the mirror here, but how did it end up in Elena's possession?"

"I don't know." I cross my arms. "Only that's not good for us, especially if she's indeed in cahoots with a demon."

Lucca passes a hand over his face, standing from his chair. "If she's a threat, we need to take care of her too."

"The warlocks of Ivern have a plan," I say.

"An absurd one. You're not going to follow through with it, Rora." Saxon tries to stare me down.

"Hey, don't look at me like that. I want to marry Calvin as much as I want to jump out of a plane without a parachute."

"I'm so confused," Vaughn pipes up. "Tell us again why you have to marry someone else if you're mated to Saxon."

"She's not marrying anyone," Saxon snarls.

A ringtone interrupts the tense conversation and I'm grateful for it. It turns out it's Cheryl's phone.

"Hello?" she answers.

Sadly, I don't have super hearing, but a moment later, she frowns. *More bad news coming our way, I bet.*

"Who was it?" Ronan snaps, growing visibly tense.

I expect the feisty redhead to snarl back, but her expression is more somber than angry. "That was Jagger. He says we need to head to Ember Emporium right now if we want to avoid a disaster."

"That's all? He didn't give any details?" Karl asks.

"No."

"That sounds like a trap," Saxon mutters. "Manu probably should stay here."

"I'm not going to stay behind. I'm not a baby."

"No, but until we hand Jacques over to the dragons, you're still a target. It's best if we don't provoke the beasts with a short fuse," Lucca argues.

I turn to Saxon. "You should stay behind too. You haven't completely healed yet."

The look of complete astonishment he gives me is almost comical, but I know it means he will fight me on it.

"You know I can't stay behind. Besides, I'm feeling much better."

Rikkon, who had been quiet the whole time, hisses loudly, and then shoves the heels of his palms against his eyes. "Fuck!"

"Ah, shit. Are you having another vision?" Saxon asks.

He doesn't answer as he rests his head in his hands. Vivienne jumps to his side and begins to rub his back. "Talk to me, Rik."

"Aargh! This hurts so much."

"Did you see anything useful? Are the dragons planning an ambush?" Lucca asks eagerly, earning an annoyed glance from his girlfriend.

"Give him a minute," she snaps.

"I see a great shadow covering the entire town … no, not shadow, more like a sentient black smoke. It has … red eyes."

My blood turns ice cold in my veins. I haven't seen anything quite like it, but that sounds like something from demonic origins. I can't simply sit around and wait for Elena to show her hand. And since there most definitely won't be any wedding happening, Ryker's plan is pretty much garbage at this point. There's only one thing left for me to do.

"You should head to Ember Emporium and see what the dragons want," I sigh.

"What about Rikkon's vision? Are we going to simply ignore it?" Vivienne asks.

"No. That sounds like something triggered by dark magic, which means it falls in my domain."

"Bullshit, Rora. I know what you're thinking. You're not going to face off against that old hag alone," Saxon retorts.

"I'm not going after Elena. There's someone else I need to see, and I have to do it alone."

"Who?" Cheryl asks.

"My mother."

My heart is heavy as I drive to my old childhood home. I texted Miranda, asking if Mom was home. I could call her directly, but I'd like to have the element of surprise. But it's not only the prospect of seeing my mother that's making my chest tight with worry. Saxon went with his friends to Ember Emporium. The last time he faced a dragon, he almost died. And from what Cheryl told us, it didn't sound like they were invited to a party.

I'm so torn. I wish I could have gone with Saxon, but I can't postpone what I have to do. We might be running out of time. This conversation with my mother can't wait until the morning, especially with Rikkon's vision hanging over our heads. No one in town is equipped to deal with a demon besides the damn warlocks, and even so, just two of them might not be enough. I have to stop Elena at all costs before she unleashes what Rikkon saw in his vision. Even if there's no solid proof that she's behind that dark cloud, my gut is telling me she's the villain.

When I park in front of my mother's house, I'm taken over by jitters. My stomach is clenched tight and my heart has decided to run a marathon in my chest. I'm not only going to tell Mom about Elena, I'm going to come clean about everything, including my bond to Saxon. *It's damn stupid that I'm feeling so nervous. I'm a grown woman, for fuck's sake.*

I get out of the car before I lose my nerve, and march toward the front door with squared shoulders. In hindsight, I've always known that it would come to this. I was in denial land thinking that I could break my bond with Saxon. We were never meant to be a one-night stand, mating bond or not. I've never connected more deeply with anyone in my entire life, but my prejudice against vampires didn't let me see what was right in front of me.

I still have the house key, but I opt for ringing the bell. A moment later, Niko opens the door sporting a Cheshire smile, and a glint of mischief in her dark eyes. I can't possibly begin to imagine what she thinks she knows, unless Miranda opened her big mouth about Saxon.

"Oh, you're in trouble." She smirks before letting me through.

"When am I not in trouble these days?" I mumble under my breath.

"Is that Aurora?" my mother asks from the den.

"Yep. The prodigal daughter returns!" Niko laughs.

Miranda joins us in the entry foyer, and without missing a beat, hits Niko upside the head. "Stop being so gleeful, brat."

"Ouch!" She rubs the sore spot, glowering at Miranda.

Niko has always taken advantage of being the youngest, and Miranda and I indulged her. We took turns pampering or protecting her from our mother's tongue-lashings or punishments. Sometimes we even took the blame for something she did.

She's the one who takes the most from our Japanese heritage, which is why she looks twelve instead of her actual age of fifteen, and also explains the reason we babied her so much. We couldn't look at her adorable face and the puppy look she's perfected without caving. That's quickly changing these days.

Our mother stops in the hallway, glaring at me so hard I almost believe she's hexing me somehow. There goes my chance to find out from Miranda what my mother knows. My guess is Calvin already went to the council to complain about me. Oh well. It saves me the trouble of telling the story from the beginning.

"I'd better go see what she wants," I say.

Wordlessly, Mom turns on her heels, and heads to her office. It's a move typical of Isadora Leal, so I follow, like she expects me to. The first thing one sees right as they enter her office is the oil portrait of my grandfather, Shiryu Takashi, one of the greatest mages of Japan. He came to Salem in an exchange program of sorts, where he met my grandmother, Sarina Meester. At the time, she was training to be the High Witch, and was kind of promised to another guy. But the stories say it was love at first sight, and since my grandfather was a badass mage, the council perceived him as a better match. So, my grandparents married for love, my parents married for love, and I'm expected to marry someone I hate. Only thinking about it renews my anger and motivation to come clean once and for all.

Already behind her desk, my mother links her fingers together, leaning her elbows on her desk. "I assume you're here to explain how you've managed to make a mess of things."

"You'll have to be more specific than that. I'm not sure which screwup you're referring to. There have been many."

"Don't even try to be a smartass with me."

"I'm not trying to be anything. I legit want to know what you're talking about. I assume it has to do with Calvin."

"Of course it has to do with Calvin. He has officially petitioned the council to end your engagement, and to remove you from the line of succession on the grounds you're associated with a Blueblood. Is that true, Aurora? Are you screwing around with a vampire?"

"I'm not screwing around with a vampire. I'm mated to one."

There. I said it. I can't believe how easy it was to utter those words out loud. But my confession seems to hang in the air, like a heavy cloud of doom. The blood drains from my mother's face, and she seems frozen in a perpetual expression of apoplexy. Her jaw eventually slackens, but it seems she's at loss for words. I stunned her into silence. That's a first.

"You what?" She presses her open palms against the desk.

"Saxon and I are mates. It's a done deal; it can't be broken."

"Bullshit, it can't be broken. I won't allow my daughter to shack up with a bloodsucker."

"No, but you can serve his king no problem. Do you even hear yourself?"

"Do you think my rebuttal of your 'bonding' is linked to prejudice?"

"You can't deny the magical community secretly loathes vampires. I never quite figured out why. Is it because they're immortals? Stronger?"

She laughs without humor, shaking her head. "All of the above, but that's not the reason I'm against your ridiculous union with that Blueblood. You can't be a High Witch and be married to a vampire. The council will never allow it."

"Why not?"

"Isn't it obvious? Power. The High Witch has always been the council's voice in King Raphael's court, but her loyalty is first and foremost to the council, not the king. If you're married to a vampire, your loyalty to us will be compromised."

I've always suspected that, but I never put much thought into it because I never imagined I would fall in love with a vampire.

I lift my chin in defiance. "If you're telling me I have to choose between being the High Witch and Saxon, I'm choosing him."

Anger sweeps over my mother's features. Even her eyeballs seem to twitch. "If you do that, if you walk away from your duties, then you're no longer my daughter. I'll strip you of your place in the council, and your training will cease immediately. You'll be shunned, forced to live as a rogue for the rest of your life. Is that what you truly want?"

Fury makes my skin tingle and my face hot. My eyes prickle, but the tears forming aren't of sadness, they're angry tears. I've always known that would be the outcome of my decision, but I had secretly hoped my mother would understand me for once. Wishful thinking.

"If that's the price to pay for being true to myself, then yes. A thousand times yes."

"You don't know what you're doing."

"No, I know exactly what I'm doing. Oh, and by the way, I had two reasons to come see you. To tell you that I'm done being your puppet, and also to warn you that Elena Montenegro has betrayed us all."

"What nonsense are you talking about now? Elena Montenegro is a pillar of the community."

"She's an evil, power-hungry witch who is most likely worshipping a demon. It was her idea to pair me up with Calvin, and you want to know why? Because the Belmonts possess the first grimoire and she covets that with a blind obsession."

Her eyebrows arch, and the blood seems to drain from her face. "How do you know they have the first grimoire?"

"She told me on the evening she asked me to steal it for her."

Mom's lips become nothing but a thin, flat line as she keeps her intense stare glued to my face. I brace for her to call me a liar. At this point, I wouldn't be surprised if she did. I am, after all, a disgrace in her eyes.

"Do you have proof of that?" she asks tightly.

The shield I thought I had in place shatters like baked clay, and I feel the full impact of her question. *My word should have been enough, damn it!*

"No."

I could have told her that the warlocks of Ivern are on to Elena, but maybe there's a reason they haven't approached my mother with their suspicions. And she doesn't deserve my trust.

"Without proof, I can't do anything."

"Bullshit. You can investigate her yourself."

"On the weight of your words?" She raises an eyebrow. "I don't think so."

I'm so frustrated, I could cry. But I won't. Not in front of her. "I wouldn't lie about something so serious. You know me better than that."

"That's the problem, Aurora. I don't know you. The daughter I raised would never, *ever*, get involved with a vampire."

"You're right. You don't know me at all. If you did, you'd realize that I'm not a puppet who blindly follows rules. I'm not someone who puts duty above family and love. You can save yourself the trouble of shunning me out of the coven, of your life. I'm walking out of my own free will."

Squaring my shoulders, I head for the door.

"If you leave now, you will never be allowed back into this house. You will never see your sisters again."

My heart twists savagely in my chest. I don't care about not coming back here, but forbidding me to see Miranda and Niko is a low blow. I look over my shoulder, not hiding an ounce of my loathing for her. "That, Isadora Leal, is a power you don't have."

36

SAXON

━━◆══════╡⟩⟩⟩⟩▸

I try my best not to show how fucking worried I am about Aurora as we approach Ember Emporium. I'm not sure why my chest feels so tight, almost as if I'm getting a premonition. She's going to see her mother, not the witch from hell. Unless she lied. I immediately reject the idea. I'd have known if she wasn't telling the truth. Now that the bond is finally solidified, I'm so in tune with her that I can almost hear her thoughts.

With a closed fist, I massage my chest, trying to get rid of the phantom pain. Cheryl, who ended up riding sandwiched between me and her brother in the backseat, turns to stare at me with her eyebrows pinched.

"What are you doing?"

I drop my hand to my lap. "Nothing."

"You're acting strange. I can sense it."

Grumbling, I look out the window. "Sure. Now everyone can

sense everything about me. Did I suddenly become a broadcasting tower?"

"Don't be so grumpy about it. You've just completed a mating ritual. Of course you're going to give off strong vibes when it comes to Aurora."

"All right, everyone. We're here. Stay sharp," Ronan announces from the driver's seat.

He parks on the side street next to Ember Emporium since we don't know what the hell we're going to find inside Larsson's business. When I turn the corner onto the main street, I notice the absence of at least half the motorcycles that are usually parked in front of the dragon's establishment. At this hour, the place should have been packed. Inside, we find it half empty as well. Cheryl walks ahead of us, veering straight for the bar where Jagger, Larsson's younger brother, is polishing a beer glass.

Immediately, I feel Ronan tense next to me, and a low growl comes from deep in his throat. "Easy there, buddy. Do not get territorial now."

He whips his face to mine. "What the hell are you talking about?"

His eyes are flashing red and his fangs are fully exposed, but his eyebrows are furrowed as if he really doesn't know what he's doing. I seek Lucca's gaze, who seems as surprised as I am about Ronan's lack of self-awareness.

"You look like you want to rip someone's head off," Lucca replies.

Ronan blinks rapidly, and after a moment, his eyes return to their natural blue color, just in time before Larsson walks into the main area, sporting a frown that means we can expect a serious shitstorm to come our way. Lucca leads our party to an empty table right in the middle of the room, the one Larsson was aiming for. If the decor of this bar were a little more rustic, I would feel transported to an old Western movie. The house might not be full, but the heavy staring could drown an elephant.

"Why did you call this meeting, Larsson?" Lucca asks.

The dragon kingpin—always dressed to the nines—unbuttons his suit jacket and takes a seat. He points at the opposite chair without breaking eye contact and waits until we're all seated to answer Lucca's question.

"As you have noticed, half my associates are gone. And do you want to know why?"

"They didn't like your management style?" I answer.

He squints while a deep rumble comes from deep in his chest. Cheryl hits me on the shoulder, then spears me with a meaningful glance. *Riight, I shouldn't antagonize the king of dragons when I'm not even recovered from the blow I received from one.*

"Earlier today, a newcomer came onto my premises," Larsson continues. "A wolf shifter by the name of Coyote, who got half my people riled up again about Gus's death. I wasn't here or I would have put a stop to it as soon as he opened his piehole." Larsson glances at Jagger, who takes the scathing, accusatory glance like a champ. He doesn't even flinch.

"Fuck," Karl mutters under his breath while Cheryl glares at Jagger.

"You couldn't have told me that detail over the phone?" she grits out.

There's a visible wince on his part and my jaw drops. Larsson can't get the guy to show emotion but Cheryl can? They're definitely more than acquaintances. I chance a glimpse at Ronan, just to make sure he's not about to pounce on the dragon shifter. Aside from the tight clench of his jaw, he seems okay for now.

"Do you know this shifter?" Lucca asks Karl.

"Yes, he's the alpha who has challenged Marcus. Why didn't you kill him on sight?" Karl asks Jagger.

"Kill him on what grounds? He came in as a patron. We don't discriminate and I didn't know who he was at first."

"Plus, we don't interfere with problems that don't concern us," Larsson adds.

"Really? I think you *do* like to meddle outside of your territory. Isn't that my mother's necklace you're wearing now?" Lucca is glowering at the dragon so hard I'm afraid laser beams are going to shoot out from his eyes. I had totally forgotten that Larsson asked Vivienne to steal that necklace from Lucca.

Returning Lucca's death glare, Larsson leans forward. "And it's because of this necklace that I'm going to give your insolence a pass."

"Could you stop with the testosterone contest for a second and focus on the problem at hand?" Cheryl interrupts. "What exactly did that snake say?"

"He said the Accords didn't exist anymore and that Gus was the first casualty of many more to come," Jagger replies. "And that it was high time shifters united to purge the vampire plague from Salem."

Karl stands abruptly, pushing his chair back so hard it screeches against the wooden floor. "We need to find that son of a bitch right now and put an end to this madness."

"You can't do anything against Coyote. You're not part of the pack anymore. If you kill him before Marcus has the chance, he will be disgraced," Cheryl retorts, but the fire in her brother's eyes doesn't extinguish.

"Does that rule apply to vampires killing that motherfucker?" I ask.

She pierces me with a satisfied glint in her eyes. "No. It does not."

At once, several ringtones fill the room. They come from my phone, Ronan's, and Lucca's. My thoughts immediately go to Aurora, but the text message is not from her. It's from Dean Davenport, the leader of the Red Guard. It says "call to arms" in capital letters and a location: downtown.

"We have to go." Ronan jumps from his chair, followed by Lucca and me.

"What is it?" Cheryl asks with round eyes.

"It's an urgent alert from the Red Guard. Coyote and your dragons must have already put in action their pitiful revolution," Lucca growls in Larsson's direction.

At once, all the shifters who were sitting in the area get out of their chairs, eyeballing our group with bad intentions. We're completely outnumbered and outgunned. Everyone here is packing some serious heat.

Larsson rises to his full height, which is a head taller than Lucca. "You'd better tread very carefully, boy. You don't want me to unleash my full wrath on you. You saw the damage one shifted dragon did." He surveys me for a second.

In true Lucca fashion, he takes a step forward, eyes glistening red, fangs bared. "I'm not afraid of you."

"You know what? Fuck you all. I'm out of here." Cheryl walks out the door before anyone can stop her.

Jagger makes a motion to follow but hesitates. He and Ronan exchange a glance that tells me they're not about to become best friends. Karl, on the other hand, does go after his sister. The wolf siblings have the right idea. We're wasting precious time dicking around.

"Hello? The text message said 'CALL TO ARMS,' not 'take your time,'" I pipe up.

Ronan pulls on Lucca's sleeve. "Come on, Luc. Saxon is right for once."

I flip him off right before I veer for the door, only to find it blocked by a bald dragon holding a rifle in a menacing manner. "Seriously, dude? What part of 'this is an urgent situation' didn't you understand?"

He snarls in response as his pupils turn into slits. *Fucking lizards with wings.*

"Let them through, Eddie," Larsson orders. "We're coming too."

37

AURORA

———✦———

It's done. I'm officially no longer Isadora Leal's daughter or next in line to become the High Witch. I thought I'd feel more devastated, but in reality, I'm partially relieved. Not being a member of the New Salem Coven any longer is freeing. Besides, I can continue learning on my own. There are other sources of knowledge besides the Council of Witches' library.

The only loose end now is Elena Montenegro. I'd thought there would be bigger consequences to doing the opposite of what I vowed to, but maybe when Ryker removed the repel spell, he also removed the hold Elena had on me.

I don't call Saxon until I put some distance between myself and the High Witch—that's how I'll refer to the woman who birthed me from now on. I also wanted to calm my nerves first. At a red traffic light, I reach for my cell phone to send him a message. If he's still meeting with Larsson, I can swing by. Call it mated female protectiveness, but I'll feel better if I'm around. He can so easily get into trouble. I wouldn't be so worried if he had been one hundred percent recovered, though. I'm not a helicopter girlfriend.

Girlfriend. The word is strange even in my head. We're more than that. We're mated, which, according to vampire standards, is like being married. The feminist in me should rebel against the idea, but she too has fallen madly in love with the cocky vampire.

My fingers hover over the digital keyboard, frozen. I didn't make the conscious decision to pause like that. When my hand drops the phone on my lap, and grips the steering wheel tightly on its own, alarm bells sound in my head.

What the fuck is going on?

My foot presses on the gas pedal, and the car peels off without me willing it so, making an illegal U-turn. My body is moving of its own accord. That's not right. Someone is controlling me as if I were a marionette. It's Elena, I'm sure of it. She must be using the blood vow to do it.

My heart races as I try in vain to force my limbs to obey my command, but nothing I do seems to work. I can't even recite out loud any type of spell. The only things I seem to be in control of are my thoughts. *Damn everything to hell! Where is she taking me?*

I'm shaking nonstop, and my pulse is spiraling out of control. My hold on the steering wheel is slippery thanks to my clammy hands. The drive takes fifteen minutes, more or less, but the nightmare is only about to start. I park my car in the exact spot I did yesterday when the bond led me to Saxon. I'm in dragon shifter territory again. But why?

I get out of the car and head straight into the woods. My pulse is drumming so fast and loud in my ears that it's all I can hear.

The forest is eerily quiet, and in my experience, when animals don't make a peep, it means they're afraid of a bigger threat.

I'm not surprised when I wind up in the same clearing where the clash between the vampires and dragons took place. Elena is waiting for me, no longer stooped over her cane, but standing tall and proud. Her white hair hangs loose, reaching her waist and contrasting with her midnight gown. Her lips are painted red, and when she smiles at me, it looks like a slash on her gaunt face.

She's still keeping my mouth shut, so all I can do is glare at her. She forces me to stop a foot away from her, right on the other side of a dark spot on the grass.

"Isn't tonight a lovely evening, Aurora? A perfect time for a celebration," she says.

Fuck you, bitch!

She chuckles, shaking her head. "Ah, I can only imagine the petty names you must be calling me. It's amusing really when I'm the one who should, by rights, be angry. You tried to screw me over, after all."

Damn, I wish I had the power to stun her with my eyes.

"What? You didn't think I wouldn't know that you were fucking around with that Blueblood? I don't know how you managed to circumvent the preventive spell I placed on you, but it matters not anymore."

Her hateful stare drifts to a point behind me. I can't turn, but I can hear footsteps crunching the grass, getting closer.

"Ah, my second guest has arrived."

When Calvin appears in my line of vision, my anxiety spikes through the roof. He doesn't seem to be here against his will.

"Did you bring the grimoire?" she asks him.

"Yes. I've got it." He looks at me with so much hatred that it feels like a punch to my chest.

My adrenaline is rising to dangerous levels, which makes it harder to breathe. The shakes racking my body are impossible to hide. Elena, Calvin, and the first grimoire. This can't end well for me. I can't even scream for help.

"Good," Elena says. "Just set it on the ground."

"Wait. You said that there was a spell in here that would make Aurora and her bloodsucking lover pay for what they did to me."

"Yes, patience, boy. First, we must finish what we started."

"What the h—"

He freezes mid-sentence after Elena throws a sparkling powder over him. He can't move a muscle besides his eyeballs, which are twitching frantically, alternating between looking at me and her.

Suddenly, I sense the power keeping my mouth shut release. "What the hell are you doing?"

"Isn't it obvious, dear Aurora? You know what I want, and unfortunately, I still need you to get it for me. When this fool here burst into the council headquarters yesterday, filled with rage and jealousy, it was easy enough to convince him to bring me the grimoire. He's dead set on making you and your Blueblood pay."

She bends over, reaching inside a large bag she has by her feet.

"What are you going to do? You can't force me to marry him."

She smiles slyly, waving a fresh vine in her hands. "Oh my dear, but I can."

Walking without any difficulty, she ties one end of the vine around my left wrist then does the same around Calvin's.

"What's this?"

"This vine represents your union. Now, the sacrifice."

She cuts me right above the knot, deep enough that immediately, droplets of blood soak the vine. Her blade strikes Calvin too, and at once, I begin to feel the tangles of earthly magic wrap around me. My stomach twists savagely, making me so sick that I'd be puking my guts out right now if Elena weren't controlling my body.

She turns her face skyward, lifting both arms above her head, and begins to chant. "Ancient gods of the Earth, hear now my prayer."

"No! I refute this vow! You c—"

With a flick of her wrist, she cuts off my ability to speak.

"In this midnight hour, I call upon the ancient powers of the moon, of the stars, of the earth, of the wind. With these sacred vines, I bind these souls through the sacrifice of spilled blood. Body to body. Spirit to spirit. Heart to heart. So must it be."

The most excruciating pain pierces through my chest. I can't feel my legs anymore, and I know the only reason I'm still standing upright is because of Elena. A scream of despair rises up in my throat, but it gets lodged there, choking me. It feels like I'm dying.

I search deep inside of me for the bond, fearing the worst. *What if Elena broke it somehow?* There's a small flicker. I can still sense Saxon, but it's not as potent as it used to be. I route all my strength to it, hoping I can reach him before Elena unleashes doom all over Salem.

Saxon, my love. I need you.

SAXON

When we reach downtown, chaos is already reigning supreme. Some buildings are in flames. There are people on the streets running around like headless chickens as they try to get away from the rioters responsible for the mess. Through the noise of shouts, breaking glass, and crackling fire, I also pick up wolves howling in the distance. I can't tell if those shifters are from Marcus's pack or Coyote's.

Karl and Cheryl quickly disappear in the dark smoke, heading in the direction of the wolves. At least there aren't any shifted dragons—*yet*. But Lucca, Ronan, and I are more concerned with finding Jacques or any of his sycophants in the crowd. It's clear that he's behind this, and knowing how the motherfucker operates, he's somewhere nearby. It's not his MO to simply stay away. That's more in line with Tatiana's style to just sit on her ass and watch the destruction from afar.

It doesn't take long for my nose to pick up the stench of the enemy even through the smoke. They have a distinct rotten smell that's impossible to miss. Killing so many innocent people throughout the centuries does that to vampires. I was lucky that I saw the light before I turned into one of those monsters.

I unsheathe my katana and glance at my friends. "Do you smell that?"

"Yes," Lucca growls. "Those bastards are near."

We break into a run, going east on Essex Street until we reach the Hawthorne Hotel where we find the bloodiest part of the fight. Immediately I spot King Raphael fighting like the beast he is. He swings his sword in a powerful arc and decapitates a bloodsucker who was dumb enough to face off against the king.

We don't pause as we join the fight. There are more than our enemies here. We also have to deal with dragons and their fucking guns, firing willy-nilly. King Raphael and his guards are all wearing bulletproof vests, just like we are. We can't die of a bullet wound, but it will slow us down, which can be fatal.

"Don't kill any of the dragons!" Ronan shouts over the cacophony.

"Are you crazy? They have assault weapons," I argue, swinging my katana when a regular vampire tries to stick me with his pitiful blade.

His head rolls off his neck in a shower of blood. It gets in my eyes, and now I'm seriously pissed.

"What took you guys so long?" Manu asks, joining us from the left.

"Why are you here?" Lucca asks.

"The alert message was sent to everyone, asshole."

She twirls around in time to knock off a gun from a short dragon shifter who came too near. To finish him off, she hits him on the side of the head with the hilt of her sword. He drops down, unconscious.

We find our rhythm, fighting side by side and carving a path through the enemy. This reminds me of the good old days, and despite the destruction and number of lives lost, it infuses me with a new sense of purpose. Finally, the bullshit treaty King Raphael signed has ended.

We manage to get near the king and his inner circle. Lucca asks him if he has seen Jacques, but the answer is no. *Son of a bitch.* Could it possibly be that he decided to sit this one out? Maybe his self-preservation instinct spoke louder than his thirst for blood.

"Saxon, watch out!" Manu screams.

I pivot on the spot, the bullet aimed at my head missing by an inch. *What the fuck!* Seeing red, I search for the motherfucker who tried to blow my brains out. I find him six feet from me. With fangs bared, I prepare to break into a run, but Ronan grabs my arm, keeping me in place.

"You go after that shifter, he's dead. We can't have that."

"Fuck that shit. He tried to kill me!"

A roar as loud as thunder makes me pause. *Fuck.* Did one of those dragons shift? A moment later, Larsson appears, still in his human form, but displaying a raw fury that shows he means business. At once, all the dragon shifters in the area lower their weapons. As for Jacques's followers, the few who survived have run away. It seems the conflict ended as quickly as it began. I can't help the feeling of disappointment. Not only did I not use all my pent-up aggression, but the vile creature we wanted was nowhere to be seen.

I'm about to lower my katana when the small hairs on the back of my neck stand on end. I turn around expecting to find the enemy, but all I see are Red Guard soldiers and the king in the center. His head is dipped low, and he doesn't seem to be breathing. Suddenly, his spine becomes taut a second before he whirls where he stands, sword raised in an aggressive stance. His eyes are bright red, and his face is twisted in blind rage. That look … it brings horrible memories to the surface. My father looked exactly like that when he killed my sister Kari.

I'm paralyzed, trapped between the past and the present. I don't react when the king lets out a roar and aims that sharp blade at my neck.

"No!" Lucca yells, body slamming his uncle before he can bring the sword down.

They fall hard on the asphalt, rolling with the impact. Lucca jumps back to his feet, his eyes wide as he stares at our king. The Red Guard is on high alert, unsure of what just happened. Their weapons are at the ready, though.

"Uncle?" Lucca asks.

Groaning, the king leans on his left forearm, pressing the heel of his right palm to his forehead. "What the hell just happened?"

"You attacked Saxon."

He seeks my gaze, confusion and regret showing in his back-to-normal dark brown eyes. "I don't remember doing that."

Lucca's face twists into a grimace as our eyes lock. He must be thinking the same thing I am, that his uncle had a momentarily lapse in his mental faculties. The malady that has been plaguing first-generation Bluebloods has finally touched the king. I pass a hand over my face, consumed with worry and doubt. What the hell are we going to do when he loses his mind for good? Will Lucca be forced to kill him?

The king gets back on his feet, then walks over. "I'm so sorry, son."

"I know."

I'm about to add one of my trademark sarcastic comments when a sharp tug in my chest robs me of words. I press a closed fist against it, not knowing where that feeling comes from, when Aurora's words sound in my head.

"Saxon, what's the matter?" Manu asks.

"It's Aurora. She's in danger. I have to go."

Without wasting another second, I take off, heading toward the place I almost lost my life a night ago.

Hang on, Aurora. I'm coming.

38

AURORA

Smiling with glee, Elena walks toward the grimoire. She picks it up with reverence, stroking the cover as if it were a treasure. Her demented stare reminds me of Gollum as he patted his precious.

"Ah, yes. Finally, after all these years, you're mine."

"You … stupid … old hag." Calvin spits the words out with difficulty. The effect of the magical dust Elena used on him must be fading. "The grimoire … only serves … my family."

Her crimson lips break into a chilling smile. "Yes, and Aurora just became your wife. She's now family."

"Were you … working with … her?" Calvin stares at me.

"Tsk, tsk. She can't answer right now. You see, Aurora was so distraught when your engagement was announced that she fell right into my trap. We're linked through a blood vow, and thus, the grimoire will work for me."

Calvin starts to laugh like a deranged person. "Go … ahead.

Try to use it."

Frowning, Elena opens the tome. Her eyes widen, and she begins to flip the pages in a manic manner. "No. No! That's impossible. I should be able to see the words."

"Who do you ... take we Belmonts for? Idiots? A blood ... vow is not enough to ... allow non-family ... access."

Elena whips her face to his, leveling a glare at him. But then she switches her attention to me, and once again, a wicked grin blossoms on her hateful face. "That's okay. I only need the grimoire for one spell. If I can't perform it, I'll just have to play puppet master for a little longer."

I take a step forward, and another. Once again, Elena is compelling my body to do her bidding.

"That's ... impossible. A blood vow ... doesn't give ... you that much ... power over someone," Calvin protests.

Wait. How does he know? Until I met Elena, I had no idea what type of things a blood vow did to a person.

"Normally it doesn't. But let's say I gave my deal with Aurora an extra punch." The bitch chuckles.

Fucker. If I had use of my arms, I'd punch her in the throat. All I can do is glower until my eyes practically pop out of my skull.

She shoves the grimoire into my hands, and commands, "Find me Ashmedai."

My tongue becomes operational again, but I discover that freedom of speech is not in my cards right now. The only word that leaves my mouth is the name she told me.

The pages begin to flicker on their own, until they stop at a chapter titled "How to Summon Ashmedai." There's a picture of a dark, towering demon with spiraling horns, orange eyes, and an expression of pure evil. Merely staring at it makes my heart shrivel with panic and darkness. There's another drawing on the page at the bottom. A pentagram, and in the middle, the same symbol I saw Elena worshipping in her apartment. Looking closely, it seems to be a logographic alphabet of unknown origin.

"What does it say?" she asks eagerly, peering at the page.

I feel a bitter satisfaction that she can't see anything, but it's eclipsed by what she's making me do now that I'm officially a Belmont. The thought makes me sick. *Don't think about that right now, Aurora.* I don't want to answer her question, but naturally, my will is worthless at the moment.

"We need to draw Ashmedai's symbol on unhallowed ground," I say.

"Yes, yes. That part he told me." She bobs her white head up and down.

"How?" I manage to sneak the question in. She must have slackened her hold on me.

"In a vision. Ashmedai has been communicating with me for decades. I'm his bride," she replies with the air of someone who is seriously enamored.

"You want to marry this?" I point at Ashmedai's picture.

She squints while her lips become nothing but a thin line. "I can't see what you're pointing at. Get to work."

"Wait, you want me to draw the pentagram?"

I'll keep asking as many stupid questions as she allows me. I have to buy time in the hopes that Saxon heard my call.

"I know what you're doing. Stop wasting time. No one is coming to save you, darling. Didn't you know? Salem is burning." She cackles like the villain she is.

"What do you mean Salem is burning?"

She snaps her fingers, pointing them to a dark spot close to her. "That's the spot the dragon shifter perished last night. He was killed in cold blood. That's the unhallowed ground you need."

Like a robot that has been programmed, I find a can of white spray paint in Elena's bag. She has removed my ability to speak again, so I perform my task in silence. Once the pentagram and Ashmedai's symbol are drawn, I read the rest of the spell. A sacrifice must be made. This can only mean one thing.

Gripped by terror, I whirl toward Calvin. She's going to kill one of us, and since she needs me to read the grimoire, that means he's the victim.

He seems to realize that too. His eyes are as round as saucers and he's sweating profusely as he watches Elena pull an athame from her bag and then drag Calvin to the center of the pentagram.

"Let me go, witch!"

"Shhh, handsome. This will be over soon."

She glances at me. "What are you waiting for? Write down that chant. Ashmedai only serves the one who summons him."

My hands are shaking as I find a piece of paper and pen in her bag to write down the demonic spell. The tremors are my own reaction to what's about to go down. *Does it mean her control over me is weakening?* I try to stop the pen from moving, but the words keep forming on the blank paper. The spell is short, and I'm done copying it in less than a minute.

"Hurry up. I've waited long enough to meet my groom in person," Elena pipes up.

I hand over the spell, making the mistake of looking into Calvin's eyes. They're bloodshot and filled with raw fear. I hated him for being such a jackass, but I never wished this ending for him. I want to say I'm sorry that I'm not strong enough to save him, but the apology gets stuck in my throat.

She makes me walk backward until I'm out of the pentagram, then she forces Calvin on his knees.

"Please, don't kill me. I'll do anything you want," he begs.

She bends over to whisper in his ear. "There's only one thing I want, and you're helping me get it."

Faster than a snake, she pulls his head back, exposing his throat. The slash comes swiftly, and I would have cried out if I could. Calvin begins to choke as blood spills freely from the cut on his neck. Elena smears her face with his blood and begins to recite out loud the spell I wrote down for her.

My knees buckle, and I fall to the ground in a heap. Tears roll down my cheeks as remorse sweeps over me. Calvin is dead and it's my fault. If I hadn't been so quick to agree to the blood vow, Elena would have never gotten her hands on the first grimoire.

The wind changes, picking up speed. Goose bumps break out on my arms as a sinister presence, wet and fouled by darkness, approaches. An oily shadow rubs against my skin, then spreads like a stain in the fabric of air, circling around Elena.

"Yes, oh great Ashmedai. You're here at last." She raises her skinny arms to the sky, letting go of Calvin, who plops forward lifelessly.

Lightning strikes the midnight canvas, followed by the loud rumble of thunder. The shadow begins to move faster around Elena, becoming a blur before finally zapping into Calvin's body. At once, I feel the bindings of the blood vow vanish. I can move my arms and legs. I can speak.

"What have you done?" I ask.

Elena ignores me. She's too busy staring at Calvin's body. I follow her line of vision, not understanding what's happening. Then, Calvin twitches, making me gasp.

Oh, no. That's why the summoning spell required a human sacrifice. Ashmedai can only manifest in this dimension by using a body as a vessel. Slowly, Calvin staggers back to his feet. The gash on his neck is sealed shut, but I know the real Calvin is truly gone. He glances in my direction, and it feels like he's sucking out all the joy from me. Gone are the whites of his eyes. Two black orbs are in their place. He blinks, and they return to normal.

"You're here. I can't believe it," Elena mumbles, drawing the demon's attention to her.

I let out a breath of relief as the vise-like hold in my chest releases. I have to get the hell out of here.

"Yes, I'm here," he says in a smooth voice, different than Calvin's. "And you are?"

"I'm Elena Montenegro. Your bride."

I slowly get back on my feet, careful not to make a sound. But my heart is pounding so hard and fast, I'm sure the demon can hear it. Holding my breath, I take a step back, wincing when a sharp *crack* sounds as the branch I stepped on snaps. Ashmedai whips his head in my direction, raising his arm and freezing me.

"Where do you think you're going, pretty face?"

"Let me go. You're free. You don't need me anymore."

His lips twist into a perverse grin. "On the contrary, my dear. It seems we never had the chance to consummate our marriage. We can't have that."

"What?" I squeak, momentarily taken aback by his declaration.

"Oh, yes. My vessel had quite an unhealthy obsession with you. I can see it all, his memories, his deep desires. He hated you as much as he desired you."

"What about me?" Elena shrieks. "I'm the one who served you all these years. I freed you. You're my groom."

Ashmedai spares her a loathing glance. "You? This pile of sagging skin and bones? You're no bride of mine."

"I was once a beauty. You can restore my youth. You have that power."

"True." He turns to me. "But I like the young witch better."

Completely ignoring Elena, he walks toward me. Fear threatens to devour me whole, but I won't let this motherfucker touch a single hair strand of mine. He might have paralyzed my body, but he hasn't cut off my magic. I channel all my power into creating a protective barrier around me. Wisps of energy crackle in the air, creating little blue sparks.

The demon stops in his tracks, raising one arrogant eyebrow. "What's this? A protective shield?" He chuckles. "That's cute."

With a wave of his hand, he dissolves my spell. *Shit. Now what?*

My attention diverts to Elena, who has produced a long sword and is running toward us. I don't know if she wants to kill the demon or me. Ashmedai spins around just as the crazy bitch raises the weapon above her head, which she loses in the next second when the sword in her hand magically transfers to his. One swipe and sayonara, Elena.

I scream despite my feelings toward her. Did she deserve to die? Yes. But now I'm alone with the demonized version of Calvin. He's still keeping me frozen. I can't recite a spell; I'm at his mercy. He steps into my personal space, and my nostrils fill with the stench of sulfur and death.

"Now, where were we?" He grabs my chin roughly, lifting my face.

Despair and fear seep into my thoughts as the demon lowers his lips to mine. Freezing magic or not, I'm going to barf all over him. Then my heart skips a beat, lurching forward not out of panic but elation. Saxon is here. He came.

"Aurora!" he shouts, not far from where I stand.

The demon lets go of me to peer over my head.

"Ah, how providential. Your vampire lover is here. Good. I get to do what my vessel couldn't." He shoves me to the ground. "Get comfortable, wifey, and watch me tear your mate to shreds."

39

AURORA

Saxon becomes a blur on a collision path to Ashmedai. He doesn't know he's not facing Calvin, but a demon who has a sword hidden behind his back. I'm free from his hold, so I do the only thing I can. I hex Saxon before he gets within reach of the deadly blade. The blast is weak since I tapped into my powers not too long ago. It only sends him back a few feet.

I brace for the demon's retaliation, but all he does is stare at me, surprised. "Ah, wifey. You're defending me?"

"I'm nobody's wife, asshole."

Saxon shakes his head and then glances at me, confusion etched on his handsome face.

"That's not Calvin. That's a demon," I say.

Saxon unsheathes his katana, getting ready to face his adversary properly. "Even better. I love a good fight."

"There won't be much of a fight, I'm afraid. I just got hitched and you're keeping me from enjoying my bride."

Saxon peels his lips back, showing off his fangs. "The only thing you'll be enjoying is the bite of my blade as it slices you in two." He attacks, but Ashmedai simply sends him flying back with a flick of his wrist.

"Arrogant fool. I'm an archdemon, master of greed and wrath. No bloodsucker is a match for me."

No.

But one thing I know is that what can be summoned can be sent back. I search for the grimoire, finding it next to Elena's bag. I crawl toward it, not wanting to draw attention to myself. Through the bond, I tell Saxon to keep Ashmedai distracted while I perform the spell. I don't know if he can hear my thoughts, but I hope he gets an idea of what my plan is.

The sound of battle recommences, and it's an effort to not look back to see how Saxon is doing. But I have to reach the grimoire. When Saxon cries out in pain, I feel it deep in my bones. I stop and glance over my shoulder. He's clutching his right arm, but he's on his feet. Blood seeps through his fingers, though. *It's just a flesh wound, Aurora, just a flesh wound. You need to get the grimoire to help Saxon.*

I finally reach the old tome, bringing it onto my lap to frantically search for the summoning spell I used earlier. I remember I had to say the demon's name out loud, which I do in a whisper. The pages flip to the correct one, but a second later, the grimoire flies out of my hand into Ashmedai's grasp.

"Oh, no, darling. You're not sending me back."

I watch in horror as the grimoire bursts into flames, turning quickly into nothing but pieces of ember and ash floating on the wind.

"No!" The word escapes from my lips in a desperate plea.

With his eyes now completely black again, Ashmedai throws his head back and laughs. The sound is as unpleasant as nails scratching a blackboard. It makes me want to crawl out of my skin and die. *No. I won't let these soiled, dark thoughts spread like a disease in my mind.* He might have destroyed the grimoire, but he hasn't destroyed my will to survive.

Roaring as loud as I can, I transmute every ounce of power I have left in me into a ball of lightning. It shoots from my outstretched hand, hitting him straight in his chest. A huge burst of light follows, combined with Ashmedai's scream. But when the light fades, he's still standing in one piece, more enraged than before. As for me, my vision is speckled with black dots and my muscles are on the verge of giving out on me. I'm completely depleted.

"You'll pay for this, witch." The demon takes a step forward, but the sharp point of Saxon's katana pierces his thorax from behind.

"No, you'll pay for hurting my mate," he snarls.

The katana's tip disappears, leaving a growing stain in its place. Ashmedai laughs again, staring at the wound. "Do you think you can kill me, bloodsucker? I'm a fuck—"

He's unable to finish his tirade. Saxon's katana slashes through his neck as if it were made out of butter, severing his head in a precise cut.

Holy shit!

In the blink of an eye, Saxon is crouching next to me with his arm wrapped around my shoulder. "My love, are you okay?"

"Yeah, I'll be fine."

His hand is shaking when he cups my face and looks into my

eyes. "I'm so sorry. I got here as fast as I could."

"Don't apologize. All that matters is that you got here."

"I love you so much. I don't know what I'd have done if I had been too late."

My heart swells with emotion, and I'd like nothing more than to bask in the feeling, but the atmosphere changes around us. The cold wind picks up in speed, bringing a foul stench with it. We both turn to the headless body just in time to see a thick, dark smoke emerge from it. Ashmedai.

"Damn it. He's not dead?" Saxon asks.

"No. I don't think demons can be killed the same way vampires can. Come on, Sax. We need to get out of here."

He stands, pulling me with him. But the smoke is massive and quickly coming our way. *Shit. What if it possesses one of us?* Shouts in the distance halt its progress. It hovers close to us like an angry storm cloud. That is, if storm clouds felt as evil as the thing in front of us.

"This isn't over," the smoke says before zapping in the opposite direction of the small group approaching.

I let out a relieved sigh, melting into Saxon's body. I'm only standing upright because he's holding me. The small group coming near us is not who I'd expect to see coming to the rescue. The two warlocks from Ivern, Ryker and Declan, Solomon, Miranda, Rikkon, and my mother.

"What the hell happened?" Ryker is the first to ask, eyeballing the carnage.

"Elena got her hands on the first grimoire and summoned a demon called Ashmedai with it."

Ryker and Declan curse out loud and trade a troubled look.

Solomon walks over to the witch's corpse and whistles. "I guess she didn't get what she thought she would."

"The demon killed her soon after he possessed Calvin's body."

"And who had the brilliant idea of trying to kill a demon by decapitating the host?" My mother glares at Saxon.

"That fucker was about to kill us both. I have no regrets," he spits back.

"Calvin was already dead when Ashmedai took control of his body," I add.

"The council will never believe you're telling the truth," she retorts. "Not after Calvin officially complained about you and your vampire lover."

"The spell for the demon's summoning is proof of that," I argue, immediately remembering that won't help me. *Damn it.*

"And where is the grimoire?" She searches the ground, wrinkling her nose as she scans past Elena's body.

"Ashmedai burned it."

She snorts. "How convenient."

"With all due respect, ma'am, we have bigger problems than your personal issues with your daughter's relationship. An archdemon is on the loose. He can possess anyone," Declan chimes in.

"Anyone? Not only his sacrifice?" My voice comes out a little high-pitched, but who can blame me?

"Summoned demons only possess the corpse of the person sacrificed for a short period of time while they gain strength."

"Son of a bitch. How do we stop it?" Saxon asks.

"We have to figure out what the demon wants," Ryker replies.

"Elena has been worshipping him for decades. She claimed to

be his bride. I know it's not much, but maybe there are clues in her apartment," I say.

Ryker and Declan both stare at me with interest.

"Actually, that's a great place to start," Ryker replies.

"He wants the Taluah Mirror," Rikkon says quietly. His eyes are a little glazed, almost as if he's in a trance.

"How do you know that?" the worst mother of the year asks.

"Rikkon has visions. It's how we knew where to find Aurora," Miranda replies.

The guy winces, pressing a closed fist against his forehead. "It's happening again. I see the demon now. He's found a new host."

With a jerky movement, he whips his head back, staring at us wide-eyed. "It's Niko."

"No," my mother mutters.

My stomach bottoms out while my body turns into stone. I'm caught between wanting to cry and scream.

"Are you sure, Rik?" Miranda pulls on his sleeve, forcing him to look at her.

"Yeah."

Saxon squeezes my shoulder, his silent way to say he's got me. "We'll find him and save Niko."

"You're no match for a demon," Declan snorts. "This is warlock business now."

"Hell to the fucking no," I shout. "My sister is in danger and you're not going to keep me, or my mate, from getting her back."

"Aurora is right," my mother says, surprising me. "You're not doing this alone. Niko's life is on the line, and I know very well you don't care one ounce about killing a child in order to collect your big prize."

"You'll only be a hindrance," Ryker argues.

"Oh shut up, you pompous dickwads," Solomon butts in. "You've done nothing but sit on your asses and let Aurora fend for herself. Now quit bitching and use your magic for something useful like getting us to Conservatorium Hotel right the fucking now."

Miranda stares at me, mouth agape and eyes a little rounder. She has never had the full Solomon experience. Our shared moment only lasts a few seconds. Declan and Ryker immediately get to work. No one escapes unscathed from the headmaster's tongue-lashing, not even uber powerful and immortal warlocks.

40

SAXON

I land in the middle of the luxurious hotel lobby alone. Aurora was right next to me before we left, but now, she's gone. My head is buzzing like there are hundreds of bees inside my skull. I'm beginning to hate warlock magic.

"Saxon?" she calls from somewhere down the lobby.

I run toward her, mindful to keep my speed down to human level. She turns the corner, almost crashing into me. Things in the clearing happened so fast, I didn't have the chance to properly look at her. There's a cut on her left forearm that stopped bleeding a while ago, but it fills my chest with anger aimed at those responsible and at myself. I should have sensed she was in danger sooner.

My protective instinct dials up to the max. I pull her into my arms, squeezing her tight. "Where were you?"

"Near the elevators." She steps back, gazing up. "We can't let the warlocks harm Niko, Sax."

"They won't. I promise."

"There you two are." Miranda walks over with Rikkon by her side.

Aurora and I pull apart, but while her gaze is trained on her sister, I'm scrutinizing Vivienne's brother. He seems different. It takes me a moment to realize what's wrong. He no longer feels like a vampire.

"Dude, your disguise is gone."

"Shit. You're right," Aurora murmurs.

His forehead crinkles. "I'm sorry. I didn't realize it. I've been having one vision after another. It's been hard to keep track of my surroundings."

Miranda presses a hand to his back, a move that feels intimate. *Ah, fucking hell.* I knew I shouldn't have trusted him to stay away from Aurora's sister.

"It's okay, Rik. I didn't notice either," she says, looking positively infatuated with Mr. Pretty Face.

"And I forgot my potion." Guilt makes him look like a lost puppy in need of rescue.

Squinting, Aurora points at the duo. "I don't know what's going on here, but you'd better get Rikkon off the streets. I don't have time to worry about his cover getting blown."

"What about Niko?" Miranda asks.

"We'll bring her back, Mir. I promise."

Looking dejected, Miranda hooks her arm with Rikkon's and steers him toward the hotel's exit.

"Don't worry about them, Rora. When this is all over, I'll set Rikkon straight."

She shakes her head. "No, it isn't fair. If there's something going on between them, who says they can't be together?"

"Uh … the law. Is your sister even legal?"

Yeah, I'm being protective. I can't help it. I failed Kari; I won't fail Aurora's sisters. They're my family now.

A deep V marks her forehead while she watches me with narrowed eyes. But I don't get to ask what she's thinking. The asshole warlocks join us and get our full attention.

"Where the hell were you? And why didn't you take us all the way to Elena's apartment?" Aurora yells at them.

"There are strong wards that prevented us from entering," Ryker retorts.

"Where are Solomon and the High Witch?" I peer over their shoulders, but aside from us and the curious hotel night staff, the place is empty.

"Right behind you," Solomon replies in his trademark grumpy voice. "Somehow, Isadora and I wound up all the way in the hotel's pool area. Go figure." He watches the warlocks suspiciously.

"What's the plan? Head to the dead witch's lair and wait for Ashmedai to come?" I ask.

"If what the Nightingale prince said is true, we need the Taluah Mirror to lure the demon into a trap."

Fuck. Rikkon's disguise has been gone for a while if the warlocks know what he is. If he's compromised, so is Vivienne. Lucca won't be happy about that.

"That's the most moronic idea I've heard tonight. Just set the trap in the mirror's current location. The demon knows it's in Elena's apartment. If you move it, he'll be expecting a trap," Solomon pipes up.

Damn. Solomon is fun to hang out with when he's doling out insults to other people instead of me.

"We're wasting time here, and I'm not convinced it wasn't on purpose," the High Witch snaps, watching the two warlocks like a hawk.

Yeah, I'm beginning to believe we might not have the same end goal here. Solomon and the High Witch head for the elevator. I let the duo follow close behind them, while I hold Aurora back.

"We need to keep an eye on those two," I tell her.

"Agreed. Their purpose in life is to hunt down demons. They won't hesitate to kill Niko if it means catching Ashmedai."

"We need a plan in case they go rogue on us."

"Each warlock carries an athame powered by a special jeweled stone that grants them the ability to kill demons or send them back to hell. If they try to kill Niko to get to Ashmedai, I need that weapon."

I nod. "You got it, babe." Aurora's eyes narrow, and quickly, I realize my error. "Sorry, I forgot."

"Come on. They'll leave without us."

"Let them. We'll take the stairs. It's faster."

"For you maybe, but—"

"Jump on, love. I'll get us there in the blink of an eye."

She grimaces but does as I ask. Even though we're in the middle of a crisis, the feel of her body pressed against my back awakens the beast. My cock twitches in my pants, proving that it definitely operates apart from my brain.

"Ready?" I ask in a voice tight with need.

"Yeah. If you drop me, you're dead."

"Woman, I take serious offense to what you just said." Before I take off, I glance at the rest of our party about to enter the elevator. "See you up there."

I don't run as fast as I can, afraid that Aurora might get sick. We make it to the top floor faster than any elevator could, though. I'm about to push the door to the hallway open when Aurora pinches my shoulders.

"Sax, wait. Can't you feel it?"

"Feel what?"

"This awful sensation that something terribly evil awaits us on the other side of this door."

I let her down, and with the loss of the contact between our bodies, it makes it easier for me to home in my senses on our surroundings. Cold dread licks the back of my neck, giving me goose bumps. At the same time, depressing thoughts sneak into my mind, bringing forth images from my past I wish to forget.

I gasp when Kari's mangled body appears in front of me like a scene from a horror movie.

"What's wrong?" Aurora steps in front of me, watching me with round eyes.

"It's … I do feel the wrongness in the air now. Let me go first."

With my katana at the ready and my body wound tight, I push the heavy metal door open, getting blasted immediately by the stench of rotten eggs. Other than the smell and the feeling of doom hanging in the air, nothing looks amiss. I step into the hallway carefully, and only when I deem it safe enough, I let Aurora through.

"Elena's penthouse is to the right."

"Okay, stay behind me."

The closer we get to it, the stronger the stink becomes. But confirmation that Ashmedai has beaten us to the place awaits us when we find her apartment door ajar. *How in the world did the demon get here so quickly?* Aurora makes a motion to enter, but I stop her.

"We should wait for the others."

"But Niko…"

"I know, my love. But we've confirmed my katana is useless against Ashmedai and you haven't recovered your strength yet."

It pains me to wait, but my need to protect Aurora is the most important thing right now. For once, I don't act recklessly like I normally do.

The *ping* of the elevator cuts through the silence. Declan and Ryker step out first with their special weapons in their hands. They're no bigger than daggers.

"Are you planning to fight a demon with that?" I eyeball their tiny blades.

"Don't underestimate something because of its size," Ryker sneers.

"Ashmedai is definitely inside," Declan redirects. "We're going in, but you'd better stay out here."

"Absolutely not," Aurora and her mother reply at the same time.

There's a shared, uncomfortable glance between them, but it breaks when Solomon opens his big mouth. "Quit trying to get rid of us."

"Fine. But let us handle Ashmedai."

"You may handle the demon once he's out of my daughter's body," the High Witch grits out, then flicks her wrist, pushing the two asshats out of her way.

She gives Aurora a crystal similar in size to the one she's holding. Both are big enough that they could break someone's skull if used as a weapon. There aren't words exchanged, but I know the gesture was a big deal. Aurora frowns, and through the bond, I pick up her turmoil.

Not knowing what else to do, I brush the back of her wrist with my fingers to let her know I'm here for her. I wish I could do more, but until we save Niko, this is the best I can do.

Declan and Ryker follow right behind the High Witch, and we stay glued to their tails. Since I can't fight the demon, I'm making it my mission to ensure those two pricks behave. If they step one toe out of line, if I so much as suspect they intend to hurt Niko, I won't hesitate to cut them in half.

"Where is the mirror?" Declan asks Aurora in a whisper.

"Down the hallway."

"Dude, just use your nose and follow the stench," I hiss.

He shoots me a scowl, which I sling right back at him.

The apartment is quiet, when suddenly, I hear low chanting in a young woman's voice coming from ahead. *Fuck.* That's Niko. Aurora shows no indication that she's heard it, though.

"Can anyone hear that?" I ask as low as I can.

"Hear what?" Ryker asks.

"The chanting."

The warlocks trade a glance, then without ceremony, they push the High Witch out of their path and dash ahead.

"What the hell," Aurora retorts, immediately motioning to follow. She only takes a couple of steps forward before she halts suddenly.

"What's the matter?" I ask.

"They hexed us!" the High Witch replies.

"Of course they did. I should have known they'd pull something shady like that," Solomon grumbles, patting the pockets of his jacket as if he's looking for something.

A moment later, there's a cry that's definitely not from Ashmedai. It's Niko.

"They're going to kill my sister!" Aurora tries to use her crystal to free herself.

They're all frozen, but when I try to move, I discover that I can. "Son of a bitch. They forgot about me." I take off after them, but when I enter the room where the infamous Taluah Mirror is, I find the two warlocks on the floor, unmoving. I don't have time to check if they're alive. I grab one of their small athames and tuck it into my pants, hiding it under my jacket. I don't want the demon to know I have it.

Aurora's younger sister stands in front of the mirror, which has turned into a portal to hell if I were to guess by the towering inferno on the other side. She turns around, looking as innocent as can be, besides a couple of details: the freakish all-black eyes and the stench of death emanating from her.

"Hello, Saxon. I was hoping you would show up. You're exactly what I need to finish my little spell."

She raises her hand, and at once, it feels like my throat has been gripped by a deadly invisible force. I'm lifted from the ground, then dragged toward the demon. She forces me down on my knees, facing the mirror. The image of the raging fire changes to a scene much more gruesome. Kari's murder.

I try to shut my eyes, but I can't. The demon forces me to watch the whole thing again. First the violent beating, then my father shredding Kari's body into pieces with his bare hands as my mother and I were forced to watch. I should have tried to stop him, but I was too afraid. My cowardice is my biggest sin, and even after I killed my father, I wasn't absolved of my guilt.

"Your sister got what she deserved. She was such a whore," a familiar voice says.

I jump to my feet, not questioning why I can move freely all of a sudden. My father is standing in front of me in flesh and blood.

I shake my head, disbelieving. "No. I killed you."

"Did you?" He raises an eyebrow. "Then why am I here talking to you?"

I stagger back, even when my vision is already tinged in red and my desire to avenge Kari all over again is bordering on bloodlust.

"You want to kill me, don't you? Go ahead, I want to see you try. You failed once, and you will fail again."

"No. This isn't happening. You're a trick, a figment of my imagination."

His face contorts in rage. He gets into my face in a split second. "Kill me now, Saxon. Prove to everyone you're nothing like me."

My hand holds the katana pummel tighter. I'm on the verge of snapping, of obeying the order to kill that's pounding in my brain, but deep down, I know what I'm seeing is not true. Ashmedai got into my head.

Instead of striking him with my katana, I cut his arm with the athame. It's only a superficial wound, but the demon steps back, letting out a roar. The image of my father morphs into Niko. She's clutching her arm while staring at me with her demonic eyes.

"Where did you get that weapon?" she hisses.

"I thought you knew everything." I smirk.

"It doesn't matter. The only way you can kill me with that is if you kill the host."

I freeze even though I knew all along that would be the case. It's probably the reason the demon decided to possess Aurora's little sister. But why would he try to trick me into killing her? It doesn't make any sense.

"Now, you interrupted me at the best part." She turns toward the mirror, which is once again showing hell. "Oh, I almost forgot. I do need to borrow something from you." She raises her arm, and my katana flies from my hand into hers.

"You see, as much as I like this host, I'd much rather have my own body back." She holds my sword with both hands, pointing it toward her stomach.

I fly like the wind, knocking the katana from her hand as I body-slam her into the mirror. Instead of crashing against the glass, I go through it. The most excruciating pain imaginable flares up everywhere as I roll over a rocky surface. My lungs immediately protest when I inhale toxic smoke.

It doesn't take long to realize where I am. I crossed into hell, and I brought the real Ashmedai with me.

41

AURORA

"Okay, I think I figured out what spell those bastards used on us." Solomon pulls a small twig from his pocket and flicks the object in the air as if it were a magical wand.

"What are you doing?" I ask.

"Warlock magic is not bound to the four elements like yours. I have to break it the old-fashioned way."

"Which is?" My mother raises an eyebrow.

"Using Nightingale magic, naturally."

"I didn't know you had that," I say.

He rolls his eyes. "Girl, where did you think my powers came from?"

"If those warlocks hurt Niko in any way, I'm going to make them pay, even if it's the last thing I do," Mom grits out.

"Nice to see that you care about someone in our family."

She flinches, which I didn't expect. "I care about you and

Miranda too. You're my daughters."

"Oh, am I your daughter now? Didn't you disown me only a few hours earlier? What made you change your mind?"

She glances away. "I … You wouldn't understand."

"Almost there," Solomon chimes in. "But do carry on. Pretend I'm not here or that there's a demon in the next room."

"No, Mother, I can't understand how you could turn your back on me. I told you Elena was evil, but you didn't believe me. You were too hung up on the fact I'm in love with a vampire."

"Got it!" Solomon interrupts again. "Thank fuck. I definitely didn't sign up to be in a *Dr. Phil* special."

Ignoring his jab, I sprint ahead, holding the crystal in my hand tight. Getting stuck thanks to the warlocks' hex served to give me time to restore my strength, and I need every bit of juice I can get. My heart is stuck in my throat when I burst into Elena's study just in time to see Saxon body-slam Niko and crash through the mirror, disappearing from view in a great explosion of bright orange light.

"No!"

I jump over the bodies of Ryker and Declan, not caring at the moment if they're alive or dead. When the light fades to a darker ochre shade, I find Niko's body sprawled in front of the mirror. Dropping to my knees, I pull her onto my lap, ignoring the warning in my head that Ashmedai could still be inside of her.

"Niko, wake up. Please." I touch her neck with trembling fingers, looking for a pulse. It's there, even if it's a little weak.

She blinks her eyes open, and it's another second before she focuses them on my face. "Rora? What happened?"

She sounds like my sister, and I don't sense any malevolent aura coming from her.

"You were possessed by a demon. You don't remember anything?"

Furrowing her eyebrows, she says, "No. The last thing I remember is going to bed."

Son of a bitch. He broke into our house despite the wards my mother keeps in place. But it's good that she doesn't remember her ordeal at his hands.

Groans and curses sound behind me. I look over my shoulder and see that Ryker and Declan are alive, both now sitting up and massaging their temples. Mom runs to us and steals Niko from my arms.

"Where's Saxon?" Solomon stares at the mirror, which does not show the room's reflection, but a barren landscape that can only be described as hellish. Dark terrain, jagged stones, smoke, fire, and lava are everywhere, but no sign of Saxon.

"I don't know. He crashed into the mirror and disappeared."

"That fucking demon turned the Taluah Mirror into a portal to hell," Ryker pipes up. "My guess is that he wanted to free his friends. Bring them here."

"You're hurt," Mom tells Niko.

I see then that she has a cut on her forearm, superficial at first glance. Then I see Saxon's sword lying not too far from her. She probably cut herself when she fell on top of the blade, but fuck, if Saxon somehow ended up in hell, he's weaponless.

"Where's my damn athame?" Ryker whines.

Facing the mirror again, I stretch my arm, but Solomon drags me back before I can touch the shimmering surface.

"What are you doing? Do you want to be dragged into hell too?"

"You don't expect me to simply stay here and not go after

Saxon. He's my mate!"

"You might not be able to come back."

"I have to try." Hot tears stream down my face.

Mom stands, pulling Niko with her. "You love the vampire that much?"

"Yes," I breathe out. "He's the love of my life."

Remorse seems to shine in her eyes. "I didn't realize you felt that way. I'm sorry."

I wipe my cheeks with the back of my hand. "Save your apologies. They're useless to me."

"If you're determined to rescue your mate, you'll only have one shot to return using that mirror." Declan walks over.

"What is it?"

"You must slay Ashmedai and use his blood to reopen the gate from your side."

"How am I going to kill him?"

"With this." He offers me his athame. "There's a cost to wielding this weapon to slay a demon, though."

"What do you mean?"

"To ignite the full potential of the Alton jewel, you must sacrifice something vital, something you don't know you want yet."

"My soul?" I stare at the small weapon in my hand.

"No, not your soul. It varies from person to person."

I take a deep breath. "That's it?"

"Yes," Declan replies.

"No, not yes," Solomon butts in, cutting a frown at the man. "You're forgetting an important detail." He turns to me. "Once you give what the jewel wants, you're bound to the creed."

"What do you mean?"

"The Alton jewel in each athame is linked to a matrix of energy. Its power is what makes it possible for us to do our job," Declan explains. "Once you're linked to the jewel, you're linked to the matrix."

"Is that bad?"

"You'll become a warlock, and your number one priority will be to hunt down demons," Solomon answers.

"No, Aurora. That's a terrible life," Mom chimes in.

"No, it isn't," Ryker snorts. "It's better than serving the king of a dying race."

There's nothing to think over. The decision is simple. I'll do whatever it takes to save Saxon, even if that requires going to the bowels of hell and losing something vital.

"Are you really going, Rora?" Niko asks in a small voice.

"Yes."

She leaves Mom's side to crash into my arms. I hug her tight, burying my face in her hair. "Take care of Miranda. You have to stick together."

"Don't talk like that. You're coming back."

"Yes, I will." I kiss her forehead, then I briefly glance at our mother.

I have nothing to say to her. Her apology came too late.

"You'll have to strike Ashmedai in his heart to kill him. Stay clear of his claws. They're deadly," Declan warns.

"Noted." I face the mirror, taking a deep, steadying breath before I step into it.

My skin prickles as if I'm being burned by ice, but when I'm through the portal, all I feel is unbearable heat. It's humid, and the fumes from the acrid smoke make me feel like I'm in a gas chamber.

I cover my face, coughing into my jacket, while keeping all my senses sharp. If this is hell, then there must be other demons besides Ashmedai.

My heart sinks when I look over my shoulder and there's nothing but darkness. The portal is shut. I need a marking to know where it was so I can reopen it, but there's no obvious landmark around here. It's hard to see anything. It's so dark and foggy, and the only source of illumination comes from the crevasses full of lava and towers of fire. I collect a few mid-sized rocks and build a small tower with them. It's the best marking I can come up with.

I'm tempted to call out to Saxon, but that would be a damn stupid move. I focus on our bond, hoping it wasn't severed when he landed here. I almost laugh in relief when I find it's stronger than ever, pulsing in sync with my heart.

The euphoria doesn't last long. I sense a second later that Saxon is in distress. I dash in his general direction, mindful of the perilous terrain. It won't do to fall into a lava pit while running like a fucking crazy person through hell. Death by stupidity is not how I want to go.

I tighten my hold on the athame, tapping into its strange power. Declan said that I must sacrifice something to the jewel encrusted in it, but he didn't say how I'm supposed to that. My hand tingles from its magic, so maybe the weapon is already searching for something I want and don't know yet. *You can take anything from me that's mine to give besides Saxon.*

My hand becomes warmer, almost to a point where it would burn, while a foreign power seeps into me, invasive and aggressive. My instinct is to let go of the athame, but I fight it. I can't fail now. Saxon needs me. The foreign force wraps around my heart, squeezing it in a barbed wire embrace. Then the image of a little girl with my eyes and Saxon's blond hair pops in my head. She smiles at me and comes running with her chubby arms open wide. But the image dissolves into dust a moment later, leaving me with the most terrible sense of loss. A sob lodges in my throat while I deal with the knowledge of what the athame took from me. My child with Saxon.

A cry of pain brings me back to the here and now, and just then the smog in front of me thins, revealing Saxon on his knees with the athame he stole from Ryker in his hand. Saxon has gashes on his forehead and arm, which are bleeding profusely. My heart twists savagely as fear spikes through my chest. I glance at Ashmedai, my mouth going dry in an instant. He's a giant with muscles capable of pulverizing anyone with a simple hit. Saxon is David and he's Goliath. There isn't a scratch on the demon's body. To me it's obvious he's been toying with Saxon until now.

I'm not sure if Saxon is aware that I'm here, and I don't want him getting distracted by my presence. I need to make an entrance, draw Ashmedai's attention. I wonder for a second if my magic works in this place, but then I decide against using it. Instead, I search the ground until I find a piece of rock that I can throw at the demon.

His tree-trunk-like legs flex, and thanks to the barkish appearance of his skin, he looks like a walking evil tree with the face of a rabid dog. He's much more terrifying in person, and he's about to charge toward Saxon.

I throw the rock with all my strength, hoping I don't miss his back. Hitting his head would give me more satisfaction, but it would also be harder. The demon staggers forward, then glances in my direction, eyes glowing orange-yellow rather than black.

"Wifey. You came for me." He smiles in a deranged manner,

showing his impressively sharp teeth. "This is going to be more pleasant than I expected."

Saxon locks his gaze with mine for one split second, which is enough to tell me I can expect a tongue-lashing from him later. He can be mad all he wants as long as he's alive. He doesn't waste the opportunity to attack our enemy while he's distracted by me, though. He breaks into a super-speed run, invisible to my human eyes. A second later, Ashmedai throws his head back to bellow out a roar, leaving his chest exposed.

I dash toward him, keeping the dagger concealed behind my back until the last second. Unfortunately, I don't possess the same supernatural speed as Saxon. By the time I'm near the demon, he's no longer distracted by his pain. He reaches for me with his claw-like hands to crush me like a bug, or worse. I duck out, missing his sharp talons by an inch, only to trip on the uneven ground and fall too close to him.

I still have the athame in my hand as I try to scramble back to my feet. I'm not fast enough, though, and Ashmedai grabs me by the ankle, dragging me toward him.

"Leave her alone!" Saxon slashes the demon's arm, only to be swatted away like a fly, disappearing in the dark fog.

"Saxon!" I cry out.

Ashmedai laughs, holding me upside down as if I were a rag doll. I'm too far from his chest to attempt a strike, and desperation is not my ally either.

No, I can't let it end like this. It's time to test if my magic works in this godforsaken place. I turn my attention inward, focusing on the power that resides in my core. At once, the spark flares to life, dissolving the fear a fraction. I'm not calm by any stretch of the

337

imagination, though. Mortal peril is something hard to ignore.

I don't dare use all my power in one spell. Instead, I transform my body into a conduit—much like the repel spell Elena put inside of me—and electrocute the demon. He lets go after a moment. I use my arms to protect my head, and then I hear a bone crack upon impact. The athame slips from my fingers as white-hot pain shoots up my arm, drawing a ragged scream from my throat.

Heavy steps approach slowly, and with them, the stench of evil. Without any weapon, all I have left is my magic. Trying to control my shallow breathing, I focus on creating the biggest ball of energy I can conjure out of thin air. It's not much—it's less than I would usually create under better circumstances—but it's all the hope I have left.

Ashmedai's dark shadow looms above me. He opens his mouth wide, exposing his teeth as he descends for the kill. I strike, illuminating the area with the brightest light any of the demons in the vicinity have seen in millennia. Ashmedai cries out, moving away. Deep satisfaction makes me forget the pain for a bit.

I roll onto my belly and crawl toward the athame. It's near; all I have to do is stretch my arm. My fingers brush against the handle, only to be crushed by Ashmedai's foot. As he breaks the bones in my hand, darkness takes over my vision for a moment. The pain is just too much.

Suddenly, the pressure is gone, and my eyesight returns to normal. Saxon is back, bloodied and covered in soot, but still fighting with everything he has. His eyes are bright red, his fangs longer than I've ever seen. No sign of the athame, though. He must have lost it.

Breathing through the pain, I extend my broken arm and grab

my weapon. There's no chance I'll be able to stab Ashmedai in my condition, but I can use the little bit of power I have to help Saxon finish the job.

I get to my knees, then slowly rise. Words pour out of my lips in a whisper, a simple spell. A gust of wind comes out of nowhere, shoving Ashmedai sideways. He peels his eyes away from Saxon for a second to glower at me. It's the opening I need. With the last bit of power left in me, I send the athame flying straight into Saxon's hand.

"The heart!" I yell just before my legs give out from under me.

Saxon leaps, burying the magical blade deep into the demon's chest. I expect a roar as loud as thunder, but no sound comes from Ashmedai. He's frozen like a statue. Cracks begin to spread through his body, slowly at first, then picking up speed as they take over every inch of his frame.

Saxon appears by my side, pulling me into his arms. I completely melt into him, relieved that our nightmare is almost over. Together, we watch our nemesis collapse on itself in a pile of dust, burying the athame with it.

"Are you okay, my love?" Saxon asks, but my mind is whirling, so I don't answer him right away.

Shit. There's no demon blood. How are we getting out of here?

42

SAXON

———✦———

Aurora keeps staring without blinking at the pile of dust that's left of Ashmedai, making me extremely worried.

"Rora?" I ask again. "What's wrong?"

With eyes as round as saucers, she looks at me. "Declan said that the only way to get out of this place was to use Ashmedai's blood. But where is the blood, Sax? There's nothing left but soot."

I open my mouth to reply when hissing and snarling sounds can be heard not too far from us. Ashmedai is gone, but this is hell. "Let's grab the athame and get out of here. We've got company."

Aurora looks over her shoulder, squinting as she tries to see the approaching danger. Quickly, I head over to Ashmedai's remains and dig our only weapon out. On instinct, I don't dust it off. It's not blood, but maybe the warlocks were wrong about that detail. I wouldn't be surprised.

"Come on, Rora. We have to leave."

"What if we can't open the portal again?" Her voice comes out as a squeak. She's panicking, and I can't have that.

I pull her to me, cupping her cheek. "We'll find a way out of here, my love. I promise."

She nods, her eyes hardening with determination. "Yes, we will."

When I step back, I see that her right hand has doubled in size, and her left arm is hanging limp by her side.

"You're hurt."

"I think I broke my arm when I fell, and Ashmedai crushed my hand under his foot."

Rage surges within me, making me wish I could kill the motherfucker again. I tuck the athame in my pants, and pick her up in my arms, careful not to jostle her too much.

"It's going to be all right, Rora."

She presses her face against my chest. "I love you, Sax."

"I love you too, Rora."

Running at my maximum speed in unfamiliar and perilous territory is not ideal, especially when I have no clue where to go. Everything looks the same here. I have to keep my speed down because one false step can be fatal to us.

"Turn left after that jagged cluster of rocks," Aurora tells me. "I remember running past it."

"Okay."

I don't hear the sound of pursuit, so I slow down. "Does this area look familiar to you?"

"It's hard to say for sure, but I think so. Let me down."

I do so as gently as I can.

"I marked the location of the portal with a pile of rocks," she says.

"Good thinking." I scan the area, and after a minute, I spot Aurora's marking. "There it is." I point ahead.

"I see nothing but gloom."

"I have other perks besides my enormous dick." I wink at her.

With a shake of her head, she says, "You're such a dork."

Still sporting a cheeky smile, I press my hand on her lower back, and steer her toward the rocks. I'd like to say I remember being here, but at the time, I was too busy fighting that fucking demon.

"Now what?" I ask.

"I don't know. Can I have the athame, please?"

"How are you going to hold it? Your arm and hand are broken, love."

Wincing, she raises her broken arm. "I can manage. It doesn't hurt as much anymore."

She's lying through her teeth, but she's too stubborn and won't relent.

"Fine. I'll pretend I believe you." I hand it over to her, pommel first. The green stone glows when Aurora touches it, and immediately, a bad feeling enters my chest.

"What was that?"

She locks her gaze with mine, and I don't like the sorrow shining in her eyes. "In order to use the athame, I had to bond with it. Its magic wouldn't have worked otherwise."

"But I was the one who killed the demon with it."

"I know. Maybe you were able to use it because we're mates."

"I don't like this at all, Rora. But let's figure out how to open the portal first."

"Yeah."

She turns to the right, shutting her eyes. The light on the stone burns brighter, creating a small halo around us. The outline of a crescent moon appears on Aurora's forehead, and when she opens her eyes again, they're glowing too. Tendrils of magic curl around her wrist, then spread up her arm, and the rest of her body. A small gasp escapes her lips, which makes my spine go rigid.

I'm about to pry the athame from her hand, but she turns to me and says, "I'm fine. The athame is healing me."

I drop my eyes to her broken hand, noticing that the swelling is decreasing. *Son of a bitch.* I'm fucking glad that the strange magic is taking Aurora's pain away, but at what cost?

When she seems to be completely healed, she raises the athame, holding it firmly in her hand, and then slashes the air in front of her while speaking words in a foreign language. Two glowing lines appear, forming an *X*. They turn into a mirror, and through it we can see the inside of Elena's apartment.

"You did it! You opened the portal."

"I guess Declan was wrong about the blood. Maybe Ashmedai's ashes were enough."

I step closer, finding Solomon and the High Witch standing on the other end, staring at us. I link my hand with Aurora's. "Are you ready?"

"Yes."

"On the count of three. One, two, three."

We both step forward, but instead of crossing to the other side, we hit an invisible wall.

"What the hell!" I frown at the mirror. "Why is it not working?"

"I don't know. Maybe I cast the spell wrong, or we did need his blood."

Solomon and the High Witch begin to speak at once, but we can't hear a word they're saying. What I can hear is the growling of something large and foul approaching. My muscles tense as I turn around in a defensive stance. A few yards away from us I spot a beast on four legs, running in our direction. *Damn it!* We're so close.

"Run, Rora!" I yell.

"No, I'm not going to let you fight that alone."

There's no time to argue. The monster is almost upon us. I'm ready to say my final words to her when something grabs my jacket and yanks me back. A terrible shock courses through my body, and then my back meets solid, smooth ground. My vision is blurry for a second, but when I can see properly again, I'm staring at a white ceiling.

"What the fuck!"

"That's what I should be saying." Solomon appears in my line of vision, his white hair sticking out and messier than normal. "Honestly, I'm sick of getting zapped because of you two."

"Rora!" I sit up at once.

"I'm here." She touches my arm with her fully healed hand.

I don't care that we have an audience, I pull her onto my lap and attack her mouth. I came too close to losing her tonight. I need the connection, to let her know how much I love her. She tilts her head to the side, deepening the kiss while her arms wrap around my neck. Nothing matters besides us and this glorious feeling of completion.

Somebody whistles nearby, then Ryker tells us to get a room. I don't want to break the kiss on anyone's account, but when the High Witch clears her throat, Aurora eases off.

"Are you two done?" she asks.

"Not by a long shot," I reply with a smile.

"That was hot," Niko says, staring at us like we're two lovers in a movie.

Okay, maybe it's best if we keep the PDA PG-13.

Aurora slips off my lap and together we get back onto our feet. She turns to Solomon. "What happened? How did you get us out of hell?"

"You can thank your mother for that. Isadora worked out the spell. We formed a magical cord that allowed me to step into hell and pull you two back."

Aurora switches her attention to her mother, not speaking for a moment. Her heart is conflicted—I can sense as much.

"What happens now?" I ask to break the tense moment.

The High Witch glances at me. "Now I explain to the council what happened."

"Are you going to tell them the truth or your version of the facts?" Aurora snaps.

The woman frowns, pinching her lips together. "I'm sorry I doubted you before. Believing Elena betrayed the coven meant everything I've done for them, every sacrifice I've made, was done for the wrong reasons. Elena was my mentor, Rora. And your grandmother's best friend."

"You never told me that."

She lowers her gaze. "I've been wrong keeping you and your sisters at arm's length."

"What's going to happen to Rora now that she's engaged to Saxon?" Niko butts in.

I choke on my saliva, which results in a coughing fit.

"We're not engaged, Niko," she replies, not glancing in my

direction.

"No. You're just married," Solomon snorts.

Aurora and I shoot him a glance.

"What?" He arches his eyebrows. "That's what being mated means."

I rub the back of my neck, feeling awkward as fuck now. It's not that I don't want to get married to her. I just never really gave it much thought. Traditional marriage ceremonies in my world are reserved only for royals.

Aurora walks over to Declan. "Here's your athame. Thanks."

"Oh, no. This is yours now. The Alton jewel has linked to your powers. It would be painful to sever the connection now."

"Does that mean that when I bonded with it, it hurt you?"

He lifts his shoulders in a resigned shrug. "It was a small price to pay. Think of it as a welcome gift to the creed."

"Say what?" I ask.

The warlocks and Aurora look at me, but it's Solomon who answers. "Aurora is a warlock now."

"What does that mean?"

"It means you'll have to cut your honeymoon short, lover boy. She needs to come to Scotland to initiate her training," Ryker answers.

"Training for what?"

"What do you think?" Declan raises an eyebrow.

"Are you a demon hunter now?" I meet her gaze.

"I guess so."

I pass a hand over my face, hating these new developments. My instinct is to say, *hell to the fucking no*, but she's my mate, not my property.

"Is that what you want, Rora?"

She glances at the warlock duo for a moment, then back at me. "To be honest, I don't know. But slaying demons and monsters sounds like an interesting career."

"And also dangerous as fuck. You almost died." I cross my arms, unable to control my frown.

"But she didn't," Ryker intervenes. "And with training, she'll be more prepared the next time."

"Saxon was the one who killed Ashmedai, not me," she chimes in.

Declan raises an eyebrow. "Is that so?"

"What does it all mean? If Aurora is a warlock now, who is going to be the next in line to become the High Witch?" Niko asks.

"Let's not worry about that now," her mother replies.

I'm still brooding when my skin begins to prickle, and a great sense of unease takes hold of me. "Uh, does anyone know what time it is?"

Solomon pulls his pocket watch out. "It's time to get your ass back home before you turn into a crisp. Sunup is around the corner."

43

AURORA

———✦———

Saxon is falling asleep on his feet by the time Ryker drops us off in our apartment. He's so out of it that he doesn't even grumble when the warlock tells me he'll be in touch. I give him a noncommittal response, which is all I'm capable of right now. I can't deal with all the changes and their consequences before I sort out my priorities.

Ryker leaves in the same manner as usual, using his warlock magic. I can't deny that learning how to do that is exciting. Leaving Saxon's side to go to Scotland isn't. But if the warlocks insist that I must leave right away, would Saxon come with me or stay?

I know something big happened downtown involving Jacques and the king. If the Blueblood wars restart, Saxon will be needed here.

"A penny for your thoughts." He walks over and pulls me into

"It's nothing. Let's get cleaned up and sleep."

He brings his nose to the crook of my neck, taking a deep breath. "I don't think I can sleep right now."

I can't possibly smell good, but my hormones don't care one bit about hygiene. I'm already melting as I lean into him, curling my fists in his shirt.

"Shower first," I say in a husky voice.

"Okay."

Holding his hand, I veer to my room, dying to get out of my clothes. They're grimy and bloody, completely ruined, good only for burning.

Once in the bathroom, I wince when I catch my reflection in the mirror. I look like a zombie extra from *The Walking Dead*. Saxon hugs me from behind, resting his chin on my shoulder. Even covered in dirt he looks like a god. It's so unfair.

"Why are you frowning?" he asks.

"Nothing."

I head for the shower, which can also be used as a bathtub. I could use a bath. My body is bruised and sore, but I doubt Saxon and I would fit in it.

"I can make it work," he whispers in my ear.

"What?"

"We can have a bath together."

Cocking my head, I ask, "Wait? Did you hear my thoughts?"

"Hmm. I'm not sure. You were staring at the bathtub longingly and I just had a vision of us in there, you riding me, surrounded by bubbles."

Desire unfurls in the pit of my stomach and heads south, pooling between my legs. My heartbeat increases its tempo, thrumming inside my ribcage.

"That's quite a vision."

He pulls his jacket off, then gets rid of his soiled shirt, jeans, and underwear in the blink of an eye. "Let's make it a reality."

"Okay."

"Here. Let me help you out of those clothes."

By the time we finally make it into the tub, I'm so turned on that it won't take much to send me over the edge. After a lot of splashing and maneuvering, we finally manage to find the right position in the tub. Saxon is big everywhere. But once we do, and he slides home, it makes all the contortionism worthwhile. We're slick and wet as we discover our rhythm. I gyrate my hips, Saxon pistons into me, our tongues mingle in the most erotic dance until my brain short-circuits.

"Sax?" I say against his lips.

"Yes, honey?" He kisses my neck, giving me delicious goose bumps.

"Bite me. Please?"

"Fuck, you don't have to ask twice."

He sinks his teeth into my skin, shooting radioactive waves of pure ecstasy down my body. I cry out his name, rotating my hips faster. With each pull from him, the pressure between my legs increases, and Saxon seems to grow larger. I have to close my eyes when the room begins to spin, and yet I see stars everywhere. My body turns into liquid fire when the orgasm hits me so intensely that I can't even scream. My voice is gone.

Saxon is busy chasing his own release. He stops drinking from me, licking the incisions shut with his tongue before he claims my mouth again. His tongue darts in ferociously, demanding, while his arms keep me trapped against his chest. He grunts against my lips, shaking violently as he empties himself into me. I keep on riding him, which only makes me shatter again.

Minutes pass before we dare to move. My heart is still beating out of sync, and my breathing is ragged. I lean back, finding Saxon staring at me with hooded eyes. There's still a hint of red in them.

"That was…"

"Earth-shatteringly amazing?" He smiles.

"Is that even a word?"

"It is now." He kisses me gently, turning my already limp body into goo.

Reluctantly, I pull away, but only so I can stare at him unabashedly. I pinch myself for reassurance that this extraordinary male is my mate, that I get to spend a lifetime with him. A sliver of sadness slides into my heart when I remember what I had to give up.

"What's the matter, my love?" he asks.

A loaded exhale whooshes out of me. "You know that in order to make the warlock athame work for me, I had to bond with the jewel. But I didn't tell you what it required of me."

Saxon's post-coital blissful expression becomes somber. "Tell me, Rora. Let me help you carry the burden."

His words almost make me cry. Through a lump in my throat I tell him the vision I saw and what I think it meant. Saxon doesn't speak for several beats, but I can read in his gaze and also sense through the bond that he's as shattered as I am.

He reaches for my cheek, caressing it with the tips of his fingers. "You couldn't have known. You did what you had to do."

"You're not angry at me?"

His brows furrow. "Why would I be angry? Your sacrifice saved our lives, and I know you'll save many others as a badass warlock. I'm proud of you."

A rogue tear escapes my eye, and Saxon wipes it off with his thumb. "I love you so much," I say.

"Not as much as I love you."

He claims my lips in a slow and tender kiss that helps soothe the pain in my chest. We'll be all right for as long as my mortal body allows. A gasp escapes my lips when sudden realization hits me.

"What's wrong? Did I hurt you?"

"No, of course not. Something just dawned on me. If I'm a warlock, that means I'm immortal."

He tenses, watching me with wide eyes. "For real?"

"I think so. Ryker and Declan are. I'm not sure how it works. But I guess I'll find out during training."

"I hate that you have to leave, but I'm fucking happy that I won't lose you in a few years," he says in a choked-up voice.

His eyes become brighter, and the raw emotion I see shining there is my undoing. I grab his face between my hands. "I want to make something clear, Saxon Hellström. You're the male I love; you're my mate. I won't go without you. If you need to stay here for a while to help the king and your friends, I'll stay too."

"But what about the training? You're part of the warlocks' creed now."

"They can wait. I'll be here as long as you have to be. And when the time comes for me to head to Scotland, you're coming with me."

"Damn straight I will. It doesn't matter where we end up, Rora. Home is where you are."

I'm on the verge of bawling my eyes out again. "Even hell?"

"Even hell."

SAXON

Life gives me and Aurora exactly twenty-four hours of uninterrupted bliss before it decides we've had enough. Lucca is the one who comes to burst our bubble. He's alone, looking somber as hell for the first time since his curse was broken.

"I'm sorry I couldn't give you more time to rest," he apologizes, then glances at Aurora.

"It's okay. We didn't expect our problems to simply disappear," she replies. "If it hadn't been you, it would have been Solomon or my mother."

"Actually, she asked me to tell you that she's spoken to the elders. You and Saxon are cleared of any charges."

I snort. "Yippee-ki-yay. Aren't we lucky?"

"Not so much. It's possible we might have lost half the support of the magical community." Lucca links his hands together, resting his elbows on his knees.

"I'm not surprised by that. Their ways are archaic. They're the type to cut off their noses to spite their faces," Aurora remarks.

"The High Witch still supports the king, but the issue now is that since you are a warlock and mated to a vampire, you can't be the next in line for that position."

"I knew that. It should be Miranda, but I was hoping to spare her or Niko the burden."

"That's the problem. Neither wants the role and your mother supports their decision. I think it's what pissed off the Council of

Witches the most."

I watch Aurora closely, noting her surprise. "I can't believe she did that."

"She seemed remorseful for the things she put you through."

"And you know what she's done to me?"

Lucca looks sheepish. "Vivi might have mentioned a few things."

She glances away, but she can't hide the distress in her heart. Our connection is only getting stronger, and I can read her like a book now.

"Where do we stand with the dragons?" I ask to change the subject. "And what happened to that outsider pack?"

"I haven't heard anything from Karl or Cheryl about the wolf business yet, but Larsson has managed to appease his people for now."

"And Jacques?"

"We believe he's no longer in Salem. We have searchers looking for him, though."

Glancing at Aurora, I ask, "Do you think Elena was working with Jacques? The timing seems too convenient to have been a coincidence."

"I don't know. It's possible. She knew that the king would eventually succumb to the disease afflicting the first generation."

Lucca's posture changes, becoming more rigid, and his eyes are guarded.

"What are you going to do about your uncle?" I ask.

His shoulders sag forward as he lets out a heavy sigh. "It's the absolute worst time for him to abdicate from the throne, but he has asked me to take a more hands-on role in his court. My time here at

Bloodstone is over."

"Which means our time is over." I can't say I'm unhappy about leaving this place, but there's Aurora to think about too. "You don't have to stay here anymore, do you?"

"No. It was only a requirement because I was the future High Witch."

"Good. When are we moving out?" I ask Lucca.

"As soon as possible. Before I forget." He pulls out a small box from his jacket pocket. "This is for you."

"What is it?"

"A gift from my uncle."

I open the box, finding a red rose pin inside. The pin soldiers from the Red Guard wear. "I don't understand. Why did he give me this?"

"He wants you and Ronan to officially join the Red Guard."

My throat closes up with emotion, and I can't think of what to say. I've trained with those soldiers, but I never in a million years expected to join their ranks. I didn't think I would be worthy of wearing this badge of honor, considering who my father was.

"This is surreal, but I can't accept it," I finally say.

"Why not?" He stands straighter.

"I'm the reason Boone was able to wound you with the vampire's bane-forged sword. If I hadn't abandoned my post to … If I hadn't neglected my duties, I could have stopped him."

Lucca stares at me with round eyes. "That's madness. You didn't abandon your post, Sax. I told you to take the evening off."

I shake my head. "I shouldn't have gone. I knew the enemy was close."

Aurora places her hand on my back. "Sax, I think it's high time you let go of your past. You're not your father. You're the most courageous and loyal male I've ever met. You saved my sister from a demon, and you went to hell for it."

"We need you in the Red Guard, Sax. You deserve it," Lucca adds.

It's hard for me to let go of the guilt. I've been carrying it for so long. But maybe they're right. I have to accept that certain things that happened were beyond my control. A burning in my eyes comes from out of nowhere. I don't want to cry like a baby, but the choke in my throat is real.

I glance up, fighting the tears. "Thank you."

The whites of Lucca's eyes are a little red now, but he keeps it together.

"You're welcome." He stands. "I'd better go. There is lots to do. I expect Aurora will be moving in with you in the mansion."

I seek her gaze, not knowing where she stands on that. "My living quarters are big enough. You'll be comfortable, I promise."

She smiles from ear to ear, making her eyes twinkle. "Sax, I'd move in with you even if your room were the size of a shoebox."

God, I couldn't love this woman more. The mating bond flares up in an instant, bright and strong. I forget Lucca and pull Aurora into my arms, crushing my lips to hers.

"Okay, then. I'd better go help Vivi with … packing."

He's out of Aurora's apartment in a flash, almost as fast as I make her clothes disappear.

"Okay, where to now?" I ask in between kisses.

She wrinkles her forehead. "Would you think I'm lame if I said the bed?"

I laugh.

"Well, my tush is sore from banging on the kitchen counter earlier," she continues.

"Rora, darling, making love to you will never, ever be lame. Besides, there's plenty we haven't tried yet on that mattress."

"Like what?" The corners of her lips twitch up.

"Have you ever heard of bondage?"

Her eyebrows arch and her beautiful hazel eyes glint with mischief. That's a shot of libido straight to my cock.

"I knew I liked you for a reason." She links her fingers with mine. "Let's go."

This is the end of Aurora and Saxon's story ... for now.
Continue reading for a teaser of Forgotten Heir.

44

MIRANDA

A week later

I've lost count of the number of times I've checked my phone. I haven't heard from Rikkon since he had the vision about Aurora. We've become close after the Nightshade Market incident, despite what everyone said. We started out as friends, but I wish we were more than that. Sometimes, I think he also wants to cross the friendship line, but he never does. And now he's radio silent.

I know nothing bad has happened to him, or I would have heard about it. And yet, my heart feels heavy all the time, gripped by anxiety and fear.

He's no longer residing in the institute. He's moved into Lucca's mansion with the rest of the gang. Aurora is there too, but I haven't visited yet. I've been avoiding seeing her because I know she's going to bring up Rikkon. I can't deal with a sermon on why I shouldn't get involved with him. The talk might be wasted anyway. It's possible that all the loaded glances and fleeting touches meant nothing. Don't people in love see what they want and not what's true?

There's a knock on the door, and then Niko walks in.

I toss the phone on my bed and grab a pillow to hug. Somehow, I need the protection, even if it's the fluffy variety.

"What are you doing? You've been moping for days." She gives my room a cursory glance and then her eyes zero in on my phone. "You haven't heard from him yet, have you?"

"What?" I squeak. "I don't know what you're talking about."

"Oh, come on. I'm not stupid. I know you have a major crush on Vivienne's brother. I don't blame you. He's hot."

Heat creeps up to my cheeks, and I can't even hide my embarrassment because my hair is tied in a ponytail.

"We're just friends."

"Shit. He has friend-zoned you? Is it because of your major age difference?" She plops on my bed, folding her legs under her.

"He's immortal, Niko. Age is irrelevant to him."

At least I hope it is.

"Your birthday is in two weeks. Eighteen is better than seventeen for sure."

I clutch the pillow tighter. "Ugh. I don't want to talk about him with you."

"Fine." She jumps off the bed. "But can I give you a piece of advice? If you want more than friendship from him, you have to pounce. Don't just wait around for him to make the first move. Take control." She slams a closed fist against her palm.

"Okay, Love Doctor. I'll definitely do that. As a matter of fact, I'm just going to head over to his place and attack his mouth."

Ha, right. Wouldn't that be something?

Niko's lips break into a wide grin. "It seems you've been thinking about doing that quite a lot. Stop thinking and just do it. Carpe noctem."

My phone decides to ping just then, making my heart somersault to the top of my throat. Niko is still watching me with a knowing smile when I flip my phone to see who texted me. It's Rikkon. *Boom.* My heart soars. *God, I have it bad.*

"By the upturn of your lips, I guess that's a message from him?"

I level a glower at her. "Why are you still here? Get out!" I toss my pillow in her direction.

"I'm leaving. Unlike you, I do have a social life. I'm going out with Troy. Don't tell Mom."

"Who is Troy?"

"A boy in my class. He works at the movie theater, which is pretty convenient."

"And why can't Mom know about him?" I raise an eyebrow.

"Because his dad runs the guild of rogue mages in Salem." She flashes me a toothy grin, and then bails.

Of course. Niko couldn't simply date someone from a regular family. Even a human would have been more preferable to Mom than rogues. I'd worry if her boyfriends lasted more than a month. Troy is the flavor of the week, hardly worth my concern.

I switch my attention to my phone, trembling as I swipe the screen to reveal Rikkon's message. There are more than one, sent an hour ago. Somehow, there was a delay on his end. Maybe he didn't have coverage where he was. The first messages are just a bunch of random characters typed in. My heart sinks. He must have butt-typed these. But as I keep scrolling, my disappointment turns into real concern. In one of them he asks me to join him at Tuck an' Roll, a dive bar in a skeevy part of town.

Fuck. There's only one reason he'd go there: to score drugs.

I should have known. With the way visions have plagued him lately, it was just a matter of time before he relapsed.

Propelled by a sense of urgency, I get dressed in warm clothes and bolt out of my room. It's early in the evening and Mom won't be home for another hour or so. I'm glad that I don't have to explain to her where I'm going in such a hurry. She's been more attentive lately, which is an improvement, but also a curse. Niko and I are too used to independence.

I open the front door with a jerky movement, not prepared for the body that falls into me. A yell escapes my lips, but then I recognize Rikkon's long blond hair under his hoodie. I stagger back, straining with the weight of his body in my arms.

"What the hell, Rikkon?"

He straightens up, looking at me through glazed eyes. He reeks of cheap beer, too. *Damn it.*

"I'm sorry, Mir. I tried to resist. But I was hurting so much. It's all good now."

I pull him inside, and then shut the door. He leans against the wall, dropping his head into his hand.

"What did you take?"

"It was just pot and a lot of beer." He hiccups.

I grab his hand and steer him to the kitchen. "Come on. We need to get you sobered up."

"How about some food? I'm starved."

"I bet you are."

I pull up a chair and force him to sit down. But Rikkon grabs my hand again, pulling me onto his lap. My pulse quickens while my heart drums like a hummingbird trapped in my chest.

"You're such a good friend, Mir." His eyes become clearer somehow as he stares into mine. "And so damn gorgeous. Sometimes it's hard to not let the lines blur." His gaze drops to my lips, and I'm pretty sure I stop breathing at that point.

He leans in and brushes his lips against mine. Electric sparks crackle where we touch, but a sense of wrongness also comes with it, soiling the moment. I pull back, then jump off his lap.

"You're drunk and high. Let's keep the lines sharp."

I turn around and get busy pulling stuff out of the fridge, but I'm screaming inside. I can't believe I ran away from him. *So what if he's drunk? Doesn't alcohol make people do what they've secretly being craving for a while?*

"What do you feel like eating? I can make a grilled cheese if you like."

The screeching noise of a chair rasping against the floor draws my attention. Rikkon is standing still, his body all of a sudden tense as he stares into the hallway.

I follow his line of vision, seeing nothing out of the ordinary. "What is it?"

"Is the Taluah Mirror here?" he asks without looking at me.

"Yes. My mother brought it home from Elena's apartment. Why?"

"It's calling to me."

He leaves the kitchen, heading straight for my mother's office where the mirror is. I follow Rikkon, feeling incredible unease now.

That mirror turned into a portal to hell. Why is it calling him? My mother keeps it covered with a black sheet for that reason. She doesn't dare to look at it, not even by accident. But Rikkon pulls the sheet off. Right now, it's working as a mirror, not a portal—at least, the only thing I see reflected is Rikkon's image.

I stay back, not daring to come any closer. Niko told me what she saw when Aurora and Saxon were trying to get back from hell. And Aurora saw something awful in it too. I don't dare risk it.

"Is everything okay?" I ask.

He neither answers nor takes his eyes off the object. Worry gnaws at my insides. *What if he's trapped in a horrifying vision?* I'm about to pull him back when he raises his arm and touches the surface. A bright flash of light illuminates the entire room, almost blinding me. I sling my arm over my face to protect my eyes. When it fades, Rikkon is sprawled on the floor, unmoving.

"Shit!" I run to him, and make sure I don't look directly into the mirror when I hook my arms under his armpits and drag him a safe distance away. Then I cover the mirror with the sheet again.

He groans, slowly coming back to the world of the living. I drop into a crouch next to him and push his long hair off his face. He blinks his eyes open, but it's another moment before he focuses on my face.

"Are you okay?"

He doesn't answer right away, and I fear he has a concussion. His eyes become rounder suddenly, and at once, he sits up, grabbing me by the shoulders. "I saw Ellnesari, Mir. Through the mirror. I saw my mother's court. I remember everything."

To Be Continued…

ALSO BY
MICHELLE HERCULES

Wicked Gods (Gifted Academy #1)

Ruthless Idols (Gifted Academy #2)

Hateful Heroes (Gifted Academy #3)

Broken Knights (Gifted Academy #4)

Reckless Times (Paragon Society #1)

Savage Games (Paragon Society #2)

Red's Alphas (Wolves of Crimson Hollow #1)

Wolf's Calling (Wolves of Crimson Hollow #2)

Pack's Queen (Wolves of Crimson Hollow #3)

Mother of Wolves (Wolves of Crimson Hollow #4)

Lost Horizon (Oz in Space #1)

Magic Void (Oz in Space #2)

Wonderwall (Love Me, I'm Famous #1)

ABOUT
MICHELLE HERCULES

USA Today Bestselling Author Michelle Hercules always knew creative arts were her calling but not in a million years did she think she would become an author. With a background in fashion design she thought she would follow that path. But one day, out of the blue, she had an idea for a book. One page turned into ten pages, ten pages turned into a hundred, and before she knew, her first novel, The Prophecy of Arcadia, was born.

Michelle Hercules resides in The Netherlands with her husband and daughter. She is currently working on the *Blueblood Vampires* series and the *Oz in Space* series.

Join Michelle Hercules' Readers' Group:
https://www.facebook.com/groups/mhsoars

Sign-up for Michelle Hercules' Newsletter:
https://mhsoars.activehosted.com/f/11

Follow Michelle Hercules on Instagram:
@michelleherculesauthor

Made in the USA
Monee, IL
07 July 2023

38762205R00215